BATMAN.

KNIGHTFALL

A NOVEL BY

DENNIS O'NEIL

Batman created by Bob Kane

ALL-NEW INTRODUCTIONS BY **DENNIS O'NEIL** AND GREG RUCKA

BARNES
& NOBLE
BOOKS
NEW YORK

2004 Barnes & Noble Books

ISBN 0-7607-5438-1

Printed and bound in the United States of America

04 05 06 07 08 09 M 9 8 7 6 5 4 3 2 1

TO MARIFRAN,

with love and no more squalor than is
absolutely necessary

Batman: Knightfall was primarily adapted from the story serialized in the following comic books, originally published by DC Comics:

Batman #488-510 (1993–94)
Batman: Shadow of the Bat #16-30 (1993–94)
Detective Comics #656-677 (1993–94)
Legends of the Dark Knight #59-63 (1993–94)
Robin #1, 7-9 (1993–94)

These comic books were created by the following people:

Editors: Dennis O'Neil
Scott Peterson
Archie Goodwin

Assistant Editors: Jordan B. Gorfinkel
Darren Vincenzo
Jim Spivey
Christopher Duffy

Writers: Chuck Dixon
Alan Grant
Doug Moench
Dennis O'Neil

Pencillers: Jim Aparo
Jim Balent
Eduardo Barreto
Bret Blevins
Norm Breyfogle
Vince Giarrano
Tom Grummett
Barry Kitson
Tom Mandrake
Mike Manley
Michael Netzer
Graham Nolan
Ron Wagner

Colorists: Adrienne Roy
Digital Chameleon

Inkers: Jim Aparo
Terry Austin
Eduardo Barreto
John Beatty
Bret Blevins
Norm Breyfogle
Rick Burchett
Steve George
Vince Giarrano
Dick Giordano
Scott Hanna
Ray Kryssing
Tom Mandrake
Mike Manley
Ron McCain
Luke McDonnell
Frank McLaughlin
Josef Rubinstein
Bob Smith
Bob Wiacek

Letterers: Jim Aparo
Ken Bruzenak
John Costanza
Albert DeGuzman
Tim Harkins
Todd Klein
Willie Schubert
Richard Starkings

With additional material adapted from:

Batman: Venom (1993)
(Originally published as *Legends of the Dark Knight* #16-20, 1991)

Editors:	Andrew Helfer	**Penciller:**	Russell Braun
	Kevin Dooley	**Inker:**	José Luis García-López
Writer:	Dennis O'Neil	**Colorist:**	Steve Oliff
Layouts:	Trevor Von Eeden	**Letterer:**	Willie Schubert

Batman: Sword of Azrael (1993)
(Originally published as *Batman: Sword of Azrael* #1-4, 1992)

Editor:	Archie Goodwin	**Penciller:**	Joe Quesada
Assistant		**Inker:**	Kevin Nowlan
Editor:	Bill Kaplan	**Colorist:**	Lovern Kindzierski
Writer:	Dennis O'Neil	**Letterer:**	Ken Bruzenak

Batman: Vengeance of Bane Special #1 (1993)

Editor:	Dennis O'Neil	**Penciller:**	Graham Nolan
Assistant		**Inker:**	Eduardo Barreto
Editor:	Scott Peterson	**Colorist:**	Adrienne Roy
Writer:	Chuck Dixon	**Letterer:**	Bill Oakley

Contents

Acknowledgments

Knightfall is a retelling as a novel of a narrative that appeared in a series of magazines published in 1992, 1993, and 1994 by DC Comics. The original story was a complex collaboration of editors, artists, and writers who often drew on work done by other editors, artists, and writers who themselves borrowed elements from work by still other editors, artists, and writers.

So a lot of people helped me put words on the pages that follow. I can't name all of them—I probably don't even know who all of them were. Batman was introduced as a comic book character in 1939 and has since been featured on radio and television, in movies, novels, short stories, and most recently, in video games. Like his superheroic predecessor, Superman, he has evolved for more than fifty years through the efforts of hundreds of creative individuals, some of whom were almost certainly uncredited.

But I can, and happily do, acknowledge those who most immediately helped me shape the contents of this book. The greatest share of the credit must go to the writers of *Batman, Detective Comics, Shadow of the Bat, Robin,* and *Catwoman,* all monthly comic books. (Portions of the narrative also appeared in *Legends of the Dark Knight* and a miniseries titled *Sword of Azrael.*) Alan Grant, Doug Moench, Chuck Dixon, and Jo

Duffy supplied ideas, plot points, and dialogue that appeared in the original stories and were from there incorporated into this novel. Both they and I were helped immeasurably by Jordan B. Gorfinkel and Darren Vincenzo, who managed a monstrously complicated publishing schedule; by Archie Goodwin, who edited the comics material I wrote; and especially by Scott Peterson, who began the project as my assistant and ended it as the editor of *Detective Comics* and was throughout a generous and enthusiastic collaborator.

We had help from a group who, though they aren't writers, nevertheless *are* storytellers and as such contributed immensely to our efforts. These are the artists who worked on the comics mentioned above: Jim Aparo, Terry Austin, Jim Balent, Eduardo Barreto, John Beatty, Bret Blevins, Norm Breyfogle, Rick Burchett, Steve George, Vince Giarrano, Dick Giordano, Tom Grummett, Scott Hanna, Barry Kitson, Ray Kryssing, Tom Mandrake, Mike Manley, Ron McCain, Luke McDonnell, Frank McLaughlin, Michael Netzer, Graham Nolan, Josef Rubinstein, Bob Smith, Ron Wagner, and Bob Wiacek. I'd also like to mention the unsung and often completely unacknowledged members of the art teams, colorists, and letterers. Our colorists were Adrienne Roy and the mysterious folk who collectively call themselves Digital Chameleon. Our letterers were Jim Aparo, Ken Bruzenak, John Constanza, Albert DeGuzman, Tim Harkins, Todd Klein, Willie Schubert, and Richard Starkings.

Fifty-five years ago, a young cartoonist named Bob Kane brought an idea to a comics publisher and developed it with an equally young writer named Bill Finger. That was the beginning of Batman and, indirectly but undeniably, this book.

And that doesn't begin to exhaust the list. Here, in no particular order, are a few other people who in one way or another contributed to *Knightfall* and deserve thanks: Peter Milligan, Ann Goetz, Julius Schwartz, Mark Waid, Marv Wolfman, Bob Le Rose, Jim Owsley, Maxine Fleckner, Carol Goldberg, Kelley Puckett, Kelley Jones, Brian Stelfreeze, Curtis King, Beth Reuter, Kirk Stowe, Susan Hall, Neal Adams, Joe E. McFarland, Joseph F. McFarland, Larry O'Neil, Roger Stern, Carmela Merlo, Zoë Kharpertian, Tricy Godduhn, Martha Thomases, Margaret Russell, Rich Kulawiec, and Sister Catherine Zimmer.

When the book was slightly more than half written, I damaged a lane divider on the Pennsylvania Turnpike by hitting it with a Pontiac. The staff of Memorial Hospital in Bedford, Pennsylvania, mended me so expertly that I was able to resume working within two weeks, and so they, too, are substantial contributors to *Knightfall*. (Nobody will ever mend the Pontiac.) Dr. Alfred Kayata of Brooklyn deserves a special mention here for continuing and amplifying the ministrations of the Pennsylvanians.

Janna Silverstein of Bantam Books made perceptive suggestions that substantially improved the entire manuscript.

And finally, my personal thanks to DC Comics' Charles Kochman, one of the best editors I've ever had. Charlie's contributions began with persuading me to undertake writing the book—he's not a fellow to be daunted by something so insignificant as an impossible deadline—and continued through supplying martial arts expertise, encouragement, and in the last, hectic fortnight, by asking questions I didn't always want to hear but certainly needed to answer.

—Dennis O'Neil
April 1994

Of Monsters and Manuscripts

At first, nobody expected *Knightfall* to be a novel, much less a *best-selling hardcover* novel—of that I'm sure. And I know it began as a comic book and morphed into several other forms and that a lot occurred in a short time, if not simultaneously. But exactly what happened when, who said what, who had which idea . . . well, I wasn't taking notes, and neither was anyone else and, frankly, none of us could have anticipated that I'd be writing an introduction like this almost a decade later because *Knightfall* the novel—not the comic book series, not the children's book, nor the BBC radio adaptation, the *novel*—was being reissued.

I'll start by giving you the story in its simplest possible form. Those with short attention spans or absolutely no interest in popular culture can read the next paragraph and skip everything else.

Okay, starkly and simply then: A writer named Peter Milligan had an idea for a story that would fill two issues of *Detective Comics*, a total of forty-four pages. Some editor, probably me, decided to expand it enormously. When news of that got out, another editor decided to render the story in other forms, among them a hardcover novel. Everything worked out well enough and the project was a big, though qualified, success.

That's the short version.

Let's begin the longer one by reminding ourselves of what comic books had evolved into by 1993, the year *Knightfall* debuted. For years—for decades!—comics were widely thought of as the dummies' art form, and then only on rare occasions were they thought of as any kind of art form at all. (The assumption may have been that semi-literate folk needed the pictures to help them understand the words.) That was changing for reasons much too complicated for discussion here; comics were not yet on a cultural par with novels, symphonies, even cinema (which is what movies are when they're in their church-going clothes), but they were becoming recognized as, at the very least, a valid narrative medium.

While comics were edging their way into a tentative respectability, the means by which they reached their audience were changing. Once, buying comics was a hit and/or miss proposition. A wholesaler dropped a wire-wrapped bundle of them at a retailer's place of business, the retailer put them on display, and a month later returned those that had remained unsold to the wholesaler. You, the avid comics reader, really couldn't be sure you'd be able to buy your favorite title every month. You *probably* could, but you couldn't be sure, because, to the guy behind the counter, one funny book was pretty much like another, and he was not in the business of guaranteeing that someone's darling would make it onto his rack.

That's how the comics retailing situation was from 1938 through the end of World War II. Then it got *really* bad.

Again, I have no intention of boring those of you not fascinated by the vagaries of the business world by detailing how changing retail patterns and the popularity of a new medium, television, affected not only comics but magazines in general. Nor will I retell the sad tale of how a few politicians and a psychiatrist or two blamed comics for what alarmists considered an epidemic of juvenile delinquency. Let's leave it at this: Soon after the end of the Big War, comic books were no longer much of a viable enterprise. Most comics publishers either ceased operations or found other wares to peddle.

I was probably fairly typical of kids who read comics in the 40s. I liked them a lot, a *whole* lot, but when I was no longer seeing them every time I went with Dad to buy a quart of milk, I stopped thinking about them. There were school activities, and TV, and movies, and dates, and plenty of teen *angst* to occupy my mind. I was too busy to notice that I missed comics if, in fact, I did. I satisfied my craving to read with novels, plays, and short stories.

In the late 50s and early 60s, the fortunes of comics improved on a couple of fronts. Two editors of vastly different temperaments and approaches—I've worked for both of them—reinvented super heroes, the costumed do-gooders who had been created by comics writers and artists and become a staple of comics publishing until the post-war implosion. These men, Stan Lee and Julius Schwartz, had remained employed as comics editors during the lean years, working for two of the remaining half dozen or so publishers still issuing comic books. Their new, sophisticated approaches made comics acceptable to the hipper variety of high schoolers, collegians, and young people in general; because of them, you weren't a dork if you liked super heroes, you were *cool*, maybe.

But without Phil Seuling, the unsung hero of comics publishing, the efforts of Messrs. Lee and Schwartz may have been in vain because for readers to *appreciate*, they must first *see*. Phil was, by profession, a high school English teacher, and by avocation a comics fan. He had an idea that would benefit him and his comics-reading friends; he would eliminate the hit-or-miss element from comics buying. He made a deal with Lee's and Schwartz's employers. If they would let him retail a few comics every month, Phil would not insist they take back any that remained unsold. It was a no-risk situation for the publishers. What they sold to Phil Seuling *stayed* sold. Phil's only demand was that he be allowed to choose his titles: Instead of some mailroom guy slapping a wire around the first bunch of books he could get his hands on, Phil would select the titles he knew his customers would want to have.

That was the beginning of the "direct sales market"—a group of independently owned shops that cater to hobbyists and collectors. As a result of Phil Seuling's efforts, comics were no longer tormented by the caprices of magazine distributors. Deal with a direct sales outlet and you, the super hero fan, *knew*, to a certainty, where and when you'd be able to get your monthly comics fix.

This did not go unnoticed in editorial offices, one of which I occupied. Editing periodicals is not always the most stable of jobs, and it is one always fraught with stress—there's always a deadline lurking in the shadows, if not plumped down in the middle of your desk—but we were doing okay.

Thanks to the direct market, we could rely on having a faithful audience. We had few artificial restrictions put on us in terms of page count, story structure, characterization. We were allowed, and even encouraged, to experiment. And—a prolonged cheer here—we had no *prima facie* restrictions regarding subject matter. Oh, we couldn't let our stories get too gory or sexual, and we had to be careful about inadvertently insulting anyone's religion, but these are taboos people who work in a mass medium must be aware of, especially people who work in comics' closest electronic equivalent, series television.

I, for one, wasn't complaining. I never really wanted to be in the business of shocking or outraging; if I had, I wouldn't have been working in mainstream publishing. But if I had an idea for a story about a real-life social issue or psychological problem, and if the subject could be dramatized in our medium, I could probably do it. Nothing was off-limits any longer just because we were doing comics; to paraphrase a company slogan, comics weren't just for kids anymore.

What you've just read might seem like a digression from the subject of this essay, which is how a novel titled *Knightfall* came to be. Not true. This book is the direct result of the odd evolution of comic books in America. *Knightfall* was not born in any one person's imagination but rather, like mythology, it was shaped by the culture and sociology of a particular group at a particular time. I gave it words and helped give it a form, but it is, again like mythology, a multi-generational collaboration. A few historical accidents and a lot of people, Phil Seuling not least among them, created the conditions that allowed us to do the work we did. I want you to understand that—hence, the history lesson, for which I beg your indulgence.

Of course, we weren't thinking about the history of our medium, or anything else particularly weighty, when we began *Knightfall*. We were just trying to do our jobs and keep ourselves entertained.

The "we" I refer to were the editors employed by DC Comics to maintain the Batman franchise. Although they're acknowledged elsewhere in this volume, I am happy to double my thanks by mentioning them again: Scott Peterson, Darren Vincenzo, and Jordan B. Gorfinkel. There we were, the four of us, occupying space in DC Comics' headquarters in midtown Manhattan, with an idea for a prolonged story and as much freedom as we could reasonably expect. As a bonus there was Batman, a character who had, at that point, been popular for over fifty years in comics, radio drama, television, and movies and who, consequently, was widely recognized. We also had a question: Was our interpretation of Batman outdated?

Our hero had remained popular for five decades partly because he had been allowed to change as the world had changed. He was physically the same caped-and-cowled guy who had first appeared in *Detective Comics* #27 (dated May 1939), and he had the same name, Bruce Wayne, but much else about him had grown and evolved. He had been, at various times, a quasi-outlaw, a police agent, a time-and-space-roving science fiction adventurer, a leading citizen and, in the irreverent 60s, a comedian. He had acquired, to quote Jack Nicholson in the 1989 Batman movie, "wonderful toys." And he had become surrounded by a textured and multi-layered milieu and a small army of friends and enemies. In 1993, he was a rather grim, extra-legal crime fighter who played by his own rules, but played by them strictly.

One of those rules was familiar to those of us who grew up in Judeo-Christian households, though followers of most other spiritual traditions would recognize it, too: "Thou shalt not kill." Earlier versions of Batman had not always abided by this. In his first story, Batman tossed a bad guy into a vat of boiling chemicals, and later, he used an airplane's machine gun on a carful of fleeing thugs. He had even, briefly, toted a holstered pistol. But since the 1940s, Batman had not taken a life, even inadvertently. "Thou shalt not kill" had become as much a *part* of Batman as the scalloped cape and pointy ears. And although in virtually every adventure he overcame foes physically—we were, after all, doing melodrama for a readership who liked action-adventure—as we interpreted him when we began working on *Knightfall*, he did not enjoy violence. It was, merely, just another one of his tools.

Beneath the grim visage and relentless mien, our Batman was pretty much an old-fashioned good guy. Not a Boy Scout—he was too edgy—but a man who conformed to the ancient Greek meaning of the word "hero," one whose task is to "protect and serve." Did that, we wondered, make him hopelessly passé? Other popular heroes, the ones we were seeing in our local theaters, embodied by performers like Arnold Schwarzenegger, Clint Eastwood, Steven Seagal and the squad of actors who answered to the name "Bond—James Bond," certainly seemed to have no compunction about using extreme violence and often quipping about it afterward.

One way to deal with hard and maybe unanswerable questions about a continuing character is not to ask them and hope nobody notices. That was our Batman strategy for years. But the question *did* exist and, to me, it was that orange elephant perched on the ottoman in the corner. With *Knightfall*, we decided to answer it—or rather, let our readers' responses answer it. I can't reveal much more about the plot we arrived at without ruining the story for those of you who are reading this essay before the novel it introduces. So let's leave it at this: We presented our readers with two versions of Batman and, although I created the "bad" one, I am delighted to report that our mail indicated a large dislike for him out there in Readerland.

We were relieved. Had our audience asked for more Bad Batmen, I don't know what I would have done. I liked my job; at times, I thought it was the best editorial gig in New York publishing. And I certainly enjoyed the movies featuring Arnold, Clint, *et. al.*, but that kind of entertainment had always been, for me, a guilty pleasure. I believed, and I guess still believe, that a culture's designated heroes should somehow reflect its values. I was much less certain about the part of heroes in *shaping* those values, but I was convinced that popular culture holds a mirror up to its world. My unspoken questions, then, were: had we, collectively, as a civilization, come to value human life so little that we found hideous forms of death amusing? And if that was true, was it part of a process I wanted to abet? If the readers favored Bad Batman, should I ask my boss to be reassigned?

I'm guessing I would have crawled into a murky crevice of my soul and found some kind of compromise. But I didn't have to. Those wonderful beings who bought our comics liked the old, virtuous, Commandment-obeying Batman, and we were free to tell our tale without worrying about what we'd do when it ended.

We didn't yet have a generic name for what we were doing and wouldn't for years, so we probably referred to it as a "crossover." Crossovers had been fairly common in comics almost from their beginnings; they occurred when a character from one title appeared in another—when, to cite an early instance, the Sub-Mariner did a co-starring turn in the Human Torch's comic. And continued stories, some quite extended, had been common in comics for decades. But *Knightfall* was to be a lot bigger and more ambitious than either a crossover or a serial. We weren't merely going to tell a year-long story, which would have occupied twelve issues of a title for a total of 264 pages; we were going to use *six* titles—the four that featured Batman, plus the two that featured his sidekick Robin and his friendly enemy Catwoman, plus a four-issue miniseries created especially for *Knightfall*. We'd involve virtually all of Batman's friends and prominent enemies, and before we were through we'd produce over 1,100 pages.

What to call this behemoth? In 1993, the answer was . . . nothing in particular. Just "*Knightfall*." Or "the stunt." But a few years ago, while writing a how-to book, I needed a name for a series such as *Knightfall*. I dubbed them "megaseries," and since nobody has to date called them anything else, we'll let the name stand.

But in 1993, we weren't worried about labels. We committed ourselves to the task we envisioned and—

Then we got busy. I began by talking with the three gentlemen our employers called my assistants and I thought of as my colleagues. The aforementioned Scott, Darren, Jordan, and I had been in a comfortable, mutually supportive working relationship for several years. We knew our characters, one another, the company that employed us, and the comics business. We were reasonably sure we could manage the demands of what we were planning. *Reasonably* sure. Not certain. We'd never tried anything this ambitious before and neither had anyone else in comics. Nor did we have the normal writer's option of completing our story and then redoing any parts that were inconsistent with any other parts. By the time we sent our last page to the printer, many, many other pages would have already been printed, sold, and read. We had to get it right on the first try or suffer exceedingly public embarrassment.

So we talked and then we called a meeting. We assembled our writers and artists at a Westchester County businessman's retreat facility and, for almost three days, we talked more. The goal was to decide exactly what our plot would be and outline the major events in it. I wanted to leave the outline just loose enough for happy accidents to happen—somebody getting an idea that hadn't occurred to anyone at the retreat—but nobody was going to be allowed to make it up as he or she went along. One thing was non-negotiable: We *had* to know how the story would end. But exactly how we'd reach our final scene . . . well, there was some wiggle room.

At the end of three days, we were satisfied that we had a good plot. We weren't surprised. I have always had a single reliable editor's trick to insure quality: use good people. Our writers and artists were, by any reasonable criteria, among the best in the world. *Knightfall* was now as much their project as ours, and though a disaster was still a possibility, the quality of our collaborators was the best possible insurance that no disaster would, in fact, happen.

No sense keeping you in suspense: No disasters happened. But we did encounter a couple of surprises along the way. One, a very pleasant one, was *Knightfall*'s success. We worked hard that year—Scott, Jordan, and Darren sometimes put in ridiculously long hours—but we were being challenged and we were exploring new territory and, even after months, we *still* weren't quite sure we could do this thing. But we could. Sales escalated and reader reaction was overwhelmingly positive (except for readers who hated our revisionist Batman, and even they often had compliments for *Knightfall* as a whole).

The BBC asked for permission to adapt and produce a full cast radio drama. We were flattered and happy to give our English brethren what they wanted. Our own company decided to license a young readers version of *Knightfall*, to be written by Alan Grant, a trusted and respected Batman comics scripter. We were looking good. If we weren't quite golden boys, we were at least gold-*plated* boys and that was enough.

Our success was bigger than we anticipated—hence the surprise—but we wouldn't have begun the series if we'd expected to fail
utterly. But our *second* surprise really did seem to come from
nowhere. My memory is fuzzier than usual here: I can't really say
when Charlie Kochman entered my professional life. Charlie was,
and is, an editor in DC's Licensed Publishing department, which
means he works on projects that use DC's comic book characters but
aren't comic books, including novel adaptations. A month or two into
Knightfall, Charlie approached me about adapting the megaseries into
novel form. Since the powers-that-be wanted the novel to be released
on the same day as the final *Knightfall* comic, I'd have just over five
months to do the job. My initial reaction was, *well, thanks for the
offer, but no way!* I mean, I had a day job and I was responsible for
scripting a handful of the *Knightfall* comics and Charlie said the novel
would have to be at least 100,000 words long and my marriage was
relatively new and there are only twenty-four hours in a day. . . . Besides, the year was ending and the Batman editor had to make at least
one business trip to the West Coast every holiday season and this *particular* Batman editor had plans to visit Missouri Christmas week. . . .
All that and write a novel with a brutal deadline? Hey, I only write fiction about super heroes; personally, I don't even own a cape.

I discussed Charlie's offer with my wife. Told her that I had it on
good authority—and I did—that when I was writing a book I was a
monster. She said okay, she'd live with a monster for a while. I continued to vacillate. Finally, Marifran said, "You'll hate yourself if you
let anyone else do it." Exit vacillation. The argument was clinched. I'd
write the novel, somehow.

For the next twenty-two weeks or so, Marifran lived with a monster and the monster was very happy at his work. I have a clue as to
why, provided by a psychologist named Mihaly Csikszentmihalyi. Dr.
Csikszentmihalyi says we're happiest when we're involved in "flow,"
which he defines as "being completely involved in an activity . . . your
whole being is involved, and you're using your skills to the utmost."
That's a fair description of me writing this book. I was focused on *getting it done* and I didn't worry much about anything else. I'd arrive
home every night at about six, eat quickly, and retire to the back room.

When the word counter on the computer told me that I'd done a thousand words, I'd stop, and the monster might spend a few minutes talking to his mate. At a thousand words every twenty-four hours, with maybe one day a week off, I calculated I could complete the manuscript and still have a little time left for editing and revision.

I bought a laptop computer, a Macintosh Powerbook 145B, and took it with me to California. Some of the book got written in hotel rooms.

Every Saturday morning, Marifran and I would drive to the King's Plaza shopping mall in Brooklyn. There we'd meet Charlie Kochman and hand over to him the work I'd completed during the previous seven days. We felt a little like spies, only instead of slipping a confederate state secrets—on microfilm?—I'd give him a small stack of typing paper. He'd thank us and vanish into the crowds, and go somewhere to do whatever it is that editors do.

We progressed apace. Comics books were written, drawn, and published. The story they told developed and grew complex, both in the comics and, at night and on weekends, in my trusty Powerbook 145B. Deadlines were met. I'm sure there were glitches—there almost always are—but none of them could have been serious because *Knightfall* was actually *getting done.* On schedule and as we'd originally planned. Me—I was never so immersed in anything as I was in *Knightfall*: editing, supervising, writing in two different forms. We moved through the fall and into the dark months and *Knightfall* marched on.

Then, another surprise—a nasty one. Marifran and I decided to make the Christmas trip to Missouri. After all, I could type in my mother's guest room as easily as in my home office. On a gloomy Christmas Eve, at about three in the afternoon, with Marifran sleeping in the shotgun seat, we were on a tollpike approximately half-way through Pennsylvania when I must have dozed at the wheel. I awoke to see the concrete lane divider in the windshield and I yelled, and then I was trying to crawl out of a shattered side window. Witnesses say our car slammed into the divider and flipped over three times. I don't know. I wasn't counting.

On Christmas morning, after the resident physician examined us in the intensive care unit, I asked him if someone could please, please go to the wreckage of our Pontiac and get my laptop, which had been unsecured in the car's back seat and must have been tossed around like dice in a cup. The doctor did the chore himself, bless him, and personally delivered the doughty 145B into my hands. It was intact and unharmed, with not a word of *Knightfall* missing from its hard drive. I never sent the Apple computer company a fan letter, but I should have.

Two weeks later, back in New York, I resumed work. The thousand-word-per-day requirement was now less negotiable than ever.

Sometime in late March, with the final deadline looming, I finished the book. For two days, a weekend, Charlie Kochman and I sat hunched over the 145B in my home office doing the final edit, with Marifran appearing occasionally to offer snacks and encouragement. We decided to add an essay on Batman I'd written for a British publisher and sent the whole package off to be copyedited.

The final *Knightfall* comic book and the novel you hold appeared simultaneously in July 1994 and we were done. *Knightfall* was history.

Now, a decade later, *Knightfall* has risen from limbo and found its way into your possession. I confess that I've never reread the novel, nor am I likely to. Looking at my published work, I tend to see only what's wrong, or what I think is wrong, or what I think *may* be wrong, and I choose to spare myself unnecessary suffering. But enough disinterested parties have liked the novel and, after all, it is being reissued, and that may mean that my colleagues and I have told a good story—which is all, really, we ever wanted to do.

DENNIS O'NEIL
DECEMBER 2003

Foreword

There was a time, believe it or not, when Batman was not to be taken seriously.

Before the feature film casting of Jack Nicholson and Michael Keaton, before the coming of the genre-shaker Frank Miller, before Len Wein and Max Allan Collins and, yes, before Dennis O'Neil. Even before the days of the Adam West TV show, with its camp-as-cool portrayal of the Dark Knight and the Boy Wonder. We're talking *waaaaay* back, in those days that the comics cognoscenti refer to as the Silver and Golden Ages, when it was as common to read a story about Batman and Robin in Space! as it was to read about their adventures in the Bakery of Doom!—with the exclamation points included, of course.

When Batman was a joke.

Oddly enough, if one goes back to the beginning—and I mean *all* the way back to the beginning—to the moment of his creation, you find quite the opposite. Not only was the Bat-Man, who debuted in *Detective Comics* #27, as serious as the grave, he was a killer himself—a vigilante who had no compunctions about putting a bullet into a madman and thus saving Gotham the time and expense of due process, or worse, the possibility of an acquittal.

But things change. Characters grow, and some of them grow with more grace and ease than others. Batman—like Superman, and to a much lesser extent, the third member of the DC Holy Trinity, Wonder Woman—is unique in that he can reinvent with a minimum of fuss. It's one of the facets of the character that accounts for his lasting endurance, one of the reasons that I am damn sure there will still be Batman stories being told for a hundred years to come. Like Superman, like Wonder Woman, Batman stands outside of time, iconic and eternal.

Or to put it another way, Thomas and Martha Wayne could be murdered in a dirty Gotham alley *tomorrow*, and the results would remain the same. A little boy would still stand, helpless, watching the life run from the bodies of his parents, watching their light fade, and in that moment, the world would still shift insanely on its axis, stealing rhyme and reason, and Bruce Wayne would still speak the same vow, would still swear to avenge their deaths, to protect the innocent, and to punish the guilty.

All you really have to do is account for inflation. The millionaire becomes a billionaire, and Batman endures.

Yet, even with this, he had become a joke. It wasn't Batman alone, of course—the same thing was going on with Superman and Wonder Woman, as well. Timeless though they might be, they had become disconnected from time; their adventures, and thus, their character, had become irrelevant.

So that's DC Comics in the late 1960s, early 1970s. Three of the greatest icons in the history of literature languishing, because who the hell *cares* if Batman and Robin foil the plot to turn all of Gotham's chocolate into soap on Valentine's Day when there's a war in Vietnam and a massacre at Kent State and a break-in at the Watergate?

Hmmm . . . look at that, what's going on over in that *Green Lantern/Green Arrow* title? Who's this O'Neil guy—wait, wait, I've heard of him before . . . maybe read a novel by him? Or some other comics? Or, oh, wait, he was a reporter, wasn't he? What's he doing writing these comics . . .

. . . where people are addicted to heroin and where that black man is accusing the Green Lantern of being a racist and where Oliver

Queen, a.k.a. the Green Arrow, is no longer a millionaire but has lost his fortune and killed a man and is now suffering from a nervous breakdown. . . .

Where, all of the sudden, comics are being relevant.

Understand, I've had the privilege of working both for and with Denny O'Neil. He is a mild man, a truly gentle soul. And if you cornered him and talked about things like artistic integrity and the courage required to tell the hard stories—the stories that everyone says nobody is going to like, the stories that, honest to God, matter— he would smile and shake his head and honestly not realize that you were talking about him. He's that kind of writer, and if he doesn't see his own brilliance, well, then, that might be a good thing; it might go to his head.

And it was *brilliant* because it was so *simple*. It was not just the addition of realism to the stories, because realism was a vein already being tapped elsewhere—though in allowing Batman to get dirty, in tearing his costume and cutting his skin and breaking his heart, he became more human; he became someone we could feel *for* as well as feel *with*. That was part of it, not all of it, because Denny took it the rest of the way. Denny made it work, writing stories that actually mattered, that transcended the medium to speak about the world beyond the Four-Colored-Page. Stories with a social conscience that no one could ignore.

Denny took it seriously—as serious as the grave—and that compelled the reader to take it seriously, too.

Reinvention. And those characters who had lost touch with the world around them suddenly came back with a shattering clarity, telling stories that made your stomach tighten and your pulse race.

Denny O'Neil is the man who wrote, and then edited, Batman for so many years.

Denny O'Neil made it *impossible* to read an issue of *Detective Comics* and think that Batman was a joke.

I've done the heavy lifting required to turn a comic serial into a novel, and I'll tell you this for nothing: it ain't easy, not by a longshot.

It requires a precise sense of narrative and an almost-intuitive understanding of drama. It requires the author to make some very difficult choices about what to keep and what to reject. A novel isn't a movie, and a movie isn't a comic, and all of these things have their own demands. The author's obligation is to serve the novel above all—and that's hard to do when the author also happens to have been intimately involved in the creation of the comic book source material.

You can write a book, put together some hundred thousand words in sequence, and that *isn't* a novel, folks. There are lots of people who can do it, too—just look around at the shelves. A novel isn't stringing together a narrative.

A novel is *about* something, and it's not just about the plot. A novel makes you feel something when its over; it lingers, and it makes you think. A novel grabs you at the start, and doesn't let go until its done, and if it works *really* well, you won't want to be let go at all.

It ain't easy, and to this day, I'm not sure I was successful.

Denny O'Neil, on the other hand, pulled it off, and managed to make it look effortless in the process. It wasn't, make no mistake, but it *looks* like it was, and that's the trick. One can read *Knightfall* and never know it was sourced from a comic; it stands as a novel. It stands on its own. Beginning, middle, and end, it resonates. It *works*.

Thus *Knightfall*—as crucial an epic as any modern tale of the Dark Knight. Conceived, in part, to cater to the hard-edged 80s Batman so popular in the films. The latest incarnation of Batman, drifting inexorably toward anti-heroism. The version whose sanity was in question, but not his viciousness or brutality. The Batman who was cool because he was a sadist, who seemed to be in it for himself.

Understand, I *hate* the film renditions of Batman. *All* of them, every last one. They insult the audience and the characters; they reduce vital supporting players like Alfred and James Gordon to jokes, to be mined for easy laughs. They oversimplify the villains—and Batman's villains, I would argue, are as complex and nuanced as any Iago or Darth Vader to have come down the pike.

But most crucially—and most unforgivably—the films stripped from Bruce Wayne, from Batman, the most critical foundation of his character.

In the movies, Batman kills.

In today's comics, Batman doesn't.

That makes the comic version a hero, and it makes the film version a murderer.

And a murderer isn't a hero, by any stretch of the imagination.

What, then, happens when the Batman becomes a killer? When the Dark Knight is beaten, broken, and falters? What happens when reinvention is again required, and everything must change?

Knightfall.

GREG RUCKA

PORTLAND, OREGON

NOVEMBER 2003

Greg Rucka is the author of numerous comic books and novels, including *Batman: No Man's Land* (Pocket Books, 2000).

Comics are grand opera.
—*Larry Hama*

Endings to be useful must be inconclusive.
—*Samuel R. Delany*
The Einstein Intersection

PART
1

 Knightfall

1

 He stands poised: weight forward, knees bent, waiting, almost ready. He scans the area and sees nothing has changed: the conical silhouette of a water tank a dozen yards away, and beyond that the bulkier silhouettes of the Gotham City skyline. Many have called it the ugliest city in the world, all sharp angles and rigid planes, black against a sky that is never blue, nor black, nor any color he can name, a sky that seems to trap light from the streets below and transform it into something wan and dingy. There are moments when he feels he wraps this sprawling, hideous metropolis around himself like a second cloak, and he knows he could never have become what he is anywhere else.

A breeze off the North River with the last nip of winter in it sends a candy wrapper skittering across the tar paper; the howl of an ambulance echoes in the street behind this building. He looks down at the skylight. He favors skylights, uses them whenever possible: the crash, the shower of jagged glass—these can work for him, frighten and startle his prey, confuse them for four or five seconds. In four seconds he can usually put one man down, sometimes two.

He tugs on the polymer line he has tied to the base of the water tank:

firm. He wraps the other end around his gloved left fist, steps to the parapet, and allows himself another few seconds to enjoy the quiet pleasure he always feels at moments like this. He has not questioned it deeply, fearing that to do so would be to skew some delicate internal equation that enables him to accomplish what he must. But he has examined himself enough to know that it is not the violence—the violence is only a tool, shabby but necessary—nor does he enjoy the dominance, the power he often exerts over other men. No, the pleasure comes from being who he is, filling the identity he created and continues to create, making this Bat-Man, this figment of his imagination, someone real, effective, formidable.

He steps over the edge of the parapet and starts his controlled fall.

A half second after he crashes through the skylight, the line in his fist grows taut. He releases it and drops the remaining six feet to the floor, absorbing the details of the loft as he falls: *Five of them, more than I anticipated. One lying on a weight bench pressing about 250 pounds: strong, an obvious danger especially if he's also agile. A second doing pull-downs on a Universal exercise machine—another jock, another danger. Between them, a thin, pale man smoking a cigarette—no problem unless armed. At the far end of the loft, the final two, turning their heads from the television they've been watching. A single light near the jocks; the television watchers are in heavy shadow. Above, a catwalk, and at the end, behind the smoker, a drop-off—a place where the floor ends twelve yards from the wall, forming a well that extends all the way to the basement, nine floors down. This is a condemned factory building; the well must have contained some gigantic machine, long since disassembled and moved.*

He lands on his toes and whirls to face the jocks, his fingers already removing a small, bat-shaped dart from beneath his cloak. He snaps it up at the single lightbulb, and as the bulb shatters he moves toward the first jock at the Universal. His eyes are covered with the night lenses that are a part of his mask; the loft and the men are a sickly green and a bit fuzzy at the edges, but plainly visible. He recognizes the jocks and the smoker: as he expected, the Manklin brothers, hired muscle with a reputation for sadism. He glides behind Angus Manklin, who has released the shoulder bar on the Universal and is blinking stupidly; Batman crosses his wrists and grabs the collar of Angus's T-shirt at the front, exerting pressure on

Angus's arteries with the edges of his hands. Angus, murmuring softly, collapses.

Chuckie Manklin has dropped his barbell and rises from the bench. A single straight punch, launched from the hip to Chuckie's solar plexus, tumbles Chuckie across the bench and onto the floor, where he folds into a fetal position and lies gasping.

Dougie Manklin, the smoker, is groping in his jacket, trying to pull an automatic from his inside pocket. A single blow to the base of his skull stills him; he slumps back into his chair, unconscious.

Suddenly there is a blast of sound from the other end of the loft, and a slug ricochets off the Universal.

"Don't shoot, ya moron," someone yells. "You'll hit the Manklins."

"I don't care who I shoot!"

The television watchers get up from their couch. The taller of them is holding a 9-millimeter automatic, the current weapon of choice on the street. He has just fired it. He is saying, "Whatever that was that come through that skylight, I want it *dead.*"

His companion cups his hands around his mouth and calls, "Angus? Dougie? Yo, Chuckie!" He waits for an answer.

The gunman fires again.

"Moron!" his companion shouts.

"I'm gettin' outta here," the gunman says.

Both men shuffle toward the front of the loft, toward a door that is dangerously close to the well. The shorter man lights a match and steps cautiously forward. He is unarmed. The gunman is a half step behind him, waving the automatic, squinting into the feeble light.

A kick spins the gun from his hand and into the darkness. A palm strike to the chin bounces him off the wall.

"Ow!" screeches the short man as the match burns his thumb. He has glimpsed what has happened to the gunman and is panicking. He runs lurching into the blackness, forgetting about the well.

The instant his left foot flails in empty air, he remembers, twists, trying to get back, but it is too late. He begins the long plunge, his lips parting to scream.

But he doesn't. Fingers close around his forearm and haul him up to safety.

Suddenly there is light from a bank of fluorescents that dangles from the ceiling. He blinks and sees his savior, a towering figure wrapped in a black cloak, its face covered by a mask with blank eyes and spiked ears. The monster, who only a second ago saved his life, hits him, then lets him slump to the floor.

Then someone behind him speaks. "You are the Batman." The voice is light, almost musical, and full of a Latino accent. The speaker stands on the catwalk above the loft, his hand still on a switch jutting from a fuse box. He is huge: seven feet tall, with an enormous chest and shoulders, a narrow waist, and thick legs. He is wearing leather: a black tank top, riding breeches, and boots. His head is covered by a black leather hood. Two tubes curl from the top and reenter the hood at the back of the neck.

"Yes," the Batman answers.

"How strange. You are a creature cloaked in nightmare. A thing of terror. Yet you will not break the Fifth Commandment. You do not kill."

"Never count on it." His hand is under his cape, uncoiling his spare, weighted line. In a moment, he will fling it like a bolo at the catwalk railing, pull it taut, and climb. "Who are you?"

"You will know my name one day. On that day, you will beg for mercy."

"You're threatening me? Get in line."

"You will scream my name. Scream it!"

The cape parts as the line is flung. For a moment, under the catwalk, the Batman loses sight of his quarry. But only for a moment. He is climbing, vaulting the railing, seeing the open window, diving through it onto the tar paper roof and rolling to his feet, all within five seconds. He spins, looking. Nothing but the familiar silhouette of the skyline. He looks upward. The hooded man now stands on the parapet of the roof of the adjoining building where the Batman had stood only a few minutes earlier. He *jumped?* Eighteen feet? Straight up? The Batman cannot follow.

Once again the odd, lilting voice calls softly: "You will scream my name!"

A moment later, Batman knows he is alone.

• • •

Three hours earlier, the Batman had been wearing a tuxedo, calling himself Bruce Wayne, and lounging in the backseat of a limousine next to a young woman named Gwenny. Gwenny was wearing a Donna Karan evening gown, and although the night was warm, a white sable stole was draped around her shoulders.

"Do you have any champagne, Brucie?" she asked, sliding open the door of the limo's portable bar.

"Darn stuff makes me giddy."

Alfred Pennyworth, in the driver's seat, glanced into the rearview mirror, pursed his lips, and adjusted the tiny receiver he wore in his left ear.

Gwenny leaned back in the seat. "I'll bet you're *fun* when you're giddy."

"Not much, really. Actually, I tend to vomit."

"Oh." Gwenny gazed out the smoked glass at the passing street scene. Then she said, "Are you going to take me to your house? Everyone says Wayne Manor is just darling! How many rooms?"

"Gee, I've never counted."

"Forty-three, sir," Alfred said over his shoulder.

"That many? What do we do with 'em all?"

"Clean them."

"Seems like a waste, somehow . . . cleaning rooms we never use."

"Not a bit, sir. The soap and water are tax deductions."

"Of course," Bruce said decisively. "Of course they are."

Alfred adjusted the tiny receiver in his ear, leaned forward, and turned a dial on the dashboard. "Weather's quite seasonable," he said.

"Oh, darn!" Bruce squirmed to face Gwenny and put a hand on her shoulder. "I feel an attack coming on."

"An attack?"

"It's an old Wayne problem. Been in the family for generations."

"What kind of attack?"

"I don't know the medical term . . . my grandfather said it was the

'Wayne clan incontinence.' I'd really rather spare you the details, Gwenny."

"If that's what you'd like—"

"Alfred, we're near Gwenny's apartment, aren't we?"

"Three blocks, sir."

"Gwenny," Bruce said, "maybe we'd better drop you off. I hate to make such an early evening of it—"

"If you're not feeling well—"

"Really hideously embarrassing."

Alfred guided the limousine to the curb, got out, and opened the passenger door. Bruce kissed Gwenny briskly on the cheek and said, "I shall call you next week. Scout's honor."

"Feel better, Bruce," Gwenny said, then hurried toward the door of her apartment building.

"Love the sable," Bruce called after her.

"Poor Ms. Gwendolyn. Another of the legion of young women who will die rather than tell their friends that notorious roué Bruce Wayne abandoned them in the shank of the evening," Alfred said, sighing. "How many of them must there be? A thousand?"

"I'm preserving their virtue," Bruce said. "I should get a medal. Or at least a merit badge."

Alfred put the Lincoln into gear and eased it into the midtown traffic stream. "You *did* invoke scout's honor, didn't you? But you were never a Boy Scout."

"I meant Indian scout, Alfred. And they were notorious liars. I've heard it was a point of *honor* to lie. If you were an Indian scout, I mean."

"You were never one of those, either."

"Absolutely right. The defense rests." Bruce straightened in the seat, and the muscles around his mouth and eyes tightened. It was the beginning of his transformation, from callow playboy to Batman. "You used the code. What'd you hear?"

Alfred glanced at the police radio on the dashboard and touched the receiver he always wore when he was playing chauffeur. It was an arrangement that allowed Bruce to masquerade as the handsome, unfocused waste of a billionaire the world thought him to be and still stay in touch with the mean streets that were his real domain. A mention of the weather meant something particularly ugly had happened.

"A massacre," Alfred said. "At Manny's Steak House on Thurston Avenue—"

"I know the place. It's a front for No-Nose Novak's operation."

"*Was.* Mr. No-Nose and seven of his associates were apparently murdered. The reporting officer sounded quite upset. 'A slice 'n' dice job' was the phrase he used. We're going to Thurston Avenue?"

"No. Commissioner Gordon will have Sergeant Bullock and Officer Montoya secure the scene. They'll find everything there is to find."

"Police headquarters, then?"

"Robinson Park."

Alfred made an abrupt left turn and accelerated. Bruce lifted a telephone, tapped out a number, and a moment later said, "The zoo."

Alfred drove onto a winding street under a canopy of trees and into a dark, silent park. He stopped near the entrance to the Gotham Zoo and switched off the engine. In the backseat, Bruce shed his tuxedo jacket. He pulled on a black trench coat and slipped on a black cowl that subtly altered the shape of his head, covering it completely except for a small area around his mouth. Later, if necessary, he would put on the full costume.

When he spoke, his voice was a rasp. "You'd better leave. Wait for me at the Cave."

Police Commissioner James Gordon was in his car, pulling away from Manny's Steak House, when the phone buzzed. Even before he picked it up, he knew that he'd hear the rasp. "The zoo." *Two words, this time. He should have saved the "the,"* Gordon thought. *Two words when one would have sufficed. He's getting to be a regular blabbermouth.*

Gordon parked at the usual place near the birdcage, got out, and patted the holstered chief's special on his belt. Robinson Park at two in the morning was not safe, even for the biggest, baddest cop in town. *Maybe I'll get to shoot a mugger while I wait.*

"Gordon."

The commissioner turned. Batman, barely visible in the shadow of the cage, did not come closer, nor did Gordon approach him. The grim game that was their relationship was played by certain rigid, unspoken rules. *No unnecessary contact. Don't ask personal questions. Keep your distance. Don't call me, I'll call you. But if you have to call, make damn sure it's important.*

"You heard?" Gordon asked.

"No-Nose finally bought it. The radio said it was bad."

Gordon pushed his glasses up his nose with his right forefinger. "Bad as it gets. They were shot. Then stabbed. Then cut."

"Any survivors?"

"They're in pieces." Gordon spoke calmly, as he always did when he was furious.

"Witnesses?"

"Nobody saw a thing."

"Any ideas, Commissioner?"

"No-Nose's been real low profile lately. He'd never have won any popularity contests, but he wasn't at the top of anyone's hate list."

"The MO sounds like the Manklins."

"I thought of them, but they haven't shown for months. We figure they're out of town."

"You're wrong," Batman said.

"I guess I don't want to know how you know." Another rule, the primary one: *Don't question my methods. Ignorance is bliss.*

"If I find out anything, I'll be in touch."

"Okay. Listen, if the Manklins *are* involved, you'd better—" Gordon stopped, suddenly aware that he was alone.

He returned to his car, hopeful and frustrated. Sometimes he despised himself for his reliance on this masked vigilante, but he knew that without Batman, his job would be impossible. Gotham City hadn't had an honest government since the Civil War. Its corruption was the butt of a thousand one-liners, the venality of its officials as much a part of the national folklore as its horrible architecture. There was never enough money for proper police training, never funds to create a decent Internal Affairs division. Gordon knew of only a dozen cops he was absolutely sure weren't dirty. Batman was necessary—a necessary evil. *Was* the masked man evil? *Well,* Gordon thought, leaving Robinson Park, *if Batman's a devil, he's my devil. I've made a pact with him and I'll keep it. Until he steps over the line. Until he kills someone. And then? The day that happens, it'll be the end for both of us, and probably for the city, too.*

2

 The sun was already high overhead when Bruce Wayne entered his ancestral home, the famous Wayne Manor. He'd hailed a cab and during the thirty-mile ride entertained the driver with a story about a thousand-dollar bet on a scavenger hunt that *seemed* to have been only a ploy to strand him in a *dreadful* neighborhood while his date went off to heaven knows where with that *vulgar* football player they'd met in a thoroughly disreputable rock and roll club somewhere in the artists' quarter—of course, he couldn't be absolutely *certain* they'd meant to ditch him, but he *did* see them kissing. Another chapter in the saga of Bruce-the-Loser. Half the cabbies in town would be laughing about it by noon.

Inside the house, he went to a grandfather clock in the foyer and set the hands at 10:47: the exact hour and minute the watch on his father's wrist had shown when Dr. Thomas Wayne had fallen with a bullet in his chest on that night twenty years ago—the night Batman was born. The clock pivoted on hidden hinges, revealing a doorway leading to a wide, uneven flight of steps hewn into the rock that supported the mansion. A hundred and thirty years ago Solomon Wayne had led black men down these steps to a place where they could hide until the Underground Railroad found havens for them. Historians agree that old Solly Wayne was greedy, cantankerous, opinionated, egotistical, frequently unreasonable, and probably a bit mad, but they also agree that he had a passion for justice. Only Alfred Pennyworth knew how much Bruce revered his ancestor's memory.

The clock swung closed behind him, and Bruce descended into the chill of a huge cavern. When young Bruce, age eight, had discovered it he had called it "the batcave"—reasonable enough, since he could see thousands of brown bats clinging to the stalactites. Over the years, he had mentally capitalized the word; to him, it was now the Batcave, and it was where he really lived—the mansion above was a mere disguise. The Cave housed a fairly complete forensics laboratory, a small gym, a telephone, a shortwave radio, a police scanner, a television set and video recorder, five cars, a motorcycle, a kitchenette, a collection of souvenirs, a desk, two chairs, and a sophisticated array of computers, two of which were networked to a high-speed Cray supercomputer in the offices of Wayne Enterprises in downtown Gotham City.

Alfred was waiting. "Tea, Master Bruce?"

"Not now, Alfred. Thanks."

Bruce shed his street clothes and most of the costume he wore underneath. Clad only in tights, he went to his collection of exercise equipment and began the lightest of the daily workouts he imposed on himself: a ten-minute warm-up jumping rope, a thousand crunches, five hundred push-ups, four hundred concentration curls, four hundred triceps presses, two hundred bench presses, a hundred squats, and the equivalent of five five-minute miles on a treadmill. As he exercised, he told Alfred of his fight with the Manklin gang and his encounter with the hooded man on the rooftop.

"Any conclusions, Master Bruce?"

"The Manklins won't win any good citizenship awards, and I'm not sorry I put some misery on them, but they weren't responsible for the massacre at the steak house. After the man in the mask got away, I went back and looked for clues. I saw no sign that their weapons had been used before they tried to use them on me, no traces of blood on their clothing.

The engine blocks on their cars were cool. I doubt any of them had been out last night at all, and if they were, they stayed in the neighborhood. I could be wrong. I could have missed something."

"They say there's always a first time."

"Right, Alfred. Maybe I missed something, but it's not likely."

"Has the Batman formed an hypothesis?"

"Yeah, but it's not one I'm happy with. It looks like the masked man killed Jimmy No-Nose and company and aped the Manklins' nasty style."

"Why?"

"This is the part I really don't like. From what the masked man said, and the gestalt of the whole incident, I have to assume that he wanted to get a look at me in action."

"Anyone you know, Master Bruce?"

"No. He might have fooled me with the voice—"

"That hypothetical first time—"

"—but not the body. He was huge, and I could see there was no padding anywhere. And he was agile. I examined the wall I thought he'd jumped up on and found a few handholds—missing bricks, mostly. So he probably climbed. But still, he'd have had to get out on the roof and up the wall in less than ten seconds. There probably aren't five men in the state who can do that, and none of them is built like a bulldozer."

Bruce finished his rope jumping and dropped to the floor to begin his crunches.

"Do we have a conclusion?"

"Not yet. But I'm worried. If I'm right, this guy committed wholesale murder just to check me out. If he'd do that, there's nothing he *wouldn't* do. We're dealing with a very ugly customer."

"I have observed that your foes are seldom Girl Scouts. Do you have a plan?"

"We can hack into the police, federal, and Interpol computers in the morning. I'll put on another face and hit the hangouts tomorrow night. I'll have Gordon lean on his snitches. When the cops are done combing the steak house, I'll have a go at it."

"The usual procedures, then."

"Which usually work, which is why they're usual."

"Indeed. Any instructions, Master Bruce?"

"Nothing."

"Then I shall leave you alone."

An hour later Bruce finished his workout, toweled himself, and sank down into a cross-legged position on a small round cushion. He closed his eyes and gradually slowed his breathing. For three hours he would sit motionless, and when he arose, he would be fully rested. He would not need sleep.

3

His name was Bane, and approximately ninety seconds after his rooftop encounter with Batman, he was cramming his bulk into the rear of a Ford Fairlane that was parked a block away. A slender, well-muscled man shifted nervously in the driver's seat and looked over his shoulder. "Go okay?" he asked.

"Interesting. He is all you said he was, this Batman."

The slender man started the car and began driving. "So you gonna be able to take him?"

"Tonight? Tomorrow? It might be, yes, I could. Almost certainly, yes. But it would be foolish to do so, my friend Bird."

"Why's that?" Bird asked.

"Because of some reasons. I do not know this city as he does. I have seen enough to know he is resourceful. These are advantages of his. I will not fight him until they are no more."

"How's *that* gonna happen?"

"I make them mean nothing. I exhaust him. I frighten him. Then I break him."

"I guess you got a plan, huh."

Bane's head dropped to his chest. He sighed and was silent.

"You okay?" Bird asked.

Bane pressed a small button strapped to his right forearm. There was a faint gurgle. A moment later, he raised his head.

"Needed your fix, huh?" Bird said.

"I do not like this word, *fix*. I am angry when you say it."

"Hey, take it easy. I ain't dissing you."

"Dissing?"

"Never mind, okay? So tell me about your plan. You're gonna exhaust Batman, you said. How you gonna do that when you don't even know who's behind that mask of his? It ain't like he's in the phone book."

"If I know the enemies of a man, I do not need his name. You will tell me his enemies."

"Not unless you give me all night and half a' tomorrow. I mean, it's a long list."

"Some of them."

"Lemme see . . . there's the Joker, Two-Face, the Ventriloquist, the Penguin, Catwoman—"

"A woman?"

"Hell of a woman. But nobody's seen her lately. The rest of 'em are doin' time—"

"Doing time?"

"In the slammer. Up the river. In jail. In *prison,* Bane!"

"Ah, prison." Bane chuckled.

"The Penguin's in Blackgate, unless he's busted out. The rest I mentioned are in Arkham Asylum."

"Two prisons in one city?"

"Arkham ain't exactly a prison. It's a loony bin . . . an insane asylum. The real crazies go there."

"But it is like a prison?"

"Tighter'n any joint I ever heard about. Maximum security. Listen, some of the cons in Arkham would make the cons back where we come from look like petunias. They say the Joker alone has killed more than a thousand citizens. I hear one shrink—psychiatrist—that examined him went nutso himself, and another joined a monastery."

"He is an enemy of the Batman?"

"Batman's the only one's ever been able to put him away." Bird glanced in the rearview mirror at the empty street behind him.

"And these others, Two-Face, the Ventriloquist—"

"Ain't in the Joker's league, but not because they ain't trying."

"All enemies of the Batman."

"He put 'em in Arkham."

"If they were to escape?"

"I guess Batman'd go after them."

The Ford passed the city limits and turned onto a small access road that ran parallel to the highway. Bird pulled into the driveway of a small motel—a collection of six frame cabins, badly needing paint and roofing. There was a crudely lettered sign nailed next to the door of a seventh, equally shabby, cabin:

OFFICE

HOURLY RATES

NO DRUGS

Bane and Bird got out of the Ford and moved toward the closest cabin.

"We got a program?" Bird asked.

"You call on the telephone. Get me five women for later. No, six."

"*Six?* Hey, Bane, I know you're a stud but—"

"Six. For after I sleep."

Bane went into the cabin and, without undressing, dropped himself onto the bed. He stared up at the ceiling, at the rectangle of light from the single window.

"*No sueño,*" he said aloud.

But Bane did dream, as he knew he would. The rectangle on the ceiling blurred, and the edges twisted and re-formed into a woman's face—

"*Madre,*" Bane murmured.

—and the face dissolved and became a building with high stone walls perched on the edge of a high cliff overlooking a placid sea—

"*Casa. Mi casa.*"

Bane squirmed and moaned. . . .

He was condemned to life in prison before he was born. His father had committed a serious crime—Bane never learned exactly what it was —and escaped while he was being taken to Peña Duro, a huge, high-walled prison that dominated the southern coastline of the island of Santa Prisca. A squad of *Los Rompos,* the tiny nation's green-shirted military police, searched for a week, in vain. Somehow Bane's father had managed to get off the island; perhaps he went to Haiti, perhaps to Puerto Rico, perhaps he got as far as Cuba. It made no difference to Santa Prisca's governor what happened to him. What was important was that someone pay for his crime. According to Santa Priscan law only a male child could serve the sentence of the father. When the green shirts came for his mother, Naria, Bane was a week away from being born. Under the medieval codes of this island nation, her unborn child was charged with the crimes of his father. Although Naria had herself done no wrong, she was taken to Peña Duro where, screaming, she gave birth. The child was born to life and a life sentence. The law made Naria responsible for her son until his seventh birthday; then she was free to go. However, once she entered the steel gates of the prison, she knew she would never live to pass through them again.

Bane would grow to manhood there, in that place of misery and despair, would learn what he knew of life, and would be given his name by a fat, cruel warden. His first memories were of cold stone floors and the rats that peered curiously at him from beneath his mother's cot. Naria must have nursed him, held him; perhaps she even crooned lullabies to him. But he did not remember her doing any of those things. When he tried to recall her voice, his mind's ear heard only whimpers and sobs coming from the next cell as, every night, guards and inmates alike savaged her. Peña Duro's authorities felt their job was to ensure that no one ever got outside the walls; they were indifferent to what happened inside them.

When Bane was six, he watched his mother die. There was nothing particularly memorable about it. She stumbled back into her cell after the nightly ordeal, sat on the cot, her back against the bars, slumped, and simply stopped breathing. Bane knew immediately that she was dead. He was familiar with death. His child's eyes had watched several men being stabbed to death, several more beaten to death. His mother's dying was normal, expected.

Guards wrapped her body in a dirty sheet and carried it away. A fat man with a cigar entered the cell, grabbed Bane's hand, and pulled.

"Come on," he said. "Got to watch your mama go to her reward."

The fat man took Bane through the gate. As they walked, Bane gazed around curiously. He had never before seen the endless blue sky, the green grass, the palm trees, nor heard the sigh of the wind and, in the distance, the roar of the ocean breaking against a rocky shoreline. Once he looked up to see what had ruffled his hair and was surprised to find nothing; he had never before felt a breeze. He and the fat man followed the two guards bearing Naria's corpse up a steep path to the edge of a cliff to a place the fat man called Punto de Tiburon.

The fat man squatted and put his face inches from Bane's; the stink of his breath made the child gag. "You know what happens to your mama now?" the fat man asked. "She gets eaten by sharks."

The guards flung the corpse, and Bane watched it drop, briefly shatter the surface of the water, and slowly sink. Bane thought he saw a dark shadow glide toward the spot where the body vanished into the green-blue depths.

The fat man led Bane back inside the prison, to a large room with white walls and a long wooden desk. The man sat in a leather-covered chair, unwrapped a cigar, and said, "Your mother has left you quite alone, little one. She has left you without a single guardian but the state. But the state is no one's mother. You must fend for yourself, little one. I am releasing you from protective custody and into the general population."

A guard took the child back to his mother's cell and locked him in. That first night, alone with the beasts of Peña Duro, Bane did not sleep. He sat hunched on the cot and listened to the sounds—the screams, cries, moans, and shrieks—he had heard all the nights of his life but had never before heeded. He squeezed his eyes shut and tried to remember what he had seen and heard earlier—sky, grass, trees, wind—but he could not.

At dawn the cell was unlocked, and Bane joined the procession of convicts shuffling along the high catwalk overlooking the mess hall. He felt a hand on his shoulder. "We will become friends today, eh?"

The speaker was a convict Bane had often seen joining the crowd that had gathered around Naria, a bulky, bald man with a ring through the left side of his nose, joined by a chain to another ring in his left ear. "You would like to be friends with me, would you not?"

A second convict stepped from the cell they were passing and said, "The boy does not want your filthy hand on him, Puerco." This man, Bane knew, was Trogg—squat, copper-skinned, his huge shoulders and arms lined with bulging veins. Bane had once seen Trogg kill another man with a single blow. "Release him," Trogg said.

"He's mine. One so small as this can slip beneath the notice of the guards. He will be useful to me."

Without warning, Trogg struck the bald man under the chin. "I said release him!" Puerco lurched backward, his body slamming into Bane. Suddenly the boy slipped over the safety rail and fell.

His eyes opened to blackness. Had his sight been taken from him? He stood, and with his hands extended, he stepped once, twice, then waved his arms. Suddenly a circle of the brightest light he had ever seen appeared in front of him and, standing in the center of the circle, a figure that was even brighter than the light—a figure that was somehow familiar. Bane's lips began to form a question, to ask who the stranger was, but before he could speak, the figure said, "Yourself."

"Myself?"

"We are one. I am as you will be many years from now."

"You are me?"

"What you will become. A physical and mental paragon. The living embodiment of human superiority. The blood of kings runs in you. The blood of your father. The world is yours and will be yours one day. Men will be like cattle before you. Like sheep. For only a few may rule the many, and you are one of a rare breed. Only one danger stands in the way of your mastering the world."

"What is that?"

"Fear. The fear that lies at the heart. Only this can keep you from what is yours. Conquer the fear in your heart and you may have anything you desire. You will be second to no man and master of all."

First the figure's voice, and then the figure itself, and finally the circle of light—these faded, and in their place, something else appeared—a giant with horns and scalloped wings that was as dark as the light had been bright—a giant bat.

The boy screamed and died.

And awoke. He was sitting upright on a bed in what he recognized as the prison infirmary. He had been in a coma for thirty-one days.

The next morning, in the breakfast line, Trogg jostled him. Bane felt Trogg's hand on his belly, slipping something beneath his shirt. In a whisper, Trogg said, "You do not have to do this."

"But I will," Bane said.

Later, alone in his cell, Bane held up what Trogg had given him: an ice pick. After dinner, he went to Puerco's cell. Puerco lay facedown on his cot, half asleep.

"Do you still want me to be your friend?" Bane asked.

The guards counted forty stab wounds in Puerco's body. They followed a trail of blood to Bane. They put metal cuffs on Bane's wrists and took him to the warden's office.

"The child has turned feral," the fat man said. "Like father, like son." It was then that the fat man gave the boy his name. "He is *veneno*. He is a bane. I will not have such abominations in my prison."

The cuffs slid down Bane's thin wrists and off; they clanked on the floor. The fat man looked at them, exhaled a cloud of cigar smoke, and said, "Listen to me, little bane. You will be thrown into the *cavidad oscuro*. The cuffs will fit snug before you come out again."

Bane stared into the fat man's eyes. "I spoke to my mother last night, my warden. She says they stoke a special fire for you."

"Throw him in the hole!" the fat man screamed to the guards. "He will have hair on his chest before I release him!"

The *cavidad oscuro* had been dug by clergy nearly three centuries ago, when the prison had been a monastery. Those sent there were told by the priests to pray for deliverance. But the only deliverance any ever found was madness or death. Bane would bow to neither. He would not surrender to fear. He would become fear.

The chamber was only eight of his child's paces long, six wide. Walls and floor were made of stone bricks. There were no sanitary facilities, no cot, only an iron grate set in the center of the floor, another in the ceiling, and a narrow ledge around the walls. He was not alone. Crabs were scuttling through the grate, and rats squeezed through a crack in the masonry. Bane found a loose brick and waited. When one of the rats came near him, he smashed its skull.

He felt water on his bare feet. The cell was below sea level at high tide; each night, the ocean would flood it. Clinging to tiny fingerholds in the walls, Bane rose with the water until he could reach and grab the ceiling grate. Hatred gave him the strength to hold on—hatred, and the promise of the man he would become. He learned to welcome the nightly visits of the sea, to fill his lungs with breath and move around below the water, sometimes capturing a fish that he would eat raw. During the day, he sat on the ledge and used his mind to travel outside the cell, the prison, to span a world of sky and grass and trees. He was happy there, in his imagined universe, until he met—

The thing he had seen in his vision—the bat-creature, the horned, winged giant, looming before him, still darker than night. But this time he did not scream, did not cower in fear. Instead he forced himself to attack. He lunged at the beast's neck, but before his fingers could close on it, a leathery wing slapped him tumbling backward. Bane scrambled to his feet and again he lunged, but the bat figure rose straight up into the shadows, higher and higher, until it blended with the darkness, until all that was visible were its gleaming white fangs.

Bane shrieked with frustration and collapsed, once again alone in his cell.

More than four thousand days, Bane was in that pit. More than ten years. He embarrassed the warden by refusing to die. Finally the warden released him, hoping that someone would seek revenge for Puerco's murder. But the fat man did not realize what Bane had become to the lost and damned of Peña Duro.

He had become a legend.

Many wanted his favor. Many wanted to serve him. One was an American called Bird.

"You got the power, kid," Bird said to him. "I seen it before. You need anything, you call on me."

"And how would I return these favors?"

"You got the magic, kid. I could use some of that. See, I'm doing life on this rock. I got screwed by some partners up in Gotham City. Guy named Novak. I'm kind of anxious to get back there and set things right. Maybe some of your magic could help me fly over these walls."

"We will talk. You will tell me about . . . Gotham."

Bird did. He told Bane of the spires that stabbed the clouds, the glittering cars that plied the pink and green and orange streets, the lavish homes lined with gold and money and the women—voluptuous women clad in silk and furs, smiling, beckoning, welcoming.

"Who is the king of this Gotham City?" Bane once asked. "Who rules?"

"Nobody, exactly," Bird told him. "I guess if you had to name one guy who's ahead of everybody else, it'd have to be Batman."

"Bat-man?"

Bane remembered his vision—the horned, winged giant that loomed over him all those terrible nights in the *cavidad oscuro*. The bat thing he had not been able to kill.

"Tell me more about this bat-man," he said, and listened as Bird spoke for hours.

Bane became a model prisoner. The warden, proud that he had tamed this animal, allowed Bane to work in the library. When part of the prison had been a monastery, the monks had assembled thousands of books; all of them were still there, and a few hundred newer volumes that had been collected over the years. Bird taught him to read, and the books brought the world to him.

As Bane improved his mind, he also improved his body. Thousands of push-ups every day. Thousands of sit-ups and pull-ups. And each day of each year brought him closer to the image of perfection in his mind.

His reign over the lost and forgotten of Peña Duro did not go unchallenged. Many coveted his position and his power, and occasionally someone tried to take them. Usually, Bane was able to discourage the rebels by breaking a few bones. But one would-be usurper would not be discouraged. He was a newcomer who called himself the Mick. He was as muscular as Trogg and as big as Bane himself. He was bald to the middle of his head; the back of his head sprouted stringy red hair that hung below his shoulder blades. His eyes were the color of stone.

The first time, the Mick came at Bane with fists. They fought for an hour, until they could fight no more. As he limped back to his cell, Bane thought he could see doubt in the faces of the convicts who had been cheering him minutes earlier. The second time they fought, the Mick used a weapon, a shiv, a jagged shard of glass with one end wrapped in tape to form a handle. He lunged at Bane from the shadows and ripped a nine-inch gash in Bane's side. Bane backed away until he hit the cell bars. Then he lowered his head and charged. His head crashed into the Mick's stomach as the glass tore another wound in his back. Locked onto each other, Bane and the Mick toppled to the floor. Bane grabbed a handful of the man's long red hair and pulled his head back. The Mick strained, veins bulging in his neck, forcing his head forward. The hair came out in Bane's fist. Bane bit the Mick's bicep. He dropped his knife but an instant later brought his knee up into Bane's groin. Bane rolled away and got to his feet. The Mick was already standing. Covered with sweat and blood, they punched, kicked, gouged. This fight ended as the first one had, with both men too exhausted to continue.

Staggering away, bleeding and barely able to walk, Bane was certain of the doubt in the faces of those around him.

"Next time," Trogg said, "you are his. Kill him tonight while he sleeps."

"No," Bane said. "I would lose respect. I will kill him where all can see."

Bane returned to the scene of the fight and found what he sought: the handful of red hair. At dinner that night, he ate hastily and left the mess hall while the other convicts were still at their meals. He went to the warden's office and put his ear to the door. Nothing. Slowly he opened the door and went inside. The room was empty. He crossed to the desk, picked up an inkwell, and spilled it on the carpet. Then he dipped a forefinger in the ink and scrawled on the wall, *El director es un canalla!* Then he dropped the Mick's red hair on the desktop.

It was crude to the point of stupidity. But the warden was a stupid man. Stupid and vindictive.

They put the Mick in the *cavidad oscuro* for three months. He might not have survived if Bane hadn't often dropped bundles of food through the grate and whispered instructions to him.

When they hauled the Mick out, no longer muscled and formidable, they bound him to a pillar in the mess hall. The warden himself lashed him with a long black whip until the Mick drooped in his bonds, unconscious.

When he had recovered enough to work, they had him dig a trench in the yard, and fill it in, and dig it, and fill it in; he did that for ten days and nights, with little rest and less food.

On the eleventh day, he begged the warden for mercy. The warden granted it, again proud that he had broken another one of the bad ones.

After dinner, Bane and fifty other inmates came to the Mick. Bane pulled a shiv from beneath his shirt, tossed it spinning into the air, caught the point delicately between thumb and forefinger, and extended the taped handle toward the Mick.

"Use it," Bane said.

The Mick stared at the weapon as though he had never seen anything like it.

"Take it and use it," Bane said.

The Mick grasped the taped end. "I thought you were my friend," he muttered.

Bane slapped him—a casual, almost indifferent swat to the cheek.

"I will break your bones, all of them," Bane said. "When you can no longer move, I will then stuff you into the hole and watch the rats feast on you."

The Mick lunged, shiv forward. Stepping aside as the Mick's momentum carried him forward, Bane stepped behind him and punched him twice in the kidneys. The Mick slammed into a wall, and Bane kicked him behind the left knee. The Mick fell, twisted around to a sitting position, and swung the shiv at Bane's shin. Bane danced back a half step, raised a foot, and smashed it down on the Mick's hand. The shiv snapped in half; a bloody shard jutted from the Mick's palm.

Bane turned to the others. "This is the man who made you doubt me," he shouted.

Bane grabbed the Mick's hair, now waist length, hauled him to his feet, spun him, shoved him into the wall, and stepped back. Bane lowered his head and drove a shoulder into the Mick's back. There was a muffled crack, and the Mick slid to the floor. He lay facedown, arms and legs flopped at odd angles. His body seemed to be empty.

"Broke his back," someone murmured.

Bane said, "I had thought to kill you. I have a better idea. I will let you live. When others look at you, they will remember this day. When I look at you, *I* will again enjoy this moment."

But an hour later, the Mick died. When the warden saw the corpse, he ordered a squad of guards to find Bane. They attacked with clubs and tear gas. When they finally brought Bane down, the warden stepped forward, took a revolver from his belt, and shot Bane in both thighs.

"Take him to the hole?" a guard asked.

"No. The infirmary."

The inmates wondered if even Bane could survive whatever the warden planned. But there was no torture. Instead, each day for a month, a doctor from outside came to tend Bane's injuries. Each day, Bird brought Bane food from the warden's own kitchen. Bird often saw four strangers, men wearing fine suits, clustered around Bane's bed, talking with the warden. When Bane was fully recovered, his arms and legs were chained, and he was taken to the warden's dispensary. The warden and the strangers were waiting. Bane was strapped to an operating table, his head and right arm were shaved, and the doctor opened a case of bright surgical instruments.

"What is the purpose of this experiment?" the warden asked one of the strangers.

"You are not being paid to know," the stranger replied.

But the doctor was friendlier. "A technique to create the perfect fighting man. We begin with a drug"—the doctor jabbed a needle into Bane's wrist—"a steroid compound I call *Venom*. It also contains elements that stimulate the adrenal glands and others that affect the corpus callosum portion of the brain."

None of this meant anything to the warden.

"If he lives through this," the doctor continued, "we will implant polyacrylamide shields subcutaneously over his most vulnerable parts—heart, lungs, kidneys, temples. He will be invulnerable to everything short of a bullet fired at close range. He will be quite the superman."

Bane coughed. His back arched, and he strained against the straps.

"The drug is taking hold," the doctor said, forcing open Bane's mouth and shoving a plastic tongue protector inside. "None of the other subjects lasted more than fifteen minutes after the initial injection."

Bane's back lifted further from the table. A front tooth cracked off at the gum. His eyes were open and bulging, the whites suddenly laced with red lines, and thick, gray tears spilled from the lower lids. His skin darkened to crimson, and the muscles beneath it twitched.

"Looks like he's having a real trip," one of the strangers said.

Bane's breath exploded from him in short gasps. The strap on his right arm tore loose from the table, and the arm shot upward; the elbow locked and the fingers curled into a fist.

Then the arm dropped, and Bane relaxed. His eyes closed, his breathing became deep and regular, and his crimson skin faded to its normal olive color.

"Well, well," the doctor said. "Our superman lives." He stuck a Syrette into Bane's right forefinger and watched it fill with blood. "I shall run some tests, and if all is well, we will continue tomorrow."

The next day the surgery began. Slits in the skin and muscle, first, and the sliding in of the polyacrylamide shields—simple stuff. Then the more complicated part: two holes bored in the base of his skull and the insertion of metal tubes. The metal tubes were attached to plastic tubes, enabling the drug—the Venom—to bypass the blood-brain barrier and be introduced directly into the brain. After each operation, the doctor expected Bane to die, and instead, after each, he recovered. But not without cost. Only four months ago, when he had been hauled from the hole, he had been as slim and hard as a poker. Now his body was a mass of lumps and bulges—the shields, of course, but also the effect of the Venom on his muscles.

He was now huge and grotesque; however, he did not mind, for he was also close to his idea of perfection.

In the sixth month of the experiment, Bird found the opportunity he had hoped for. The doctor had been careless, leaving a vial of Venom on the table next to Bane's bed. Bird did not understand all that was happening to Bane, but he had overheard some of what the doctor was trying to accomplish and he knew the drug was an essential element in it. Such a drug had to be enormously valuable. When he was taking away Bane's dinner dishes, Bird grabbed the Venom and hid it under the tray. Bane saw the maneuver and smiled.

If he ever got out, Bird could sell the drug for a small fortune. *If.*

At nine in the morning, they came for Bane. Four of the strangers armed with tranquilizer guns. They handcuffed and led him toward the gate. Bane realized that if they ever got to wherever they were taking him, his chances for escape would be greatly diminished; he would be on unfamiliar turf dealing with enemies much smarter than the warden.

The gate swung open and for a moment Bane was transfixed: the sky, grass, trees . . . and, on the road outside the walls, what looked like a steel box mounted on wheels—obviously a mobile cage of some kind, a cell stronger than any in Peña Duro and perhaps a foreshadowing of life to come. He couldn't let them put him inside it.

He held his breath until he was sure his skin was darkening, until he was certain that what he was about to do would be convincing to his captors. And then, as they were passing through the gate, he wheezed and folded himself at the waist.

"Help," he gasped.

"The sonnabitch's having a seizure," one of the strangers said. He squatted and looked up at Bane's face. "What's goin' on? You need a doctor—"

Bane kneed him in the chin, whirled, and drove his head into the second man. The third man got his gun up and fired a tranquilizer dart that struck Bane in the temple and buried itself in a plastic shield. Bane kicked him in the belly, hopped over his body, and ran, leaving all three strangers lying in the road. The path he was on angled steeply upward, and suddenly Bane recognized it. Eleven years earlier, he had walked it with the corpse of his mother.

Behind him he heard a siren and shots. Something struck him in the lower back and knocked him sprawling in the dirt—a rifle bullet, hitting the kidney shield. He scrambled to his feet and ran. At the top of the path, he paused and looked back. Guards were pouring through the gate; guards were firing from the top of the wall.

He scanned the area: sky, grass, trees—and far below, the ocean that had swallowed his mother.

He jumped.

He hit the water feetfirst and plunged downward. He knew how to hold his breath and how to swim—he had had plenty of practice in the hole. But the cuffs were a problem; he did not know how to swim without his hands. He focused, sent his will coursing through vein and muscle, seeing the chain between the cuffs part, seeing his arms spread wide and—

The chain snapped.

A long, dark shape passed between him and the sunlight. From his reading, he knew this had to be a shark. The shark that had feasted on his mother? He began to swim away. The shark dived, moving quickly. In seconds it would catch him. His fingers scraped along a sandy bottom and closed on something: a rock. In the hole, he had used stones to smash the rats. Was *this* hole so different? He twisted and saw through the blue-green murk a white snout and two rows of glistening teeth. He swung and struck the beast just above its eyes. Again. And again. The shark's fins had stopped moving and blood was diffusing in the water around it. *You want to eat me? I will show you who gets eaten.* Bane bit into the white skin and tore away a chunk of gristle. Then he plunged his hand into the hole he had made and grabbed a fistful of gore and yanked it out.

Bane surfaced beneath an overhang, found fingerholds in the cliff, and waited until he had stopped panting. Then he swam along the base of the cliff until he came to a beach. He crawled onto the glittering sand and stood. On the horizon, he could see the walls of Peña Duro.

He stayed on the beach until night. A cold wind blew from the sea, and the waves slapped the sand loudly. In the distance Bane saw brief flashes of light. He walked until he came to a path that paralleled the shoreline. The flashes of light were directly overhead now, and fat rain-drops began to smack him. At first the storm disturbed him, but after an hour, he admired its impersonal fury. Occasionally, the lightning revealed the silhouette of the prison. It took him most of the night to reach one of the walls. He lay flat against it. He knew the routine of this place as well as he knew his own heartbeat. This was Saturday—actually, Sunday morning. On Saturday night, the warden left Peña Duro to visit a village nearby. He returned at dawn, always drunk, sometimes accompanied by a woman.

Bane waited. He could see clouds now, ashen against the pale sky. He heard the growl of an engine: the warden's ancient station wagon, struggling up the road. The station wagon stopped in front of the gate, and the warden climbed out and swayed, clutching a bottle in both hands, the stump of a cigar clenched in his teeth.

"Open up," he shouted.

Bane ran. He punched the warden in the face and caught the sagging body as the bottle and the cigar hit the ground. He groped beneath the warden's raincoat and found the revolver. A spotlight swept past him, stopped, swept back.

"Let him go," someone called.

The warden squirmed in Bane's grasp. Bane's blow had not been hard.

Bane pressed the barrel of the gun to the warden's temple and shouted, "Send out Bird or the warden dies."

There was no reply.

"Tell them," Bane said into the warden's ear.

"*You!*" the warden gasped. "You're dead! My men saw blood—"

"Tell them!" Bane repeated, pressing the gun barrel harder.

"Do as he says." The warden's voice was shrill.

Still no answer.

Bane lowered the revolver and shot the warden in the left leg. The warden screamed. Bane let him fall. Bane shot the warden's right leg. He pressed the gun barrel to the warden's head and looked up.

From the top of the wall: "All right."

Minutes passed. The gate swung open. Bird, Trogg, and an inmate named Zombie trotted to Bane and the warden.

"I knew you'd come back for us, Magic Man," Bird said. "I hope you don't mind my bringing some pals. These guys'll be plenty useful, believe me." He turned to his companions. "Didn't I *tell* you he's got the magic?"

Bane nodded toward the station wagon. "You drive," he said to Bird.

"No good, Magic Man. They'll have this island sealed up tight. We need a chopper."

"A chopper?"

"A helicopter. An airplane."

"Tell them."

Bird shouted instructions, and then they got into the station wagon.

"It'll take 'em a while to get here," Bird said. "But they'll come, don't you worry."

The warden was huddled in the backseat, palms pressed to the bloody holes in his legs. He was sobbing.

"Can't we shut him up?" Trogg said.

"I like to listen to him," Bane said.

A few minutes later they heard the *chup chup chup* of an approaching helicopter. It dropped from the clouds and landed a few feet away.

Bane handed Bird the gun. "Get us out of here," he said.

"You got it, Mister Magic."

There was only the pilot in the aircraft, a young man wearing a military uniform. Bane, Trogg, and Zombie bundled the warden into the rear compartment; Bird sat next to the pilot and aimed the revolver at him.

"Up, up, and away," Bird said. "Take 'er south. I got connections in Venezuela."

"I . . . I have always treated you well," the warden said to Bane between sobs. "Your mother, too. Without me, who knows what would have happened to you?"

The blur that was Santa Prisca was receding in the distance. Ahead of and below them there was only the sea. Bane slid open the door and grabbed the warden by the collar of his raincoat.

"You know what happens to you now?" Bane asked, his hand on the back of the fat man's head. "You get eaten by sharks."

The warden fell, flailing and screaming.

During the three months it took Bird to arrange travel north to the United States, Bane questioned him continuously about Gotham City. Although Bird boasted of the glories of other places—New York, Los

Angeles, Chicago, St. Louis, Metropolis—Bane always brought the conversation back to Gotham.

"Why you so hipped on the Big G?" Bird once asked.

"I do not know," Bane replied slowly. "But tell me again what you told me in Peña Duro."

Bird spoke for an hour. When he was done, Bane said, "This Batman. What of him?"

"Nobody knows who he is or what his game is. But Gotham after dark is *his*. He's taken down every major player in the city. The only ones who aren't scared of him are *crazy*."

And now Bane knew why he was so obsessed with Gotham. Perfectly logical: it was where fear ruled. Conquer fear—conquer the bat—and you own the city.

"When the Mick challenged me . . . if he had won, he would have ruled the prison."

"Yeah, Magic Man, but there's no *way* you're ever gonna lose."

"It is so—"

Bane groaned and opened his eyes. He was disoriented, as he always was when he came from his past. Slowly, he became aware of the room around him—the motel room just outside the Gotham City limits. The rectangle on the ceiling was bright and sharp: sunlight. He must have slept for hours. He was hungry. And where were Bird and the women?

4

 James Gordon had driven out of the parking lot behind police headquarters and was entering the freeway before he became aware that he was not alone in the car. Batman arose from the backseat and said, "Good evening, Commissioner."

"I've finally figured out how you do that. You're one of those ninjas, aren't you? You learned it in Japan."

"Correspondence course," Batman said. "It was either ninja or air-conditioning repair, and I already had a black suit."

"Okay, I asked. What's on your mind?"

"What's happening with the army?"

"How do you know about that?" Gordon looked at his passenger in the rearview mirror.

"Lots of radio transmission in code on the military bands. Too much smoke for there to be no fire."

"Somebody ripped off a supply of rockets," Gordon said. "The little kind, the ones you aim from your shoulder."

"Antitank?"

"Something like that. The feds aren't telling us dumb flatfoots much, but I gather the operation was slick as ice."

"How many, Commissioner?"

"As I said, our federal brethren aren't into sharing. My guess is a lot. More than a dozen."

"Anything else unusual happen lately?"

"Same old same old," Gordon said. "Six hookers turned up dead this morning. Necks broken. The ladies of the night are always getting killed, but usually not six at a shot."

"And they usually die of gunshots or stab wounds."

Gordon nodded.

"That it?" Batman asked.

"One more odd one. Eight moving vans were stolen from a rental outfit."

"The prostitutes are probably a coincidence, but the rockets and vans might be connected."

"How so?"

"Terrorist weapons."

"Could be, I guess," Gordon said. "Use the vans as giant bombs."

"Exactly. Fill a truck with explosives or magnesium shavings, detonate it by remote control, and you can take out a bridge or tunnel—or almost anything else."

"I'll put out the word."

"Commissioner, I'd like you to do me a favor."

"No kidding? I never thought I'd hear you say that."

"Someone was at the Manklins—"

"So it *was* you who put them away. How'd you know where to find them?"

"People should be careful what they say in sleazy bars. The scuzzball on the next stool might be me."

Gordon shook his head in wonder. "What can I do for you? You said there was someone . . ."

"Big. About seven feet tall. Strange body—too lumpy to be either an athlete or bodybuilder. I'd say there was surgery involved. He's very fast and he speaks with a Spanish accent. I've come up with zilch on him."

"Then I probably won't do any better, but I'll see if it rings a bell for anybody."

"Thanks."

"This guy important?" Gordon asked.

"I think he did the job at the steak house."

"Not the Manklins?"

"For once in their foul lives, they're innocent. They've been framed."

"I almost wish I hadn't heard that."

"You've still got plenty of past crimes to hang on them."

Gordon braked at a red light. "Can I drop you anywhere? Opera maybe? Basketball game? Costume party?"

He turned around to look, but the backseat was now empty.

5

Bane watched Bird, Trogg, and Zombie eating, stuffing themselves with pizza, hamburgers, potatoes. There was no conversation. The cabin was silent except for the sounds of their chewing and an occasional rattle of a wrapper. He was pleased. The robbery at the military depot had gone well. He now had three dozen excellent military rockets.

It had been Zombie's idea, and Zombie had supplied the information they had needed to carry it out. Zombie wasn't the man's real name, of course, nor was it a prison nickname. It was a military code name. Zombie had been a covert operations officer—a former navy SEAL who had gone into business for himself. He was an expert in demolitions, counterterrorist tactics, sabotage, assassination. He had been put in Peña Duro after he was caught trying to mine the harbor at Guantánamo Bay, the US naval base in Cuba. Wounded, he had been stupid enough to seek help in Santa Prisca. He had been betrayed by men he thought were allies and taken to the governor, who believed that Zombie might be traded to the group that had hired him, a cadre of Middle Eastern terrorists. But the terrorists weren't interested. The governor had ordered Zombie imprisoned while he negotiated a deal with the American CIA. Bane was grateful to Bird for introducing him to this very useful fellow.

Bird was himself extremely useful. His former career as a smuggler, thief, and extortionist had given him extensive knowledge of the criminal community in the United States and the Caribbean. The hundred thousand dollars in Bird's Swiss bank account had financed the trip from Venezuela, the motel hideout, and the supplies needed to rob the military depot. Like Zombie, Bird had made the mistake of trusting Santa Priscans. In partnership with a man named Novak and a group of Santa Priscan nationals, he had arranged to deliver a load of cocaine to Gotham City. His partners had decided that Bird's share of the profits was better spent elsewhere. It took only a brief meeting with a police chief and a briefer meeting with the island's chief judge to put Bird behind the gray walls. It could have been worse. The judge had been perfectly willing to put Bird in front of a firing squad, but Bird's former associates weren't cruel men.

Trogg was the third pizza eater and the only one who hadn't been framed. He was also the most innocent of the three. He had been imprisoned for the crime he had committed, but it was the *only* serious crime he had ever done. A drug dealer's driver had decided that Trogg's niece would make a nice trophy and tried to drag her out of the café where she worked as a waitress. Trogg hit the driver once, cracking his cheekbone completely in half. The case wasn't important enough to take to court— not prudent to waste valuable state's time on an illiterate laborer. In Santa Prisca, police captains have limited judicial powers. So a Capitán Juarez sentenced Trogg to twenty years in Peña Duro. He had been inside exactly four of those years the day he punched Puerco and had served just over sixteen the day, four months ago, he had accepted Bird's invitation to step through the front gate and join Bane.

"Finish your meal," Bane said to the three. "Then we plan the next phase of our work tonight." He turned to Bird. "Telephone your friend. Six women for later."

"Hey, Magic, is that a good idea? Considering the . . . problems you had last week—"

"*I* had no problems. *They* did. They were unable to do what I paid them for."

Bird wiped his mouth with a paper napkin and said, slowly, "This is wacko, but you don't think the drug maybe . . . got in your way?"

"It was *their* fault. Make the call."

"You got it."

While Bird used the telphone, Bane refilled the vial strapped to his right forearm with Venom. He had a large supply of the greenish liquid, again thanks to the resourceful Bird. The first thing Bird had done when they arrived in Gotham was to visit an acquaintance in the pharmaceutical business. Bird produced the Venom he had stolen from the warden's infirmary and asked the chemist if he could analyze, and then duplicate, the formula. When Bird and Bane returned the next day, the chemist was grinning.

"Hey, *dudes,*" he said, tossing his head and flipping his long blond hair out of his eyes. "This stuff is *righteous.* All those steroids and colloids and shit . . . Wow. You know?"

"You have the formula?" Bane asked.

The chemist held up a sheet of computer paper. "All printed out and everything. Man, I was so impressed I ran off *two* copies."

Bird, standing behind Bane, put a forefinger to his lips, signaling the chemist to stop talking. But the chemist had snorted six lines of coke earlier and was not receptive.

"Two copies?" Bane asked quietly.

"One for myself. Not that I need it. Man, I was so impressed I *memorized* it. Last night, man, I dreamed that *Madonna* came to me wearing nothing but a steel bikini and, dig, she *sang* the formula to me. To the tune of 'Material Girl' I think it was. Yeah, and then she took off her steel bra and there it was *tattooed* on her bazongas. You think there is a *way* I am *ever* gonna forget that?"

"In about a minute," Bird murmured.

But it took Bane much less time—only a few seconds—to snap the chemist's neck.

Another chemist friend of Bird's, cautioned to be discreet, actually synthesized a supply of the Venom. Bane's trial-and-error taught him that he needed two hits each day, spaced twelve hours apart. The apparatus implanted in his body at the prison worked perfectly: when he pressed a button on the vial strapped to his wrist, sending a premeasured dose through a tube to a conduit sunk in his skull and into his brain, he was fine. If he delayed pressing the button by so much as an hour, he became nervous, his mouth dried, his vision blurred. If he delayed longer, his limbs spasmed, and the world around him melted and he hallucinated—

—the bat-thing, looming out of the darkness, mocking him—

Bane pressed the button, felt the warmth spread from the top of his head down to his jaw, and from there to the tips of his fingers and toes. He relaxed.

". . . I sent for the girls," Bird was saying. "Be here at midnight. That okay? I told 'em to bring some oysters. Lotta oysters."

"Let us get to work," Bane said. He swept the pizza cartons from the table and spread out a blueprint.

"This is a schematic of Arkham Asylum," Bird said to Zombie and Trogg. "They rebuilt it a coupla years ago 'cause the old place had revolving doors. Worse security than the country clubs at Allenwood and Danbury. This area here"—he pointed to a shaded area on the schematic—"is where they store the real nutcases. The Joker, Two-Face, Abattoir, some others. Mostly, these guys don't see the light of day. Their food is sent through dumbwaiters. The corridor outside the cells is lined with heat detectors, motion detectors, pressure-sensitive flooring. Monitors in the sewer and water lines. TV cameras. A mouse gets in there, the alarm goes off, the whole joint is flooded with gas. Coupla dozen guards with Ingrams are here"—he pointed to another area—"on twenty-four-hour alert. Signals sent to the cop house downtown and the marine base. Oh, and there are battery-operated backups in case the electricity goes out."

"Very nice," Zombie said.

"What is in the walls?" Bane asked.

"Hell, Magic, whatever is in walls," Bird said. "Steel. Masonry. That kind of stuff."

"The rockets we took, they can destroy steel and masonry?"

"I don't know why not," Bird said.

"They can," Zombie said.

"Good," Bane said. "We will need a helicopter, parachutes, and gas masks."

"You going to stage a prison break?" Zombie asked.

"Yes," Bane said.

"Look, Magic," Bird said, "this is gonna cost big time, and the stash I got in the Swiss bank is just about gone."

"I have money," Zombie said.

"Yeah?" Bird asked.

"More than enough."

"Leave me," Bane said. "Call when the women arrive."

Trogg went into an adjoining cabin where he slept. Bird and Zombie walked across the parking lot to a vending machine near the motel office door and got colas.

"Zombie, old buddy, I gotta ask," said Bird. "What're *you* getting from this? I mean, Santa Prisca is history. You're a free man. You could take that money you say you got, hop a plane, and *zam*—you're in Tahiti or someplace checking the action. Why stick around?"

"I once thought I was a genius. I once thought I was the avatar of the great conquerors of history: Alexander the Great. Genghis Khan. Caesar. Von Clausewitz. Grant. Rommel. Patton. But I was wrong. Caesar would not have botched mining Guantánamo Bay. Rommel would not have trusted fools. Patton would never have allowed himself to be put into Peña Duro. I am of high competence, but in the end, I am ordinary. Bane is not. Nietzsche said that man is a rope stretching between animal and superman. Bane is the superman. I want to witness his becoming. I want to serve him."

It was the most Bird had ever heard Zombie say. "I gotta tell you, it sounds *good*. Sounds *right*."

A black limousine turned into the parking lot from the access road. Bird and Zombie watched six women in short skirts climb from the backseat.

"I hope those babes got a lotta life insurance," Bird said.

6

 Tim Drake entered the shed behind his father's mansion and went to the cistern. He twisted a knob, and as the water drained away, he removed his sweatshirt and jeans. He looked down at what he wore beneath them —boots, cape, green tights, and a red tunic emblazoned with a stylized *R*. One of Bruce's rules: once you descended into the Batcave, you left the name and identity you were born with behind. In the Cave, Tim was Robin, and he had to dress appropriately.

"I don't get it," he had once said to Alfred. "What difference do *clothes* make? Bruce isn't . . . *weird,* is he? Some kind of fetishist?"

"Not as you mean it," Alfred replied. "I am by no means certain I have all the details clear in my mind, but I can give you the gist of it. Sometime in his early travels, Bruce encountered a tribe of Native Americans—in Alaska, if memory serves. Like many if not most tribal people, they had rituals involving masks of gods. When they put on the mask and raiment of a god, they *became* that deity. They donned the mask not to hide, but to *reveal* something greater than themselves that was within them. The mask was a *trigger,* if you will. To wear the mask in the wrong context was to cause confusion, perhaps to render the god impotent. To participate in the ritual without the mask was to mock the god, with terrible consequences."

"Bruce believes in that stuff?"

"He believes in the psychological principles behind it."

"Was this a rule for the first Robin? Dick Grayson?"

"Yes. And Jason Todd, the *second* Robin."

The cistern was empty. Tim climbed in, placed his palm against a stone, and pressed. The bottom of the cistern slid aside, and Tim—now Robin—dropped to the floor of the cave below. He took a small flashlight from his belt, switched it on, and followed the beam for a mile to where the tunnel widened to the huge chamber under Wayne Manor. Moving toward the bank of computers, he stepped onto a section of the cave floor that was actually plastic camouflaged as rock; this, he knew, would activate an alarm in the house, altered to sound like a noisy refrigerator motor starting. Unless Alfred was busy with a tradesman or running an errand, he would be down shortly.

Robin sat at the computer console and tapped the "message" key. The smallest of the screens in front of him brightened: SOUTH AFRICA. So Bruce wanted him to hack into the South African embassy's data system and feed its code into the Crays. Okay, that meant Bruce hadn't gotten a line on the guy he met after the Manklin takedown. Robin had already gotten into systems of eight other embassies, the FBI, the CIA, Interpol, navy intelligence, the army's Criminal Investigation Division, Scotland Yard. Also, reluctantly, the Gotham City PD: it wasn't likely that Gordon would withhold information, but it was at least possible that the commissioner had missed something. Robin started tapping keys.

"Are we making progress?" Alfred said from behind him.

"I don't know about *we*, but *I'm* not. Hey, Alfie, give me a break. I just got here."

"Can I get you some refreshment? I've just baked some fat-free brownies."

"In a while, maybe."

"How is your father?"

"No change. He's mostly vegged out. Sits in his wheelchair staring at nothing." Jack Drake had been desperately ill for more than a year, ever since he and Tim's mother, Helen, were imprisoned by Haitian terrorists.

Jack had emerged from the ordeal with a torn body and a broken mind; Tim sometimes envisioned his father's spirit as a sodden, inert lump. Helen had died in a filthy hut.

"What does the new doctor say? Dr. Kinsolving, is it?"

"Shondra Kinsolving. She says not to hope too much, but she might be able to bring him back at least part of the way."

"Let me reiterate that if there is anything I can do—"

"Thanks, Alfred. Appreciate the offer. What's up with Bruce? I haven't seen him in weeks."

"He has been concentrating on his duties at Wayne Enterprises. The police have been managing without Batman's help. As you may have noticed, the city has been relatively quiet of late. I think that may have Master Bruce a trifle worried."

"Why?"

"For all his rationality, he has his superstitions. One of them is that after every lull there is a storm."

"Waiting for the first thundercrack, huh? You believe he's right?"

"Let us say that I believe he is seldom wrong."

"No argument there—hey, what is *this*?" Robin peered at the closest of the screens. "I think I may have just found a crack in the South African armor. Yeah, this *has* to be the password."

Robin typed and waited for the computers to do their work.

7

 The inmates at Arkham Asylum ate well. No gray institutional glop on plastic trays for them. Arkham didn't have a cook, it had a real *chef*. His name was Edward Cheatley, and he had learned his art in Paris and Rome. A few years ago, he was widely hailed as "the Wolfgang Puck of the East Coast." That was before he served his girlfriend's husband a delicious foie gras seasoned with strychnine. The husband survived, but Eddie's career didn't. He'd done a nickel at Blackgate and found that upon his release he couldn't get a job cooking at a taco stand. He had been rescued from a job cleaning rest rooms at a downtown bus depot by Jeremiah Arkham, the executive director of the asylum.

Jeremiah was called by Vicki Vale of the *Gotham Gazette* "a bizarre combination of knee-jerk do-gooder and Torquemada"; he believed in insulin shock, electroshock, isolation, prolonged confinement in straitjackets, sleep deprivation, and such original measures as putting three inches of water in a bare cell, removing an inmate's clothing, and turning off the heat. But he also believed in second chances. He had taken Eddie away from the rest rooms and told him, earnestly, "These men in my care have grave problems. But, dammit, they're *human beings,* regardless of how sick and depraved and disgusting they might be, and they deserve the benefits of fine cuisine."

Tonight, Eddie had prepared something simple: roasted Cornish game hens with a strawberry compote, dilled potato salad, steamed green beans, and for dessert, chocolate truffles. He arranged each meal on a china plate and glanced around the kitchen to be certain that the guards were adhering to Jeremiah's dictum to "leave Edward alone. He is an artist, dammit, and artists have to be trusted." Then Eddie slipped a folded piece of paper into each game hen. Probably a few of his diners would get a bite of paper before they figured out they were receiving messages, but that was all right. His old jail buddy, Bird, had paid him twenty large in used bills, and for that kind of money he was willing to compromise a little poultry.

Bruce Wayne was tooling his scarlet Lamborghini with a dented right front fender away from the Hotel François, where he had attended a chicken dinner in honor of Mayor Armand Krol, when his police scanner reported a "special four-nineteen." "Special four-nineteen" was one of Gordon's codes. The commissioner wanted to see Batman immediately. Bruce used the car phone to arrange a rendezvous and parked in an all-night garage. "Don't know where the darn tree came from," he said to the attendant, staring ruefully at the dent, which he had carefully pounded into the metal a week ago; it never hurt to reinforce the city's image of Bruce Wayne's ineptitude.

He took a briefcase from the passenger seat, tipped the attendant a hundred, and strolled to the riverfront. Concealed by a stand of trees on the strip of park between the river and the street, well away from the walk and its mercury vapor lamps, he removed a cape and mask from the briefcase and put them on. He pulled the cape around him to conceal his tuxedo and waited.

Gordon arrived five minutes later.

"What's on your mind, Commissioner?" Batman asked.

"More hookers. Six more dead hookers."

Gordon usually didn't bother him with ordinary street crimes. "Something special about them?"

"They all had bats carved into their bodies."

"I see."

"Nobody's reacted yet, not officially, but you can imagine what kind of word is going around."

"What do you think?"

"You don't really want me to answer that. But somebody's tipped the press. The *Gazette* won't play the story big, but the *Star* and the *Whisper* will and so will Channel Six. You have any ideas, I'd better hear 'em."

"Nothing tangible, Commissioner. Just a hunch."

"Spit it out."

"The man on the rooftop. Find him and you have your killer."

"What's the connection?"

"Only this: these murders don't make sense, and neither does he."

The conversation was over. Gordon turned to gaze at the river, confident that within seconds he would be alone.

Bane was pleased with himself. Cutting the bats into the women's flesh had been an inspiration. It was an ancient strategic principle: turn your enemy's friends against him. The police had to be the Batman's allies; it was logical. And Bane's careful study of Gotham City had taught him that although the police were slightly corrupt—compared to the Santa Prisca militia—they would not ignore wholesale slaughter. Especially not wholesale slaughter linked to someone much disliked. Not everyone believed Batman existed, and among those who did he was not universally popular: the underworld feared him, as was to be expected; the liberals among politicians and churchmen decried him as a vigilante, which he most certainly was; and many ordinary policemen felt he threatened the respect they needed on the streets—"You ain't no Batman" was often among the jeers they heard. Now they had an excuse to withhold cooperation, if not hunt him down.

The women had served a purpose, after all.

"Get me six more," Bane told Bird.

"Afraid no-can-do, Magic," Bird said. "You damage the merchandise. The boys aren't letting you have any more."

Bird was refusing him? Bird was *daring* to refuse him? Bird could be broken like a twig—Bane realized that the time for his dose had passed. He pressed the button on his arm and, a moment later, felt warmth. He relaxed. He would be generous; he would ignore Bird's insolence—for now.

"Perhaps you're right," Bane said. "Perhaps the six last night were enough."

"We got a program?"

"Make certain the helicopter is ready. Have Zombie check the weapons. In less than twenty-four hours, we will strike at this Arkham Asylum."

"Consider it done, Magic Man."

Bird's tone was servile, almost fawning. Bane decided to forgive him.

8

The first alarm sounded at eight the next evening—an explosion in front of the Harvester's Bank and Trust near Robinson Park. Within the next five minutes, there were six other explosions, all near banks. Police dispatchers spoke rapidly into their microphones, and sirens began to wail in the streets.

At 8:30, a school bus parked in a garage burst into flames, igniting several other buses nearby.

At 8:45, the huge Reuter Lumberyard, the state's largest, caught fire.

Sitting in a helicopter at a private airstrip near the motel, Bane listened to the police and fire dispatches. He twisted in his seat to face Zombie, who sat in the pilot's seat. "You have done excellent work," Bane shouted over the roar of the engine. "It is time to visit Arkham Asylum."

Zombie pulled at the controls, and the aircraft rose into the air.

Bane saw the ground drop away. He stifled an urge to laugh with sheer pleasure. He was where he should be, high above the earth and its tiny creatures. The horizon tilted, and Bane leaned forward in his seat, filling his eyes with a god's view of creation.

•   •   •

Batman paused to listen to the radio report the lumberyard fire. Then he continued curling the two-hundred-pound dumbbell.

"Shouldn't you be reacting?" Alfred asked from his chair near the computers. "It's most unlike the Dark Knight to ignore blatant criminal activity."

"I'm not a 'dark knight' except to third-rate journalists with turgid prose styles," Batman replied. "And I'm not ignoring anything. I'm waiting. Fires in a garage and lumberyard, explosions *outside* banks . . . obviously diversions."

"Who is diverting whom from what?"

"Somebody's diverting the cops from wherever the real action is going to happen."

"And where might that be?"

"I don't know. But I will."

". . . *explosion at Arkham Asylum* . . ." the voice on the radio squawked.

"That's it," Batman said. He put down the dumbbell and pulled his mask into place.

"The limousine, Master Bruce?" Alfred asked.

"No. I'll go alone. You alert Robin."

"But isn't it a bit early?" Bruce's firmest rule: Batman never appeared before dark, and seldom before eleven.

"Can't be helped, Alfred."

Batman left the gym area and strode to the cluster of vehicles. He got into a low, matte-black sports car, a vehicle Alfred had once dubbed "the Batmobile." It was basically a Maserati, much modified, with a racing engine, one-way bulletproof glass, bulletproof tires, a security system that included a small thermite bomb, which would melt the car to slag if anyone penetrated its other defenses, and a lot of electronics. Batman settled into the seat, which was made from a mold of his body. He touched a switch. Concealed television cameras with infrared lenses scanned every path and road within two miles of Wayne Manor. Batman peered at a television screen on the dashboard: nothing. He started the engine and guided the car along a winding ramp and out of the Cave into an equipment shed adjoining the tennis courts behind the house. From there he drove to a small dirt road that wound around the estate, glancing often at the television monitor, and finally onto the beltway. He turned away from Gotham City; Arkham Asylum was in the opposite direction.

Earlier, the world's most notorious madmen had enjoyed some light reading with their excellent Cornish game hens. The note was brief: *Explosions at about nine tonight. Exit from the rear. Guns will be in the yard. Be prepared to deal with the gas.*

Harvey Dent—known as Two-Face—touched the horrible scars caused by acid thrown at him when he had been a district attorney. "Escape? Yes!" Then he touched the side of his face that was not disfigured. "Not a good idea, Harv. The doctors are *helping* you here."

He took out his two-faced silver dollar and gazed first at the side that he had once scored with a knife and then at the side that was still mint. Jeremiah Arkham had allowed Harvey to keep the coin. "It provides a ruminative focus for him and should hasten his progress," Jeremiah had explained to his fellow psychiatrists, who had gazed at the floor and shaken their heads.

Harvey spun the coin in the air, caught it in his right hand, and slapped it onto his left wrist. The scarred side was up.

In an adjoining cell, the Joker read the note and clapped his hands. "Goody goody goody," he said in a falsetto voice, and giggled. "Mayhem and murder and maybe much maleficent mischief."

The bright red lips slashed across his white skin curled upward into a smile. "Of course," he said in a low baritone, "hurting people really isn't done in the best circles."

His lips curved down. And up again as the Joker said, falsetto, "So I'll do it in a *straight line.*"

Most of the other inmates in the ultramaximum security block—the Scarecrow, Maxie Zeus, Killer Croc, Mr. Zsasz, Poison Ivy—read their notes quietly and wondered if what they read could possibly be true.

The note meant nothing to Amygdala. He couldn't read.

To Abattoir, the note confirmed what he already knew, that it was his destiny, preordained by the universe itself, to flee incarceration and find his remaining family members, whose blood would nourish and empower him.

The Ventriloquist removed one of his socks, put his hand into it, formed a crease in the cloth with thumb and forefinger, and said, "What is your opinion, Socko?"

"It's the real goods," Socko said as the Ventriloquist's lips moved.

The corridors of the asylum were quiet—none of the usual howls, grumbles, laughter. The entire institution seemed to be waiting.

Bernie Intaglia munched his pastrami and rye and eyed the bank of monitors in front of him and his partner, Harry Humes. He and Harry were working the eight-to-four A.M shift in Arkham's main security complex.

"Harry," Bernie said. "You notice the loonies are all reading something? I seen that one take it outta his chicken."

"You sure you don't belong in there with 'em?"

"No, look."

Harry looked. "Yeah, you're right. Prob'ly one a Arkham's ideas. You wasn't here yet when he had 'em all saying the words to the national anthem backwards. Did I tell you about that?"

"A lotta times."

"You wanna talk about a loony, Jerry Arkham's the *champ*."

"So we shouldn't do anything about the reading?"

"Make a note in the log. What harm's reading gonna do?"

Bernie continued eating his sandwich.

Zombie steadied the helicopter above Arkham as Bane took aim through a scope mounted on the rocket launcher.

The first rocket blew a hole in the roof of the ultramax block, destroying most of the gas delivery system. The second blasted an inverted V in the rear wall of the yard. A third took out a chunk of the asylum itself.

Alarms blared. Ten uniformed men grabbed Ingram submachine guns and burst into the corridor outside the guardroom. But they couldn't get far: the explosions had activated motion sensors that in turn had slammed steel fire doors down at each entrance to maximum security. The entire block was sealed off.

The helicopter landed in the yard. Trogg tossed out crates of weapons —grenades, Uzis, Browning automatics.

Bane launched his fourth rocket; another section of the wall crumbled.

Lights flashed on switchboards at the Riverside Coast Guard base and, thirty miles away, the Gotham City Police Headquarters. Detective Renee Montoya, working the afternoon shift as watch captain, put out an emergency call. But the tactical unit squads were scattered around the city, securing various banks. Even if the streets had been clear, it would have taken them at least fifty minutes to reach Arkham. And the streets *weren't* clear: there was still some evening traffic.

Montoya's counterpart at the Coast Guard base, Ensign Lawrence Tibbet, flipped open the procedures manual. He thumbed pages frantically. What the hell was he supposed to do? "Ah, there it is," he murmured. In the event of a signal from the asylum, he was to "render all possible assistance." But what did *that* mean? Scramble the base's chopper? Not possible: the chopper's transmission had been on the fritz; its engine was strewn all over the landing pad. He picked up a phone and called Washington.

Bane and Trogg were inside ultramax firing their fifty-caliber Desert Eagle Magnum automatics at cell doors, blasting away the locks. The doors slammed open, and the inmates began to fill the corridor.

The Batmobile was a mile away, one of dozens of cars beginning to lose speed; ahead, a tractor trailer had overturned, blocking the beltway. Batman hesitated only a moment, then spun the wheel, cutting across three lanes of traffic to a beltway entrance. He was met by a van driving up the ramp. He swerved off the ramp onto the grassy slope that bordered it. A moment later he sped off the grass and onto the street below.

He was now a block from the asylum, in a neighborhood of dilapidated frame houses, untended lawns, and rusting vehicles. He gunned the engine. Skidding around a corner, he saw Arkham and a column of smoke rising from it. In the twilight, it was difficult to see everything, but he registered that there was an inverted V shape in the wall of the yard. Figures were tumbling through it and into the street. A helicopter was rising overhead.

Two men in inmates' jumpsuits were running up the sidewalk toward him, holding carbines at port arms. He braked the car. The inmates passed it. Batman slid out and caught them from behind. He slammed their heads together, and before they had hit the sidewalk, he was whirling in the opposite direction, running for Arkham.

He had gone only a half block before another inmate leapt at him from between two parked cars, swinging an empty beer bottle at Batman's head. Batman caught the man's wrist on his left forearm and, pivoting, guided the bottle around, past its target. He continued the pivot, bringing his right elbow up into his attacker's chin, and was again facing the asylum, continuing to run.

Overhead, Bane was observing the scene through night glasses.

"He is here," Bane murmured.

"Right according to plan, huh, Magic?" This from Bird, who was aiming a 30.06 deer rifle down at the asylum, occasionally squeezing off shots at guards who dared show themselves.

In the twin green circles of the glasses, Bane saw Batman glide through the hole in the wall and leap at an inmate who was standing over the weapons crates, handing out guns. The man fell immediately. But what had this Batman done to him? Whatever it was, it was too quick for the eye to follow.

Bane swept the glasses away from the yard. A tactical squad van was rounding the corner and screeching to a stop. Cops wearing armor poured from the doors in the rear and sprinted toward the asylum.

Bane returned the glasses to their original position: Batman was now facing two Arkhamites. One swung at him. Batman blocked the blow with his forearm and stepped forward to drive his stiffened fingers into the man's solar plexus; in the same instant, his leg levered out to catch the second man in the belly.

"He is truly formidable," Bane murmured.

The tac squad cops, now wearing gas masks, were pouring through the breached wall, firing tear gas canisters.

Batman hadn't recognized the men he'd dropped. They weren't among the dozen he had helped put in Arkham. Which was not good. Those twelve—they were the most dangerous. The only reason some of them were kept alive was that they were so deranged, psychologists demanded to be able to study them. Whole textbooks had been scrapped after the authors spent a few days in Arkham. Batman lowered the night lenses over the eye holes in his mask; the spotlights had been shattered by gunfire and the area was almost entirely dark now. He scanned the yard and saw a tall, thin, unmistakably pale figure edging toward the inverted V. This was the Joker, surely the most depraved sadist who had ever lived. At least Batman could stop *him*—

A cop stepped in front of Batman, pointed his service revolver, and said in a voice muffled by his gas mask, "Freeze!"

He dipped the barrel of the gun. "On the ground."

Batman dropped onto his right hand and, using it as an axis, pivoted his entire body. His boots swept the cop's feet from under him. The cop landed flat on his back and never saw Batman vanish into the shadows.

Outside the wall, other police units were arriving. The street was a chaotic welter of flashing lights, blue-uniformed bodies, cruisers, vans. Sirens screamed and growled. The air was scented with smoke and tear gas. The Joker could be anywhere. Batman knew that in seconds he might be recognized and he would have to escape again. He didn't want to hurt another officer.

He ran.

In his car, he picked up the phone and tapped out the number of Gordon's mobile unit.

"One of your men tried to arrest me," he said when Gordon answered.

"Yeah, you're wanted for questioning. The hookers. I stalled them as long as I could."

"Can you get it lifted?"

"Maybe. But not right away. It would help if you could tell me who *did* carve up the women."

"The man on the rooftop."

"Batman, you've got to give me something more than a *hunch*."

The car was gliding down the dark street, away from the asylum. In the rearview mirror, Batman saw the blinking red lights of the police cruisers.

"You heading toward Arkham, Commissioner?"

"Right. Should be there in a couple of minutes. You?"

"I'm leaving the neighborhood."

"It's over?"

"Your people can handle it from here. I stopped six of them. A lot of others got away, including the Joker."

"Any ideas? Inside job? Outside job?"

"There was a helicopter. The break probably originated from there, possibly with inside help."

"You got a guess about who was in the chopper?"

"No."

No guess. A hunch. The *same* hunch. The man on the rooftop.

At three the following morning, Bane, Zombie, Trogg, and Bird were at the motel, eating pizza.

"Hoo-*eee,*" Bird howled. "Boy, what a caper! It's gonna be a hot time in the old town tonight with all those loonies on the loose. Lock up your wives and daughters! Hell, lock up your *dogs!*"

"Do you consider the operation a success?" Zombie asked Bane.

"I saw him again, which is what I wanted to do most. He is strong. But I will study him and I will know his weakness. And if I ever see him again, I will recognize him. There is an added benefit. Many of the . . . *lunatics?*—many of them escaped. If what Bird said is true, he will try to catch them. This must weaken him. I only hope it does not weaken him too much."

"You want to kill him yourself."

"Yes."

Bane turned in his chair and closed his eyes. In a moment, he was again feeling the damp chill of the *cavidad oscuro* and watching the bat-thing loom in the darkness, rise, and escape. But no. That part of the vision would not come to pass. He would catch the bat and break it, and then he would fulfill his destiny—first Gotham and then the world would be his. He need only confront his nemesis and destroy it, and he had already begun to do that.

Batman spent the rest of the night in the Cave, monitoring police calls and the computers downtown. By dawn, a hastily convened task force consisting of representatives from the state police, the Gotham City PD, the prison authority, and the mayor's office had arrived at a tally: twelve million dollars' damage—

"How can they care about *that?*" Alfred muttered.

—and a dozen inmates escaped, including some of the worst: the Joker, Two-Face, the Ventriloquist, Amygdala, Killer Croc, Abattoir, Mr. Zsasz, Poison Ivy, Firefly, Maxie Zeus, the Scarecrow—all life-takers, all ruthless, all once captured by Batman.

"I'll start with the Ventriloquist," Batman said. "He used to run with a gang. I've kept tabs on most of the members. I'll put on a disguise and—"

"If I may, Master Bruce. Wouldn't it be a good idea to get some rest first? Aren't the chances slight that this Ventriloquist fellow would reveal himself so soon? Haven't you *already* been up for over forty-eight hours? And isn't it likely that once your pursuit begins in earnest, you may be awake for days on end?"

"Any more of your polite questions, Alfred?"

"Now that you mention it . . . a chap far more inquisitive than myself *could* ask, if he were feeling intrusive, why you feel this is your problem, this plague of lunatics."

"What do you think I might answer this nosy, hypothetical chap?"

"Far be it from me to attempt to penetrate the labyrinth of your formidable intelligence, but if you insist—"

"I do."

"You might reply that the incarceration of these fiends is a responsibility you have bestowed upon yourself and that self-assumed responsibilities are the only ones a man dare not deny."

"Why might that be, do you think?"

"Because, you could conceivably say, these responsibilities and the

actions issuing from them are what define a man, and without such definition a man has no genuine being."

"I guess I could say that. If I were of an existentialist persuasion."

"I, of course, am a lowly servant, barely literate, utterly unacquainted
with the works of Sartre, Kierkegaard, Dostoyevsky, Kaufmann, Jaspers,
Camus, and their ilk, and thus unable to advance such an hypothesis."

"Then how do you know their names?"

Alfred arched his brows. "I *do* dust the books in the library."

"You've made your point. I'll catch a couple of hours' rest."

"What a splendid idea. I shall have a hot, nourishing meal for you
when you awake."

10

Batman seldom needed more than two hours' sleep, and when he did sleep, he almost never dreamed. Years ago, he had sought out a martial arts master in the mountains of Korea, and in the eleven months that he had studied with Kirigi, he had learned a technique that the ancient Korean refused to name—a combination of relaxation and visualization that penetrated below the conscious and subconscious, below personality itself, and put him in a state of complete serenity.

—Dreams cleanse the garbage of the mind. Go to a place where there is no garbage . . .

But he could not go to that place, so deep within him. Not now. Because of something that had happened earlier—an asylum inmate leaping at him from between two parked cars . . .

So he dreamed.

Young Brucie, tired and happy. Up late, way past bedtime on a Friday night. Birthday treat. The movies with Mom and Dad. A favorite of Dad's: The Mark of Zorro. *The guy in the mask and cape. Horses and swords. The most exciting thing Brucie had ever seen. Leaving the the-*

ater, walking along the dark street, his hand in Mom's. Suddenly, Mom's fingers tighten and she gasps. What is it? A man coming from behind parked cars.

—Gimme money.

Dad steps in front of Mom and Brucie.

—No. Go away.

A sound like a firecracker. Dad falls. The man reaching for Mom, grabbing the pearls around her neck. Another firecracker. Mom falling, the pearls hitting the sidewalk, rolling into the gutter. The man running away. Brucie looking down at Mom and Dad. Not moving. Blood all over them. A child screaming—

Bruce awoke and was staring straight up into the shadows that hid the roof of the Cave. He focused on a time sense within him and learned that only fifteen minutes had passed since he first lay down. Only fifteen. Not enough time. He closed his eyes and tried to relax past the garbage, the memories—

Young Bruce, wandering the globe. A university here, an apprenticeship there. Paris, Chongju, Cape Girardeau, Manchester, Bhopal, even Krasnoyarsk and Zimbabwe, anywhere there was anyone who could teach him anything he might find useful.

—What a waste, the ladies of Gotham would say.

—That handsome young Wayne, why, he can't seem to stick with a single, solitary thing.

—Not the man his father was.

—If it wasn't for all that Wayne money, he'd be out on the street begging for quarters.

Home now, sitting in the library of his family mansion, staring out the windows at the twilight, wondering. He would fight crime. He would take his childhood trauma and mold it, fashion it into something useful. But how? Suddenly the window in front of him shatters, and a bat flaps into the room. In that instant, before the shards of glass strike the rug, that fast, he performs a profound act of creation; he creates a kind of person who has never before existed. He creates himself.

He says aloud, "Criminals are a superstitious and cowardly lot. I must be a creature of the night. I shall become a bat."

It is at once the silliest and most profound thing he has ever uttered. . . .

And he awoke. Two hours had passed, but he felt completely unrested. Was he becoming ill? He would do a body scan—later. After he had located Killer Croc. Or the Scarecrow. Or the Joker. Yes, he might allow himself the luxury of illness after the Joker was safely jailed. Or Two-Face. The Ventriloquist. Maxie Zeus. Amygdala. Or any of the others.

11

Maxie Zeus, once Max Zlotski, the short, chubby Ventriloquist, and the lumbering giant called Amygdala scattered and went their separate ways into the woods.

Maxie was running easily, as befitted the god he knew himself to be, although he was still wearing a straitjacket.

"It is my will that I be thus bound," he told his loyal subjects, the grass and trees. "It pleasures me to deny myself my omnipotence as it pleasured me to bring wrathful lightning bolts upon the place where it pleasured me to be incarcerated. They thought to imprison a god? Ha! Do the fools not realize my might—"

One of his loyal subjects, a maple tree, reared up before him and he ran into it. He broke his nose and fell unconscious.

The Ventriloquist was in the woods, well out of sight of anyone on the road. Arkham was a mile behind him, a cluster of suburban bungalows just ahead. The night was chilly and dark, but there was a reddish moon shining through the leaves.

The Ventriloquist was gasping. He sat down, his back to a tree trunk, and panted. When he had regained control of his body, he considered his situation and panicked. He didn't know what to do. He needed someone to tell him. He needed Scarface, who was his friend . . . no, he was his *dummy* . . . no, that wasn't right either. He didn't know *what* Scarface was, but he did know that Scarface talked and told him what to do. The doctors called it "multiple personality disorder." Scarface said the doctors were full of it.

Where *was* Scarface? Hiding in this tree? Maybe he could chop it down and get a knife and carve and carve and carve until he found Scarface? No, probably not.

No Scarface. Not now. Socko would have to do.

Hastily, frantically, the Ventriloquist once again pulled off his shoe and sock. He fit the sock over his hand and formed a crease with his thumb and forefinger.

"Socko," said the Ventriloquist, "have you seen Scarface?"

"No, I haven't seen your friend Mr. Scarface," Socko said as the Ventriloquist's lips moved.

"I really must find him and I can't do it alone. Could you help me?"

"I can try, Mr. Ventriloquist."

From behind him someone said, "Could I help too?"

The Ventriloquist and Socko turned. Amygdala was standing by a white oak, dappled by the moonlight. The Ventriloquist—and Socko—had to crane upward to see him; he was nearly nine feet tall. His head was rather small at the top and wide at the jaw. The rest of him was elephantine, particularly his hands, which were as large as Sunday hams.

"Amygdala is very dangerous," the Ventriloquist whispered to Socko. "The doctors at Arkham experimented on his brain. He's quite uncontrollable."

"Then we must be very cautious if we're to use him," Socko whispered back.

"You may help me find Scarface, Amygdala," the Ventriloquist said. "I am the Ventriloquist."

"What's your little friend's name?"

"Uh . . . Socko."

"Am I supposed to get my medicine soon?"

"We will find you some medicine as soon as we find Scarface," the Ventriloquist promised.

Socko nodded in agreement.

Batman spun the wheel and headed toward the asylum. The police radio had just reported that two beat cops, acting on a tip from some kids, had found Maxie Zeus, still straitjacketed, his tongue out to catch drops of blood dripping from his broken nose, babbling about "Nectar." Earlier, a bird-watcher had seen Maxie with the Ventriloquist and, a bit later, had seen the Ventriloquist joined by Amygdala. If the Ventriloquist and Amygdala were in the vicinity, they might still be together. Which would simplify a small part of his task.

I'll take any lucky break I can get.

With or without luck, he'd probably have a challenging evening. The Ventriloquist wouldn't be a problem unless he'd hooked up with his former pals, but Amygdala was huge and, unless sedated, capable of ferocious rage.

How long since he's had his last jolt of Thorazine?

Amygdala waited outside while the Ventriloquist and Socko entered the Tap Room, a tavern once frequented by his criminal associates. The Ventriloquist wrinkled his nose—he disliked the stale alcohol smell of places like this, but in this line of work, they were practically a necessity. He looked at the bar and at the tables: a bartender and seven customers, six men and a young woman.

"No familiar faces," said the Ventriloquist.

"Ask anyway," Socko said.

The Ventriloquist cleared his throat and raised his voice. "We're looking for Scarface. Have any of you gentlemen seen him?"

For a moment the chatter of conversation stopped. Seven drinkers

stared at the short, bald man with the thick glasses standing there with a
sock on his hand. The woman giggled, and her companion laughed, and
then the rest of the drinkers roared.

"Laugh at Socko, will you?" said Socko. "Well, chuckle all you want
at *me*—"

Amygdala suddenly filled the door.

"—but I think you'd best take my pal more seriously."

"You are laughing at my little friend?" Amygdala shouted. "*Nobody*
laughs at my little friend!"

The Ventriloquist and Socko sat at the bar, sipping somebody's abandoned chaser as Amygdala wrecked the room.

Batman had heard the call on the police radio: riot at a joint a few
miles from the asylum. When he arrived, there was already a police
cruiser parked outside, and two cops were talking to a woman whose arm
was in a sling. Batman stopped in the shadow of some trees and touched a
switch. The car's aerial tilted and swiveled to point at the woman. It was
now a powerful directional microphone.

". . . monster, like something from a circus . . . little guy . . . had
a sock on his hand . . . hurt Billy and Al and them . . . Looie put a
knife in 'is back and he don't even notice . . . musta killed Looie . . .
guess I was lucky . . . only threw me across the room . . . said they
was looking for some kinda face . . ."

Scarface.

The police radio squawked: "Silent alarm at Joy-Boy Toys, Laneer
Road store."

Batman saw that the cops interviewing the woman had heard it. They
moved toward their vehicle. But they wouldn't be going in the right
direction. Joy-Boy Toys had moved from its Laneer Road location to a
small shopping center; apparently nobody had bothered to inform the
local cop house. The Wayne fortune was based on real estate; Bruce
Wayne spent a half hour a week scanning the realty news for potentially
useful information.

Batman would arrive there first.

. . .

The Ventriloquist was unhappy. Oh, he'd found the toy store and the puppet department and he could see well enough in the light of an electric sign, but "What *trash!*" the Ventriloquist grumbled. "*Look* at these things! A stupid frog and a stupid teddy bear and a stupid *butterfly*. A *butterfly!* Absolutely *out of the question!* that any of these could take the place of Scarface!"

Batman stepped from behind a counter. "Time for you to come with me, Ventriloquist."

"I'll go along quietly, Batman. No trouble from me. No sir."

"Look out behind you," Socko said. "A monster!"

"I'm not in the mood for old jokes. Lose the sock. Keep your hands where I can see them." Suddenly Batman realized he was being stupid. Amygdala *was* probably nearby and might well be preparing to attack—

From behind him: "Leave my friends alone!"

Sausage-sized fingers closed on Batman's neck and shoulder. It was Amygdala.

How can he move so quietly?

Amygdala hoisted Batman over his head.

"I'll hurt you. I'll hurt you real bad!"

Batman was able to will himself to relax as Amygdala hurled him into a shelf. He landed on his feet as Baby Brandie dolls squeaking "Mama" clattered to the floor all around him. He rolled into a forward somersault and brought both his boots up into Amygdala's belly. The giant didn't seem to notice. He grabbed Batman's ankles—how *could* the giant move so fast?—and whirled, flinging Batman into a toy train exhibit. The table that held a tiny town cracked in two, and Batman fell amid tiny houses and stores and boxcars. Amygdala lunged. Batman's kick caught the giant beneath the chin and snapped his head back. But it didn't stop him. Batman put both feet against Amygdala's chest and tried to force him away. Amygdala's fist dropped like a wrecking ball into Batman's shoulder. Immediately Batman's left arm went numb. Batman shoved aside the half-table to his right—a tiny city hall hit him on the forehead—and rolled. As Amygdala struggled to stand, Batman seemed to rise from the floor. His left leg shot out. His foot slammed full force against Amygdala's temple. The giant stared, as though he didn't quite understand what had happened.

My best tae kwon do move and it didn't stop him, Batman thought. *Back to the drawing board.*

He dropped to his shoulders and used his forearms to propel himself upward. His legs locked around Amygdala's neck, and as he squeezed the carotid artery he grabbed a pair of ankles the size of fire hydrants and pulled. The giant toppled, still in Batman's grip. The floor shook, and a Baby Brandie squeaked, "Mama." Batman sat up, astride Amygdala's chest and, still squeezing with the legs, locked his fists together and brought them down on Amygdala's forehead. Again. And again. Squeezing and hitting.

Amygdala relaxed and began to snore.

The store was empty. The Ventriloquist had fled. *But he couldn't have gotten far. Which direction? Toward the woods?*

Batman heard the screech of brakes in the parking lot outside. The police cruiser. The cops had finally found the right address. He was wanted for questioning. The Ventriloquist would have to wait. He'd have to let a killer escape.

He had no choice.

Batman had come in a rear window. He left the same way, got in the car, and released the brake. He let the car roll almost to the road before starting the engine and then switched on infrared beams visible only through a specially tinted windshield. No cop in the world could catch him now.

12

 In the Batcave, Alfred had a medical kit waiting. Batman shed his mask and tunic.

"Extraordinary bruise on the shoulder, Master Bruce. These ladies you see—they can be quite *physical.*"

"Anything broken, Alfred?"

Alfred's fingers probed. "No, but there is some separation at the joint and"—more probing—"the wrist is sprained. There is some pain, I imagine."

"There will be when the adrenaline wears off."

"I could give you a painkiller," Alfred suggested tentatively.

"Don't use them."

"As well I know. But I always feel obliged to ask. Was our venture successful?"

"Half," Bruce said. "Amygdala's back in Arkham by now. But the Ventriloquist got away."

"You can console yourself with the knowledge that you apprehended the more dangerous of the duo."

"Alfred, maybe you didn't hear me. The Ventriloquist escaped. And before that, the Joker escaped."

"And you blame yourself."

"Who else?"

Alfred sighed. "Get some sleep, Master Bruce."

"I could lie down. But I couldn't sleep."

Alfred was shocked. Batman had never admitted a lack of control over himself before.

Alfred and Tim Drake were in the billiards room of Wayne Manor, the only room in which there was a television set. They were watching "Midnight Ramblings with Mitzi Manners," Gotham's leading local talk show. Mitzi, a young woman with long, straight auburn hair and the kind of pretty face that is instantly forgettable, was interviewing Dr. Simpson Flanders, a clinical psychologist who was, in appearance, her male equivalent.

"What can we expect from the mass escape from Arkham, Doctor?" Mitzi asked, smiling.

"Excuse me for saying so, Mitzi, but I think the media are acting a bit . . . hysterical." Dr. Flanders held up a book, glanced at a monitor, and adjusted the angle of the book so the camera saw its title. "As I've detailed in my current book, *I'm Sane and So Are You,* these patients are merely misunderstood. They are crying for help."

"There have been a dozen homicides since the breakout," Mitzi replied, the smile segueing into a pert frown, the chirp in her voice taking an edge. "We're talking about the most dangerous collection of psychopaths ever assembled. They are hardly 'misunderstood.' "

"That's your innate prejudice toward the mentally divergent. Mitzi, Mitzi, these patients are lost. Confused. They cannot operate in the outside world. You think they are a danger to society?"

"Rot," Alfred said, thumbing the remote and switching off the set.

"I think he may have a point," Tim said. "They *are* crying for help—at least some of them are. But that doesn't change the fact that they're killing innocent people."

"It's a bit late to begin one of our philosophical discussions, lad. Hadn't you better be getting back home?"

"No hurry. Dr. Kinsolving's got Dad at her clinic overnight for tests."

"And that young lady friend of yours—Ariana, is it?"

"Helping with inventory-taking at the family store."

"Homework?"

"Alfred, come *on!* I've got a couple of history chapters and a chapter of *Great Expectations* and I've got till Monday."

"Timothy, would I be correct in assuming that you're waiting for Master Bruce?"

"Well, I haven't seen him since the breakout. How's he doing?"

For a moment, Alfred was tempted to lie. But Timothy Drake had been Batman's apprentice for a year now, ever since he had done what the best criminal minds in the country had failed to do—deduced Batman's identity. The day Tim first came to Wayne Manor offering to help, Bruce and Alfred knew that this young man—this *child*—was potentially Bruce's equal. If he were to assume the cape and cowl someday, only the truth would serve him.

"Not good," Alfred said. "I think he's been remarkably successful. He thinks he's a dreadful failure. He's personally apprehended seven of the twelve escapees and he's done it while having to elude the police. The police themselves claim that they've taken Maxie Zeus, but he did them the service of running into a tree. I make the score Batman seven, Gotham's Finest zero."

"But he's not satisfied, huh?" Tim said.

"Lad, for years I've wondered what Bruce's tragic flaw might be. I believe I now know. He takes on too much. He feels responsible for every life those psychopaths have taken simply because he has *made* himself responsible."

"Is he holding up?"

Alfred sighed. "For the time being. He is probably the best-conditioned human being on the planet, and he knows every mental and physical technique there is. But I fear that even he is approaching his limits. He hasn't rested in five days, and I doubt he's had more than a few bites of food."

"What can I do to help?"

"Tim, if I could think of anything, I would have told you before now."

"I'm beginning to feel guilty myself. Maybe if I'd gotten the identity of the guy on the rooftop, but . . . zilch-o. I even hacked into the South American prison computers—Batman said the guy had a Latino accent, remember? My Spanish is sketchy, but I boned up on the words for 'escape,' 'riot,' and 'fleeing' and programmed the machine to flag them. Like I said, zilch-o."

"Is it possible that a prison might not have a computer system?"

"Maybe. Batman would know. I wouldn't."

13

When Bane had first arrived in Gotham City six weeks ago, he seldom went outside during the day. *All that light, all that space*—disconcerting for one whose life had been bounded by prison walls until only recently. But lately he had taken to walking in an open park area near the motel during the early afternoon, squinting, peering at the horizon, testing how far he could see. Zombie and Bird walked with him.

"We ready to make our move on ol' pointy ears?" Bird asked Bane.

"Don't call him that," Zombie said. "It shows you're not taking him seriously."

"I don't have to," Bird replied, jerking a thumb in Bane's direction. "Magic here does. We got a program yet, Magic?"

Bane remembered choosing the time and place of his confrontation with the Mick. "We must find him. We must learn where he lives. How he lives."

"Not so easy, Magic," Bird said. "Nobody knows what kinda face is behind that mask, much less where that face hangs. It's not like plenty haven't tried to find out."

"He always has the element of surprise," Bane said thoughtfully. "If we knew where he was coming and when, we might be able to learn where he started from."

"Sounds like the Magic Man's getting a glimmer," Bird said.

Bane looked at his watch, pressed the stud on his arm, and let the Venom warm him. Then he scanned the horizon.

"You really *must* rest," Alfred said. "I'm afraid I must insist."

"I caught a few minutes' relaxation while I was on stakeout," Batman replied, shedding his mask and cloak. Alfred followed him across the Batcave to the communications area, where Robin was busy scanning the display on the computer screen.

"When?" Alfred demanded.

"When what?"

"When did you catch those 'few minutes' relaxation'?"

"Sometime. Recently."

"Today?"

"Maybe yesterday." Bruce turned and said, "What difference does it make?"

"I will not dignify that with an answer," Alfred said, and added, "*Master* Bruce."

Bruce joined Robin at the computer. "Anything?"

"A lot. But nothing on who your mysterious Mr. Rooftop might be."

"That's all that's important."

"You could get an argument on that from the FBI and Interpol. Looks like an arms shipment might be passing through Gotham Harbor—"

"Let them handle it."

"Guess they'll have to."

Robin turned from the console and looked up at Bruce. He had never seen his mentor looking like this: deep gray circles beneath the eyes, pale skin, hair unkempt, and three days' growth of beard. "You haven't been around much lately."

"I've been busy. You may have heard."

"I heard what Alfred was saying, and if you don't mind my butting in, it sounded okay—"

"I *do* mind. Look, you're thirteen years old—"

"Fourteen. Had a birthday yesterday."

"You're a kid. You don't understand as much as you think you do."

"No argument, and no offense—"

"Quiet!" Bruce turned a knob, and the hiss of a police radio echoed through the cave. The dispatcher's words were garbled, barely discernible in the rattle of static: "Zsasz . . . killer recently escaped from Arkham . . . Bates School for Women . . . hostages . . . send tactical squad . . ."

Bruce dropped his head into his hands. "I was afraid of something like this."

"Hostages," Robin said. "Could be bad."

Bruce moved toward the cars, grabbing a fresh mask and cloak as he passed a clothing rack.

"What can I do?" Robin shouted after him.

But Bruce was already in the Batmobile; he might not have heard the question. The car sped up the ramp.

"Who's this Zsasz?" Robin asked Alfred.

"A very twisted specimen, I'm afraid. He has murdered hundreds of people, most of them innocent and helpless. Each time he kills, he makes a small cut in his own flesh. As a result, he is covered from head to foot with tiny scars."

"And he's in a school—"

"Full of innocent girls."

"Take a look, ladies," Zsasz said, ripping open the front of his shirt.

The fifteen young women at the other end of the library stared at his scarred chest.

"A map of hardened blood charting my every sin, all my glory . . . each scar a kill . . . *Look* at you, too terrified to whimper. But deep inside, where all the red is so barely bound, I know you're asking, 'How many of *us* will become part of *him?*' Maybe all of you, maybe only some . . . but surely at least, say, *three* of you. One thing is *certain* . . . I intend to *savor* this night in peace, and the *surest* way for you to get under and into my skin . . . is to make a *fuss*."

Zsasz did an about-face and strode out the door. The women heard it lock behind him.

"Locked us in . . . gonna die," Marcy Hickenlooper moaned.

Janine Maxweather was pacing furiously. "We should have jumped him—ripped his eyes out."

"Easy to say now . . . now that he's gone," Nikki Jones said.

"What about the window?" Darlene Doyle asked.

Senta Jernigan shook her head. "Not without a crowbar." The school board had recently put bars on all the windows in the building—"Can't be too careful," the board president had told the faculty.

"I heard sirens a while ago," Mattie Roberts said. "The police are outside. They'll know what to do."

Janine stopped pacing and joined her schoolmates. The girls clustered together in the center of the room and stared at the floor.

Lieutenant Arnold Kitch of the tactical squad raised his umbrella. The mist of a few minutes ago had become a hard October rain. The two dozen other cops, not equipped with umbrellas, huddled near the cars and vans, getting soaked. They were all waiting for Kitch to say something.

"Benson," Kitch snapped in his best commander voice.

"Yessir," Officer Lamar Benson replied, almost saluting.

"Sitrep!"

Benson sidled closer to his boss, but Kitch did not extend the hospitality of the umbrella. "Most of the girls got out the back. They're already on their way to the hospital for trauma counseling."

"Satisfactory."

"Still, some fifteen resident students unaccounted for, sir—and one of the escapees claims she broke free of a group Zsasz was herding into the library."

"Her condition?" Kitch demanded.

"Pretty hysterical, but convincing."

"Any other intelligence?"

"That's it, sir."

"We can't plan without more information. Some volunteer will have to go in."

"I'll do it, sir," Benson said. "My brother Milt was one of the guards at Arkham—one that didn't make it."

Benson went to the open back of the tac squad van, shed his uniform jacket and cap, and replaced it with a heavy, bulletproof vest and a visored helmet. He fastened a small transmitter to the vest. He dropped his service revolver on the floor of the van, took a .44 Magnum automatic from a gun rack, and holstered it.

Kitch accompanied the officer to an open basement window. He bowed his lips toward a small microphone pinned to his lapel and said, "Testing."

"Loud and clear, Lieutenant," Benson said, tapping the side of his helmet. "You say it, I'll hear it. I may not be able to respond, but I'll tap my own mike every two minutes to give you an okay."

"Ten-four," Kitch said.

The Batmobile was ninety yards away, its microphone aerial aimed at Kitch and Benson. Batman heard the conversation between the officers and, through night-vision binoculars, saw Benson squeeze himself through the basement window. Batman removed his mask and made an adjustment on the tiny receiver built into it; now he would be able to monitor Kitch and Benson.

Kitch was bad news. If Gordon had been commanding the unit, or even Bullock, Batman might have been able to ask for cooperation, despite the order to question him about the murdered hookers. But Kitch was the foremost Batman-hater in the department.

Kitch's voice: "Benson?"

Tap tap.

•   •   •

The tac squad cops had the old school building surrounded and bathed in harsh light from their cruisers. If Batman tried to follow Benson, he'd have to fight his way through a mob of uniforms. Maybe he could disguise himself as a cop? No, Kitch was an ambitious martinet, but he was also cool and observant. He wouldn't be fooled.

There had to be a way.

Batman got out of the car and looked upward. Through the rain, he could see the skeletal branches of an irregular line of trees that extended to within a few yards of the school roof.

"Benson?"

Tap tap.

Batman jumped, caught a low limb, and began climbing.

Benson lifted the moisture-fogged visor of his helmet. There wasn't much light—just the red glow from an exit sign. But it was enough. He was in a corridor on the first floor of the school. If what the escaped student had said was right, the library should be just around the corner.

He unholstered his gun, flattened himself against the wall, and inched forward.

Cautiously he turned the corner. Still all clear. To the left, a pair of lockers; directly ahead, the double doors to the library. Benson had to assume Zsasz was inside. Okay, he'd blast the lock, go in fast, and smoke the bastard.

He spoke into his mike. "Lieutenant, I'm going into the library."

Then he felt something cold and hard on his throat and, an instant later, saw a dark stream spurting from beneath his chin. The gun slipped from his fingers, and he fell on top of it.

Lightning ripped across the sky and Batman tensed. As thunder boomed, he leapt and hit the steeply canted roof. His boots slipped on the wet tiles. He dropped and allowed himself to slide to the roof's edge and then off. There was a row of small windows just below the eaves. Batman caught the rain gutter and swung. Glass shattered. He arched his back, straightened his arms and legs, and went through the window.

A uniformed cop trotted to Kitch. "Lieutenant, I think I just saw somebody on the roof. In the rain and all, I couldn't be sure—"

"Just a second," Kitch said. He pulled his lapel microphone to his lips and said, "Benson. Answer me."

Kitch waited, listening to the faint crackle of static and the hiss of the rain.

"It would be better if I was at the school," Commissioner Gordon was saying to Mayor Krol. "I was on my way when I got your call—"

"Don't waste my time telling me what I know."

Gordon took a deep breath. They were in the parlor of the mayor's mansion. Krol sat in a leather throne behind a large oak desk. He did not offer Gordon a chair. "Well?" Gordon asked.

"Well what?"

"What can I do for you?"

"You can stop screwing up," Krol said.

"How have I done that?"

"Your men should have dealt with the breakout from Arkham. Maximum force."

"Mayor—"

"I think you'd better call me 'Your Honor.' "

"*Mayor* Krol, I had only a handful of men there—"

"Because the discipline in your department is so lax it takes your people forever to respond. And when they *did* respond, they pussyfooted. Does the phrase 'shoot to kill' have any meaning for you?"

"Not in those circumstances. There was too much confusion, too many innocent bystanders—"

"Excuses. Always excuses. While the city goes to hell."

"If we had more funds—"

"Yes, yes, it's always somebody else's fault. Well, listen to me, Mr. *Commissioner,* one of my friends has a daughter at Bates School and if anything happens to her, I'm holding you personally responsible."

"Is that all?" Gordon turned to go.

"You'll leave when you're dismissed," Krol snapped.

Gordon stopped. "Yes?"

"Even if my friend's kid isn't hurt, Gordon, I think you might consider an early retirement. Before you *get* retired."

Gordon was at the door. "If you'll excuse me, I've got a job to do."

Zsasz entered the library, dragging Benson's corpse, and locked the door behind him. The girls gasped. "Well, ladies, one of you won't be my first victim tonight. That honor goes to *this* fool."

He held up a knife, grinned, and cut a small slit in his forearm. Smiling, he watched a rivulet of blood trickle across his skin.

"We're gonna die, gonna die, gonna die," Marcy Hickenlooper crooned.

"Please don't hurt us," Nikki Jones said.

Janine Maxweather picked up a chair and ran at Zsasz. The killer stepped to the side and kicked the girl's knee. Janine sprawled forward; the chair slid across the floor and hit a table.

Zsasz stood above her, delicately testing the point of his knife with a forefinger. "Now let me see. Who will be number two?"

Janine glared up at him.

"I think I will choose—" He stepped away from Janine and grabbed Marcy's wrist. "Yes, yes. You, my puling little bitch. *You* will be number two."

Marcy fell to her knees. Zsasz twisted his fingers in her hair and pulled back her head. He smiled at the girls. "Now watch, ladies. Watch and learn."

•　　•　　•

The light in the corridor was bad, but Batman was wearing night-vision lenses.

Where's the library? Around that corner? Yes, double doors and lockers—lockers with a stain on them. Reddish liquid still wet, still trickling down to the floor.

There was no more time. He kicked the lock on the double doors and slammed them open. Zsasz looked up from his blade, which was just indenting the skin on Marcy Hickenlooper's throat.

"That's enough blood for one night, Zsasz," Batman said.

"The police!" Mattie Roberts said. "I *told* you!"

"Ah, but he's not a cop," Zsasz said. "He's just like me—a stalker in the dark . . . a figure of fear . . . a predator."

Zsasz pressed his blade further. Marcy moaned.

"And you love it," Zsasz said to Batman. "Don't you? Especially when you bring your prey down."

"I don't kill," Batman said.

"Ah, yes. Your 'saving grace'—the one factor that allows the zombies to sanction your actions . . . that and your choice of victims, of course. But you'd like to kill them, if only they'd let you get away with it. Because that would make your work so much easier, wouldn't it? And *ever* so much more satisfying."

"You're wrong."

"And you are what my shrinks call 'in denial.' We *are* the same. We both like to come up on them in the dark, feeling the forbidden power of it, seeing the fear slashed in their faces. We crave it."

Benson dead on the floor, Batman thought. *I've been too slow. And I'm not nearly fast enough to reach him before he slits that girl's throat.*

"We're not the same," he said.

"Ah, there *is* one difference," Zsasz said. "I stalk the fresh ones, the *clean* ones, while you stalk the ones fouled with blood . . . me and mine. So I know the thrill from both sides . . . unlike you! But I suspect that's already begun to change, hasn't it?"

The girl on the floor by the table—she's begun to crawl toward Zsasz. What does she have in mind?

"What do you mean?" Batman asked.

"Someone loosed the hordes of Arkham. All your most dangerous prey. Which means someone has it in for you—"

—*the girl is next to Zsasz's leg. He's so intent on me he doesn't see her—*

"—someone who may be stalking you right now, waiting for the right moment of *fear* and *weakness* . . . the perfect moment to *pounce.*"

Batman raised his hands to his face. *Anything to keep his attention on me for another second—*

Janine Maxweather bit Zsasz on the ankle. He howled and slashed at her with the knife, and as she was rolling out of the way Batman leapt. Zsasz flung Marcy at him; instinctively, Batman caught her. Zsasz thrust the knife at his face. Batman's head moved a half inch, and the blade missed.

Zsasz hopped over Janine and sprinted for the doors. Batman lowered Marcy to the floor and followed.

The corridor, pale green through the night lenses, seemed empty. No, something was rounding the corner. Zsasz would stop and wait, knife ready.

In Batman's ear came Kitch's voice: "*All units. Two minutes, we're going in.*"

Batman ran and somersaulted past the angle of the corner. Zsasz's blade caught the tip of his cape. Batman rolled to his feet, turned. Zsasz's feet were apart, knees bent, blade held low and canted upward: classic knife fighter stance. He jabbed. Batman pivoted out of the way, grabbed Zsasz's wrist in his left hand, and brought his right elbow down on Zsasz's arm. Bone snapped. Batman forced the killer to his knees.

"I'm right and you know it," Zsasz said through clenched teeth. "Finish it. Kill me."

"*No!*" Batman shouted, and hit Zsasz on the side of the head with a clenched fist. Zsasz fell on top of Batman's boots. Batman kicked him over and stared down at Zsasz's face. "I'm *not* like you. Hear me, killer?"

"Yes you are."

Batman raised his fist above his head. His arm was rigid and trembling.

"Losing control?" Zsasz taunted.

"To hell with it," Batman said, and broke Zsasz's jaw.

"Freeze!" The command had come from behind Batman. The cops had finally arrived. He knew there was probably a gun aimed at his back and behind it someone with a lot of questions he didn't want to answer. He ran for the nearest door, which led to a classroom, and continued running until he flattened and dove through a window. Then he vaulted to his feet on the wet grass and sprinted in a zigzag path for the trees and his car. Behind him came shouts. A shot, fired blindly. The cops were looking into darkness. They couldn't see him, couldn't see his dark costume in the rainy night. He was safe.

14

 Bane watched Batman's race from the school to the car. He lowered his night-vision binoculars and said to Zombie, "Follow him."

Zombie pushed the yoke of the helicopter's controls. The craft descended toward the winding ribbon of road and paced the car below.

Bane adjusted the headset he was wearing and listened to the crackle of the police transmissions. He glanced at Zombie from the corner of his eye. Zombie was valuable, perhaps more valuable than Trogg or Bird. He was a pilot, a technician, a warrior. And he had ideas. It had been Zombie's idea to monitor the police band. When Bane heard of the hostage situation at the school, it had been Zombie who knew that Zsasz was one of Batman's enemies.

Batman had always proceeded from secrecy and surprise. *This* time, Bane knew where he would be going, and approximately when. The helicopter had arrived after Batman was already in the school, but Bane had scanned the area and, despite the rain, was able to spot the Batmobile. Then he had simply waited. And now he was following his prey home.

Suddenly the helicopter lurched and the cabin was bright with a reddish glare. Zombie struggled with the controls. A thunderclap momentarily deafened Bane. He felt panic. "We were hit by lightning," Zombie yelled.

Bane scanned the road below, in vain. In the few seconds Bane was not looking, the Batmobile had vanished. Furious, he slammed his fist into the bulkhead beside him.

"Hey, Magic, take it easy," Bird said. "Bad break. Coulda happened to anyone."

Bane clamped Bird's cheeks between an enormous thumb and forefinger and said, "If I hear any more of your insolence, I will kill you slowly."

Bird paled and mumbled an apology.

Bane fumbled under his jacket and touched the stud on his arm. A few seconds later, the warmth of the Venom suffused and calmed him. He returned his attention to the road. Batman's car had vanished somewhere in the area immediately below. That was information which might yet be useful.

Tim was watching the late news when Dr. Shondra Kinsolving entered the room. Dr. Kinsolving stood behind Tim's chair and watched with him. A young, bearded newsman was praising the courage of Janine Maxweather, a junior at the Bates School for Women. Her classmates all agreed: *Janine* had defeated Zsasz. Batman had merely cleaned up after her.

Tim thumbed the remote and turned to look up at Dr. Kinsolving. "How's Dad doing?"

"Very well," Dr. Kinsolving said, coming around the chair to face Tim. "You understand, I can't promise anything—"

"Sure."

"—but I think we can hope for a partial return of lower-body movement by Christmas. After that . . ." Dr. Kinsolving shrugged. "We'll have to wait and see."

"Even that would be great," Tim said. The other doctors—the best specialists in the world—had given up hope. Jack Drake would never return, they'd said, though the body he'd once inhabited might continue breathing for another couple of decades. As a last resort, the family attorney had contacted Dr. Kinsolving. She was a duly licensed physician, true, but she had a reputation for unorthodox methods. Nobody knew exactly what her methods were, and she evaded questions, but the experts agreed that she couldn't be achieving her results with normal allopathic medicine. Consequently, the medical establishment mistrusted her.

Tim didn't. From the moment they'd first met, he'd sensed a special quality in her. She seemed utterly calm, completely self-possessed, infinitely gentle; but those were traits he'd encountered in others. Dr. Kinsolving was more. But Tim lacked a concept for *what* more she was. He gazed at her, searching again for clues. She was a tall black woman who habitually wore severely tailored suits. Her hair was cropped close to her skull. She wore no makeup, and her only jewelry was a pair of gold hoop earrings. Tim wouldn't call her beautiful, but only because the word seemed inadequate. She was something *beyond* merely beautiful.

"I left your father with Mrs. McIlvaine," Dr. Kinsolving said. "I'll try to look in tomorrow afternoon. If anything happens in the meantime, you have my number."

"Thanks, Dr. Kinsolving."

The woman nodded briefly in acknowledgment and left the room. A minute later he heard her car in the driveway. He thought about putting on his Robin costume and going to the Batcave. After the encounter with Zsasz, Bruce might need him. But he'd been up almost twenty hours. He was at the absolute limit of his endurance. After he slept—*then* he'd help Bruce.

15

 Without breaking stride, Jean Paul Valley scanned the wide lobby he was entering; he already knew the location of the elevators, security desk, potted plants, and computerized office directory—the general plan of the Wayne Building's ground floor—as he knew the particulars of each of the skyscraper's other forty-six levels. But he needed to assure himself that nothing was out of place, that everything was completely ordinary. And he wanted to close his eyes for a second, to allow for the change from the hot, bright October sidewalk he'd just left to the shadowy coolness of the lobby. A second was all his eyes required to adjust to the change from glare to fluorescent twilight.

He did not return the nod the lobby security man gave him as he hurried to the locked door marked EMPLOYEES ONLY behind the desk. The man muttered, "Creep," as Jean Paul unlocked and opened the door and went into the lounge behind it. Jean Paul did not look at the clock above the coffee machine; he knew he was thirty minutes early, as he had been every working day since he'd joined the Wayne organization six months ago. There was no need to visit his locker; he was already dressed in his uniform and carrying his five-celled flashlight.

He sat next to a Formica-topped table and waited.

.   .   .

Alfred saw Bruce slumped in front of the television in the library, watching the late news. The room was dark except for the glow from the tube.

". . . Ms. Janine Maxweather is the girl of the hour, if not the year," a gushy young woman standing in front of the Bates School was concluding.

"Is this young woman the paragon the media are portraying, Master Bruce?" Alfred asked.

"She had guts, all right."

"Perhaps she should be the recipient of a Wayne Foundation Scholarship."

"Her father is Rory Maxweather. He has more money than I do. Maybe we could give a scholarship in her name to some kid in the inner city."

"I trust that Batman did more than ride Ms. Maxweather's coattails." Alfred listened to the wind driving rain against the windows, waiting for Bruce to reply. Finally, he said, "I trust—"

"I heard you, Alfred. And you're wrong. If it hadn't been for Janine Maxweather, the other girl—Marcy—would be dead. I stood there for a full two minutes doing nothing but listening to Zsasz rant. I couldn't think of anything *to* do. I was stupid."

"Oh, surely—"

"He was taunting me. Claiming we were alike. I denied it, but . . . he was right, Alfred. I broke his arm. That ended the fight. But then I hit him. I broke his jaw and maybe fractured his skull and if that cop hadn't arrived, I would have hit him again."

"I doubt it."

"I don't."

"You can't know what you would have done—"

"Neither can you."

"—but based on a vast amount of experience in very similar situations, it is quite safe to assume that you would have controlled yourself."

"Once, I would have agreed with you. A *month* ago, I would have agreed. But now—"

"Now you are exhausted. You are stressed beyond what the human nervous system can bear. Within the past six days, you have dealt with Zsasz, Scarecrow, Maxie Zeus—"

"Zeus screwed up. He caught himself."

"Please don't interrupt. You also apprehended that Poison Ivy woman and Killer Croc. You *must* rest."

"Not while the Joker and Two-Face—"

"—and Abattoir and the rest of the foul crew still roam free. I have heard it, Master Bruce. Your detractors claim you are obsessed to the point of madness. Your reply has always been that you are aware of your obsession and choose to let it govern your life. It is the choice that proves your sanity. Madmen have no options."

"Okay. Your point?"

"I fear you have crossed the line. You know you should stop what you are doing. You know that unless you rest, you will make a mistake that could cost a life—yours or someone else's. Yet you are unable to do so. What does that make you?"

"A guy in a cape with bats in his belfry."

"Normally, I would applaud your attempt at humor. But not now. You are evading the question."

"Can't this wait?"

"Until when? Until there is a Marcy Hickenlooper lying in her own blood?"

"Alfred, maybe I *am* loopy. But I'm not going to quit now. End of discussion."

"There is an alternative. Seek help."

"Phone my friendly neighborhood psychiatrist and say, 'Doc, I'm this masked vigilante and I'm having a rough time—' "

"Not that kind of help. Have Master Tim accompany you."

"No chance. He's just a kid. I won't throw him against the likes of the Joker." *I won't risk losing him like I lost Jason Todd.*

"Of course not," Alfred said. "But he can work with the electronics. He can perform simple surveillance. He can drive the vehicle, if need be." *And he can remind you that you're human.*

"Okay, I'll consider it," Bruce said.

"I have another suggestion."

"Okay."

"Enlist the aid of Jean Paul Valley."

"No way."

"Before you decide, consider. He is as adept with computers as Master Tim. He is *almost* as good at combat as yourself. He has proven himself to be virtuous—"

"I barely know him."

"He saved your life."

"And I'm grateful," Bruce said. "But what you're suggesting is that he become some sort of auxiliary Batman."

"Would that be so terrible?"

"It might be. For him."

"And it might be worse for you if you *don't* confide in him. He might be a necessary evil."

"I'll think it over, Alfred."

Bruce rose, and Alfred saw him clearly. For a moment, Alfred was startled at the resemblance between Bruce and his father. In the pale glow of the television, Bruce looked like Dr. Thomas Wayne had looked when he came home after a long session in the operating room that had ended in failure.

16

Jean Paul wasn't sure whom he wanted to hear his prayers. On his knees in a room at the executive gym on the twenty-seventh floor of the Wayne Building in downtown Gotham, Jean Paul was praying as he had prayed every night since early childhood. But to whom? Not the Lord—those were different prayers. To St. Dumas, then, founder of the Order? Yes. But did he have the right to speak to the Venerable Dumas? Was he not excommunicated from the Order, and if he was, could he still invoke the saint's name? He didn't know. But he had to pray to someone, just as he had to continue drawing breath, and that someone had to be Dumas—there was no other choice for him. But when he closed his eyes, he did not see the saint as depicted in old woodcuts and the modern paintings they inspired; Paul saw his father. He knew enough psychology to explain this, but he believed in the Order far more than he believed in Freud.

Jean Paul finished his devotions and rose. The gym was deserted, as was the entire building except for a couple of security men. Jean Paul shed his black T-shirt and picked up a heavy broadsword. For a moment he held the haft in front of his face, as he had been taught, and then he began the slashes, thrusts, parries, and jabs that constituted the Devotion to the

Most Blessed St. Dumas through the Use and Manipulation of Bladed Weapons. Batman once told him that this was what the Asians called a *kata,* an intricate series of moves meant to simulate and improve combat skills. If that were true, the Oriental warriors must have learned it from the Order.

Several times, in moods of adolescent rebellion, he had tried the Devotion *without* praying first and had stumbled and fumbled and finally hurt himself. So he knew that what his father had told him was true; without aid and succor from the saint, he was no more than the inept bumbler the world believed him to be.

The Devotion concluded, he put on his shirt and a uniform jacket over it. He got his five-cell flashlight from his locker and began to patrol the building.

Batman stepped from the stairwell, stood just outside the red glow of an exit sign, and waited. He could hear Jean Paul's footsteps fifty yards down the corridor—firm, sharply defined steps; Jean Paul was not shuffling, not sauntering, not moping through the boring job of checking things that never needed to be checked; he was walking like a man fully alert and focused. That was good.

Coming closer. Now only a dozen yards away. Batman tensed. He felt as though he were about to step off a precipice. He had always admitted the possibility that one day he might have to reveal his identity to an outsider, but he had never thought that in doing so he would be admitting weakness. Because that's what he was doing—conceding that Alfred was right. He *was* exhausted, stressed almost beyond endurance. Too weak to continue his crusade alone.

Jean Paul became visible, a moving shape against the deep darkness of the corridor. He wasn't using his flashlight; he was trusting his night vision. Again, good. Jean Paul stopped. He was sensing something ahead of him; again, good.

"Hello," Batman said, stepping into the light.

Jean Paul's body instantly shifted into the state of alert relaxation

Batman had observed only in Zen masters and the greatest martial artists, poised on the cusp between readiness and action.

"Take it easy," Batman said. "I'm a good guy." His fingers moved to the lower edge of his mask and he hesitated. *Was this really necessary?* "I'm called Batman," he said finally, peeling away the mask, "and I'm also Bruce Wayne."

Zombie spread a map out on the table and motioned Bane, Trogg, and Bird closer. Zombie used his forefinger to trace a winding blue line. "This is where we last saw Batman's car, heading for this area here. Unless he went over twenty miles of back roads to the beltway, he had to have gone to one of six estates. They're all owned by very rich men. Vincenzo, Peterson, Wayne, Higgins, Drake, and Gorfinkel. We can eliminate Higgins and Gorfinkel. Higgins is ninety-four and Gorfinkel died last year— his seventy-year-old widow lives in the house with a few servants, all of whom are past fifty. We can probably eliminate Drake. He was tortured by gangsters in Haiti a few years ago and he's been confined to a wheelchair ever since."

"Maybe he's faking it," Bird said.

"Maybe," Zombie said. "But it's more likely that Wayne, Vincenzo, or Peterson is the Batman. Vincenzo was an Olympic athlete, the decathlon, and he now runs a bottling company. Peterson is the CEO of a company that manufactures cameras. He played baseball in college. Wayne is a screwup. His money comes from real estate. He's also got an investment firm and Waynetech, a research outfit. He doesn't go out in public much, but when he does, he usually makes a fool of himself. He dropped out of a dozen colleges and if he hadn't been lucky enough to hire top men, he would have been broke long ago."

"Perhaps it was not luck," Bane said. "Can you get me pictures of these men?"

"No prob," Bird said. "I got connections at Channel Six. They'll have files on them."

"Get me these pictures," Bane said. "They will tell us something."

• • •

Jean Paul gazed around at the Cave, awed. He had known of its existence—Bruce told him about it a few hours ago—but he had pictured some cramped hole with a bench and a couple of chairs. Not . . . *this*. This vast subterranean *cathedral*. These machines. This gymnasium, and the cars, the trophies, the racks of costumes, and the makeup table—

"Master Bruce would like you to familiarize yourself with everything here," Alfred said. "It should take you several days."

"My duties at the Wayne building—"

"You are on special assignment for the duration."

"Mister Pennyworth, what's this about? If I can ask."

"Master Bruce is engaged in a prolonged and very difficult task. No doubt you've seen the reports of the Arkham escapees on television—"

"I never watch television. Excuse me for interrupting you, sir."

"Quite all right. As I was saying . . . Batman is in a stressful situation. He may not be able to do all he feels he must. His tasks could conceivably force him to focus his energies elsewhere for a time. In that eventuality, he would ask you to assume the mantle of Batman until such time as he is able to return to his normal mode of existence. Even if that does not come to pass, he might need your assistance."

"Excuse me, sir . . . are you saying he might want me to *be* Batman?"

"In extremis, perhaps. It is not likely to happen, but one of Batman's rules is to always prepare for any eventuality."

Jean Paul went to the rack of costumes, removed one, and held it against his body. It would fit. He and Bruce Wayne had nearly identical builds. But would it be blasphemy to actually *wear* this strange vestment? He hoped not. He would pray to St. Dumas for guidance.

17

It was a strange experience for Robin to be riding shot-gun in the Batmobile. He was familiar with the car, of course; he'd seen it in the Batcave, and he had even sat in the driver's seat when Batman wasn't around. But he'd never thought he'd be in it while it was cruising through the canyons of the financial district.

Earlier that night Alfred had finally told him about his predecessor, the *second* Robin, Jason Todd. Jason was a street kid who had helped Batman catch a group of young thieves who operated from an orphanage. Despite Jason's obvious hostility and resistance to discipline, Bruce had liked him, had finally asked him to live in Wayne Manor and eventually to become Batman's assistant. The arrangement was not an easy one. Jason was moody and sometimes disobedient. But he was also smart and coura-geous.

"I think Bruce saw something of himself in the lad," Alfred explained. "They were both orphans and, like young Bruce, Jason was trying to make the best of a painful circumstance."

But Jason *wasn't* an orphan. While helping Batman investigate a lead to the Joker, who was involved in an arms-smuggling deal, Jason had discovered that his mother was probably still alive, somewhere in the

Middle East. Without telling Batman, or anyone else, he pursued her. At a lonely oasis in the Sinai desert, Jason and his mother were killed in an explosion—almost certainly a trap set by the Joker. Bruce never mentioned Jason. But there, in the Cave, Jason's Robin costume was encased in glass: a memorial and perhaps a reminder.

Robin wasn't used to riding beside someone in silence. "How are you doing with the Joker?" he asked, more to make conversation than to get information.

"Looks like he's hiding on the other side of the river. I don't know where yet." Batman's voice always lowered, almost to a whisper, when he spoke of the Joker.

"Seems quiet tonight," Robin said.

Batman nodded.

"We after anybody in particular?"

"Two-Face."

"That's why you went into the catamaran exhibit at the boat show, and the shack behind the Doublemint billboard?"

"Right."

"I'll check the police scanner."

Robin twisted a knob, and the car was filled with the crackle of radio transmission: ". . . domestic disturbance . . . warehouse fire on Hickson and Front . . . shooting . . . liquor store holdup in progress . . . ice cream truck reported missing . . ."

All the violence, all the pain, all the terrible things man did to man. The city only *seemed* quiet. The city was *never* quiet, and never would be. Robin thought he saw Batman grimace, but in the dim light from the dashboard, he couldn't be sure.

The Happy Freez truck was parked outside the mayor's mansion, blocking the driveway, when Krol's chauffeured limousine arrived at eleven.

A uniformed officer got out of the limo and sauntered toward the truck. He approached the driver's door; through the window the officer saw a figure dressed in a purple suit and floppy green hat with a huge, round red nose—obviously an ice cream peddling clown. The officer rapped on the glass. "Move it, funny face," he shouted.

The clown rolled down the window. "Are you His Honor the illustrious Mayor Krol?" the clown asked, and giggled.

"Do I *look* like him?"

"Wel-l-l . . . no. I've heard *he's* handsome."

"You gonna move this thing or am I gonna move it for you?"

"Please! Such a *harsh* tone of voice. It positively frightens me to pieces."

"Listen—"

"No sir, Mister, *you* listen. I have a *present* for the mayor, from the girls at the Bates School. They want to thank His Honor for all his help during the recent unfortunate bloodletting."

"What kind of present?"

"Do I look like I'm driving a fur truck? Maybe you think I've got a load of diamonds in here. Baseball cards? Yo-yos? Krugerrands? Penny stocks? *Ice* cream, you ninny! I have got a whole quart of Rocky Road and if that is not His Honor's fave, it *ought* to be, 'cause it is delicious." He reached into a cooler on the seat beside him and produced an ice cream bar on a stick. "Our newest flavor—Mocha Java Splendor. Try some."

"Kinda chilly for this stuff but . . . what the hell!" The officer bit into the ice cream bar.

The clown got out of the truck with a quart package and began mincing toward the mayor's limo.

"Hey, I didn't say—" The officer gasped, clutched his throat, and as his mouth widened into a grin, collapsed.

The rear window of the limo dropped, and Mayor Krol called, "What's happening with Smith?"

"He had a seizure."

"Johnson, see what's the matter with him," Krol told his chauffeur.

The clown held out the quart package. "You scream, I scream, we all scream for ice cream," he sang. "Could I please hear you scream?"

"He's dead," Johnson yelled.

The clown was pulling a silenced automatic from under his coat as he turned. He fired, hitting Johnson once in the chest. Johnson fell atop Smith.

"What the hell—?" Krol started to open the door of the limo.

"That's right, Mayorsy-wayorsy," the clown said, removing the red nose and gesturing with his pistol. "C'mon out and join the fun. Oh, allow me to introduce myself." He swept off the hat and bowed from the waist. "I am often known as 'the sadistic fiend from hell,' or 'the Clown Prince of Crime.' But you can call me the Joker."

As soon as the radio reported that Krol's chauffeur and bodyguard had been found dead by a passing patrol car, Batman spun the wheel of the Batmobile and sped up a side street. The neighborhood was old, dating back to before the Civil War, and the streets were narrow and winding. Yet Batman was able to power the car through them as though he were alone on a six-lane freeway. Robin had never seen driving like it.

There was already a cluster of vehicles by the steel gate when Batman braked the car. "Stay put," he told Robin.

Batman joined Commissioner Gordon, Sergeant Harvey Bullock, and Officer Renee Montoya, who were standing over the bodies of Smith and Johnson while a uniformed cop took pictures. Harvey was, as usual, feeding himself from a carton of doughnuts. He was a slob: his fedora was on backward, his belly showed through a gap in his shirt and overhung his belt, and his shoes were so scuffed that it was impossible to say what color they had been originally. In contrast, Montoya was slim and rigid as a rapier, a woman of starch and creases. They were two of Gordon's best.

"Hey, hey, looky who's here," Bullock said through a mouthful of doughnut. "Our prime candidate for America's Most Wanted."

Batman ignored him. He stood squarely in front of Gordon and said, "I've heard you want me for questioning. I'm surrendering myself to you, Commissioner Gordon."

"Lemme put the cuffs on him," Bullock said, fumbling in a pocket.

"That won't be necessary," Gordon said.

"May I ask what you've learned," Batman said to Gordon.

"Not much. Prowl car spotted these two. One of 'em's Krol's driver, the other's his bodyguard. We've already searched the mansion. No sign of Krol. The maid says he hasn't come home yet."

The photographer looked up at Gordon. "Okay to turn 'em over, Commissioner?"

"Do your job, son. The medical examiner's already seen 'em."

Batman contemplated Smith and Johnson. He peered at the rictus of a grin on Smith's face, took a small flashlight from under his cloak, and played it on both bodies. He knelt and put his face close to a splotch on the front of Smith's raincoat. "Commissioner, I need to look under him."

Gordon hesitated. "Okay, but don't disturb anything more than you have to."

Batman rolled Smith partway onto his right side and shined the light under him.

"Krol's been kidnapped by the Joker. They're in a Happy Freez ice cream truck, probably heading for the Lower Island Tunnel. Get on the horn and get them stopped."

He sprinted for the Batmobile.

"Wasn't there something about him bein' wanted for questioning?" Bullock asked.

"You heard him, Sergeant. Get the tunnel patrol and tell them to stop any Happy Freez trucks they see. Tell them to use extreme caution."

But the call came too late. When the Happy Freez truck stopped at one of the tollbooths at the Gotham end of the tunnel, the clown driving had handed the attendant an ice cream bar instead of three dollars. The truck sped away, smashing through the thin wooden gate, and entered the tunnel. A second later, the booth exploded.

"Little leftover plastique from a deal with some confreres in the Sinai," the Joker said over his shoulder to Krol, who was bound and gagged with tape and sitting in a puddle of melted ice cream. "You can never *tell* what use you'll find for the darned stuff."

The Joker braked. Ahead, bursts of red light bounced off the white tile walls of the tunnel.

"Well, suh, the poe-leece done got far end of this here pipe all clogged," the Joker said in a deep, heavily accented voice. "Dang my soul if'n they ain't. Guess this here party's a'gonna git *mighty* innerestin'."

It had been obvious, of course, Batman thought as he careened through the streets of the lower city. *The grin on the bodyguard's face— the Joker's special poison. The splotch on his clothing—smelled like ice cream. The stick under the body confirmed it. Earlier, somebody reported a stolen ice cream truck—not usual this late in the year. So the Joker had taken the truck, poisoned an ice cream bar, conned the guard into eating it, shot the chauffeur, and taken Krol—*

"Are we heading for the tunnel?" Robin asked.

"Yes."

"Wouldn't it be faster to take the bridge?"

"You heard the radio. Fire on Hickson and Front. The bridge will be blocked with fire equipment."

And the Joker's on the other side of the river. He always hides out in remote areas, and even if he hasn't this time, it would be risky for him to drive such a recognizable vehicle in the city late at night. He could be holed up in a garage but—no. The river's the best bet.

Ahead, past a bus terminal, barely visible in the darkness, they could see a column of smoke rising, gray against the deep blue of the sky. The Batmobile screeched around a corner and stopped. Traffic was backed up from the entrance to the tunnel, which was partially collapsed. Smoke rose from the rubble.

The phone buzzed. Batman punched a button and heard Gordon: "You there?"

"Yes."

"Joker's trapped in the tunnel. Cruisers on the other side, some kind of explosion on this—"

"I'm looking at it."

"Then I'm maybe three minutes behind you. We've been communicating by phone in case he's monitoring the police band. Look, you can skip this. My people can handle it."

Since when! Batman broke the connection and turned to Robin. "I'm going after him. Now listen to me—*stay in the car.* Do *not* follow me under any circumstances."

Because the Joker killed Jason.

"Do you understand?"

"Okay, sure," Robin said.

The Joker ran up to an alcove in the tunnel a hundred yards ahead of the Happy Freez truck, deposited two ice cream bars, and ran back. He climbed into the cab and placed his palms flat against his ears.

"Ka-boom!" he said.

And an explosion shattered the tile wall and collapsed the ceiling.

Dust filled the air. Krol gasped and coughed beneath his gag, but the Joker seemed unaffected.

"Now this is a real sticky situation," he said conversationally. "Actually, it's not so much *sticky* as *wet* and that is a very important distinction. *Attendez-vous, mon frère,* and dig what I'm laying down. You see, we are, at this moment, under the Gotham River which don't plant taters and don't plant cotton, but enough of this agricultural chit-chat. The point is that the big bang you just heard undoubtedly opened a crack or seven in the tunnel and even as we speak said moisture is seeping in and will soon trickle and I am quite confident—and I mean this seriously—will shortly thereafter *gush* in a *torrent* and anyone hereabouts who can't grow some world-class gills in the world's biggest hurry will be in Titanic trouble. Glub glub. Does that include you, Mayorsy-wayorsy?"

Krol tried to speak but uttered only a muffled grunt through the tape.

"Me, I don't plan to drown," the Joker continued. "Not tonight. Because—*I have a plan.* But you guessed that, did you not? Ah, once upon a time, you see, I planned some dreadful mischief. Naughty me, I was going to blow up all the bridges and tunnels at the height of rush hour and cause the early demise of . . . oh, thousands of solid citizens, would you say? Tens of thousands? Lots, anyway. But I never quite got around to it. You know how it is, a man gets so darn busy with the little murders and tortures—everyday acts of random, ruthless mayhem—that he neglects the really *creative* part of his soul. What I did was, I got hold of the plans for this particular tunnel. Why, the geniuses who constructed this public work put in a whole slew of *smaller* tunnels for wires and telephone lines and—yucky!—*sewers.* I know where they are."

Something had begun to drum on the top of the truck. The Joker put a hand to his ear and struck a listening pose. "Hark! The pitter-patter of rain on the roof. Well, it *was* rain before it became Ol' Man Gotham. Was that ten centuries ago? I forget. If I ever knew. *Any*hoo, I am prepared to make you an offer. I will take you with me. You won't have to grow gills. But—and you knew there would be a *but,* didn't you?—if I do, I swear, promise, attest, and aver that when we are safely away, I will cause you prolonged pain such as you cannot imagine."

The sound on the roof grew louder.

"What'll it be?" the Joker asked. "Death by drowning now or hideous agony later?"

Krol grunted.

"Can't *heearrr youuu,*" the Joker crooned. "Tell you what. I'll elucidate the possibilities one at a time. You just nod when you hear something you like and yes, they *do* call me Mr. Fair. Now, *numero uno*—you grow gills."

Krol shook his head violently.

"*Numero dos*—and I gotta tell you, this is the one *I* like—death by ghastly torture later."

Krol bobbed his head.

"Mister Mayor, I like your enthusiasm, I really do. And I gotta tell ya, the choice you made was the choice with *heart.* Now let me see . . . how the *heck* do I get us outta here?"

Batman ran among the stalled cars and trucks until he came to the collapsed entrance to the tunnel. Smoke was boiling from somewhere in the rubble, mixing with the pall of dust that hung in the air. He paused to survey the scene for a moment before leaping to the top of the cab of a semi, and from there to a jagged gap in the masonry. He squeezed through it and found himself in a crawlway over the main roadbed. He pulled a small flashlight from his belt and in its beam saw that part of the crawlway had fallen into the tunnel. The hole was big enough to accommodate him. He dropped onto the roadbed, letting his legs fold under him, rolling, coming to his feet. The main lighting system was out, but an emergency generator was powering small auxiliary bulbs every twenty-five feet. They barely glowed; Batman kept a grip on his flash.

Ahead, a minivan was stopped, its engine still running. As Batman ran past it, the driver called, "Mister, what's happening?"

Batman paused. "Turn off your motor and sit tight." He could see that the driver was a chubby, middle-aged man; four chubby children were in the seat behind him. "Help is on the way."

I hope.

He ran on, past a battered old Volkswagen bug, two white subcompacts, and a green pickup. It was nearly midnight; traffic had been sparse when the explosions occurred. That was fortunate: a rush-hour bombing would have caused panic and chaos.

Gordon had said the far end of the tunnel was blocked. It was possible that the Joker had somehow gotten around the barriers, but if he hadn't, Batman should be seeing the Happy Freez truck soon.

Water splashed on his cowl. A dozen rivulets were pouring from cracks in the masonry. Batman shined his flashlight upward and saw new cracks opening, new streams of water.

The river's going to come roaring in here. Those people will never get out in time.

Suddenly, he felt as though his bones had been sucked away. He could barely stand. He remembered that he hadn't really slept in days—he'd lost count of exactly how many days—and for the last week he had taken all his nourishment in bites as he worked. He leaned against the curved tile wall. Maybe if he just rested a while . . .

No. Not when I'm so close.

He forced himself onward. He rounded a curve in the tunnel and saw the Happy Freez truck. Bursting into the cabin, he swept his light around. A litter of wrappers and cartons and splotches of melted ice cream. But no Krol. No Joker.

Batman left the truck and continued running. He was splashing now; the water was almost ankle-deep. He was nearing the far end of the tunnel; the Joker *had* to be somewhere close.

Robin switched his attention between the police band and the regular AM radio signal, specifically the all-news station WGNS. The police calls were for medics, ambulances, and rescue equipment. Listening to them, it was possible to guess what was happening in the tunnel. But the excited announcer on GNS spelled it out: ". . . tunnel personnel at the scene say water is already flooding in, weakening the structure that was already weakened by half-completed repairs. It may only be minutes before the tunnel completely collapses, trapping up to a hundred motorists. Once again, two explosions at the Lower Island Tunnel—"

And I'm supposed to just sit here in the car, Robin thought. *I could be out there helping, but Bruce said not to move. Okay, he's the boss. Maybe I should turn to a music station. Maybe I should get into some rock, or rap as long as I'm just sitting here. I'll turn off GNS and go to Rockin' Robbie Kowalski over on WBAH and hear the latest from Sonia Dada or somebody.*

But he didn't.

The Joker pushed Krol ahead of him. They were in a narrow space between the tiled wall of the tunnel and the steel and concrete shell that encased it. On one side they could hear the murmur of engines from the cars trapped in the stretch between mounds of rubble and an occasional angry horn; on the other side, silence. Millions of tons of river made no noise. The Joker had a flashlight he had taken from the Happy Freez truck's glove compartment. He shined it over Krol's shoulder.

"Only a little further, Your Honorness," the Joker said. "We should come to a nice ladder and then, if you still agree to our bargain, I'll untape your hands so you can climb. But I will keep one end of the tape stuck to you and I'll be holding the other, and if you try anything *precipitous,* I shall break your leg. I think we can all agree that *that* is the proper course of action here."

Krol grunted.

They came to a wall. The Joker's beam swept upward. No ladder. Just holes in the cement where a ladder had *been,* and a dark stain that was visibly spreading downward.

"They have made my purloined plans *obsolete.* They have *changed* things. And do you know what? *They. Did. Not. Call. First!* I must confess my disappointment. And my hurt. I am wounded, yes I am."

A fat drop of water splashed on the top of Krol's head.

"Uh-oh," the Joker said. "That is, if you were to ask me, Mister Mayor Troll, either the morning dew arriving way ahead of schedule, or a *bad sign.* It may mean that Ol' Man River is a-comin' in. What *kind* of city are you running where bodies of excessive moisture do not keep to their proper places?"

The Joker grabbed Krol's shoulder and spun him around. "Back the way we came, Troll."

Batman reached the tunnel exit. It was as blocked as the entrance. A frail man in a three-piece suit had taken a shovel from the trunk of his car and was digging at the rubble. At the rate he was going, he'd be free and clear in about three months.

No sign of the Joker or Krol. Batman tucked away his flash and slid the night lenses over the eye holes in his mask. Maybe they'd improve his vision. Maybe he'd see something he'd missed. He retraced his steps, scanning the walls as he moved.

And there it was. A metal door in an alcove. Probably a maintenance access. *Why didn't I spot it before? Because I was exhausted? No excuse.*

He felt pressure on his calf, above the top of his boot. Water. Now more than a foot high. Soon—within minutes—he'd be standing in a huge, submerged grave. He still had time to escape, to return to where he'd entered. He might be able to take some of the trapped motorists with him. But then what about the mayor? And the Joker?—would *they* drown? Would the world finally be rid of the Joker? No way to be sure.

Batman had seen him survive explosions, gunfire, electrocution, falling from aircraft, and yes, even plunging to the bottom of the Gotham River. What reason was there to believe that the odds would finally catch up to him?

Batman stepped toward the door, halted, and stepped back.

He couldn't decide where to go, or what to do. It was the most terrifying moment of his adult life.

". . . have Palmer Haas, the chief engineer at the Lower Island Tunnel on the line," the WGNS announcer was saying. Robin turned up the volume. "Mr. Haas, can you tell us what the situation is?"

"Hard to say. None of our people are . . . oh, my heavens!"

"What is it, Mr. Haas?"

"The pressure reading just changed. It probably means that the roadbed is filling with water."

"How many people are trapped there?"

"Seventy-five, eighty," Haas said grimly.

"Can you give us an estimate of their chances? . . . Mr. Haas? Chief Engineer Haas? . . . We seem to have lost contact with Chief Engineer Palmer Haas . . ."

Stay in the car, Bruce had said.

While innocents drowned?

No.

Robin opened the door and began running.

Palmer Haas ran to the construction foreman. "How's it going?" he gasped, adjusting his hard hat.

"We've had the backhoe working ever since the explosion," the foreman said. "But hell, it'll take another hour 'fore we even get a little hole dug through."

"Do we have any explosives on the site?"

"Yeah, we been blasting all day—"

"Use them," Haas ordered.

"Hell, man, somebody's on the other side they're gonna likely be blown to bits."

"We've got to take the chance."

The foreman shook his head, shrugged, and trudged away.

Robin used Batman's route: pavement to the top of the semi to the jagged gap. Crawlway. Hole. Down to the roadbed—

He landed in waist-deep water. He waded forward. Slowly. He flattened his body and began to swim, a shallow crawl. Slow, but faster than walking. There were a few bulbs at the top of the wall still glowing. In their dim light, he saw people sitting on top of cars.

"Can you tell us what's going on?" a man yelled.

Robin lowered his feet and stood. "No sir. Not sure myself."

Then he remembered the radio in his tunic, one of many devices Bruce had insisted be incorporated into the costume—devices Jason Todd hadn't had. He pulled an earpiece from his belt, made an adjustment on his buckle, and heard nothing but static. *Too far underwater.*

He resumed swimming.

His belly scraped asphalt. The water was calf-deep here. On his feet, he splashed ahead, calling instructions to everyone he saw.

Then he saw the Happy Freez truck and, in the beam of headlights, Batman, unmoving, staring at a wall.

The Joker yanked Krol's collar. The mayor jerked to a stop inches from the door.

"Not so fast, Troll. I'm not sure we want to leave our hidey-hole just yet."

The Joker positioned Krol in front of the door, kicked it open and shoved Krol out. Krol stumbled and fell facedown in the water.

· · ·

A second earlier, Batman had heard someone call his name, turned, and saw Robin splashing toward him. He waved: *Go back!*

He heard the sound of rusty hinges and turned again. Someone—Krol —was falling. Behind, in the doorway, was a familiar silhouette: the Joker.

A slab of tile and cement tore loose from the ceiling and fell between Batman and the Joker. An edge struck Batman just above the ear. His bulletproof cowl absorbed much of the blow, but still the force of it knocked him to his knees.

Robin kneeled at his side, saying words Batman couldn't quite hear above the gush of the water that was pouring over them from above. Batman shook his head, closed his eyes, opened them. A clown's motley trousers and floppy shoes were in front of him, and another voice was screeching. From the corner of his vision, he saw Robin jerk away.

He wanted to move. He *needed* to move. But he couldn't.

Robin, intent on Batman, hadn't seen the Joker until a floppy shoe kicked him in the face.

"You little dickens!" the Joker screeched. "I killed you in the Sinai! I did!"

White-gloved fingers closed around his throat and squeezed. Weight on his head forced him under the water.

"This time you'll *stay dead!*"

Robin reached up, found the waistband of the Joker's motley trousers. He pulled, shifting his center of gravity, and the weight lifted. He burst into air, choked, and gasped. The Joker was sitting next to him, already swinging. A white fist slammed into Robin's jaw, and again he went under. He kicked out, struck something. Robin groped blindly and touched the wall. He leaned on it, gathered his legs under him, and stood.

His vision filled with dust and debris, and he realized that he had just heard an explosion. The lenses of his mask were clouded. He tore it off.

Smoke was billowing from the exit. He saw a clown shape shambling away deeper into the tunnel and Batman standing, visibly trembling, his cloak mottled with gray powder.

He's been standing there, Robin thought. *Just standing there.*

Batman looked around and slowly shook his head.

"Do you know where you are?" Robin shouted at him.

Batman nodded and stumbled after the clown. Robin grabbed him by the cloak. "Batman, *no!*"

Batman swept a hand backward, trying to free himself. But the effort was feeble. Robin tightened his grip. He knew, with absolute certainty, that if Batman pursued his enemy, they would both die. But he couldn't use force on his mentor, he just couldn't. He had to *say* something.

"Krol . . . needs your help."

Who? Who needs my help? Who's speaking to me?

Krol lying facedown in the water.

Krol needs my help. But I can't help Krol. Because . . . the other is more important. Isn't it? Isn't it more important than saving Krol, this other thing?

In his ear, a familiar voice: "Help me with Krol."

His mother and father dead on the street. Was that more important than Krol? Avenging their murders, yes. That was the other thing—dealing with thieves and murderers. But why? So innocent people would not lie with their faces paling, their limbs splayed and growing cold.

Krol was dying. A hand on his arm, the voice: "Come on."

Moving toward Krol. So Krol would not die as his parents had died. That was more important than anything.

Krol being lifted. Was he lifting Krol? Men in coveralls and high rubber boots milling around them, taking Krol, babbling.

The voice: "This way."

A bright place. A shadowy place. A dark place.

The voice: "We can hide here. I don't think anyone saw us go in the confusion. I radioed Alfred. He'll pick you up. I'll go back for the car."

Whatever that meant. Whatever any of that meant.

18

 Bane sat alone in front of the television screen in the motel office, watching the videotape Bird had brought to him.

First he saw news footage of Daryl Vincenzo, a solidly built man with a dark mustache and a curiously deferential manner.

"No," Bane said aloud.

Next, Cotter Peterson—younger and slimmer than Vincenzo, a lean, all-American boy type in his mid-thirties.

"No," said Bane.

Finally, Bruce Wayne: tall, handsome, but vacuous. Shambling walk, slouching posture, empty grin.

"Him," said Bane. "The manner is a mask. Beneath it is steel."

He went to the door, opened it, and shouted, "Come."

A minute later, Bird, Zombie, and Trogg entered the office.

"You have the maps?" Bane asked Zombie.

"Yes." Zombie unfolded a geological chart and spread it on the floor in front of Bane. "As you can see, there are a lot of caverns in the area."

"Batman would choose to live in a cave," Bane said. "He comes from the cold and the dark."

"You sound like you know him," Bird said.

"I do. I met him in the *cavidad oscuro*."

Bruce—or was he Batman?—lay on the hard stone of the Cave floor. His eyes were closed, but his breathing was irregular. He was awake. He was in a region past sleep, past exhaustion.

The Joker had escaped.

He had failed.

Bane was rigid on the motel bed, his muscles tense and bulging. He had been sucked into his old dream, and now he advanced toward the bat-thing, strode into the bleak, cold night of the monster's cave—strode alone because he knew this battle would have to be fought as Bane had always fought his important battles, without friend or ally, with no one to share either victory or blame. The bat was a presence rather than a thing seen. Only its eyes were visible, glittering in the dark. With a roar, Bane charged, grasped the bat in his massive arms, and began to squeeze, knowing that this time, finally, he would triumph.

"Is he sleeping, do you think?" Tim asked.

"I hope so," Alfred replied. "But I doubt it."

They were sitting in the large, coppery kitchen of the manor. Alfred nodded toward the refrigerator. "I have some excellent low-fat apple pie—"

"No thanks." For almost a minute, there was silence. Then Tim asked, "How's he doing?"

"I fear for him, lad. I've never seen him like this and I am at my wit's end. He does not respond to joking, to scolding, to simple logic. If I thought I could get him to a good psychiatrist—"

"How about a regular doctor?"

"Doubtful. But worth a mention. Lord knows, his body needs attention. Do you have someone in mind?"

"Shondra. Dr. Kinsolving."

"The physician attending your father?"

"She's worked wonders for Dad," Tim said. "There's something about her . . . she's more than a doctor. She's like a witch or something. I mean a *good* witch, if there is such a thing."

"I believe the literature admits of the possibility."

"I can feel some kind of power coming off her."

"Is she attractive?"

"It's not *that,* Alfred. I'd recognize lust. Not that I've had much experience with it."

"You're young. How are you otherwise? That business in the tunnel must have been as harrowing for you as for Master Bruce."

"Tell me about it. I didn't realize how bad it was until afterward. At the time, I was too busy just getting through it to notice."

"You did well. Hiding Bruce in the construction site, driving the automobile back here by yourself—"

"*That* would have given some traffic cop a cow if I'd been stopped."

Alfred smiled. "You did what the circumstances demanded."

"One thing bothers me. I almost let Mayor Krol drown while I was talking to Batman."

"May I remind you that His Honor *did* survive—"

"No thanks to me. I mean, I could've pulled his head out of the water at least. But all I could think of was Batman and the Joker."

"As I said a moment ago, you're young. You lack experience."

"*He'd* never make a mistake like that."

"Bruce? In the first year of his career as Batman, he erred frequently. Sometimes nightly. But he never erred the same way twice. That may be a lesson you can learn from him."

"Sounds a lot harder than algebra." Tim glanced at his watch. "Hey, I gotta run."

"Schoolwork?"

"Something better. A date."

"Your young Russian immigrant friend Adrian?"

"*Ariana.* See you, Alfred."

Alfred went to the window and watched Tim bicycle in the direction of his father's house. Today he was Tim, not Robin; the Cave was off-limits to Tim. Alfred wondered if the youngster knew that Bruce Wayne didn't have dates, not real ones, not ones that admitted the possibility of a relationship. The hardships Bruce routinely endured were far more than physical; Batman could have no lover and remain Batman. Alfred did not wish that kind of loneliness for Tim.

The limousine stopped in the motel driveway at precisely nine o'clock. The driver tapped his horn. Bane, followed by Zombie, Bird, and Trogg, came from the office. They all got into the rear seat of the limo, and Bird rapped the plexiglass partition that separated the passenger area from the driver's seat. "Hit it, bro."

"Where to?" the driver asked.

"Just drive. We'll give you directions," Bird said.

"We're going to find Batman?" Zombie asked.

"Not yet," Bane said. "I want to look at the city."

"The master surveys his realm," Zombie murmured.

"Downtown Gotham, m'man," Bird told the driver.

The limo turned from the motel parking lot and sped down the road. Bird, Trogg, and Zombie sat upright, rigid in their seats. Bane leaned back, put his hands behind his head, and relaxed.

The movie had been okay . . . okay, *better* than okay, and the walk back to Ariana's was even better than the movie. She and Tim weren't exactly touching, not quite, except when their arms sort of accidentally collided, which was actually pretty often, but there was a potent *possibility* of touch and Tim found that just a bit dizzying.

They stopped at the doorway next to Ariana's family print shop and stood a foot apart. Ariana brushed back a strand of her long black hair. Tim looked into her enormous gray eyes.

"Well," Tim said.

"Uh huh," Ariana said.

"You *really* liked the movie?"

"I told you I did," Ariana said gravely. "Didn't you believe me?"

"Oh, sure. I didn't think you were . . . weren't being truthful, completely, exactly."

Ariana's face was tilted up, her eyes wide, her lips slightly pursed. Some kind of invitation throbbed in the air between them, and Tim couldn't believe that he was sure what it was.

Tangle with a maniac serial killer—no prob. But *this*—

He bowed toward her, bumped her nose with his. Skin slid against skin and lips touched briefly but significantly.

"Well, good night," Ariana said.

"I'll call you tomorrow," Tim said.

Ariana unlocked the door, glanced back, and closed it.

I'm pretty sure I am now recognizing lust, Tim thought. *Pretty sure. Having experience with it, too. Little experience, here, no doubt about it. Very little experience. But I'm still young.*

19

Alfred went through the clock and into the Cave. Bruce was still lying on his pallet, eyes squeezed shut, body rigid. Clearly not resting properly.

"Go away," he said, not moving.

"Very well."

Alfred slowly climbed the steps to the manor, closed the clock behind him, took a feather duster from a closet, and entered the library. He swiped at the leather-bound Mark Twain first editions. Always keep busy, was his motto. But tonight, the chore was not therapeutic. If something happened tonight, Bruce—Batman—would not be able to cope. If *anything* happened. Suddenly the sturdy walls of this grand old house seemed frail and the darkness outside full of menace.

He picked up a phone and dialed.

Jean Paul was finishing his third nightly round of the Wayne Building when the phone buzzed. He removed it from his belt, spoke his name, and listened.

"Mr. Valley, Alfred Pennyworth here. Mr. Wayne's man. I wonder if you would be so kind as to drop by the manor."

"Now?"

"If you could."

"I'd need Mr. Wayne to authorize my leaving my post."

"Actually, that's why I'm calling," Alfred said brusquely. "Mr. Wayne is indisposed and we might require your services."

"You're sure this is all right with Mr. Wayne?"

"I am reasonably certain he would not object."

"Well . . . I'll have to take a taxicab," Jean Paul said. "Wouldn't I? I'm sorry . . . I don't drive."

"A taxicab is an excellent idea," Alfred assured him. "We will reimburse you the fare."

"It'll take an hour."

"Shall I expect you at eleven?"

"Twelve. It'll take me some time to get a taxicab."

"Twelve, then. Good-bye for now, Mr. Valley."

The city outside the limousine was dazzling. Bane leaned back in the cushions and gazed through the smoky glass at the blaze of colored lights and sleek women wearing fur, the towering buildings, the stately homes, the cathedrals, parks, and rows of shops, the restaurants, the hotels, the theaters and clubs—all of Gotham's riches.

"Where to now, Magic?" Bird asked.

"Stop at the next corner."

Bird relayed the instruction to the driver.

"Everyone get out," Bane said.

Zombie and Trogg nodded and obeyed. Bird said, "Hey, big M, was it something we said?"

"Don't question him," Zombie growled.

"Okay, okay," Bird said, climbing onto the sidewalk.

"The driver too," Bane said.

Zombie and Trogg moved around to the driver's door.

"You heard him," Zombie said.

"No way I can leave this vee-hic-le," the driver said. "Company rules."

Zombie pulled the door open and Trogg hauled the driver out and threw him across the hood onto the sidewalk.

Bane got into the driver's seat. He had observed the operation of the machine. Making it function would present no particular difficulty. He touched the controls, peered at the gauges behind the wheel, and satisfied he understood them all, steered into the traffic stream.

"Where's he going?" Bird asked.

Trogg spoke for the first time since they had left Santa Prisca. "Kill the Bat."

Tim entered his father's house thinking of Ariana. He expected to still be thinking of her until he fell asleep and maybe immediately upon awakening in the morning and maybe during the day when he had a spare moment.

Usually when he taxied in from the city this late, the house was dark. But he saw a light under the door to the recreation room. He looked in. Shondra was in the big leather chair, reading a book. She looked up and smiled.

"Working late, Dr. Kinsolving?" Tim asked.

"I was until a while ago. Your father may need me later—"

"Is something wrong?"

"No, no, your father is doing well. I just want to observe the results of something I tried. It seemed wasteful to drive to Gotham and back. I thought I'd sleep on the couch here, if you don't mind."

"I *do* mind, Dr. Kinsolving. This house has twenty-three rooms and at least half of them have beds. Take the one at the end of the hall upstairs. Bed's as big as a football field."

"Thank you, Tim."

"Sure. Well, see you."

Tim waved and went up to his room. His bed was as big as a football field, too, but he didn't feel like occupying it. What he wanted to do was call Ariana, but it was almost midnight, much too late. Maybe he could hack around on the computer for a while, have another shot at the task Batman had given him. They *still* didn't know who the guy on the roof was.

When Alfred heard a car stopping outside the main entranceway to the manor, he thought Jean Paul had arrived and opened the door. But the car wasn't a taxi, it was a limousine, and the man striding toward him certainly wasn't Jean Paul Valley. Alfred remembered Bruce's description of the strange figure in the Manklin brothers' loft and, shocked, knew that this was the brute Batman had been seeking.

He swung the door shut but before he could turn the lock he was slammed against a wall.

Bane shouldered the door aside as it rebounded and stalked into the foyer.

Alfred was seeing double: two huge brutes wearing hoods with hoses coming from them tromping across two rugs toward two grandfather clocks . . .

He shook his head and said, "We aren't receiving callers this evening, sir, but if you leave your card—"

"Where is he?" Bane demanded.

"Master Wayne? Out enjoying the company of some young woman, I should think. He mentioned a new comedy club—"

Bane turned to the clock. Alfred wondered how Bane knew, then realized that he must have noticed Alfred glance at the clock.

Master Bruce is in no condition to deal with him. I suppose it's my show, though I do wish Jean Paul would arrive.

Bane was grasping the clock, pulling at it. Alfred picked up a lead glass vase and swung it at the back of Bane's head. It shattered. Bane glanced over his shoulder.

He grunted. "Do not do that again."

Sound suggestion, considering the effect it had. Alfred looked for another weapon.

A creak and a splintering, and then the right side of the clock tore loose, revealing the entrance to the Cave. No weapon. In desperation, Alfred lunged at Bane, hit him on the side with both hands. Bane's elbow shot back like a piston, striking Alfred in the chest, leaving him unable to move as he sank to the rug.

Bane started down the steps.

Bruce heard the clock break and boot soles scraping on the stone stairway, descending. He rose from his pallet and waited as the footfalls came closer. Someone was violating the Cave. He should be alarmed, should be already in motion, attacking. But his emotions were as heavy as sludge, and his body was obeying his emotions.

The man stepped into the light.

"We've met before," Bruce said. "The rooftop."

"You are Bruce Wayne. You are Batman."

For a moment Bruce considered lying. But he was standing unmasked, wearing Batman's clothes, facing a stranger who obviously knew his secret. He felt a pang of anger. *He has no right to know.* He calmed himself with a deep breath. Anger would gain him nothing, and lying would be stupid.

"Okay, let's say I am," he said.

"I have known you since I lived in the hell of a dark hole thousands of miles from here. I have known you in my dreams. And I escaped from that hell—from my *dreams*—for one reason only. To find you—and to break you."

"Did you free the Arkham inmates?"

"Yes."

"Was it about *me?* You wanted them to wear me down? Weaken me? All the wasted lives . . . it's been nothing but that? You'd kill for *that?*"

"I would kill for anything. I would kill to silence a grating voice. To darken the light in eyes that dared to look at me."

"You revel in violence and I grow sick of it."

"Do you?" Bane laughed.

"I've spent my life fighting your kind of madness and now . . ."

Bruce stopped speaking. Now he knew that he had told the truth—he did hate violence—but that this man, this Bane, was right in laughing, too, because Bruce embraced what he hated. Why had he never seen the contradiction? Because he had never allowed himself to?

After a full minute he said, "You may be the most insane creature I've ever faced. Don't you know what you are? Don't you see the ugliness, the inhumanity?"

"Words," Bane said.

Bruce reached over his shoulder and began pulling his mask into place.

"You cannot hide," Bane said.

"I'm not hiding. I'm becoming."

"We begin," Bane said. He pressed the stud strapped to his arm.

Bruce saw Bane's skin flush and his muscles swell.

What is it? What's he done to himself?

Jean Paul felt like cursing himself. There he was, standing outside the Wayne Building for fifteen minutes looking for a taxicab to hail before he realized that at this hour on Saturday night taxicabs did not come into this area, which was devoted to the higher kinds of financial business and was virtually deserted after six on Friday evening. Could one telephone for a taxicab? Surely that must be possible, but how? And where did one find a public telephone amid these towering, windowless walls? He had left his portable cellular phone in his locker; it was part of his uniform and he had changed to street clothing. He could reenter the building, but he still wouldn't know the procedure for summoning a taxicab.

He began walking. A few blocks away there was a brightly lit thoroughfare. Surely he'd be able to find a taxicab *there*.

Alfred could not breathe, but he was not dead, so oxygen must be reaching his lungs somehow. He couldn't stand, either, but he could drag himself across the rug, inch by inch, to the high table and the telephone on it. When he got there—*if* he got there—he would think of someone to call.

"Tim, are you still awake?" Shondra Kinsolving stood in the door to Tim's room.

"Yes ma'am." Tim turned from his computer. "Why? Do you need something?"

"No, but come and look at your father."

Tim followed Shondra down the hall to his father's room. It was the largest in the house, outfitted as a complete medical facility.

Jack Drake lay on his bed, eyes closed, chest lifting and falling regularly. Tim was always astonished at how old and pale and delicate he was, this tycoon who, a couple of years ago, was a hearty man's man, exuding machismo from every pore, as big and fierce as Bruce Wayne. But Bruce never strutted his toughness nor boasted of it, and sometimes Jack Drake had.

"There doesn't seem to be anything wrong," Tim said.

"No, Tim. There's something *right*. He's off the respirator." And he was: the apparatus was on the floor, unused. "It's the first real progress he's made," Shondra said.

"That's good, isn't it? That's really good?"

"Really very good."

"I don't know what to say. . . . Thanks, Dr. Kinsolving. Thanks a lot."

"You're welcome, Tim."

Batman settled the mask firmly on his face and was immediately disappointed. Always, until this moment, putting on the mask gave him a sense of *otherness*, and with it a feeling of power. But now he was simply a man with his face covered, a man who had exceeded any measurable capacity for fatigue, stress, and exhaustion days ago. But, he reminded himself, he had studied with the world's finest martial artists and had surpassed all of them; he had been in a thousand battles and lost none; he was in the Cave that was his real home. Exhausted or not, he could defeat this strutting maniac.

He leapt.

Bane caught him in midflight and hurled him into the computer bank. A monitor toppled and imploded. Batman's reflexes, trained by hundreds of hours of Kirigi's drills, saved him from serious injury; he let himself go limp, bounced off the console and to the floor. He was on his feet in a second. Bane hadn't moved. He stood like a stone pillar, waiting.

And suddenly Batman knew he had been mistaken—he could not beat his enemy.

No! If I think that, it's true.

He went at Bane with his favorite kung fu move: jump high, extend leg in kick—

Bane caught his ankle in one hand, swung him around, and threw him against a wall. This time his reflexes were slower; he hit the wall hard.

Slowly, leaning against the wall for support, Batman got up.

Every muscle sluggish and trembling . . . all strength stretched and sapped . . .

He circled Bane, feinted, and put hip and shoulder into a straight left to the belly. Bane did not move.

"You are already broken," Bane said.

Tim was just getting into bed when the phone rang. At first he thought it was one of his nerdy friends from school playing a joke; he could hear only a gasping.

"Okay, Ives. Ha ha ha. Now can you find something constructive to do, like pick your nose?"

But then he heard Alfred's voice, hoarse and tortured. "Get help . . . Master Bruce . . ."

For a moment Tim couldn't grasp the meaning of what he was hearing. "Bruce is in trouble?"

"Yes."

"Bruce or Batman?"

"Get help . . ." There was a thump, as though the phone had been dropped.

"Alfred? *Alfred!*"

Tim heard only the murmur of the open line. *Get help? From whom?*

Then he was running, down the back steps, out into the yard, across to the shed. He was about to break Bruce's rule; he wasn't wearing his Robin costume, but he was certain that something was terribly wrong in the Cave, or the manor, or both. Robin or Tim Drake—what difference did it make? As long as someone went to do whatever had to be done.

It had been stupid to try . . . what? *something!* Batman couldn't remember what it had been stupid to try. *Oh, yeah, sure—unarmed combat.* That was stupid. He was outmuscled. But he'd been outmuscled before—most recently, by Amygdala. And he'd won.

He reached beneath his cape and found the small, bat-shaped *shuriken.* Batman snapped the darts toward their target. They struck Bane, lodged in his skin. But he did not react with so much as a twitch.

Must be some kind of subcutaneous implant . . . he didn't even feel my punch . . .

Batman backed away, toward a display of weapons he'd collected during his years of globe-trotting. He grabbed a boomerang and spun it across the Cave. It splintered on Bane's chest. Batman's fingers closed around the hilt of a *katana.* The razor-sharp samurai sword—*that* would slice through the enemy's protection. Rip into his chest, into his heart—

"You'd like to kill them if only they'd let you," Zsasz had said. Batman's fingers uncurled.

I'll have to outthink him.

But his brain was a sodden lump in his skull.

Bane advanced. Not hurrying.

He's enjoying this.

Batman moved farther back, away from the pool of light, into the damp chill of the Cave. Bane stepped into the shadows with him.

Total darkness. That's where I'll have an advantage.

He slid the night lenses into place and continued edging backward.

• • •

The cabdriver was drunk and English was obviously not his first language. Or second. Or third. When the taxicab passed the same intersection for the third time, Jean Paul opened the door and got out. With the driver shouting at him, Jean Paul dashed through the traffic to the sidewalk. The cab screeched away. Jean Paul scanned the avenue. A few passenger cars, a delivery van. But no more taxicabs. He glanced at his wristwatch. Almost one o'clock. Two hours since Alfred Pennyworth's call. Jean Paul hoped the matter was not urgent.

Tim ran the mile from the shed to the main area of the Cave in six minutes. He stepped hard on the artificial stone; Alfred would hear the alarm and know he'd arrived.

That is, if Alfred is in condition to hear anything.

"Batman!" Tim shouted.

The word echoed, then faded to silence. Tim went to the work area and saw a computer screen lying shattered on the floor. A few feet away, a broken boomerang.

"Batman!"

Echoes, and silence.

Someone was calling him, far away. He didn't know who, and he didn't care, not at the moment. He moved deeper and deeper into the cavern, where he had not been since he first discovered it, so long ago. Then the Cave had promised wonders, his for the exploration. Now it promised safety. In the green glow of his night lenses, he saw treacherous cracks in the stone floor and abrupt drop-offs, walls that projected sharply and unexpectedly outward, stalactites and stalagmites as pointed as spears. His breath exploded in tiny clouds before his eyes, and he heard the flapping of bats' wings in the vaulted ceiling above him and, somewhere nearby, running water. Here, the Cave was cold, damp, dangerous. There were a hundred ways for a man to injure himself, especially if he were coming in the dark. Any one of them would do.

His enemy's boots scraped and thudded on the rock, advancing.

Batman could not count on the man injuring himself. He would have to attack—but attack from an unexpected place, by surprise, cloaked in darkness. Surprise and darkness—they would surely give him the advantage he needed.

The scraping and thudding were closer.

Batman levered himself up onto a narrow ledge about six feet from the floor. He tested the width and braced against the wall behind it. Perfect: wide enough to jump from and high enough to let him land on his quarry with maximum impact.

He waited.

The footfalls hesitated, stopped, and began again.

His enemy came into sight, stepping cautiously, blindly but calmly exploring the area ahead with his toe, waving his extended hands.

Batman leapt.

But his timing was not right. Instead of bringing his weight down directly on Bane's head and shoulder where he could get his forearm against the arteries in his neck, he hit Bane's left shoulder, and slid down his back. He grabbed for the tubes on Bane's hood. Bane slapped his hand away. He groped for Bane's throat. Bane caught his wrist, bowed at the waist, and pulled Batman up and over. The green-glowing cavern spun, and then Batman was on his back, looking up at Bane, looking up at Bane's massive boot descending—

His ribs splintered beneath his tunic, and pain blazed in his chest. The boot descended again, black and green, filling Batman's vision, and then there was no color at all.

Bane bent, groped, found Batman's cape, and grunted in satisfaction. He straightened and turned and began to drag Batman back toward the manor.

●　　●　　●

Tim entered the manor from the secret doorway. The grandfather clock that concealed it was hanging from one hinge. Tim quelled an urge to panic and began to search the house.

He found Alfred in the bathroom next to the foyer. The old man's shirt was draped across the bathtub, and he was peering down at a mottled purple bruise near his solar plexus. His face was ashen, and his hands trembled.

"Alfred, what happened?"

"Tim, don't mind me. Master Bruce . . . in the Cave . . ." Alfred's body was shaken with a spasm of coughing.

"Whoever did this to you is in the Cave? With Batman?"

Alfred nodded yes.

"I didn't see anyone . . ." But he knew it was a huge cavern.

Tim helped Alfred to a chair. He went to the telephone in the foyer and called his home number. On the eleventh ring, Shondra answered.

"Shondra, I'm at Bruce Wayne's. There's been an emergency . . . maybe two . . ."

"I'll be right there, Tim."

Tim was crossing the foyer to where he'd left Alfred when he heard the sound of something bumping on the steps leading to the clock.

Bane filled the doorway. He glanced at Tim and strode into the house, dragging Batman behind him.

Tim jumped at Bane, and Bane swatted him aside. Tim slid across the parquet floor and crashed against a table.

Bane dragged Batman outside, across the lawn, to the limousine. He opened the door, dumped Batman in, went around the hood, and got in the driver's side.

Tim stumbled onto the lawn just as the limousine was circling the driveway. Squinting, he was able to see and memorize the license plate.

Halfway to the gate of the estate, the limousine passed another vehicle, a taxicab. A few seconds later the cab stopped and Jean Paul got out. Tim, just inside the door to the house, moving toward the bathroom and Alfred, heard it and met Jean Paul coming up the walk.

"Can you drive?" he asked.

"No."

"Then it's up to me. Come on!"

Tim and Jean Paul ran into the house, to the kitchen. Tim grabbed a set of keys from a pegboard in the pantry.

"What's happening?" Jean Paul asked.

"No time to explain."

Tim opened the side door that led to the carport where the Buick station wagon Alfred used for local errands was kept. When he and Jean Paul were in the Buick, he fumbled the key in the ignition and started the engine.

Okay, just relax and do it. No problem here. You've driven Dad's Porsche around the grounds often enough. And you handled the 'mobile a couple of nights ago. Put the sucker in gear and—

The station wagon rolled down the driveway to the gate.

Which way? Left would take us through twenty miles of back roads and eventually to the interstate. Right leads to the beltway and the city. What would Bruce do? Play the percentages. Yes. A lot more possibilities to the right.

Tim turned to the right and stepped on the gas.

Bane had trouble finding the ramp that led to the highway. After three tries, he finally saw the sign with the arrow and sped onto the beltway.

Batman groaned and stirred. Bane punched him.

Bane turned onto the exit marked DOWNTOWN GOTHAM CITY. He was disappointed. He had never been in a city this early in the morning. Where were the people? He expected the crowds he'd seen earlier, thronging the sidewalks, dashing across the intersections, shouting and cursing and laughing. But the streets were almost empty. He saw three men gathered around a fire in a trash barrel. They would have to do.

Tim saw twin taillights bobbing up the ramp. The Buick was still a half mile from the beltway, so he couldn't be certain the lights belonged to the limousine. But the odds were with him; at this hour, this far from the city, there wouldn't be many drivers on the road. He fed the wagon more gas.

Jean Paul sat on the forward edge of the seat, straining against the safety belt.

Once on the beltway, brightly lit by mercury vapor lamps, Tim was certain that he *was* following the limo; despite the distance, he could see the big car clearly.

He wasn't sure what to do next. Try to overtake the limo? *Then what? Rescue Batman? Fight whoever's inside? Maybe there are a lot of them. Maybe there are a lot of them with guns.* Tim chose merely to follow, maintaining the half-mile gap. When the limo reached its destination, wherever that might be, he could devise a tactic—he hoped.

The limo turned into the downtown shopping area—a maze of narrow streets; if Tim lost sight of the limo, he might never see it again. But he had no trouble keeping it in view; the driver went down Adams Boulevard, the city's widest and brightest thoroughfare.

"He's stopping," Jean Paul said.

Tim pulled to the curb. *Now what?*

Bane pulled Batman from the car. He paused, dropped Batman to the sidewalk, and pressed the stud on his arm: the sweet warmth of Venom . . .

The time had come to decide what to do with his enemy. Kill him? A death, painful but swift? No. That would destroy this Batman, but with little satisfaction. Bane remembered what he had said to the Mick: *"When others look at you, they will remember this day. When I look at you, I will again enjoy this moment."*

If that had been true of the Mick, an annoyance hardly worthy of Bane's attention, how much more was it true of Batman? To conquer the enemy—that was admirable. But to break him, to watch him writhe helplessly, to hear him plead for mercy—that was magnificent. A man who could do that would have cause to fear nothing.

"I will keep you in a cellar," Bane said aloud. "Once a week I will have them drag you across the floor by one foot—"

Bane could see it. Batman, pale, blinded by light, smeared with filth, dressed in tatters, so thin his ribs almost burst from his skin, his arms and legs flopping, drool leaking down his chin. "Give him a cockroach to eat," Bane says. "Give him a live mouse. Then put fire to his feet. I want to hear him scream."

The brief vision had the power of a prophecy.

Effortlessly, Bane lifted Batman high overhead and looked around: there were the three men warming themselves at the fire in the trash barrel; an old lady wrapped in a dark shawl shuffling past them; a delivery van stopped at a traffic signal; and a block behind him, a station wagon similar to the one the warden at Santa Prisca had owned.

"*Look!*" Bane roared. The men, the old lady, even the van driver turned their eyes toward him.

"*I am Bane. I am the king of Gotham City.*"

He raised his knee and smashed Batman down on it.

PART 2

 Knightquest

1

Batman awoke and became aware of what was happening as Bane hoisted him into the air. He knew, with absolute and terrible certainty, that Bane planned to break his back. ". . . king of Gotham City," he heard and realized he had one second to save himself.

As Bane dropped him, Batman was able to twist to the left. He hoped to take the main force of the smash against Bane's knee on his ribs. But he did not twist far enough. He heard and felt bone break, and then he was on the cement looking up at Bane.

Bane, head thrown back, howled in triumph.

Batman tried to move and couldn't. Bane looked down at him.

"I leave you now," Bane said. "But I will soon return. Think of that. Think of what I will do to you."

Tim and Jean Paul reached Batman as Bane was climbing into the limousine. "I'll get him," Jean Paul said.

"No! That's not important. Help me with Batman."

"It *is* important."

Jean Paul ran for the limousine, but Bane had already guided it away from the curb. Jean Paul chased it for a block. Finally he allowed his steps to falter and stood in the middle of Adams Avenue watching a pair of taillights recede.

Tim was speaking to Batman when Jean Paul returned. "We'll get you to a hospital—"

"No hospital," Batman said, his voice raw and barely audible. "Home."

The three men had left the warmth of the trash barrel fire and were gathered around Tim and Batman.

The old lady joined them. "I ain't got time for this now. But I'll light a candle at Mass."

She hurried away.

Tim looked up at Jean Paul. "Help me get him to the station wagon."

"Perhaps we shouldn't move him—"

"Do as he says," Batman whispered.

The men from the trash barrel stepped aside as Tim and Jean Paul lifted Batman, trying to keep his body as still as possible, and carried him to the station wagon. They laid him flat on the backseat and got in the front. Tim put the wagon in gear and edged into the center lane, peering intently ahead, looking for potholes.

"How's he doing?" Tim asked Jean Paul.

"I think he is unconscious."

"No," Batman said. "Awake. Get costume off."

"You want us to undress you?" Jean Paul asked. "Why?"

"Secret identity."

"That matters at a time like this?"

"Don't *argue* with him," Tim snapped. "Just do as he says." But Tim thought that Jean Paul might be right. Maybe they *shouldn't* remove Bruce's costume; maybe that would injure him further. He suddenly wished he was older and much, much smarter.

He glanced over his shoulder: Jean Paul was pulling the tunic from Bruce's body. It was too late to second-guess himself; the harm, if any, was already done.

Tim watched the sky lighten ahead of them as he drove off the beltway. When he passed the gate to Wayne Manor, sun was flickering in the branches of the big oak near the house. He parked in the carport next to a Honda he recognized as belonging to Shondra Kinsolving and left Jean Paul with Bruce while he went inside.

Alfred and Shondra were in the drawing room having tea.

"I came right after you left," Shondra said. "We've been waiting. I've tended to Mr. Pennyworth's injuries—"

"Nasty fall," Alfred muttered.

"—and he said something had happened to Bruce Wayne."

Alfred nodded. He was still pale, but he was no longer trembling, and he was sitting erect in his chair. Apparently, his injuries weren't too serious.

"Bruce has been in a car crash," Tim said. "He's outside."

Shondra was already on her feet, picking up a medical bag that had been on the floor next to her chair. She and Alfred followed Tim to the carport. Shondra opened the door nearest Bruce's head, peered at him, and touched his neck.

"We'll need a stretcher."

"I'll get it," Alfred said, hurrying away. Tim knew that Alfred would have to go into the Cave. He would be gone for at least a few minutes.

"What happened?" Shondra demanded.

"Took wrong turn," Bruce said hoarsely. "Went off road."

"Should I telephone for an ambulance?" Jean Paul asked.

"No ambulance," Bruce said.

"That will have to be my decision," Shondra said. She went around the wagon and opened the door on the opposite side, knelt by Bruce, and probed his legs. Tim and Jean Paul watched, saying nothing.

Alfred appeared with a folding stretcher on his shoulder. With Shondra supervising, they removed Bruce from the wagon, laid him on the stretcher, and carried him into his first-floor bedroom. Shondra opened her bag, removed several instruments, and began a thorough examination.

Alfred, Tim, and Jean Paul went into the kitchen. "Is it as bad as it appears?" Alfred asked.

"It is terrible," Jean Paul said.

"Let's wait for Shondra's decision," Tim said.

A short time later, Shondra joined them. "Not good," she said briskly. "He's massively bruised, probably has some internal injuries, and I think his spine is broken. I'll need X rays to be sure."

"Would that mean paralysis?" Alfred asked.

"It might. It'll be weeks before we know anything. Right now all I can do is guess, and I'd rather not. I'll need hospital facilities. I'll arrange for them now. Tim, he wants to see you."

Tim didn't want to leave the kitchen. Everything was happening too quickly; he needed time to assimilate, to understand. Again he felt his inexperience as a terrible burden. But Bruce had called, and he had to answer.

He crept into the bedroom. Bruce lay under a single sheet. His head did not move when he spoke. "You've got to help Jean Paul become Batman."

"Jean Paul?" Tim moved close to Bruce's head.

"That guy . . . took me out. Dangerous. Must be stopped. The Arkham inmates, too . . . half of them still loose."

"Commissioner Gordon—"

"Police will do what they can. Won't be . . . enough. Need Batman. Need another Batman."

Is that possible? Tim wanted to ask. *Can there* be *another Batman?*

Bruce's eyes closed. His breathing was shallow. "City's going to hell. Too much for Gordon. You're too young. Jean Paul is the only choice. Show him. Teach him."

"Bruce, you're jumping to conclusions. You'll probably be back in action in a week or two—"

"No. Not soon. Maybe never. Up to you and Jean Paul."

Shondra entered and said, "The ambulance will be here shortly. I'm taking you in for tests and X rays."

"Don't want—"

"Not relevant, Mr. Wayne. I'll get the information I must have about your condition and then we can discuss bringing you back here. Provided you're willing to pay for a lot of equipment and full-time nursing. The hospital would probably be cheaper—"

"Don't like hospitals. Full of sick people."

"All right."

"I'll see you later," Tim said to Bruce.

"Don't forget to do what I asked you."

"On my way."

Tim went into the kitchen. "Jean Paul," he said, "you're about to get one hell of a promotion."

Until a year ago, Jean Paul Valley hadn't known that he was a trained assassin. If he had bothered to think about it, he would have realized that his was not a normal existence, but he would not have guessed the reason for the abnormalities: he was being taught an array of skills that were close to supernatural and with them, an absolute ruthlessness. His father deliberately kept him unaware that he was being dedicated to the Ancient Order of St. Dumas, to a life of terror and violence in what was presumed to be a just—no, a *holy*—cause.

To his teachers, young Jean Paul seemed to be a typical nerd. He got excellent grades, and he was certainly no discipline problem, but his social skills were close to absolute zero. Everyone agreed that he *could* have been a success with the girls: he was tall, slim, with pale blue eyes and gleaming blond hair—his was the kind of unthreatening masculine beauty that adolescent females often find highly attractive. But if any of the young women spoke to him, he stammered and fled. He was no better with the boys. The only way he could relate to others was with a scrupulous courtesy. More than one of his teachers used the word "creep" when Jean Paul's name was mentioned in the faculty lounge. The kinder among them made excuses for the boy: he was, after all, practically an orphan; he had no mother, and his father seemed to be absent most of the time; he was a latchkey kid with a vengeance.

What they couldn't know was that Jean Paul *wanted* to be friends with them, desperately. But his father had forbidden what he termed "any unnecessary fraternization with the unsaved." His father's teachings made it clear that anyone who was not a member of the Order of St. Dumas was unclean at best, standing with one foot in hell at worst. The problem was, there didn't seem to *be* any members of the Order of St. Dumas except Jean Paul and his father.

Having no conversations with his peers—or for that matter with his teachers—Jean Paul could not know that other children did not have gaps in their memories. Nor that these inevitably occurred following those occasions, usually late at night, when his father either used a hypodermic needle on him or slowly spun a shiny gold medallion. Nor could he know that youngsters did not normally grow in quantum spurts, increasing tremendously in strength or agility virtually overnight. All this Jean Paul Valley considered part of the natural process of growing up because there was no one to tell him it was not so. If someone had bothered to ask him, he would have claimed to be quite ordinary.

Until the night his dying father crawled to his door. Jean Paul was living in a small apartment near the campus of Gotham University, where he was a graduate student majoring in Computer Science. The apartment was like most of the places Jean Paul had lived, small, dingy, out-of-the-way—in fact, accessible only through a door that opened on an alley. Jean Paul was, as usual, studying—not Computer Science, which he found vaguely interesting and not difficult, but one of the history books his father insisted he read. It was a heavy, leather-bound tome that bore no title and related incidents in what the author claimed was "the pinnacle of human achievement, the flowering of civilization"—the Crusades. Jean Paul had just taken off his glasses and was rubbing his eyes when he heard what sounded like a scratching at the door. He ignored it, as he ignored most things. But the sound persisted. Finally Jean Paul investigated and found a man sprawled in the alley. His strange costume was ripped in a dozen places, and he was bleeding from several wounds in his chest. Jean Paul felt panic: what was he supposed to do? What action would accord with the precepts of St. Dumas? What would his *father* do? Then, bending down, he realized that the man *was* his father.

"Inside," his father gasped.

Jean Paul managed to lift the older man and take him to the apartment's single bed. "There's a doctor on call at the university," he said.

"No doctor," his father said. "No one must know."

"Know what?"

"Of Azrael."

"Azrael?" The name sounded familiar, but Jean Paul could not remember when or where he had heard it.

"Listen," his father said, "here is what you must do. Strip me. Abandon my body to be found by strangers—"

"No!" Jean Paul cried with a force that surprised him. He did not know he was capable of such emotion.

"—and then open the package I gave you last year. It contains what you need. I have failed. You must not."

Jean Paul waited for him to say more, but his father merely stared at the ceiling. Finally Jean Paul realized that his father was dead.

He felt tears forming in his eyes, and then something deep inside him seemed to shift, and there was no more grief, only a need to obey. He was a loyal disciple of St. Dumas, and unquestioning obedience was the first of the Order's precepts. He pulled the strange garments, already stiff with dry blood, off his father's corpse. He worked quickly, calmly, with no emotion whatever.

He waited until three in the morning. Then he hoisted the body over his shoulders in a fireman's carry and hurried to the end of the alley. He looked both ways, like a schoolboy crossing an intersection alone, and then lumbered to the nearest corner. He dropped his father's remains head down in a trash barrel and returned to his apartment, satisfied that he had done well.

The package his father had mentioned was in a bedroom closet. It contained instructions to call a telephone number to say, "All praise to the Most Blessed St. Dumas," and to wait for further instructions. It also contained forty thousand US dollars in small, worn bills. Jean Paul followed the instructions. Fifteen minutes later the phone rang and the person on the other end told him to leave the country. He was to travel by commercial aircraft to Switzerland, where he would be met by someone who would escort him to his final destination.

A day later Jean Paul was in a Land Rover being driven through a snowy valley between two towering mountains. The driver was a large man wearing a black watch cap, black pea coat, black trousers and boots, and black sunglasses; he said nothing.

The silent man stopped the Rover in front of a weathered frame chalet and pointed to it. Jean Paul approached cautiously. The door swung open with a loud creak of hinges, and Jean Paul was staring through it into the interior of the chalet. Then he lowered his gaze and saw a gnome—a stunted person barely three feet tall. Its—*his*—body was as round as a barrel; arms and legs seemed to protrude from it, rather than be part of it. His head and lower face were covered with red-brown fur; his face was flat, simian. He was clad in a rough brown robe.

"I am Nomoz," he said in heavily accented English. "I am your teacher."

"Teacher of what?" Jean Paul asked.

"We do not have a formal name for it," Nomoz replied, leading Jean Paul and the silent man into the chalet to a roaring fire in a huge stone fireplace. "We call it 'the System.' "

"Like a computer operating system?"

Nomoz laughed: *Hyeh hyeh hyeh.* The sound was like cracking ice. "Com-*pu*-ters? No, no—*hyeh*—com-*pu*-ters." He looked up at the silent man. "Heinreich?"

Heinreich slapped Jean Paul hard across the face.

Feeling tears spilling down his cheeks, Jean Paul asked, "What did you do *that* for?"

"You let him strike you so?" Nomoz demanded. "You do not strike him back?"

"Well, no . . ."

"Not even if he tells you that your father was a member of a secret organization that dates back to the fourteenth century and that he—*hyeh* —killed fourteen men, two women, and an eleven-year-old child?"

Heinreich slapped Jean Paul harder.

"That your father was a liar and a failure?" Nomoz added.

This time, Heinreich struck Jean Paul with a closed fist. Jean Paul fell backward and lay flat on the floor, his glasses hanging by one temple piece. He tasted blood. "Why are you doing this to me?"

"To hurt you. To show you how weak you are. To prepare you to become Azrael."

Months later, after the ordeal and all that followed it were over, Alfred told Jean Paul what had been happening in Gotham City while he was in Switzerland learning of his heritage. They were sitting in Wayne Manor's spacious library. Alfred offered Jean Paul tea and, when the younger man refused, poured himself a cup and relaxed in an overstuffed leather chair as Jean Paul perched on the edge of a footstool.

"As you know, there was a major panic that resulted in several deaths when your father fell from that balcony. No one could explain exactly what happened," Alfred began. "Naturally, Master Bruce was interested. It seems that in the middle of the annual Gotham City Founders Day parade something dropped from the sky and landed in the middle of the Equestrian Club's marching unit. Several horses stampeded, trampling a number of spectators including a young woman named Sherri Port. Ms. Port was with a television crew chronicling the event. That gave Master Bruce a personal reason to investigate—Ms. Port was an acquaintance, one of the few women he had ever dated twice.

"The eyewitness accounts were confused, but several of the more lucid testimonies agreed that the thing that had caused the stampede was a human body clad in some sort of medieval costume. One man said it was a 'falling angel.' That *ensured* that Master Bruce would involve himself—falling angels and sudden death are an irresistible combination for the Batman."

The *falling angel* was Jean Paul's father, but neither he nor Bruce Wayne knew that then.

The detective work was, for Batman, almost ridiculously easy. First, determine where the man had come from. Simply look up and see the terrace of a high-rise apartment building's penthouse. Find out that the penthouse belonged to a Carleton LeHah. Confirm that LeHah was a Swiss importer the CIA believed to be involved in the international arms trade. Late one night, drop onto the terrace from a hang glider and, using infrared equipment, find traces of blood and a spent 9-millimeter slug coated with Teflon. Next, go to a nearby building owned by Wayne Realty and put a laser microphone in an empty office, aim it at LeHah's living room window, and attach a voice-activated tape recorder.

"The microphone picked up vibrations in the window glass of LeHah's domicile," Alfred explained. "It translated them into sounds, including human speech. When Master Bruce checked the tape machine, he heard LeHah planning to transport illegal warheads to Switzerland. At that point, Bruce Wayne, the notorious wastrel, decided on a skiing vacation in the Alps. Naturally, his faithful butler accompanied him to warm his mittens."

While Bruce and Alfred were following LeHah, Jean Paul was simultaneously being disillusioned, enlightened, and trained to be an avenging angel. His teacher was Nomoz. The gnome—the word *dwarf* somehow failed to describe him—told Jean Paul about the Order of St. Dumas. Jean Paul had heard of the Order, of course. His father had drilled him in the rituals and precepts but had never explained what the Order was, nor described its functioning.

Quite simply, the Order of St. Dumas was the wealthiest organization in the world. It had been formed by a zealous lieutenant of the Knights Templar during the latter years of the Crusades. Dumas and his followers found the Knights Templar, those dedicated, fanatic warrior priests, to be lax and unenthusiastic in the bringing of holiness to the heathen hordes and, incidentally, relieving the heathen hordes of gold, silk, gems, and anything else of value that could be loaded on horseback. Dumas formed his own army, prosecuted the Crusades years after Rome had declared them at an end, and answered a protest from the pope with the demand that he, Dumas, be declared blessed. The pope refused on the grounds that this honor was reserved for those saintly folk who had gone on to their heavenly reward, generally after some years had passed. Dumas retaliated by slaughtering the papal emissaries, declaring himself not merely blessed but canonized, and disappeared. Virtually overnight, the entire Order, some several thousand strong, vanished like smoke in the wind. They dispersed into every civilized country on earth and, with the loot from their holy mission, became bankers, merchants, and heads of state. During the first century of their covert activities, rumors occasionally started concerning a secret cabal—sometimes people said it was called the Illuminati. Dumas's successors encouraged this falsehood; a little misdirection never hurt.

The Order gave nothing away, engaged in no charity, paid no taxes. By the time Columbus stepped onto the shores of the New World, the Order's wealth was incalculable, its members the richest men on the planet. But membership in the Order, with all the privilege and luxury that accompanied it, had a price: absolute obedience. It was one of Dumas's precepts that if anyone betrayed the Order—and disobedience was a prime betrayal—an avenging angel named Azrael would come to mete swift and merciless punishment. This was no idle threat. The dozen or so members who did disobey during those early centuries were hacked to pieces, often in front of witnesses who described an angel with a flaming sword appearing from nowhere to strike the victim.

Only a few in the Order's innermost circle knew that Azrael was a man whose angelhood was a combination of psychology, theatrics, and technology. The psychology and theatrics changed little over the centuries, but the technology evolved with the times. Initially, Azrael's flaming sword was an iron blade with a piece of cotton soaked in coal oil wrapped around it. By the nineteenth century, it was a hollow piece of perforated steel containing a sodium rod that its user ignited immediately before making his appearance. The weapon Jean Paul's father had used was forged from tungsten; its haft was a tube full of a plastique compound that could be ignited by thumbing a button and was propelled through the holes in the sword by a tank of compressed air hidden in the costume's sleeve. The costume itself was a soft, extruded plastic of crimson and scarlet that would protect the wearer from anything short of an exploding bullet, or one coated with Teflon, which is what Carleton LeHah fired at Jean Paul's father when Azrael appeared on the balcony of LeHah's penthouse.

"He is a—*hyeh*—blasphemer and apostate," Nomoz told Jean Paul. "He seeks the riches and power of the Most Holy Order for himself. The Azrael who was your father failed to punish him. You must."

"I am to be the new Azrael? Why?"

"Your father and his father and his father—all were blessed with this sacred task. It is an hereditary privilege, all praise be to St. Dumas. Give thanks." Nomoz bowed his head.

Becoming the new Azrael was mostly a matter of running up the snowy mountainsides and lifting weights—a physical regimen any professional football player might adopt. The rest of the skills and knowledge Jean Paul already had. His father had been imparting them to him almost from the day he was born. The injections, the swinging medallion were preludes to his father reaching down past Jean Paul's mind—to parts of the soul psychologists don't even suspect exist—and twisting, wrenching, remolding: a technique first used by Chartrien Dumas and perfected for six centuries. There were gaps in Jean Paul's memory, but not in his experience. Without knowing it, he was charged with angelic zeal and lethal abilities.

When Jean Paul had been in Switzerland a month, Nomoz declared him ready to be Azrael and gave him a mission: find and punish Carleton LeHah. It was not especially difficult: the Order's resources were vast. Bruce Wayne also had considerable resources, and the finest investigative mind alive. But he was not infallible: he was capable of mistakes and he made a serious one in a West Berlin hospital. As Batman, he had traced LeHah to the medical facility and cornered him in a storage room. LeHah had smashed a five-gallon jar of ether on the floor next to Batman, and as Batman struggled to overcome the narcotic fumes, he had been beaten senseless.

Later, in the back of a van parked under a tree on a country road, LeHah had removed Batman's mask and recognized Bruce Wayne from society-page photographs. LeHah was delighted. He was richer by far than Wayne, and so ransom was not a consideration. But surely he could find uses for Wayne's resources, particularly those connected with Waynetech, with its laboratories full of cutting-edge technology that could be converted into weaponry.

In a private jet, LeHah took Wayne to an oil refinery he owned in New Mexico and began trying to separate Batman from his secrets. But Bruce Wayne's mind was almost as conditioned as Jean Paul Valley's. He had never benefited from an Order's System, but since age fourteen he had been investigating the regions below human consciousness, training himself in hypnosis and meditation, learning from a psychologist in California, a yogi in India, a sideshow performer in Florida, and a patient in a London hospital for the insane, among others. LeHah's sodium Pentothal was ineffectual, as were scopolamine and various hallucinogens. Finally, LeHah decided that the old ways were the best ways. He bound a shirtless Bruce Wayne to a pillar in the refinery's underground storage facility and applied a white-hot bowie knife to his flesh. That didn't work, either.

"Sooner or later, I *will* break you," LeHah said. He was holding a knife in his right hand, a small blowtorch in his left.

"Not in this world," Bruce said.

"Then I cut your heart out."

Bruce kicked the knife from LeHah's hand.

"Little trouble hanging onto your torture implement there?" Bruce asked pleasantly. "Maybe if you tied it to your fingers? Little pink bow, maybe?"

"I do not need a blade," LeHah said. He dropped the blowtorch on the floor, reached behind his back to a holster on his belt, and produced a 7.65-millimeter Beretta.

And a voice roared, "No!"

Azrael, in all his angelic ferocity, a flaming sword in each hand, filled the doorway. Nomoz, grinning, stood beside him.

"Know that men call you *liar!*" Azrael cried. "Know that men call you *betrayer!* Know that men call you *defiler!*"

"How many times must I kill you?" LeHah shrieked. "I can kill you again."

He fired. Some of the slugs hit Azrael's plastic garments and either bounced off or embedded themselves short of his body. Others punched holes in pipes that ran along the low ceiling; crude oil dribbled out.

There was a dull *whoosh* as the oil seeped onto the still-flaming blowtorch. A fiery wall sprang up with Azrael and Nomoz on one side, LeHah and Wayne on the other.

"Now we watch the infidels—*hyeh*—burn," Nomoz said.

Azrael removed his cloak and started toward the wall.

"Where are you going?" Nomoz demanded.

Azrael looked at Bruce Wayne through the flames. "I can't leave a man to die."

"Azrael does not rescue. Azrael—*hyeh*—avenges. Come. Our work here is finished."

Azrael ignored him. Protected by his costume, he went through the fire and severed Bruce's bonds with one of his swords. LeHah leapt at him, swinging the Beretta. Azrael stepped backward and thrust out his sword. LeHah gasped and looked down at blood welling from a gash in his chest. He dropped to his knees and then pitched over onto his side. Azrael wrapped Bruce in the cloak and again breached the blazing wall.

Bruce waved his arm at LeHah, barely visible through the fire. "We can't leave him."

"Defiler," Azrael murmured.

With Nomoz hopping behind him, he carried Bruce up a steep flight of steps and out into the cool New Mexican night. When they had gone a hundred yards, the refinery exploded, gouting debris high into the dark sky.

"You disobeyed!" Nomoz screamed. "You disgrace your mission as an angel of vengeance."

"I am not an angel," Jean Paul replied quietly, removing his helmet. "I am a man. My name is Jean Paul Valley. That was my father's name, too."

"Know that you are excommunicated! Know that you are cast out! Know that you are an abomination!"

Nomoz hobbled out of the glow of the burning refinery and vanished into the darkness.

Jean Paul returned with Bruce to Gotham City aboard a Wayne jet. Alfred met them at the airport and led them to the waiting limousine. Jean Paul accepted Bruce's offer of a ride to the city. As Jean Paul was getting out of the car in front of his apartment, Bruce said, "I haven't forgotten that I owe you my life. If there's anything you need, please call me."

"I'll be fine," Jean Paul mumbled and dashed away.

"He seems like a nice young chap," Alfred said.

"Nice? He's no nicer than I am."

"You're not nice, Master Bruce?"

"Only in polite company. We'll have to keep an eye on young Mr. Valley."

A week later, Jean Paul telephoned and asked to see Bruce. The next morning he arrived at Bruce's Waynetech office with his hair newly trimmed, wearing a dark brown suit, purple tie, and black loafers.

He sat in the chair opposite Bruce and stared at the rug. "Do you think you could give me a job?" he blurted. "The university . . . I don't feel I belong there anymore."

"I'm sure we can find you something," Bruce said, smiling.

Jean Paul accepted a position with the private security organization that guarded all of the Wayne facilities—the downtown office buildings and the sleek, modern Waynetech laboratories just beyond the city limits. He was a model employee. But he would win no popularity contests. More than one of his colleagues used the word "creep" when his name was mentioned in the office cafeteria.

2

The morning after Bruce Wayne went into the hospital, Alfred looked for a likely place for an accident. When he found a suitable area, he drove the Buick to the manor and met Tim. Alfred got into the Lamborghini, Tim into the Buick, and they went to the soon-to-be accident site. It was on a lonely back road with woods on one side and a deep ditch on the other. They pushed the Lamborghini off the road and down the steep incline into the ditch. Its front end banged into a tree.

From the road, Alfred and Tim stared down at it. "Looks hardly scratched," Tim said.

"Just a moment," Alfred said and went to the station wagon. He got a heavy sledgehammer from the trunk and, with Tim following, stepped and slid into the ditch. For five minutes they took turns smashing the hammer onto the car.

Panting, Alfred stepped back. "A proper job, I'd say."

"Looks really banged up," Tim agreed. "Now what?"

"We summon a tow truck and express regret at the fate of so excellent a machine."

"They'll think Bruce is a terrible driver."

"They already do. It's what he wants them to think."

"Alfred, doesn't it bother him, to look like such an ass when he's really . . . really something?"

"I believe it secretly delights him."

"One hell of a promotion," Tim Drake had called Jean Paul's elevation from security guard to masked crime fighter. Part of Jean Paul feared that Tim's words were more accurate than he knew. He was in the Cave now, standing in front of the rack of costumes. Jean Paul took one down, hefted it. Featherlight—made from silk and a synthetic fabric, useless as armor and highly impractical on a cold Gotham night, but excellent for situations demanding acrobatics and probably quite comfortable when worn beneath a business suit. He replaced it and removed another. Heavy—Kevlar tunic and cloak, radio and night-vision gear in the cowl, a belt laden with tools—an excellent garment to wear to a firefight and well suited to basic breaking and entering. Like a debutante trying to decide on a ball gown, Jean Paul held the costume to his body and stepped in front of a mirror. It was not like his Azrael garb. It was dark and demonic. But was it evil? If so, was it a seductive evil, a *comfortable* evil?

"Looking good," Robin said, coming down the steps. "Drive the girls wild. You ready?"

"I suppose so."

"Okay, first we deal with the transportation problem. You been taking those driver's ed courses Alfred signed you up for?"

"I completed the course today."

"You think you can handle the 'mobile?"

"Yes."

"We'll see."

They went to the customized Maserati. Twice, before they reached the Cave exit, Jean Paul almost steered the car into a wall. This vehicle was not like the one he had learned to drive at the school; it was almost perverse—he barely twitched the wheel and the car veered wildly.

"Take it easy," Robin said.

"I am driving," Jean Paul said brusquely, clearly not wanting to discuss the matter.

"You might get an argument from the car about that."

Jean Paul stopped just outside the Cave exit.

"What's wrong?" Robin asked.

"Be quiet."

Jean Paul did as he had been taught to do: uttered an invocation to St. Dumas. He felt a crater open somewhere within his soul and from it flowed the skills and confidence he needed.

He put the car in gear and drove smoothly and flawlessly to Gotham City.

3

"Word has gotten around," Bird said to Trogg, Zombie, and Bane. "And the word is, bye-bye Batman."

"Good," Bane said.

"We got a program?" Bird asked.

If Bane had spoken truthfully, the answer would have been no. He hadn't thought beyond the breaking of Batman. Somehow, Bane assumed that once he did that, his course of action would be obvious. It wasn't.

"What is the criminal organization closest to here?" he asked Bird.

"Closest like in geography? Hell, Magic, that'd have to be the Talliarico gang. They hang in a clubhouse in North Gotham, ten, eleven miles down the pike."

"We will go see them tonight."

Bird grinned, and Trogg and Zombie nodded.

Bruce Wayne had been in the hospital for ten days when Shondra Kinsolving brought him his ten-o'clock orange juice and good news.

"You can go home today," she said.

"Well, Dr. Kinsolving, that is *certainly* a day brightener," Bruce said. He was sitting up in his hospital bed and had been staring at a game show on television when the doctor walked in. "Some of these nurses are absolutely rude. And it is such a strain for my butler to smuggle decent food past the harridans."

"Don't you want your test results?"

"Oh, absolutely."

"It's all pretty much as I guessed. Your spine is fractured, but while the spinal cord is severely traumatized, it is not quite severed. You also have broken ribs on both sides, a lot of bruises and contusions, and some internal bleeding, but those are things we can handle. The broken spine is the problem."

"So what's the bottom line, *mein Doktor?* I'm to be the wheelchair kid from now on? Worse than that?"

"It's much too early to tell. The injury was bad, but you *are* in excellent overall condition—the best I've ever seen. We'll just have to see how you respond to treatment."

"You're the doctor."

Shondra perched on the edge of the bed. "Several things about your case puzzle me, Mr. Wayne."

"Such as?"

"Your injuries aren't consistent with an automobile accident. What exactly did happen?"

"Darned if I know. One minute I'm driving along happy as a pig in a sty and the next—*zammo!* I wake up in my bed and you're standing over me."

"I see."

"Anything else, Doctor?"

"Your body. I've never seen so many scars. Some are quite fresh— there's a burn mark on your shoulder that has to be less than a year old. There are bullet holes, knife slashes, even a puckering that must have been caused by acid. It isn't the body of an unemployed—"

"—wastrel? Playboy?"

"The point is, Mr. Wayne, you're not what you seem to be."

"Then what *am* I?"

"I don't know. If I had to guess, I'd say a 'warrior.' "

"Don't I wish! Women *adore* those macho types. But, alas, the truth is more prosaic. In my youth, I played dangerous games. I lost a lot. Losing gave me the souvenirs you mentioned. I do hope you're not disappointed."

"If that's your story, I suppose you'll stick with it."

"Like glue."

"Mr. Wayne, it would be better if you told me the truth. Much, much better. For both of us, but especially for you. I can knit your bones together, I can pump you full of drugs, I can even supervise physical therapy, but I can't *heal* you as long as you insist on lying to me." She stood and walked to the door. "Have a nice day."

Bruce lay back. The banter, the phony nonchalance, had exhausted him. A part of his mind registered the television game show because a part of his mind always registered everything, but mostly he was considering Dr. Shondra Kinsolving. She was asking to know his secrets. He couldn't possibly tell them to her, but he found the prospect of doing so intriguing and oddly attractive.

"How did it go last night?" Alfred asked. He and Tim were in the kitchen of the manor eating low-fat apple pie and drinking cider.

"Depends on what you're judging. I guess it went okay."

"Jean Paul was a satisfactory stand-in for Master Bruce?"

"Like I said, okay," Tim said.

"You are not terribly convincing."

"Okay, Alfred, I'll tell the truth. He scared me."

"Jean Paul?"

"The same. I never saw him being Azrael, so I don't know how he was—"

"Ferocious, according to Master Bruce," Alfred murmured.

"—but as Batman . . . he was everything Bruce wants people to *think* he is."

It began shortly after they arrived in Gotham. Robin hadn't planned for anything to happen this first night out. He thought it best if Jean Paul merely got used to the idea of being Batman. But minutes after they passed the city limits, the police dispatcher alerted patrol cars of a possible break-in at a tool and die factory on the North Side near the river. Robin told Jean Paul—Batman—to ignore it.

"It's the kind of thing Gordon's people can handle," he said. "Not for us."

"It's a crime, isn't it?" Batman demanded. He sent the car hurtling down an alley and screeched onto a street, empty except for a stripped and burned remnant of a van and a few sheets of newspaper fluttering in the gutter. They were ahead of the police cruiser, assuming Gotham City cops would bother to answer a lousy burglary call. As they arrived at the factory, a Lincoln town car was roaring away. They followed the Lincoln sixteen blocks to an auto paint shop.

"Okay, let's call Gordon in on this," Robin said. "He can take it from here."

"No," Batman said. "I'm Batman now and this is what I do. I catch criminals." He got out of the car. Robin set the alarms and safeties and joined him.

Batman was stalking toward the paint shop's door.

Robin whispered, "Give me a minute to do a recon. I'll get on the roof and check for skylights—"

Batman did not break stride.

"Hey, we're not even sure these guys *did* anything—"

Batman kicked in the door.

Oh boy. Robin followed him inside.

They were in a large, open area filled with paint sprayers, tool benches, and two cars with newspapers taped around them. It smelled of grease and enamel and something less pungent and less pleasant, perhaps of human origin. Three men were gathered around the open trunk of the Lincoln removing small power tools from it.

"Surrender!" Batman commanded.

He doesn't have the chops for it, Robin thought. *He doesn't sound like he means it.*

The men, dressed in jeans and denim jackets, coveralls, and greasy chinos, looked at Batman and each other.

They're psyching themselves to resist. This is where Bruce would make a move, before they talk themselves into fighting.

A man in a ponytail swung a wrench at Batman's head. Batman hit him once, and he fell and lay still. A second man, this one in a short, spiky brush cut, was bringing a heavy hammer from high above down at Batman's head. Batman caught the man's wrist, punched him in the stomach, twisted the hammer away, and levered the peen up and into the man's chin. From four feet away, Robin heard bone crack. Batman, still holding the hammer, turned to the last of the thieves and said, "Your turn."

Batman raised the hammer.

Robin stepped between him and the thief. "He's not resisting."

"Good. I won't give him a chance to change his mind."

"Not with the *hammer!*"

Batman tossed the hammer spinning back over his head, stepped around Robin, kicked the thief in the stomach, kneed him in the face, brought clasped fists onto the nape of his neck, and when he was lying in a pool of grease, kicked him in the head.

"That's not tough," Robin said. "That's sadistic."

"You think so? Maybe you're too softhearted for this kind of effort."

You arrogant creep, Robin wanted to say. *Your first night out and you're telling me how to do the job.*

But he didn't. Not to Jean Paul and not at all until he was eating pie in the kitchen with Alfred the next day.

"He may have overreacted because of nerves," Alfred said.

"It was his manner as much as what he did," Tim said. "So . . . self-righteous."

"Give him another trial run," Alfred said. "If you still have misgivings then, perhaps you should voice them to Master Bruce."

"Okay, if you think I absolutely have to. But he's got enough to think about."

Alfred carried dirty dishes to the sink. He glanced over his shoulder to see Tim with his chin cupped in his hands, staring at the wall.

4

Shondra had been gone for five minutes, but Bruce still felt her presence in the room. She was a good doctor, of that he was sure. But she was more than that. He felt an almost tangible energy coming from her, and when it touched him he felt something he hadn't experienced since early childhood: peace.

The first hours after the injury, as he slipped in and out of consciousness, were a torment of fearful possibilities: *What if I never walk again? What if I never* move *again? What if it affects my mind? What if I can't be Batman—?*

Then would he be anybody? He'd been Batman since that night in front of the theater. That night all three Waynes died. Oh, it took the ghost called Bruce another decade and a half to find an identity, but he died with his parents nonetheless, and the world was a limbo until he created and then inhabited the Batman.

This creation of his, this Batman, was trained, intelligent, and to a certain degree intuitive. But he was also physical. Could he exist without the physicality? No, not as Batman. Then as *what?*

He didn't want to answer that question. And when Shondra was around, he didn't feel the need to.

It was four in the afternoon. She was due back at ten the next morning. Only eighteen hours. Not so long to wait.

"So whaddaya hear, Montoya?" Harvey Bullock asked through the half doughnut he had stuffed in his mouth.

"You're disgusting, Harvey," Renee Montoya replied. They were in the main police headquarters in downtown Gotham, the only two detectives left in the building. The rest were scattered throughout the city, tending to Gotham's main after-dark business—crime.

"Okay, I'm disgusting." Bullock stuffed the other half of the doughnut into his mouth and said again, "So whaddaya hear?"

"Nothing more than you've heard. Somebody or somebodies entered Vic Talliarico's club last night and blew him and six pals away. Lots of spent shells, but no witnesses and nothing we can use. End of report. Commissioner Gordon's got a dozen guys knocking on doors, but in that part of town—"

"Yeah, nobody heard nothin'. What I gotta wonder, apart from who done it, is how it's gonna affect the rest of the mooks in town."

Montoya shrugged and walked to the other side of the squad room, where she couldn't hear the sound of Bullock chewing.

"Nothing?" Bane said. "Our killing of the Talliarico men accomplished nothing?"

"Hey, Magic," Bird said, "you gotta give these things time. The word's gotta get around—"

"*Time?* It has been a week since I destroyed Batman. How much more *time* will we need?"

"I have a suggestion," Zombie said.

"Yes?" Bane stared at him across the motel table.

"We have been striking at random at whatever target presents itself. This is not the way to accomplish our ends."

"Well, I don't know about that," Bird said. "We wanna be the only outfit around—"

"No!" Bane said.

"No, Bane wants to lead *all* the outfits," Zombie said. "We hit the top. This man Bressi."

"Tony Bressi?" Bird asked.

"Why?" Bane asked Zombie.

"He is the leader of the largest and most powerful organization in the city," Zombie said. "The others defer to him. Control Bressi, and you have a hold on the rest."

Bane leaned across the table until his face was only inches from Bird's. "Why did you not tell me this?"

"Well, be fair, Magic. You didn't *ask*."

"Bad answer," Zombie murmured.

Bane moved an inch closer to Bird and said, "Do not speak that way to me again."

"Hey, Big M, no offen—" Bird's voice lowered and stopped.

Bane straightened. "Let us discuss our offensive against Bressi," he began.

Bruce could feel some kind of energy seeping from Shondra's fingertips into the top of his spine and down his back—a pleasant, warm tingling. She was humming softly, tunelessly.

"May I ask what you're doing?"

"A trick I learned years ago," Shondra said.

"Does this trick have a name?"

"Probably," Shondra replied pleasantly as she increased the pressure on Bruce's back. "Most things do."

"Ah, the enigmatic healer."

"If you like. You have your secrets, I have mine. The difference is, mine won't kill me."

"And mine will?"

The tingling grew stronger, almost unpleasantly strong, like an electric current passing through Bruce's bones.

"They *are* killing you, Bruce. Oh, don't mistake me. You're doing remarkably well. It's been less than two months since the accident, and you've regained most of your upper body movement. You're able to sit in a wheelchair at a point when most men would still be flat on their backs. Frankly, you're incredible. But I suspect that's because you have good genes. Mother Nature has been very kind to you. But you're not helping her. You're not allowing your body to recover as completely as it could."

The tingling stopped, and Shondra moved around to the front of the bed.

"You're holding so much in, you're impeding the natural processes," she said. "Sometimes you make me angry and I feel like just bailing out and letting you and your damn secrets perish together."

"Why don't you?"

"Would you like me to?"

"No, no, I didn't mean that," Bruce said quickly.

"Then I'll answer you. And the answer is, damned if I know. Normally I can't stand men like you. The smug rich with their little secrets and their little plans—"

"Is that what I am?"

"Only what you'd like me to think you are. Or what you'd like *you* to think you are."

She leaned over the bed and kissed him abruptly, quickly, on the lips.

"I'm sorry," she said, straightening. "That wasn't professional."

"Perhaps not. But it *was* therapeutic."

"I wonder how many women doctors you've used that line on."

"None, Shondra."

"I think that's the first completely true thing you've ever said to me. Maybe you've made a start."

"Toward telling the truth or toward getting well?"

"In your case, they may be identical."

Shondra moved closer. For a moment Bruce was certain she would kiss him again. But she straightened and walked quickly from the room, as though she were already late for an important appointment.

• • •

"Bane," Jean Paul Valley said.

"Huh?" Robin looked away from the computer screen to where Jean Paul was running on the Cave's treadmill.

"Bane," Jean Paul repeated. "Bruce Wayne said the man who broke him was Bane. We're going after him."

"A couple of objections to that, Paul. One, Bruce said not to. Two, we have no idea where to find him, much less what he's up to."

"One, I don't care what Bruce said," Jean Paul replied. "He is a helpless cripple—"

Helpless cripple? You coldhearted jerk.

"—I am the Batman now. Two, this Bane is a criminal. We will locate him by questioning other criminals."

"Listen, Paul, you're the *fill-in* Batman. You wear the suit only until Bruce is well."

Jean Paul hopped off the treadmill, dropped to the floor of the Cave, and began doing push-ups. "He will never be well. I am the Batman, period."

Arrogant creep.

"Okay, let's pretend I didn't hear that," Robin said. "Just exactly which criminals are we going to talk to?"

"I've been reading Wayne's computer files. Anthony Bressi seems to be some sort of important crime boss."

"Tough Tony? Yeah, he was definitely on Batman's list of future projects."

"We'll start with him." Jean Paul was now doing his push-ups on only his left hand.

"I'm almost afraid to ask, but what do you have in mind? Call him up, make an appointment?"

"Don't be stupid."

Robin left the computer bank and squatted down to where his face was even with Jean Paul's. "I'm trying to be funny. So I'm not a comedian. But I'm not stupid, either. I assume you plan to bust into Bressi's scene."

"According to the files, he owns a place called the Skytop Club."

"Yeah, and the building that's under it. It's downtown, somewhere near the bridge."

"How late do these nightclubs stay open?" Jean Paul was pushing up on only his left thumb and forefinger.

"Depends. Liquor laws say not past two A.M."

"We'll go there at two-thirty."

Great, and I've got an algebra exam in the morning. "Okay," Robin said, "I'm in." He stood and shut down the computer. "But I'm gonna catch a few Zs between now and then. You might want to get some sleep, too."

"I don't need sleep."

"I'd like to answer that, but we already know I'm not a comedian."

"Yes. We do." Jean Paul grunted and began pushing up on his *right* thumb and forefinger.

5

 It was after midnight when Bird entered Bane's cabin.

"Do you have them?" Bane asked.

"Piece a' cake, Big M. We got us a couple of brats and Tough Tony's got some bodyguards to bury."

"They were hard to kill?"

"Not for Zombie. It's like that guy was *born* with a gun in his hand."

"You have done well."

"Hey, happy to be on the team."

The digital clock on Bruce's bedside table read 2:14. He had been trying to sleep since ten. None of the hundred and fourteen techniques he knew for inducing states of rest, ranging from simple relaxation to somnambulism, were working now.

Maybe Shondra's right. Maybe I've got to just let go. Maybe I won't recover until I . . . tell her?

But how could he do that? Only a few people on earth knew he was Batman, people who were as dedicated as he was, and he sometimes regretted the circumstances that had forced him to share his secrets with them. Was it fair to burden this woman, this doctor, this *healer*, with knowledge that could get her killed?

But if he didn't, would she be able to help him? She herself thought not. And if she failed, he would never put on the mask again, would never be Batman.

Would never be Batman . . .

Was that unthinkable? Was it a possibility? Suddenly he realized that he had a choice. He could choose to be Bruce Wayne, no double identity, no secrets apart from the secrets every rich man had, and then he would have no problem with telling Shondra.

Listen, darling, I used to be this dark avenger—"But I'm not anymore," he said aloud, and the sound of his voice startled him. "I'm not Batman anymore."

That was probably true. And if it wasn't, he could make it true.

And maybe he should.

At six in the morning, Bruce reached for the telephone. He started to call Shondra's office, then realized she wouldn't be there this early. He remembered that she'd said she'd be staying with Jack Drake. He started to call Drake's number and stopped. It wouldn't be fair to wake the Drake household because Bruce Wayne had something he wanted to say.

And I shouldn't say it on the phone.

Finally he telephoned a car service and asked to be picked up in thirty minutes. He got out of bed slowly, barely able to move in his hips-to-shoulders body cast, and put a robe on over his pajamas. He lowered himself into his wheelchair and rolled past Alfred's room.

No point in waking the old guy.

But why not? He was about to follow Alfred's advice. Why shouldn't he share his intentions with his oldest and closest friend?

Because this is private. This is the most private thing I've ever done.

What? Telling a doctor something the doctor needs to know?

No. Letting someone into my life. Letting a woman in. That hadn't happened before. Not to the armies of Barbies and Cyndis and Carols and

Megs and Debbies—the flight attendants, the lawyers, the business-women, the debutantes, the journalists. None had been given a glimpse of what lay behind the famous Bruce Wayne impersonation.

He wheeled himself to the front door and waited. He was feeling an emotion utterly alien to him. He wasn't sure what it was, but he guessed *exhilaration* might be close.

There was a cold wind blowing through the shattered window of the Skytop Club's office, but Tough Tony Bressi wasn't feeling it. He was on his knees looking up at the blue-gloved fist poised above his face and, beyond the fist, at the mask.

"Tell me about Bane," Batman said.

"No way."

Batman slapped Tony's nose. A bone cracked, and blood trickled into Tony's mouth.

"Take it easy," Robin said from the doorway.

"Bane," Batman repeated.

"Lissen," Tony Bressi said, "you take your best shot at me. You give it all you got. But I ain't saying nothing about him."

Robin stepped forward. "You're scared, aren't you?"

"Of *you?*" Bressi sneered.

Robin turned to Batman. "There was a squawk on the police radio last night. A couple of Tony's employees shot to death in a car. All of a sudden, I'm wondering who else was in that car. Maybe Tony here wants to tell us."

"My kids," Tony mumbled. "He said he'd send 'em home in pieces."

"Unless?" Robin asked. "There has to be an 'unless.' "

"He wants to take over. Everything. Every operation in Gotham."

"Now we're getting somewhere," Batman said.

"Getting somewhere?" Robin asked. "Care to explain?"

"Not in front of him," Batman said. He cuffed Bressi's ear. "You're not going anywhere, are you?"

Bressi shook his head.

Batman led Robin to a telephone alcove on the far side of the nightclub. As he spoke, he stared past the cluster of tables and chairs to where Bressi was kneeling beneath the shattered window. "Tough Tony can get me closer to Bane."

"Bruce said we shouldn't take on Bane. Not now."

"I wear the mantle of the Bat. I make the decisions. Bane is mine and mine alone. You can help me or you can stay out of the way."

Robin started to reply, but Batman was already moving across the room.

Batman hit Tough Tony Bressi again.

"There's no need to beat him like that," Robin said.

"You shut up," Batman shouted.

Robin looked at the three men tied to a pillar, at the smashed windows of the abandoned warehouse, at the litter on the floor, and finally at Tony Bressi and Batman.

He's out of control and there's not much I can say in front of Bressi without blowing our cover.

Batman glared at Bressi. "Now—do we have an understanding, Tough Tony?"

"Yeah, sure," Bressi said, wiping blood from the corner of his mouth with the back of his hand. "You keep the boys"—he nodded toward the bound men—"here till I convince Bane we're gonna hand 'em over to him and the unions they control with 'em. So he hands over my kids."

"And when the release is set, you get word to me."

"Got it."

"Then get out of here and start contacting Bane's people."

"I'll do it," Bressi said. "You know I'll do anything to get my kids back."

"Forget your kids, Tony. You cross me and I'll kill them myself."

Robin turned away. Bressi was a killer a dozen times over, and a drug dealer, and he was probably party to even slimier things. But it was painful to see the naked desperation in his eyes when he spoke of his children. And what was in Batman's eyes, behind that mask? *What kind of childhood did Jean Paul have?*

.   .   .

The driver wheeled Bruce out to the town car, helped him into the backseat, and stowed the wheelchair in the trunk.

"Name's Benny," the driver said. "Yer that Bruce Wayne, ain't'cha?"

"The one and only."

"I heard about you totalling the Lamborghini. Too bad. 'Course, in my perfessional opinion, you drive the car you can handle. Maybe the 'ghini was a little too much for you."

"Obviously."

"Boy, I'd like to get *my* hands on one a' them babies."

"Ask Santa. Very politely."

"Hey, I just thoughta something," Benny said. "Ain't you got a chauffeur? How come you need *me?*"

Bruce tried to answer the question for himself. What he was about to do was somehow *intimate*—too private to share with anyone, even Alfred. *This must be how a man feels when he's proposing marriage. But that's not what I'm doing today. Is it?*

"It's his day off," he told Benny.

Bruce directed the driver to the Drake estate, a little more than a mile away. Benny stopped by the main entrance to the huge old Georgian mansion next to a green delivery van marked SPRANG FLOWERS and helped Bruce into the chair.

"You want I should wait?"

"No need. Somebody here will drive me back." *Somebody named Shondra Kinsolving.*

Bruce propelled himself to the front door and reached for the bell push. He hesitated. Did he really want to do this?

The front wheel of the chair accidentally bumped the door. It swung open. Well, nothing unusual there. Whoever belonged to the delivery van was probably making a delivery. A bit early for it, but maybe the Drake household was early rising.

Then why am I tense? Why are all my alarm systems jangling?

Bruce pushed inside. He was in a wide foyer, not unlike his own. There was an elevator directly in front of him and an alcove to his left.

"Hello!" he shouted.

A man stepped from the alcove. He was wearing a red ski mask and he carried a submachine gun.

Kidnappers? Must be. No problem. I can be all over him before he presses the trigger—not in a wheelchair.

Bruce rolled toward the gunman. "Am I early?" he asked. "I wasn't sure if the invitation said seven A.M. or seven P.M., and wouldn't you know that I can't find the darn thing—"

Close enough. Bruce grabbed the barrel of the gun with his left hand and drove the stiffened fingers of his right into the man's solar plexus. The man doubled up, staggered a step backward, and straightened.

That strike should have taken him out.

He punched Bruce. Then he moved behind the chair and tipped it forward. Bruce tumbled onto the carpet. He tried to get to his feet, but the body cast wouldn't let him move.

I'm lying here like a turtle on its back, helpless.

He heard the elevator doors slide open and saw feet. Ten of them. Six wearing combat boots, two in sneakers, and two in high heels.

"Get 'im outta the lift," someone said.

"We're bloody well trying," someone else said.

Then a voice he recognized: "Bruce!"

It was Shondra's voice. He struggled to move his neck, to do the simplest damn thing in the world, to look up, just look up—

Two men were carrying Jack Drake, who was lying on a stretcher; both wore red ski masks. A third man in a red ski mask was dragging Shondra across the foyer.

Got to do something.

The kidnappers took Jack Drake and Shondra through the door to the outside. Bruce tried to roll himself over onto his belly. He heard an engine start and a car—*no, the delivery van*—screech down the driveway. After a long minute, he succeeded in rolling onto the front of his body. He reached out, pulled himself a few inches, and repeated the process, and repeated it, and repeated it. Almost ten minutes later, he reached a table with a telephone on it, knocked it over, and used the phone to call Alfred.

In ten minutes, the kidnappers could be halfway to the next state.

Bruce lay on the floor, utterly exhausted, until Alfred came.

•   •   •

By the time Bruce gave his statement to the police, was driven home by Alfred, and went to bed, it was noon. He slept until eight the following morning. When he opened his eyes, Alfred greeted him with a tray bearing tea and toast.

"I'm not hungry," Bruce said.

"We are rather overdoing the invalid impersonation today, aren't we?" Alfred asked.

"What the hell does *that* mean?"

"All this week you've been your normal self, allowing for your infirmities. Now, suddenly, you remind me of Garbo playing Camille. Try putting the back of your wrist to your forehead and sighing—really quite effective, properly executed."

"I suppose you have an alternative suggestion."

"None you haven't thought of yourself, Master Bruce."

Bruce took a slice of toast from the tray and bit into it. "You think I've been feeling sorry for myself because I was so useless at the Drakes'. Maybe so. But maybe I just needed a few hours to process what happened."

"Judging from your past performance, you should have done that processing in about four seconds."

"There *is* no 'past performance,' Alfred. Batman has always dealt with violence. Bruce Wayne has seldom dealt with anything more urgent than cotillion invitations. Violence is new territory—for Bruce."

"And how is he feeling about it?"

Scared. But not even Alfred is going to know that. "I'll handle it. How's Tim?"

"Distraught, as you might well imagine. He's been down in the Cave all morning working the computers. Keeping busy, probably trying not to worry about his father."

"Ask if he'll talk to me."

"I can guarantee that he will."

Bruce ate the rest of the toast. As he was finishing the last sip of his tea, Tim entered the room. The boy's hair was only half combed, the collar of his white shirt was soiled, and his eyes were unnaturally bright.

Seeing the grief and terror in Tim's face stunned Bruce. He had never learned to empathize, nor to express sympathy. His parents were slain before they could teach him.

Finally he found refuge in a cliché. "Tim, I'm terribly sorry."

"I know, Bruce."

"I wish I could have done more."

"I guess you did all you could."

"The police are sometimes very good at this sort of thing. I'm sure they'll have news for you soon."

"Okay. If that's all—" Tim went to the door, paused.

"If there's anything I can do—"

Tim turned and came to Bruce's bedside. "Bruce, you're a detective. You're the best in the world. So how can you lie there and ask if there's anything you can do? Find my father. Find *Shondra*, if you don't care about my father."

"You know that's not fair, Tim. Jack *and* Shondra are important to me."

Especially her. Especially Shondra.

"Then look for them."

"The police—"

"If the police were any good, there wouldn't *be* a Batman."

"Tim, that's the problem. I'm not Batman—not now. Maybe never again."

"Your legs are temporarily out of commission. But you've told me a million times that the *mind* is what fights crime, not the body."

Bruce stared at the bedclothes. "Okay. Get me a pencil and paper. I'll make a list of things you'll have to get for me. Another list of things for you to do."

"Back in a minute."

"Tim?"

"Yeah?"

"Have you asked Jean Paul to help?"

"No. This . . . isn't his style."

6

 Jean Paul finished his daily prayers to St. Dumas. He felt stronger than ever physically, but his soul was troubled. Sometimes he wondered if he weren't already in hell, being punished for some hideous sin. This world, full of crime and sorrow, couldn't be the earth. It seemed to him that it must be a grotesque distortion of the real earth, an earth seen in a funhouse mirror. So it was either a nether realm or a nightmare. But if it were a nightmare—whose?

Trogg, Bird, and Zombie watched Bane playing with the Bressi children on the floor of the motel cabin. At first the huge Santa Priscan had been hesitant; he approached the boy and girl cautiously, as though they were exotic and perhaps dangerous beasts.

"He's curious," Zombie said. "He's never seen children before. Not this close."

"Hell," Bird said, "the kind of life he's had, he's never even *been* a kid."

Gradually, Bane relaxed, and after an hour he seemed to be enjoying himself with the young Bressis, neither of whom was yet in school. The children, after getting past their fright at the unfamiliar surroundings, liked Bane, too.

"Tonight he may kill them," Bird said quietly. "That gonna be a problem, you think?"

"Not for him," Zombie said. "He's who he is."

Trogg nodded.

Bruce was just finishing a scan of Jack Drake's stock portfolio. He had already examined documents pertaining to Drake's business, real estate, and philanthropic interests; these, mostly in the form of computer printouts, were stacked on the floor next to his bed.

"Anything?" Tim asked.

"Your father isn't long on friends, and like any wealthy man, he has a few enemies. But I don't see how anyone could profit from his kidnapping —or his death, for that matter. Revenge? Possible, but not likely. We table that and consider other possible motives. Terrorist attack? Possible. Ransom? Very possible."

"Wouldn't they have contacted us by now?" Tim asked anxiously. "It's been thirty-six hours—"

"Not necessarily. Sometimes they let the victim's family stew."

"Then we're at a dead end."

"Not at all. Did you hack into the police computer?"

Tim handed Bruce a printout. "Stolen vehicles for the past week. A delivery van like the one you described was stolen Monday morning and abandoned last night—"

Bruce scanned the page and nodded. "On Harlen Road. Okay, that figures."

"How?"

"Harlen Road's near Elbert Field. It's a small private airfield. No commercial traffic. Too small for a 707, but large enough for a Lear Jet."

"You think they took my father out of the city? Out of state?"

"No. Out of the country. To Great Britain."

"Why there?"

"A number of reasons," Bruce said. "Their accents—English or Scottish. One of the kidnappers referred to the elevator as a 'lift.' That's British. The guy who dumped me was carrying a Sten, a vintage World War II commando weapon. Again, British. Nothing even remotely conclusive, but maybe a starting place. So here's my hypothesis: four masked Brits took your father and Shondra to Elbert Field and loaded them onto a private plane—they couldn't use a commercial carrier for obvious reasons. They took off for parts unknown, but they may be headed across the Atlantic."

"Should we get in touch with somebody over there? Scotland Yard? Interpol?"

"The red tape would be impossible, Tim, even if we got Gordon to make the request. No, we do it ourselves, as always. Get into the FAA net. Find a flight plan for a private plane going from Gotham to England, Ireland, Scotland, or Wales. If you strike out, we'll try something else."

"I'm on my way."

"And send Alfred in."

Bruce stacked the printouts together, evened the edges, put them on the floor, and waited.

Bane, bare to the waist, was watching the evening news on television when Bird entered the cabin.

"Magic, you got a minute?"

"What is it?"

"Listen, if we're gonna consolidate our hold on Gotham, I think we oughtta really put the squeeze on once we get the unions, 'cause now that Batman's back—"

"Batman is not back."

"But he is . . . a lotta Bressi's boys got taken out by him when he busted into the Skybox . . . and he may even know we got Bressi's kids stashed away—"

Bane stood abruptly and held his clenched fists in front of his chest. "It's not him. It's nothing but a costume. I broke the Batman and I will crush the pretender."

Bane was standing close to Bird, looming over him. Bird edged back until he was stopped by the wall. Bane quivered with anger. Then he pressed the stud on his arm, felt the rush of the Venom, and a moment later relaxed.

Zombie came into the cabin. "Bressi just made contact," he said. "Says the unions are ours. Wants his children back."

"Good," Bane said.

"I don't know about this, Bane. If Batman's squeezing Bressi—"

"I told you, Bird. Batman is broken."

"All right . . . whoever's in the outfit . . . what if he's using Bressi to—"

"Then you will take Zombie and Trogg and find out when you supervise the return of Bressi's children."

Bane returned his attention to the television.

Robin climbed from the Cave to the cistern, pressed the hidden control that flooded it, shed his costume, and put on the jeans, sweater, and jacket he'd left there earlier. Wearily, he walked through the crisp October evening toward his house—his *empty* house. His father and Shondra had been gone more than thirty-six hours. Bruce was involved in the case, and that was cause for hope. If anyone could find Jack Drake and Dr. Kinsolving, Bruce could. So maybe he should try to stop worrying about them.

But he had no reason to stop worrying about Batman . . . *no, dammit, he's not Batman. He's Jean Paul Valley in a Batman suit and he said he's going after Bane. Tonight. I can't let him do it. He's getting meaner and meaner with each passing night. Part of it must be that training Bruce said he had—the "System." All that hypnosis, and the drugs—we still don't know how much his brain was washed. But that's not the only thing that's changing Jean Paul. It's also because he's shutting me out, trying to go it alone. Alfred says the same thing happened to Bruce when Jason Todd died. The Batman started getting darker and darker without the balance of a Robin to ground him, keep him sane. But what if Jean Paul won't let me keep him sane? Should I tell Bruce he made a mistake? No, not yet . . . not while Bruce is trying to find my father. And trying to recover from a broken back. Besides, Bruce didn't make a mistake, not in the areas of skill and confidence. Jean Paul's the only one who could wear that cape.*

The Georgian mansion was quiet. To Tim, the silence seemed tense and brooding. He climbed the rear staircase, entered his room, and flopped down on the bed. Tonight could be wicked.

Bruce put down the phone and turned to Alfred. "That confirms it. A private jet took off from Elbert Field about four hours after the kidnapping."

"Destination Heathrow?" Alfred asked.

"No, a smaller field near somewhere called Monkleigh."

"Ah. About sixty miles outside London. Predominantly rural area. Quite picturesque, if you enjoy that sort of thing."

"You know it, then?"

"I spent some time in the neighborhood in my youth, sir. I haven't been near it in almost thirty years, but I expect it hasn't changed much."

"We'll see. We should be there by tomorrow morning."

Alfred frowned. "You're serious about pursuing the kidnappers?"

"Why wouldn't I be?"

"Your injuries—"

"That's one of the reasons for doing it. Shondra Kinsolving seems to be the only doctor who can do anything about my back."

"Master Bruce, surely in all the world there is at least one other physician who's capable of ministering to you."

"Find that person and we'll discuss it."

Bruce picked up the telephone.

Alfred's frown deepened. "You're arranging transportation to England?"

"Yes. Unless you'd prefer to do it."

"I would rather not. I will abet folly, if I must, but I refuse to initiate it."

Alfred turned abruptly and left the room.

. . .

Jean Paul awoke and blinked, struggling to remember where he was. Yes, yes, the Cave. But what was he doing here? He looked down at the workbench in front of him. There were tools, an elaborate drawing, and next to it, part of his Azrael costume, the left gauntlet, the one that contained the compressed air apparatus. It had been modified and, although he had no memory of doing it, Jean Paul knew the work was his. The equipment, designed to blow flame through a hollow sword, would now propel the small darts Batman used at tremendous speed, greatly increasing their effectiveness as weapons.

Tonight, perhaps, he would use them against Bane.

He said a prayer of thanks to St. Dumas.

The Waynecorps Lear Jet took off smoothly, banked over the city, climbed, and settled into a course for England. Bruce wheeled himself to the cockpit and chatted with the pilot for a few minutes. He had qualified to pilot small jet aircraft the month he'd returned to Gotham City, more than a decade ago, and he kept his license current, but he hadn't flown anything larger than a Beechcraft in years. He asked the pilot several laymen's questions and, when he returned to the main cabin, knew all he'd ever need to know about a recently installed Loran system.

"Do we have a plan?" Alfred asked.

"A rough one. First we should conjure up a couple of new identities."

"May I ask why?"

"We may have to do some pretty open investigating, the kind Bruce-the-klutz-Wayne and his dim-witted servant wouldn't be capable of."

"Dim-witted?"

"Okay, not-incandescently-bright-but-devilishly-handsome servant. Anyway, we may not be able to play dumb, not continuously. So we'll be someone else. Two someone elses."

"Bertie Wooster and Jeeves," Alfred said. Then he added: "A devilishly handsome Jeeves."

"Wooster's as dumb as Wayne. And Jeeves isn't handsome. No, I think I'll be Sir Hemingford Gray and you'll be Charles, his chauffeur. That shouldn't be much of a stretch for you, being a chauffeur."

"Doomed to be typecast forever." Alfred sighed.

"The pay's good and the work's steady."

"Half of what you say is perfectly correct. Exactly how do we accomplish these transformations?"

"With clothing, forged documents, some makeup, and"—Bruce's voice rose a half octave and became a phlegmy whine—"a bit of the old vocal acrobatics, d'yew know?"

"No. But I trust I shall learn."

"No doubt."

"Master Bruce, are you certain this is a good idea? You know every private detective in the world. Wouldn't one of them be better suited for this work? That fellow from St. Louis, Timothy Trench—"

"—is good, and Joe Potato and Christopher Chance are better, and several others are as good as Potato and Chance. But none of them is good enough."

Bruce settled back in his chair and stared at the darkness outside the window.

7

 They had been hidden in the warehouse among some wooden crates for almost an hour, and Robin could sense Batman getting impatient. When Bruce Wayne wore the mask, Batman could wait for hours, motionless, calm, breathing slowly and deeply. But Jean Paul's Batman fidgeted, constantly shifting his weight, adjusting the bulky gauntlet he wore on his left arm, clenching and unclenching his fists. And it was contagious: Robin found himself resisting the temptation to squirm.

It was after one by Robin's watch when they heard the squeak of the door below opening. A tall bald man entered, pushing Tony Bressi's children ahead of him. He was followed by a thin blond man and a squat, powerful man with coppery skin.

"Yo, big Tony," the blond man called, " 'member me? Bird." He waved a hand at the bald man. "This's my guy Zombie and this"—he waved at the squat man—"is Trogg."

Bressi, who had been pacing the littered floor next to the stacked crates, turned and started forward.

"Here's your kids, Bressi," Zombie said, "and for your sake I hope you came to collect them alone."

"You think I'm crazy enough to cross you?" Bressi protested.

Robin saw Batman stand and knew that in a moment something would be terribly wrong. It was too soon; they should stay concealed.

"*Where's Bane?*" Batman shouted.

"Up there—*waste him!*" Zombie yelled.

Batman was swooping down from the top of the crates as Bane's three men were pulling automatics from under their jackets and Robin was calling, "Not yet! Not till the kids are in the clear!"

He's so hell-bent on shock and pain that he doesn't even hear me.

Batman landed next to Zombie and smashed him to the floor. He spun and struck Trogg with the gauntlet; even from thirty feet away, Robin could see flecks of blood flying from Trogg's face as Batman's blow landed.

Bird had time to get his gun clear and was aiming it at Batman's back.

"Behind you!" Robin shouted.

Batman twisted, sweeping his arm around, and three darts sprang from the gauntlet. They hit Bird in both shoulders. He yelped and dropped his weapon. Batman crossed to him and punched him unconscious.

The fight was over. Bressi gathered his children in his arms and clung to them. Robin dropped from the crates to the floor and ran to where Batman was lifting Zombie off the floor by his collar.

"*Where's Bane?*"

The man's head lolled.

Robin grabbed Batman's arm. "Hey, can't you see he's out of it? You knocked all three of them silly. They'll be lucky to be able to talk by next Wednesday. And what's with the gonzo blitzkrieg? Those kids—"

"—were never in danger, never in the line of fire," Batman said. "All the heat was on *me.*"

Robin heard a siren outside coming closer, and saw Batman stiffen.

"Police?" Batman asked. "Did you call them?"

"I thought we could use some help with the mopping up—"

Batman was stalking out of the light, toward the rear door. "That was stupid—a mockery of everything we're supposed to be."

He vanished into the shadows. Robin ran after him.

• • •

In a small hotel a couple of miles from London's Heathrow Airport, Bruce Wayne was transformed into Sir Hemingford Gray. Dark brown hair was thinned with clippers until the scalp showed through it and then dyed a dingy gray; matching sideburns and mustache were glued into place; foam pads were inserted between gums and cheeks. But the primary disguise was not cosmetic. Years ago, a Russian theater director, a disciple of Stanislavsky, had taught Bruce a trick that had never gotten into any of Stanislavsky's books, if, indeed, Stanislavsky had ever heard of it.

Darken the room. Sit absolutely still. Visualize the character you want to become. Use all your senses. See how he stands, sits, lies, walks, gestures. Hear his voice in speech, song, laughter, in anger, glee, and mourning. Smell his skin. Taste what's inside his mouth. Feel the texture of his skin, his hair, his beard. Know this person. Then visualize yourself as completely as you can—and, again, amplify sight with the other senses—and place yourself next to him. Now, bring his body into yours and rest until you are used to it.

Sir Hemingford Gray, age ninety minutes, looked up and said, "What d'yew say, Charles? Shall we be off?"

"Absolutely, Sir Hemingford," Charles, né Alfred, said.

An hour later, they were driving in an open car through rural England. The weather was brisk. Charles wore a heavy overcoat, suede driving gloves, and a wool cap with earflaps; Sir Hemingford was wrapped in a heavy blanket.

"Wouldn't it be wise to put the top up?" Charles asked.

"Not a thing a Gray does, coming back to England after so long. Got to smell the air, d'yew know?"

They ate lunch in a small roadside pub outside the village of Monkleigh and asked the innkeeper for directions to the airfield. It was only a few minutes away.

"Not much of an airport," Charles said.

"Bloody small," Sir Hemingford said.

There was one landing strip, two hangars, and an office. The only plane in sight was an ancient Piper Cub parked near one of the hangars. Charles stopped the car in front of the office, and Sir Hemingford, leaning heavily on two canes, got out. He banged into the office and thumped his cane on the floor. A young man in a white shirt with the sleeves rolled to the elbows looked up from a *Daily Mirror*. "Yes?"

"Yew from around here?" Sir Hemingford demanded.

"Yes sir. I was born in the village—"

"Y'know my family. The Grays."

"I don't believe I recognize the name—"

"Damned fool took off in his bloody airplane with my rifle, d'yew know. Well, where is he?"

"Who?" The young man folded his paper and set it aside.

"The damned fool who has my rifle. Elephant gun. Big bugger. Said he'd wait for me. *Well?*"

"If you could be more specific—"

Sir Hemingford thumped his canes on the floor. "The damned fool I met in Gotham City. Took my rifle and my bag and said he'd give me a lift here. Jet plane. Little one."

"You must mean Mr. Asp."

"That his name? S'pose it is. Should've arrived yesterday."

"Last night. He's renting Monkleigh Hall."

"That's him. Told me he was renting some-bloody-hall. *Well?*"

"Well what?"

"Where the bloody hell is Monkleigh Hall?"

"Just the other side of the village—"

"Y'know, m' lad, yew could save yourself a lot of time if yew'd just answer a man's questions!"

Sir Hemingford Gray stomped out. Charles was waiting by the car.

"I had a look through the window of the hangar over there," Charles said. "There's a Lear Jet inside."

"Very good. On our way, then. Next stop, Monkleigh Hall."

•   •   •

When Robin came out of the tunnel and into the main chamber of the Cave, he saw Jean Paul, in the Batman costume but without the mask, sitting at the workbench.

"Paul?"

When Jean Paul showed no sign of having heard him, Robin went to the bench. Jean Paul's eyes were unnaturally wide; his hand, holding a drafting pen, was moving mechanically over a piece of paper. Robin leaned closer to see what Jean Paul was drawing. It looked like a much-modified version of the costume he was wearing.

He's in a trance. He's in the System.

Jean Paul's eyes closed for a moment, and when he opened them, he turned to Robin and said, "You're looking for Bruce? He's on a trip—Bruce and Alfred. They called. They apologized for not getting in touch with you. It has something to do with your father."

Tim Drake, inside the Robin garb, felt a flash of elation.

"Bruce said he'd call you the first chance he gets," Jean Paul continued. "He told me to move in. To mind the store, he said."

Robin nodded. "How are you doing, Paul? Pretty rough, last night."

"I'm fine. I'm sorry we had to argue like that."

"Yeah, me too. So what are you doing?"

Jean Paul looked at the drawings as though they were alien artifacts. "This, you mean? Just some . . . designs. The costume needs . . . improvement. Hadn't you better be getting home before you're missed?"

"Guess so. Catch you later, Paul."

"Sure. Later."

Jean Paul bent over the bench and began to move the pen.

The woman who was behind the counter of the Monkleigh post office was *sure* she remembered Sir Hemingford Gray's people, and seeing as how Sir Hemingford was practically *family,* she didn't see a thing wrong with telling him as much as he wanted to know about the new tenants at Monkleigh Hall.

"An American named Benedict Asp," Sir Hemingford said as Charles inched the big car through Monkleigh's narrow, winding main street. "He's had the house for a month. Lots of company, d'yew know. Foreign blokes. The missus in the post office said she heard 'em talking foreign, anyway."

"I suppose you *must* be Sir Hemingford at all times?" Charles asked, sounding like Alfred.

"Better safe than sorry, eh?"

"Right-o. Have we a plan?"

Sir Hemingford had opened a leather attaché case and was examining a round device the size of his smallest fingernail. "Direct assault—that's the British way. Combined with a lot of sneakiness. I learned that from the French."

Batman glided silently, swiftly over the roofs of Gotham City. In the distance, the river, gleaming in the moonlight; below, the rigid geometry of the streets, pale orange in the glow of the vapor lights. Although he'd been a student at a local university for six months, the city was still mostly new to him; he had seldom left the neighborhood of the campus until the night his dying father had crawled to his door. He'd learn all the secrets soon enough, though.

The mantle of the Bat was his.

Bane must fall if *Gotham* was to be his, too.

But Bane still ruled the night. He must find the monster and then the night, the city, everything would be his and he would make it righteous.

He entered Gotham Police Headquarters through a lavatory window on the third floor and went down the corridor to Commissioner Gordon's office. Gordon looked up from a report he had been studying. "New suit? Nasty looking. I can't say it's an improvement on your usual costume."

"I'm not asking for compliments."

"I've been expecting you," Gordon said. "You've been very active lately. My detectives have been cleaning up after you."

"That's what I'm here about," Batman said, remembering to speak in Bruce Wayne's rasp. "What have you learned from Bane's stooges? Have they talked?"

"Bullock and Kitch have been working them for close to twenty-four hours. Getting nowhere. I don't think they're going to rat Bane out."

"Where are you holding them?"

"The city detention center over on Girard. But not for long. The feds are crying for a shot at them. And the governor wants them separated and placed in maximum security in a hurry."

"Interesting."

"I assume you're after Bane. How do you plan to find him?"

Batman turned away. "I'll keep that to myself for now. The less you know, the better."

"That *does* seem to be the procedure these days."

8

For the fifth time Shondra examined her prison. Eighteen by twenty-six paces. Stone walls. No windows. Low ceiling with heavy oak beams across it. A thick oak door with a large, ancient-looking lock, probably pickable if she knew anything about picking locks. Obviously the cellar of a house—originally a wine cellar, probably. It was furnished with a table, a chamber pot, a daybed, and a hospital bed. That's where Jack Drake was lying, asleep, the transparent plastic mask of the respirator over his face. The respirator itself was hooked to an electrical cord that snaked under the door. An identical cord led to the table and to the single lamp on it.

Jack wasn't faring well. The violence of the abduction had sent his system into shock. His skin was ashen, and despite everything Shondra had been able to do, he was breathing in shallow gasps. He had been in a coma since they'd boarded the aircraft somewhere outside Gotham. His condition was critical. He would die unless Shondra got the medical supplies she needed.

She sat on the edge of the bed next to her patient, checked the respirator, and tried to think.

What do I know? Long plane trip. Six, seven hours. If we went west, we're on the West Coast—California, Washington, Oregon. If we went east, we're out of the country. England, France. I'm betting on east.

When they had landed, Jack was already unconscious. Their kidnappers had taken him off the aircraft first, then blindfolded Shondra and led her to a vehicle. There were no city sounds, just a gentle sigh of breeze and, she was pretty sure, the chirping of birds. They had driven about thirty minutes.

And down steps, and here we are. Here we've been for hours. How much longer before we find out what's happening? What do these bastards want?

Sir Hemingford and his man, Charles, checked into an inn the post-mistress had recommended—their only choice, really, since the next nearest hotel was forty miles away. A woman who looked remarkably like the postmistress except for thirty extra pounds, and was in fact her sister, showed them to a large, comfortable room, announced breakfast at six-thirty sharp, and bade them a good night. Sir Hemingford sat on the bed, leaned his canes against the wall, and began trembling.

"Master Bruce!" Alfred said, hurrying to his side.

"Not Bruce. Hemingford." Sir Hemingford waved him away. "It's nothing. Just tired. Be fine in a little while."

He lay down, and a moment later, his breathing slowed and deepened. Alfred—he couldn't think of himself as some ridiculous *Charles*—covered him with a quilt.

This had better not go on for long. He's a sick man. He can't take much more stress.

The sleek black Jaguar sedan stopped in front of Monkleigh Hall, and a beefy man in a blue blazer and black turtleneck got out. The door to the house opened, and Benedict Asp trotted down the stone walk.

"Ah, Colonel Vega," Asp cried. "Yuri! Welcome to Monkleigh Hall, my humble abode."

Asp was short and wiry. His white hair was thin in front and pulled into a floppy ponytail in back. His face was sharp, ferretlike, and he wore large, wire-rimmed glasses. He was dressed in a green T-shirt, leather vest, jeans, and hiking boots. He shook hands with Vega.

"I am ex-colonel now, Benedict," Vega said. "Glasnost was not good for my department. Our funding ceased abruptly. Such is democracy, I suppose."

"Not necessarily, sir. There are ways and means—especially in England. They love their secrecy here. Most helpful to such as ourselves."

Asp led his guest into the house and down a steep flight of steps to a heavy oak door. He unlocked it with a large brass key, swung it open, and ushered Vega inside.

"Colonel Yuri Vega, may I present the eminent American physician, Dr. Shondra Kinsolving."

Shondra turned from Jack Drake and stared.

"Benjamin—*you!*"

"It's Bene*dict* now—*Sandra.*" To Vega, he said, "Forgive me, colonel. I neglected to mention that Dr. Kinsolving is my sister."

Vega bowed.

Sir Hemingford Gray had been pounding the door with his cane for a minute when Benedict Asp, yawning, opened it.

"Don't s'pose yew have a decent breakfast inside?" Sir Hemingford said.

"Begyerpardon," Asp said. "Who are you?"

"Who the bloody hell do I look like?" Sir Hemingford demanded as he pushed past Asp and entered the main hall of the old house. "Sir Hemingford Gray. Well?"

"Well *what?*"

"Well, where's breakfast? Some kidney pie to begin with—"

Asp rubbed his eyes with his palms. "Do you know what time it is?"

" 'Course I do. Almost six. High bloody time I had some kidney pie and—"

"Listen, Sir Hungerford—"

"Hemingford. American, eh? Explains it."

"Explains what?"

"Why yew aren't offering me breakfast."

Sir Hemingford was circling the room, occasionally planting his canes firmly on the hardwood floor and bending to examine the surface of a table or chair.

"I'm afraid I must ask you to leave," Asp said.

"Not until you tell me, I bloody well won't."

"Tell you what?"

"How long you plan to stay here?" Sir Hemingford's voice was tense and exasperated.

"What business is that of yours?"

"Because I used to visit this place. When I was young. Before Father packed the lot of us off to Africa and a bloody bull elephant did for my legs. Always liked Monkleigh Hall. Thought I might buy it."

Asp gestured toward the door. "Perhaps if you came back later—"

"Dinner? What'll you serve? None of that American food! Nothing that comes from a tin! Beef and porridge—that's a *proper* dinner."

"We can discuss it this afternoon."

Sir Hemingford stomped to the door. Asp scurried around him to open it.

"Yew're not half bad, for an American. What did yew say the name was?"

"Benedict Asp."

"Ass? As in donkey? Maybe yew *are* half bad. Must be a reason for a name like that."

In the car, driving away from Monkleigh Hall, Sir Hemingford said, "Stop round the next bend."

Charles parked the roadster under a clump of trees. Sir Hemingford opened a leather briefcase and took out a pair of headphones. He touched a knob inside the case and listened intently for a few moments.

"Working," he said.

"How many bugs did you manage to plant?" Charles asked.

"Only three." Sir Hemingford switched on a tape recorder. "If we don't get anything from them, we'll try the laser equipment."

Charles got out of the car and began to search for a place to hide the electronics.

"No," Shondra said. "I told you twenty years ago, Benny—I will not do it again."

Asp went to where Jack Drake was bound upright in a chair. A respirator covered the lower half of his face, and the hiss of his breathing was the loudest sound in the cellar. Asp slapped him.

"You sick brute," Shondra said, starting forward. Yuri Vega caught her arm.

Asp struck Jack Drake again. Drake's head snapped back, and the hiss became louder.

"Stop!" Shondra cried. "Whatever it is you want me to do—I'll do it. Just don't hit him anymore."

"Excellent," Asp said. "Colonel Vega? You would perhaps do the honors?"

Yuri Vega rolled up his left sleeve to the elbow and produced a gravity knife from his hip pocket. He snapped it open and, smiling, laid the edge on his bare arm. With a quick, deft motion, he sliced open his flesh.

"My dear?" Asp said to Shondra. He stood beside her and closed his eyes. Reluctantly, Shondra did the same. They became very still. He paled a bit, and her dark skin became still darker. The muscles in Shondra's face relaxed; her hands rose, as though on strings, flattened, and made small circles in front of her; her lips parted, and she began to hum tunelessly.

Yuri Vega looked down at his arm and gasped. The blood was drying; the raw, red flesh visible through the gash was vanishing; the skin was closing, knitting together. In thirty seconds, the wound was gone; it left no scar.

"Satisfied, my dear Colonel?" Asp asked.

"It is impressive, yes," Vega said. "But I must see more. You have demonstrated healing. Now show me killing."

He waved the knife and grinned.

Lieutenant Kitch and Sergeant Bullock had been in the tiny interrogation room for six hours, first with Bird, then with Trogg, and now with Zombie. There were a dozen empty paper cups on the single table and a mound of Bullock's cigar butts in the ashtray.

"You guys are never gonna see the light of day, you know that?" Bullock asked, leaning over the seated Zombie.

"Are you trying to frighten me, Sergeant?" Zombie smiled. "With what? Imprisonment? I have served hard time in Peña Duro, the hellhole of the universe. Your prisons are soft, easy."

"Sure, they're country clubs," Bullock agreed. "But you'll serve alone. The feds are coming tomorrow and splitting you and your two bunkies up. You'll be counting the years in separate pens. Hard time is harder without friends."

"And what must I do to save myself? Surrender Bane to you? I would die first. I would die smiling."

"Get this goon outta here before I put a slug in him," Bullock said to Kitch.

"Let's go," Kitch said, opening the door. "We're finished with you."

"Imagine my relief," Zombie said.

A uniformed officer led him away.

Bullock lit a fresh cigar. "I should have guessed. These guys are toughing us out. We don't have one damn clue about who Bane is or what's going on in this city."

"We have his gang," Kitch said. "We'll have him next."

"Yeah, and world peace, love, and harmony. You sound like a runner-up for Miss America. Only one way we're gonna get this Bane and it's got nothing to do with playing by the rules."

• • •

Jean Paul finally found what he was looking for in Batman's private computer files: floor plans for the Gotham City House of Detention on Girard Street. Gordon had said Bane's men were being held in the lockup on the top floor. Good. It would not be difficult. But he didn't have much time. He would have to act tonight.

Bane finally identified the emotion he was feeling. He was tranquil. He had never before been away from the sound of human voices, not even during the years he spent in Peña Duro's hole. Though he could not always see other human beings, he could feel their presence, an almost tangible weight on him, unending and oppressive, and always he heard them: laughing, moaning, shouting, sometimes screaming, and occasionally shrieking. Always there was the sound of voices. Until now. He despised Trogg, Bird, and Zombie—especially Zombie—for being so stupid as to get caught. But he was also grateful to them. Their absence confirmed for him what he wanted to believe: he was totally self-sufficient. He needed no one. People were mere tools, to be used and discarded.

He wondered if kings felt like this. *No,* he decided, *probably not.* Kings were human and weak and he was something *beyond* human.

He tapped the stud on his arm and as the Venom flooded him he laughed in contempt for humanity and all its shabby, stupid weakness.

•   •   •

"So what'd you tell 'em, Zombie?" Bird said, pacing the cell. Zombie sat on his bunk. Trogg squatted in a corner.

"Don't be absurd," Zombie said. "I told them nothing."

Bird stopped abruptly. "Lissen, I'm getting spooked. You think Bane will free us?"

"Only Bane can know what he will do. If it serves his purpose, he will act. If not, then we must wait. We offer them nothing. They have nothing to interest us."

Bird slid down the wall and sat next to Trogg. "I don't like the idea of doing time. But I done it for worse reasons. Only thing I'm gonna miss is watching Magic in action—"

There was the crash of breaking glass and a parcel dropped from the cell's only window.

"What the hell?" Bird muttered.

Zombie untied the string that held the parcel closed. He removed three gas masks from the paper wrapping. The straps of one were wrapped around a note.

Watch and wait.
—B.

"It's him," Bird whispered.

Zombie lifted the final item from the parcel. It was a small, round piece of plastic explosive with a tiny detonator stuck into it. "For the lock," Zombie said.

Suddenly his eyes stung, and his throat was burning. He slipped one of the gas masks on and threw the others to Bird and Trogg. He could hear a guard in the corridor outside choking. He pressed the plastic charge against the door lock, snapped the detonator, and ran to the far side of the cell. There was a brief, bright flash, and a sound like someone kicking a cardboard box.

The door swung wide.

Outside the air was filled with white mist. Zombie, Bird, and Trogg jumped over the sprawled bodies of two guards and ran to the barred gate at the far end of the narrow corridor, which was partially open. A third guard, gasping and stumbling, stood in their way. Trogg picked the man up and hurled him against a wall.

They were in a narrow stairwell.

"Up there," Zombie said.

They dashed up a steep flight of steps, went through another door, and found themselves on the roof of the building. The street, eight floors below, was filled with police cars and uniformed officers.

"No good," Zombie said. He ran to the rear of the building. There was a rope ladder that dropped to a dark alley. In the faint light from a few windows, Zombie could see a dark sedan waiting for them. He motioned to the others. "Come on."

They climbed down the ladder, peered into the car to make certain it was empty, and piled in. A moment later Zombie guided it from the alley and into the busy Saturday night traffic.

"I *knew* Magic would come through for us," said Bird.

Zombie sped through a red light and drove toward the motel. Bane would be waiting there.

Batman smiled. He was less than a mile away from the jail, sitting in the 'mobile and watching a dot crawl slowly across a phosphorescent screen. The transmitter he'd hidden under the left front fender of the getaway car was working perfectly, as he knew it would; he'd gotten it from the electronics bin in the Cave, and Bruce Wayne always bought the best. The gas masks had come from the Cave, too. Only the gas itself gave him any problems; he'd had to mix it himself, but again the Cave had provided raw ingredients and lab equipment. The formula, he had discovered, he already knew, as he knew—praise be to St. Dumas and the System—a *dozen* suitable formulas.

He checked the position of the dot and put the car in gear. Bird, Trogg, and Zombie were doing exactly what he planned for them to do—lead him directly to Bane.

• • •

Bullock, Montoya, Warden Froman from the House of Detention, and Gordon were gathered in Gordon's office. It was eleven, an hour after Bane's three men had escaped.

Bullock blew smoke into Warden Froman's face. "So which one a your boys is dirty?"

"You want to explain that?" Froman asked.

"The bustout was an inside job—hadda be. Somebody knew the layout and somebody cut the alarm wires. So who was it?"

"Listen, fat man, get your cigar out of my face and get your *face* out of my face or—"

"Or what?"

Montoya laid a hand on Bullock's arm. "Take it easy, Harv."

"Good advice," Gordon said dryly. "You may be right, Sergeant Bullock, and you may not be. We don't know enough yet to make the call. I can think of at least one other possibility. At least one."

Bullock inspected the glowing end of his cigar and grunted.

Bird's body crashed through the cabin window. Bane jumped from his chair and ran to where his aide lay. Bird was breathing, but his clothes were tattered and his face a mass of bruises and blood. Someone had beaten him mercilessly. There was a note pinned to his shirt:

> *Meet me atop the Neenan Building. 10 tonight.*
> *—Batman*

Bane didn't know what time it was. About eight, he guessed.

"I broke him," Bane said. "I did it once. I will do it again. I will do it forever."

Bane stepped over Bird's body and left the cabin.

Outside, he found Trogg and Zombie slumped against the wall of the motel office. Their clothes were torn. Zombie was bleeding from a scalp wound. Trogg's left eye was swollen shut, and his mouth was a red smear.

Zombie looked up at Bane. "It was Batman. He jumped us."

"Get in the car," Bane said.

10

Batman moved swiftly and silently up the fire escape. Below him lay an overflowing dumpster and an alley; above, the roof of the Neenan Building with a huge electric billboard that overlooked Adams Boulevard— at ten on Saturday night, the busiest avenue in Gotham. People would see him destroy Bane, and yet the battle would be so high off the ground that nobody would be able to interfere, at least not until it was over.

By tomorrow morning, the city's criminals would know that Batman had destroyed Bane. Batman would again be supreme.

And Jean Paul Valley was Batman.

"You're sure this is a good idea?" Zombie asked as he steered the car off the freeway at the Adams Boulevard exit.

"Yes," Bane said.

In the backseat, Trogg grunted and wiped his wrist across his bloody mouth.

"You know there'll be thousands of people there?"

"Yes. I want them to see. Before, the first time, only a few saw. This time, I want the whole city to know I broke the Batman."

"We may have problems getting away afterward," Zombie said.

"We will deal with them." Bane's fingers hovered near the stud on his arm, but he did not touch it. Not yet.

Batman planted small explosive charges in the stairwell and on the top landing of the fire escape. After Bane arrived—*if* Bane arrived—he would detonate the charges. He and Bane would be alone on the rooftop.

He moved to the edge of the roof and looked down. Gothamites scattered like confetti, coming out of theaters, entering restaurants, pausing to examine store windows, to buy food from cart vendors, to scan billboards. Cars, vans, trucks, bicycles, people on roller skates and skateboards. Shouts, roars, laughter. To Jean Paul, it was a neon-lit version of hell.

Bane left Trogg in the alley near the fire escape with a gun and orders to prevent anyone from climbing it. Five minutes later, he knocked out a night watchman in the lobby of the Neenan Building and posted Zombie near the entrance to the elevator. Then he entered the elevator and rode it to the top floor. He got out and went up a short, narrow flight of steps, opened a door, and stepped onto the tarred rooftop.

He looked around. Garishly colored light from the sign and the signs on adjoining buildings momentarily dazzled him. He squinted, searching for the Batman. Was it possible the fool would not come?

"Show yourself!" Bane shouted.

A dark blur against the blaze of color dropped from the top of the sign.

"I'm here," Batman said.

"Good," Bane said. He touched the stud and felt the warmth, the strength, gush through him.

. . .

Just before he leapt from the top of the sign, Jean Paul, who once was Azrael and now was Batman, murmured a special prayer his father had taught him. It worked as it always did, to sharpen his senses and focus his attention.

He saw Bane's fingers move to his arm. He noted the tubes leading from the arm to the back of Bane's head.

That's a source of power for him!

"You're different," Bane said. "You're only pretending to be him."

"No. I am the Batman. The only Batman."

"Soon," Bane said slowly, "you will wish you were not."

The thing he touched is on his left arm. So he's right-handed.

Batman began gliding to the left. Bane moved with him. Slowly they circled some invisible point between them until Batman raised his gauntleted arm. There was a faint hiss, and three darts sprang out and flew toward Bane's throat. Bane raised his arm, and the darts embedded themselves into a subcutaneous plastic sheath.

Batman kicked Bane in the chin. Bane's head snapped, and he stepped backward. Batman punched him in the jaw. Bane took another step backward. Then Bane struck back. The blow to Batman's chin was swift and totally unexpected. The world tilted, and Batman was looking up at the smoky sky. Bane landed atop him and immediately punched him in the face. Batman's mask absorbed some of the blow but not enough: ugly flowers suddenly blossomed behind his eyes, and something screeched in his ears. Bane raised his arm for another strike. Batman reached up and cupped his hands around Bane's neck and pulled as he levered his legs upward; Bane tumbled forward and Batman rolled out from under him, up to a standing position.

Bane's momentum had taken him to the edge of the roof. Just as he was scrambling to his feet, Batman kicked him in the chest. Bane teetered and fell backward.

. . .

When Ed Switzer didn't make his regular eleven o'clock call-in, Marian Dilby, night captain at Acme Security, Inc., phoned Ed at the Neenan Building. After forty rings, she hung up and got on her radio. Acme was shorthanded that night, so instead of summoning one of Acme's patrol cars, she called the cops. She told the dispatcher at Gotham PD that the night watchman at the Neenan Building wasn't responding. The dispatcher went on the air with it.

Harvey Bullock was only two blocks from the Neenan Building when he heard the alert.

"What the hell," he muttered, and keyed his microphone: "Bullock here," he told the dispatcher. "I got the Neenan thing."

Bane did not fall far. He caught the fire escape and dangled.

Batman saw Bane hanging and realized he had forgotten to detonate the charges.

He pressed a button on his belt. There were two dull explosions. Dust billowed from the wall where the top of the fire escape had been bolted to the brick facade, and the fire escape pulled free and began to fall into the alley.

Bane fell with it. He released his grip, dropped twelve feet into an open dumpster, and sank into garbage.

I can't let him escape. Batman fixed his line around the base of the sign, tossed the other end over the roof's edge, grabbed it, and rappeled down.

He hit the alley just as Bane was climbing from the garbage and saw a second man emerging from the shadows, aiming a gun.

"No!" Bane yelled at Trogg. "He's mine."

Trogg lowered the gun.

Batman leapt at Bane. Bane brought his elbow around, but Batman ducked under it and hit Bane in the stomach. As Bane backed away, he reached for the stud on his left forearm.

His power source.

As Bane touched the stud, Batman grabbed the tubes that led from

Bane's arm to the back of his head and pulled. A fine mist sprayed from the tube into the empty air.

Suddenly the alley was lit by two bright beams and a hoarse voice commanded, "Freeze!"

Bullock had steered his car to the rear of the Neenan Building. That's where most of the skels operated, in the back, in the dark.

He got there in time to see the guy in the funny suit—Batman—hurting the other mook. That's when he got on the horn and yelled "Freeze!" Then he pulled his piece and got out of the car. Batman turned to look at Bullock, and the other mook punched Batman in the head. Then the mook took off running. Bullock thought about shooting him and decided not to. Paperwork'd be a bitch. Instead he got on the horn and called for backup.

Bane had to get away. The police—he couldn't deal with them and the man in the mask, whoever the bastard was. Not without Venom.

He had to get the Venom into his brain. But how? He had the drug—there was a vial full of it strapped to his arm. But how could he put it into his blood? Drink it? Perhaps. That could work, but it would be slow, would have to seep through his stomach and intestines, and it might lose potency in the process. What *could* he do?

Bane ran.

He would get away. He would find a doctor who could reattach the tubes. He would flood himself with the sweet warmth. He would find the man in the mask and break his bones one at a time until he was nothing but a sack of agony.

There was something ahead. A flight of steps leading up to an elevated train platform. Good. A train could take him away, perhaps take him to the motel cabin where he could rest and think about finding a doctor.

He sprinted up the steps and past a small booth. Someone in the booth yelled at him. Bane continued running until he came to a turnstile. He jumped over it and was on a narrow platform overlooking the train tracks.

He looked to the left, to the right. A round light was growing in the darkness, a rumble was becoming louder. A train was approaching. Bane waited until it had screeched into the station and hissed to a stop. Doors slid open and Bane entered a car. The doors slid shut, the brakes hissed, and the train swayed as it moved out of the station. Bane momentarily lost his balance and clutched the overhead rail. A few of the dozen passengers glanced up, briefly surveyed the newcomer, and returned their attention to their magazines, books, newspapers, or the floor. This was Gotham City; sweaty, battered men in weird clothing were nothing remarkable, particularly late at night.

Bane was safe.

From a block away, Batman had seen Bane run up the steps, had seen a train coming to a stop. Bane was escaping. He could not permit that. He uttered a prayer to St. Dumas and scrambled up the steps.

He was vaulting over the turnstile as the last car was passing the far end of the platform. He ran and jumped. His fingers closed around a U-shaped bracket, and his toes found purchase on a narrow ledge rim of metal under the car's rear door. He peered through a dirty window set in the top half of the door and saw that the car was empty except for a shabby old woman whose legs were shielded by two overflowing shopping bags.

The train dipped sharply to the left as it rounded a curve. Batman clung to the bracket until the train was again upright. He pulled at the door handle. It wouldn't open. He drew back his gauntleted fist and smashed it through the plexiglass window, which buckled inward and fell to the floor in one piece.

Batman squeezed through the opening.

"Get outta here," the woman with the shopping bags said.

11

Bullock saw Batman enter the transit station and figured the mook had to be there too. Then he saw the
train and knew they'd probably both be on it. He told
the dispatcher what he knew and added, "The train's
an express. It won't stop till it hits Riverside. Get some
uniforms down there to meet it."

The dispatcher reported Bullock's transmission to Commissioner
Gordon. Gordon slammed down the phone. He was shrugging into his
overcoat as he trotted to the elevator that would take him to the garage.
Police Headquarters was only a couple of minutes from Riverside. He
could be there when the train arrived.

The doors between the cars weren't locked. Batman ran forward until
he reached the front of the train. The car was empty except for Bane, who
stood gripping a metal pole. Batman lowered his head and charged. His

head and shoulders struck Bane, and locked together, they stumbled backward. Batman brought his knee up into Bane's belly and slammed his gauntleted palm up into Bane's chin.

The train slowed as it pulled into Riverside Station.

Batman's shoulder pressed Bane against the car's center door as he punched Bane's midsection with both fists. A rib cracked. The door slid open and Bane, grunting, fell backward. Batman stepped from the car and stood waiting. Slowly Bane raised himself to one knee and looked up. Batman did not move. Bane lurched to his feet and stumbled away. In two strides, Batman caught him, spun him around, and kicked him off the platform to the track bed.

Gordon and Bullock burst through a gate and ran to the edge of the platform. They saw Bane lying across the tracks with Batman straddling him, knees bent, arm drawn back, huge fist cocked.

"Kill me," Bane whispered. "There is nothing for me now. Kill me."

"We'll take over now," Gordon called from the platform.

Batman's arm trembled. A blow from his gauntleted fist would crack the skull, jelly the brain—

"Don't do it," Gordon yelled.

"Kill me."

"No," Batman said. "You're broken, Bane. Blackgate Prison can hold the pieces."

Batman waited until Gordon and Bullock jumped from the platform to the tracks before turning and walking through the darkness of the tunnel.

Later, Batman went to the Cave and shed his mask and costume. Then Jean Paul sat alone in the dark and pondered: Why *hadn't* he killed Bane? Standing above him there on the tracks, fist raised, clean, righteous rage coursing through him, he had been filled with the conviction that killing Bane was a holy chore. But he hadn't.

Because that's what Bane wanted? Yes, of course. Death would have been too easy. Bane will suffer far more if he lives. Azrael knows only death. Batman can punish in many ways.

Jean Paul smiled. He had his answer.

Jean Paul Valley was no longer Azrael.

Jean Paul Valley was now Batman.

But who was Jean Paul Valley?

The late afternoon sun slanted in through the single window, making the largest guest room in the inn surprisingly bright. Soon, within the hour, the light would dim and the night's chill would claim Monkleigh. But for now both the village and the inn it served were warm and pleasant.

"Nothing, Master Br—Hemingford?" asked Alfred, who was no longer pretending to be Charles.

Bruce switched off the tape machine he had been listening to for the past hour. "Nothing. Either they're not a very talkative bunch or they're doing their conversing away from the mikes I planted."

Alfred frowned. Bruce was no longer being Sir Hemingford except when others were present. A bad sign: normally, he would have relished the discipline the constant masquerade required.

He must be perpetually exhausted. "An alternative plan, then?" Alfred asked.

"Not yet."

"In that case, may I suggest dinner. You haven't eaten since last night."

"I'm not really hungry," Bruce snapped.

Alfred was not intimidated. "Undoubtedly true, and also quite beside the point. You *must* eat—"

"Okay, compromise. Drop me off at the surveillance point—maybe I can see more than I'm hearing—and then go into the village and get some supper. Bring me something. Some fruit."

"All carbohydrates and no protein—"

Bruce held up his hands in mock surrender. "Okay, okay, by all means, protein. Fish. A fish sandwich and the fruit."

"Very well."

It was evening when Alfred helped Sir Hemingford from the car to the clump of trees. Across an open field, they could see Monkleigh Hall, a large, graceless structure of no particular architectural style, entirely black except for disharmonious green trim on the eaves. The sun had gone down; the sky was the color of pearl and full of crimson streaks.

"I shall return within the hour," Alfred promised.

Sir Hemingford was already scanning Monkleigh Hall through powerful binoculars. "Take your time."

Benedict Asp led Yuri Vega into the wine cellar and smiled at his sister.

"Now we are ready for the real test," Asp said. He pointed to two metal caps that resembled unpadded cyclists' helmets resting on the table. Each had a single cable that sprouted from the back and led to a fiberglass case the size of an automobile battery.

"Nothing doing, Benny," Shondra said.

"Colonel?" Asp said to Vega. "Perhaps you would do the honors."

Vega crossed to where Jack Drake was tied to a chair. He lifted Drake's left hand and broke the index finger. Drake's face twisted under the respirator mask, and he whimpered.

"Don't," Shondra pleaded.

"How nice of you to agree to cooperate," Asp said, placing one of the caps on Shondra's head.

"What is this thing?" Shondra asked.

"Something the excellent Soviet scientists under Colonel Vega's command developed before his foolish superiors disbanded the department and . . . there was more to it, Yuri?"

"Put me under house arrest," Vega said.

"As you may know, my dear," Asp continued, "our Russian friends had quite a healthy interest in the paranormal. They saw it as a possible source of weaponry, and I daresay we're about to prove them right. These helmets"—Asp put on his cap—"capture and store the energy you and I know so well. That much has been proven. Colonel Vega believes that once it is stored, it can be amplified and directed. That is what we shall establish tonight."

"What do you want me to do?" Shondra's voice was flat and resigned.

"Nothing awfully dreadful, I assure you. Simply do what you have done before with such success. Colonel?"

Vega took out his knife, opened it, and sliced open the top of his left wrist.

"Heal him," Asp commanded.

Shondra and Asp: eyes closed. Skin changing. Hands up and circling. Humming—

—inside her skull: a shriek, as thick, horny fingers jabbed into her brain—

"No, Benny, please," she whispered.

—but the fingers jabbed and tore and twisted—

Shondra's hands and head fell, and then she slipped to the floor and lay still.

"She is dead?" Vega asked.

Asp knelt beside Shondra. "No, merely in shock. She'll recover nicely."

"What of this?" Vega held up his left wrist. The cut was open and leaking blood.

"I'm afraid you'll have to put a bandage on it," Asp said. "I *did* warn you, you know. The energy got diverted. Now let's go see how effective it was."

Vega sucked blood from the cut and fumbled in his pocket for a handkerchief.

Alfred shivered. He had decided to leave the car with Sir Hemingford and walk into Monkleigh. Now, as he approached the outskirts of the village, he was wishing he had worn a coat. A cold wind was rattling the leaves around him, and his sweater was not proof against it, not at all. Ah, well, no matter. A bit of chill wouldn't harm him and in a minute or two he would be at the inn, sipping mulled cider in front of a fire and perhaps enjoying a bit of a chat with the plump proprietress. He would have to hurry, though. Sir Hemingford *was* wearing an overcoat, but still, in his condition, it wouldn't do to leave him in the weather for long.

Something was ahead, directly in Alfred's path, just outside the inn. He drew close and caught his breath. It was a man, the village constable, his legs tangled in his bicycle frame. The lights from the inn windows shone dully in his open eyes. Alfred didn't need to touch him to know he was dead.

Alfred ran the few steps to the inn and went inside.

"Hallo," he called. "I need a doctor—"

There was a powerful smell of frying meat in the air. Alfred dashed into the kitchen. The proprietress was sprawled across the stove, her cheek resting on a skillet. Alfred grabbed her apron string and pulled her off; her body slumped to the floor.

"Oh my dear Lord," Alfred whispered. He looked around. There was an old-fashioned dial telephone on the wall near a butcher block. Alfred scurried around the block and stumbled. Another woman was lying in his way—the postmistress. He reached over the body and got the phone. He dialed the operator. After twenty rings, he hung up.

Shivering, not with cold this time, he returned to the main room of the inn. He heard a car pass outside and went to the window. A black Jaguar was just rounding one of the main street's bends, the same black Jaguar he had seen parked in front of Monkleigh Hall.

"Master Bruce!"

Alfred went to the dead constable and, keeping his eyes averted from the corpse, lifted the bicycle. He had to pull hard to free it from the constable's legs. "Forgive me," he murmured.

He mounted the bike and began pedaling toward Monkleigh Hall. Master Bruce was alone, almost helpless, and Alfred felt certain that whatever monstrous evil was happening in the village originated in that grim, black dwelling.

Behind him, there was a dull explosion; the kitchen window of the inn erupted outward, and flames began to curl around its edges.

12

 Sir Hemingford saw Benedict Asp and another, larger man get into the black Jaguar and drive away. That could mean the house was empty. This might be the only opportunity he'd have to search it. But it was a quarter mile away across open ground in the dark. Only a few months ago, none of this would have been a problem. The dash across the field would have taken only a minute, and he would have negotiated the uneven terrain effortlessly, either by using special lenses or simply relying on his own extraordinary night vision. But now—the trek would be painful and slow on foot; in the car parked behind him, it would be much faster and easier. *If* he could drive the car, which he doubted. So he'd have to travel on his own power, and injured as he was, he might not get to Monkleigh Hall within the hour, and once there, it would take him even more hours to conduct any kind of search. He could get lucky, of course. Asp and his companion might be gone until tomorrow, and whatever he needed to find—something to do with Shondra and Jack Drake?—could be in plain sight. But did he dare take the chance?

Everything was so complicated. Actions that he once would have taken without thought had to be considered and debated—

Alfred. Where was Alfred? Alfred could drive, and keep a watch outside Monkleigh Hall while Sir Hemingford conducted at least a cursory search. How long did it take to buy a fish sandwich? He looked at the road to Monkleigh and saw an orange glow in the sky above the town. A fire. Alfred would want to help; that explained why he wasn't back yet.

Sir Hemingford heard the purr of a high-performance engine and put the glasses to his eyes. The Jaguar had returned. Asp and the other man got out, Asp opened the trunk and, with his companion's help, removed a woman. Sir Hemingford had seen enough death to recognize it, even from a distance. Asp and the man carried the body inside. Sir Hemingford put on his earphones. A moment later:

"Look, not a mark on her. Not a clue to testify as to how she died. And all done by the power of thought," Asp said.

"You can perform the autopsy yourself, Benedict?" A Russian accent.

"Certainly, I was at the top of my class in medical school."

"A pity the lady doctor is not able to do it."

"Shondra has been of ample help already tonight, wouldn't you say? Let the poor dear have her rest."

So Shondra is inside the house. And she is helping Asp.

"What do you expect to find when you cut her open, Benedict?"

"That she died of accelerated health. Her metabolism, including her immune system, went into overdrive. The strain killed her."

A hoarse chuckle: the Russian. "Too much of a good thing."

"Exactly. I'm finished with my preliminary examination. The more detailed autopsy can wait. I'll collect our fair accomplice and her patient and we can be on our way. Why don't you pack and see to the car, Yuri?"

Sound of footsteps receding.

They were getting ready to leave. With Shondra. With Jack Drake. *Where is Alfred?*

It was ghastly. Alfred had returned to the inn to help with the fire— caused by a rupture in the fuel line or some such, no doubt. He got a pail of water from the pump in the yard and took it into the kitchen. Flames were creeping up the wall behind the stove and across the linoleum floor. Alfred flung his pail's worth of water and went to the sink for a refill. Four more times he emptied the pail; the fire was then contained in a small area around the stove, balked by wet wallboard and linoleum. Alfred pulled down window curtains and used them to beat out the flames. He stood, panting, covered with soot, trying not to look at the postmistress and the hideously burned proprietress.

Where is everyone? Surely, the rest of the villagers must have seen the flames by now.

He dropped the curtains and went outside. Looked left and right, up and down. The village was quiet.

"Hallo?" he shouted.

Could they all be dead?

Gripped by a terrible certainty, he trudged toward the nearest house, already knowing what he would find inside, already dreading it.

Shondra was adjusting the flow control on Jack Drake's respirator when Asp entered the cellar.

"Come. We're leaving. Our task here is done."

"Benny—what did we do? What did *I* do?"

"Something that will make me one of the richest men on earth. I will buy you an *exceptionally* nice Christmas gift."

"I'm not going," Shondra said.

"Don't make me hit you again."

"You promised that we'd cure Jack Drake."

Asp glanced down at Drake. "Did I?" He snatched away the respirator. Shondra grabbed at it. Asp slapped her.

"He'll *die*," Shondra cried.

"If you give me one more moment's trouble, yes, he will. And you will watch. Take notes, if you like." Asp dangled the respirator mask in front of Drake's face. Drake was gasping; his skin was becoming mottled.

"All right, I'll do whatever you say," Shondra murmured.

"That's my girl." He handed the respirator to Shondra and stood aside as she tugged it into place over Jack Drake's nose and mouth.

"Now help me carry him to the car," Asp said. "Unless you'd rather leave him here."

Sir Hemingford could drive. Not well, but he could get where he was going. He couldn't use his legs, but he was able to push the car's accelerator and brake with one of his canes as he steered with the other hand. He bumped along the wide arc of the road, hoping he'd meet someone—preferably Alfred or a constable, but *anyone* would do.

The road was deserted.

Stopping was awkward. Trying to shift into neutral as he steadied the wheel with an elbow and jabbed at the brake, he momentarily lost control. The gears shrieked, and the car lurched to a stop fifty yards from Monkleigh Hall. A front tire slid into a ditch, and the entire car canted sharply to the right. He briefly remembered all the times as Bruce Wayne he'd *faked* bad driving.

Sir Hemingford got out and leaned heavily on his canes.

Only about fifty yards. Nothing but cake.

Move forward. Put a cane out in front, lean on it, pivot, swinging the opposite side of the body forward, put the other cane in front, lean, pivot, swing . . .

Only fifty yards.

Ahead he saw Asp and the Russian carry out something wrapped in a rug that had to be the corpse and dump it in the trunk of the Jaguar.

Lean, pivot, swing . . .

The Russian got into the driver's seat as Asp vanished into the house again.

Only about twenty yards now.

Asp reappeared. He and a woman were supporting Jack Drake between them.

The woman was Shondra. Tall, stately, dark skin glistening in the light from the open door—unmistakably Shondra Kinsolving.

Lean, pivot, swing . . .

Ten yards.

"I say, where the bloody hell's the path to the inn got to?" Sir Hemingford shouted. "Getting so a man can't depend on anything. Not the England of our fathers, d'yew know?"

"I haven't time for you, old fool," Asp said.

Sir Hemingford craned his neck forward and squinted. "Dr. Kinsolving, isn't it? D'yew remember, we met in the States, in Gotham City."

Shondra continued walking.

Bruce had to communicate with her, regardless of the risk: he spoke in his normal voice. "You wondered how many women doctors I'd used a certain line on."

Shondra halted and stared at him.

"You? Bruce?"

"You know this man?" Asp demanded.

"Mistaken identity," Shondra said.

"Shondra, if he's holding you against your will, speak out," Bruce said.

"Whoever you are, let me make it quite clear—Mr. Asp and I are old friends. I am his willing *business partner*. Do you understand?"

The Russian said, "What is the trouble?"

"No trouble," Shondra said.

"Yuri, perhaps you'd care to deal with this imbecile," Asp said.

Vega stepped behind Bruce and wrapped a beefy forearm around his neck. Shondra and Asp, with Jack Drake still between them, moved toward the Jaguar. Bruce brought one of his canes back beneath his elbow and into Vega's belly. Vega's grip loosened, and Bruce hooked the cane around the Russian's ankle and fell forward, pulling Vega's leg from under him. Bruce broke his fall with a forearm and rolled with his momentum as Vega pitched backward and hit the grass.

Asp was opening the rear door of the Jaguar, ten feet from Bruce's head. Shondra was supporting Drake alone.

Can't let them leave with Drake. Got to chance hurting him—

Bruce hooked the other cane around Drake's calf and pulled. Drake slipped from Shondra's grasp and fell sideways onto the lawn.

Vega was on his hands and knees, crawling toward Bruce. Bruce flipped a cane, got an overhand grip, and drove the small end into Vega's chin.

"Let him go," Shondra was saying.

Let who go? Drake?

Vega was shaking his head. Bruce jabbed first his left cane into Vega's temple and then his right. From the top of his vision, he could see Asp's legs disappearing into the left side of the Jaguar.

A car door slammed and an engine rumbled.

Vega's elbows bent. His face hit the grass, his legs straightened, and he lay still.

Tires spun on gravel, and the Jaguar roared away.

Bruce tried to roll over and couldn't. It wasn't the pain—he could enter into the pain and get past it, the way the Korean master Kirigi had taught him long ago—it was the body cast. It was imprisoning him.

Bruce grasped a tuft of grass and pulled himself onto his stomach. He inched forward, dragging his legs, until he could touch the side of Drake's neck. He should have felt a pulse. But he didn't.

Can't use CPR. Can't get in the correct position—the damn cast . . .

Drake's respirator mask and tank were lying next to his shoulder. Bruce put the mask in position.

"Come on, Jack. Breathe. You can do it."

Something that was tan and crimson burst in front of Bruce's eyes, and fatigue coursed through him.

Can't pass out. Not while Drake has a chance.

From far away, from the bottom of some well somewhere: "Master Bruce!"

Another tan and crimson burst, flaring past the edge of his vision and slowly receding, congealing into a nose, a thin mustache—

"Master Bruce."

Alfred? Maybe not. Probably an hallucination. But maybe not. Just in case: "Alfred, Jack. Needs help. Doctor. The village."

What was Alfred saying? Nobody in Monkleigh? Was that it?

Someone coughed.

"He's alive," Alfred said.

Bruce started to protest. *Of course I'm alive.* Then he realized that *Jack Drake* had coughed, that Alfred meant *Jack Drake.*

It was okay to pass out now.

13

"The doctors seem cautiously optimistic," Alfred said.

Across an ocean, seven thousand miles away, Tim Drake sighed and relaxed his grip on the phone. "Did they say when he can come home?"

"No, but I shouldn't imagine it will be anytime soon," Alfred said. He was lounging in an overstuffed chair in the penthouse suite of a London hotel, holding the telephone in one hand and a teacup in the other. "You have to remember, he has been through quite an ordeal."

"But he's okay."

"All things considered, he is doing remarkably well," Alfred said.

"What about Bruce?"

"He is in the hospital room next to your father."

"His back? Is it worse?"

Alfred hesitated before replying. "Let me just say that it is certainly not better. Now that he has rescued your father, we can hope that he will entrust the fate of Dr. Kinsolving to others, behave sanely, and take care of himself."

"Tell him he'd better. Gotham needs him."

Alfred sipped tea. "Which brings us to another topic. How is Jean Paul faring?"

"Well . . ." The transatlantic line hissed. Finally, Tim said, "He's really effective."

"That does not exactly answer my question, Timothy."

"I don't know how to say this—"

"English sentences are sometimes generally acceptable."

"Alfred, I think he may be loony."

Alfred put down his teacup and frowned. "Any particular reason?"

"A lot of things. When he's out on a case . . . he's really brutal. Almost sadistic. And lately, he's gotten really secretive. He's always going out alone. He won't tell me where he's headed or even what he's working on."

"I suppose much of that may be normal, given the stress he must be under."

"But that isn't all. He's shut me out of the Cave."

"Beg your pardon?"

"He's blocked off the entrance from the cistern. The car entrance can only be opened from the inside or by code—"

"Is that all?" Alfred said.

"I've saved the best for last. Or maybe I mean the *worst*. Anyway . . . he's nailed Bane. Sent him to jail."

"I suppose we should celebrate."

"Alfred, Bruce told Jean Paul to stay *away* from Bane."

"I am well aware of that."

"You think you should tell Bruce?"

"I wish I knew, Tim."

Alfred heard Tim break the connection and stared at the phone for a full minute before hanging up.

A primly efficient nurse was helping Bruce Wayne button his shirt when Dr. Rogers Holder entered the examination room, holding a sheaf of papers.

"Hurting then, Mr. Bruce Wayne?" Dr. Holder spoke with a thick

Yorkshire accent. He was in his fifties, mostly bald, thin, wearing heavy glasses and a lab coat. A stethoscope dangled from his neck.

"Are those more test results?" Bruce asked, nodding toward the papers.

"They are. But you haven't answered my question. Are you hurting?"

"Yes, I am."

"Well, best get used to it. Because that's what the rest of your life will likely be all about. Pain. And you brought it on yourself. You're a fool, Wayne. An arrogant, overmonied, irresponsible fool."

The nurse glanced at Bruce and bustled away.

"I take it the prognosis is not favorable, Dr. Holder?"

"It could have been. If you'd acted sanely when you first injured yourself. If you'd stayed home and minded a good physican. But no. Not you. Not the Gotham City playboy. You had to traipse around the world doing heaven-knows-what. Pleasuring yourself, I shouldn't doubt."

"What I did was . . . not much fun."

Dr. Holder slammed the papers down on a tabletop. "You ask is the prognosis favorable? No sir, it is not. I'd say you've doomed yourself to a life of pain and paralysis."

"Is there anything I can do? A doctor could do?"

"Perhaps. They've had some success with transplanted fetal tissue in spinal trauma cases. Get yourself to a good surgeon and let him go to work. Do it immediately—today—and there might be a chance. Wait even a week and . . ."

"Thank you, doctor."

"I don't *want* your bloody thanks."

The nurse reentered and helped Bruce finish dressing.

Alfred covered Bruce with a blanket and crossed the room to the telephone. "I shall check us out of here at once. While the staff is preparing the bill, I shall charter an airplane. We can be back in Gotham City by this evening. I shall have someone from the hospital waiting—"

"We're not going home," Bruce said.

"But Dr. Holder said—"

"We're staying until the job is done."

"But you've accomplished what you set out to do. Jack Drake is safe. You rescued him." Alfred's long face was pitying, but his voice held a note of outrage. "Now take care of yourself. Let someone else finish it."

"By the time that 'someone else' got started," Bruce said slowly, "more lives would be lost. Maybe a lot more. Have you forgotten Monkleigh?"

"Of course not." Now Alfred sounded angry.

"That quaint English village became a charnel house. Within seconds. Because of Benedict Asp and Shondra Kinsolving."

Alfred went to the window and stared down at the bustling midday traffic in the street below. "That's what's really driving you, isn't it? Dr. Kinsolving. You feel betrayed. She was a woman you had come to . . ."

"Love? Maybe. I don't know. I haven't had much experience with love. But I *do* know I was on my way to tell her everything when she and Jack Drake were kidnapped. Only she *wasn't* kidnapped, was she? She was part of it—part of whatever put all those bodies on the streets of Monkleigh."

"You may be judging her too harshly."

"No, I'm not. I haven't got evidence that would convict her in a court of law, but I don't *have* to have that kind of evidence. I'm not a judge, or a lawyer, or even a cop. I have the luxury of being able to decide for myself."

"Some would question your use of the word 'luxury.'"

"That would be their privilege."

"Have you ever wondered why Asp bothered with Mr. Drake?" Alfred asked. "Why stage the abduction? Why didn't Dr. Kinsolving simply go to Asp on her own?"

"We'll have the answer to *that* when we find Kinsolving."

Shondra had driven only a few miles when Asp ordered her to pull over. "Not until we reach a police station," Shondra said.

Asp produced a small leather case from his pocket. He removed a hypodermic needle from it and, without warning, jabbed it into Shondra's shoulder. "It should hit you in a few seconds," Asp said casually. "It's a quite potent hallucinogen—quite potent. Makes LSD seem like aspirin. If you'd like to continue driving, well . . . the trip will be most interesting. I wonder how many innocent people you'll kill."

Suddenly there were eight different roads in front of the windshield, in eight different colors, skewing in eight different directions. Shondra stopped the car. "I suggest you climb into the backseat and enjoy yourself," Asp said.

But Shondra did not enjoy herself, and was not enjoying herself now. She was in a cottage somewhere, she thought, in Scotland. But she did not know *why* she thought she was in Scotland; something she had heard or seen while she had been hallucinating, perhaps. Hours later, as she was coming off the drug, when the world was again more or less solid and normal, Asp had hurried her into this room and bound her to a chair. Then he'd gone to tend to the car, leaving Shondra to ponder the mistakes she'd made.

The worst had been abandoning Bruce—if that *was* Bruce under those whiskers. She'd made an instant decision—the kind she was no good at— based on sketchy information. Jack Drake needed more medicine than Shondra had available, more than Asp was going to allow her. Bruce just might have a chance against the Russian, but not against Vega *and* Asp. So when Asp had climbed into the seat next to her and ordered her to drive, she had, thinking she'd go only as far as the first place she could to get help for Bruce and Jack Drake and a constable for Asp and Vega. But they'd met no one on the road. And again, she'd underestimated Asp: she should have known that he'd have a weapon—if not a gun, then the hypodermic he *did* have.

Shondra strained her wrists against the loops of rope around them. There was some play; Asp had done a sloppy job of tying her up. If he'd be gone just ten minutes. . . .

She looked out the window. She was pretty sure the sky was darkening—only pretty sure because she had seen the sky do many bizarre and ugly things recently. How long *had* they been driving? At least eight hours. For her, a preview of a sinner's eternity. Asp passed the window and, a moment later, entered the cottage. Shondra tugged at the ropes. Her left wrist was half free.

"What next, Benny?" Shondra asked. "Fists? Whips? Thumb screws? Something even nastier? Because I won't cooperate with you now that you can't threaten me with Jack Drake's death."

Asp grinned. "My dear Shondra, you wound me with your accusations. How many times must I tell you"—he grabbed her hair and forced her head back, then lowered his face until it was almost touching hers—"I abhor violence."

"If someone can hurt you back. I noticed how quickly you abandoned your friend Yuri when he was getting beat up."

"Shondra, Shondra," Asp chuckled. "Sir Hemingford Gray did me a small service there. I was finished with bearish Yuri. I had what I wanted from him—the amplifiers. One way or another, he and I would have parted company within a day or two. I didn't particularly want to kill him, and thanks to Gray, I didn't have to. I say it again—I abhor violence. But not so much that I will hesitate to use it, dear sister. I will prevail. And when I do, I will be able to demand anything from anyone on earth because I will be able to kill at a distance and there will be nothing that can stop me. It is something only gods could aspire to. Until now."

"Does the word *megalomaniac* have any meaning for you, Benny?" Shondra could feel her own warm blood on her wrist and hand; she had torn away skin. But the loops were at her knuckles. Only a bit more—

Then her hand was free! She was still partially bound to the chair, but her left hand was loose. As Shondra was getting to her feet, she lifted and swung the chair at Asp's head. It connected. The high back snapped off at the impact, and the last of Shondra's bonds fell to the floor.

Asp was glassy-eyed, blinking, rubbing the place where the chair had struck him.

Shondra bolted for the door, opened it, and faced a huge man, almost seven feet tall. He had a jagged scar across his forehead. He wore round glasses tinted dark blue, a black, sleeveless T-shirt, and black jeans. He hit her.

"Silly slut," Asp said, looking down at her. "Did you think I'd leave this room unguarded? This is Fritz, a valued associate from my drug-running days. I arranged for him to meet us here the day before last. Fritz, this is my sister Sandra . . . ah, but you've *already* met."

Asp grabbed Shondra's hair and dragged her to another chair. With Fritz's help, he again bound her. Fritz tested the knots; they were secure and tight. Asp left the room and returned with a small leather case. He took a hypodermic from it.

"I've been to that show," Shondra said. "Don't you have any other tricks?"

"Ah, my dear, this *is* another trick. Entirely. During my years as a . . . ah, supplier of custom pharmaceuticals, I experimented with a great many compounds. You will remember that I *am* a genius and consequently I was uncommonly successful. Now this"—he held up the needle —"began as a truth serum. Some Latin American customers found other uses for it. It is quite excellent at neutralizing willpower."

Asp injected Shondra with the drug. Waiting for it to become effective, he said conversationally, "Pity we lost Drake. We might have gotten another couple of days out of him before we lost him *permanently*. But he was in sorry shape. Sooner or later, I would have had to find another way past your inhibitions."

"Why didn't you use . . . drug from the . . . beginning?" Shondra felt as though she were speaking through a mouthful of molasses.

"Ah, the gallant lady seeks to combat my little pharmaceutical miracle with conversation," Asp cried. "And I, generous fellow that I am, see no reason to deny her. Well, Drake was a target of opportunity, dear sister. You were with him when my associates found you. It would have been *wasteful* not to use him."

Shondra struggled to form the words she wanted to say. "How'd you locate me?"

"How did I locate you? Is that the question? The answer is, not easily. For years I searched for my beloved sibling, on and off. But other matters kept distracting me. Finally I followed a few suggestions of Yuri's and my associates were able to trace you. You know the rest."

Shondra strained against the ropes.

Asp turned to Fritz. "There's a matter I wish you'd attend to. An English nobleman named Sir Hemingford Gray. He apparently knows my dear sister, and he was instrumental in freeing Drake. He is obviously not the twit he pretends to be. I consider him a danger. See if you can find him."

"Then what?"

"Eliminate him."

Shondra slumped in her chair.

14

Bruce finished pasting the muttonchop whiskers onto his face. He had already dyed his hair and inserted the cheek pads. "Sir Hemingford lives," he murmured.

"I thought we had retired Sir Hemingford," Alfred said.

In Sir Hemingford's voice, Bruce said, "Not a bit of it, old dog. Sir Hem might still be useful to us, don't y'know? For one thing, if the yank Wayne had rented this house, there'd be a pother in the tabloids. Wayne the billionaire is news whilst Sir Hem is just another dotty British eccentric."

He smiled Sir Hemingford's smug smile into the mirror and picked up a telephone.

"Calling Master Timothy?" Alfred asked.

"Right-o. Asked him to do a spot of work for me, don't y'know?" Into the phone: "Hallo Tim?"

"How's my dad?" Tim Drake asked from seven thousand miles away.

"Doing well. Doctors here say he has a good chance. We'll keep you posted."

"I haven't thanked you for saving him—"

"Not necessary, lad."

"About that information you asked me to get . . . I hacked into the med school records and learned that Shondra's name isn't Shondra Kinsolving. It's Sandra Asplin. She's from a little town upstate called Slag Lake. She was adopted when she was six by Mr. and Mrs. Amos Asplin. Mrs. Asplin is still alive, still living in Slag Lake."

"Very good. We'll be in touch."

"May I speak to him?" Alfred asked.

Sir Hemingford handed him the phone.

"Timothy? Hello, lad. How . . . is everything?"

"Jean Paul, you mean? I haven't seen him. I guess he's locked in the Cave."

"No news is good news, eh? I'll be in touch. Cheers, lad."

Alfred gave the phone back to Sir Hemingford.

"Anything else on your mind, lad?" Sir Hemingford asked.

"Not . . . a lot. Some things. I guess they'll keep till I see you again."

"Not the sort of matter you'd care to discuss on an open line, that it?"

"I guess not," Tim murmured.

"Right-o. Keep well."

As Sir Hemingford was cradling the receiver, he glanced into the mirror he'd used to put on his disguise and saw a man wearing a ski mask lifting a handgun. He flung the phone sideways, ripping the cord from the wall in the process, and yelled, "Alfred—*down!*" The phone crashed through the window and hit the gunman in the face. Sir Hemingford hobbled to the window in time to see the gunman top a fence and vanish into the next yard. He hung one of his canes over his left wrist and grasped his ribs with his right hand.

"You've hurt yourself," Alfred said.

"Not now. There may be others. Call the police."

Sir Hemingford, pale and trembling, followed Alfred into the hall, which had no outside windows, and sat while Alfred spoke to a desk sergeant.

"Your hit man *failed?*" Benedict Asp shook his head.

"He's a good man," Fritz said angrily.

"Not good enough, evidently."

"There's another possibility."

"Is there?" Asp raised an eyebrow.

"Maybe this Hemingford guy is better than he looks. From what you told me, he handled the Russkie, too."

"You have a point," Asp said. "A very good point. Sir Hemingford Gray is much, much more than he appears to be. He is, in point of fact, a danger to me." He went to where Shondra lay handcuffed to a bedpost and looked down at her. She was unconscious, breathing heavily through her mouth; her dark skin glistened with a patina of sweat. "Perhaps dear sister Sandra here is the answer to Sir Hemingford Gray."

Bruce Wayne glanced briefly at the lights of Gotham City from the window of the Lear Jet, then turned to Alfred and said, "We'll get a room in Gotham tonight and get an early start to Slag Lake in the morning."

"May I ask why we are not returning to the manor?"

"For one thing, it's on the other side of town. Way out of our way. For another, I don't want Jean Paul to feel we're intruding on him."

"You didn't *give* him the house."

"No, Alfred, but I want him to have a free hand, at least until he feels easy in his new job."

"I never thought of being Batman as a *job*."

"Vocation. Mission. Hobby. Whatever."

"What do we hope to accomplish in Slag Lake?"

"We've hit a brick wall going forward. So we'll go backward. To where Shondra—or *Sandra*—began. Sometimes there's a clue to the present in the past."

"The story of your life," Alfred said dryly.

Shondra twisted in the chair, straining against the ropes that bound her, eyes squeezed shut, teeth clenched.

"—remember, my little Sandra," Asp said. "Remember the house in Slag Lake—"

—pretty little white house with a wide front porch and a green lawn and a picket fence—

"—and our dear mother Minnie Asplin—"

—thin woman wearing a faded housedress, always twisting her fingers nervously or tugging at the ends of her brown hair, always apologizing—

"—and most of all, remember daddy dear, Amos Asplin—"

—almost as thin as Minnie, shiny black hair slicked back, three-piece suit neatly pressed, gold-rimmed glasses glittering—

"Remember how he was a pillar of the community, active in church affairs and the Rotary and the town council. Remember how everyone admired him, praised his generosity and kindness, particularly his kindness in adopting a little black child from the city, providing a home and all the benefits of life in an ideal American community."

"I remember," Shondra said.

"Remember how he would beat you and scream names at you. 'Dirty pickaninny slut.' You hated him. Remember the time I tried to interfere and he pushed me away? I hit my head on the table and he said, 'Serves you right.' And Minnie just stood there doing nothing, as usual. You hate her, too."

"Yes," Shondra murmured.

"Later, you tried to help me. You touched the cut on my head and at first nothing happened. But then—"

Kneeling by her little white brother, dabbing at his tearstained cheeks with the hem of her dress, Sandra put her finger on the ugly cut just above his hairline and—

"We connected," Shondra murmured, and a smile tugged at the corners of her lips.

—felt their minds rush together like separate streams of water melding into one and become energized—

Shondra's smile widened.

—the edges of Benny's skin drew close and knitted together—

"And then one day he came in with the whip. Do you remember what happened next, Sandra?"

Shondra bit her lower lip. A thin trickle of blood slid down her chin.

. . .

"That cut on the boy's head healed right up," Minnie Asplin told Bruce Wayne and Alfred.

"Go on," Bruce said.

They were in the living room of the Asplin's white frame house in Slag Lake. Bruce occupied a large, worn easy chair with lace doilies on the arms, Alfred sat on one end of an equally worn sofa; and Minnie Asplin perched on the front edge of a wooden rocker. Her fingers twisted nervously as she spoke.

"Pretty soon they was healing other folks hereabouts," Minnie said. "Got quite a reputation for it. Seems like neither one could do much alone, but when they put their heads together . . . Well, some as called it a miracle. 'Course Amos, he hated it. Said it was an abomination. Said it was the devil's work. He beat the girl worse'n ever."

Alfred regarded Minnie Asplin. *She's lonely. She's glad to have someone to talk to, even potential enemies.* "May I ask why you did not interfere with such barbarity?" he asked.

"Them days, a wife done as her husband told her."

"Mrs. Asplin, forgive me," Bruce said. "But Mr. Asplin was obviously a racist. So why did he adopt a black child?"

"What I finally figured out was . . . he wanted someone he could feel good about hurting. Feel righteous, using a belt on something he thought was evil."

Alfred bowed his head. "Good Lord," he murmured.

"What finally happened to him?" Bruce asked.

"One day, he was meaner'n usual. He come in with an old buggy whip he found somewhere. Said he was going to take the skin off her. He goes into the bedroom where the two of them was and he raises that whip and all of a sudden he grabs his chest and just keels over. Dead as a doornail, he was."

Minnie stared at the carpet, rocking gently.

After a minute, Bruce said quietly, "And then?"

"Sandra, she was scared. She swore she'd never use what she called her 'power' again. Pretty soon she run away. I got a card from her years later. She wrote as how she changed her name and gone to medical school."

"What about the boy?" Bruce asked.

"He run away a couple of days after Sandra. I never heard a word from him. I don't know if he's alive or dead."

Alfred glanced at Bruce. Bruce shook his head *no*.

Suddenly Minnie stopped rocking. Her thin hands went to her chest and she started to stand.

"Mrs. Asplin!" said Alfred, also rising.

Minnie's legs folded and she sat on the arm of the rocker and, when it overturned under her weight, fell to the floor. Her left leg twitched twice, and she lay still.

Alfred knelt next to her and put his finger on a thin wrist. He looked to where Bruce was still sitting in the easy chair. "She's dead, Master Bruce."

"Just like the people in Monkleigh," Bruce said.

15

"We did it," Benedict Asp said, clapping his hands. "I *know* we did. I could *feel* it." He leaned over and kissed Shondra on the cheek. She did not respond; her eyes remained closed. "I was sure you had the hate in you yet. I just had to get past your silly superego."

"Exactly *what* did you do?" Fritz asked.

Removing the psionic cap from his head, Asp said, "We killed the old witch, just as we killed her husband twenty years ago. Only this time we did it from seven thousand miles away."

"That's good, huh?"

Asp removed Shondra's cap. "*Very* good. Eventually, it will make us very rich men. The richest in history, in point of fact. First, however, we have one more annoyance to take care of. Its name is Hemingford Gray."

Bruce Wayne used the car phone, and a Texas drawl, to call the Slag Lake sheriff's office and report a death in the Asplin house.

"I feel dreadful, just leaving her like that," Alfred said from the front seat.

"Me too," Bruce said. "But there was nothing we could do for her. The funeral home will get a large, anonymous donation to pay for her funeral."

The car was passing a sign which read:

LEAVING SLAG LAKE

HAVE A NICE DAY

Alfred stepped on the gas.

Bruce removed a laptop computer from a leather case, plugged it into a telephone jack, and began tapping the keys.

"Getting something from Master Tim?" Alfred asked.

"A computer feed."

"Another modern miracle—Master Timothy operates a keyboard in Gotham and you share the results in a speeding automobile two hundred miles away."

"They also have indoor toilets these days," Bruce said.

Bruce adjusted the brightness control on the computer screen. "Tim's gotten a make on Benedict Asp. His real name is Asplin, of course. Benjamin Asplin. Adopted at age three by Mr. and Mrs. Amos Asplin."

"Evidently not for the same reason his sister was."

"True. Old Amos apparently wasn't into beating *white* children. Benjamin has quite a history. Brilliant student. IQ of one-eighty. But he flunked out of medical school after he was caught selling organs from fresh corpses."

"Charming."

"Next he seems to have gotten into the designer drug business. He was also involved with the Russian KGB. The CIA thinks he spent time at their parapsychology lab in Moscow. Then he vanished for a dozen or so years. The feds assumed he was dead."

"Master Bruce, the various authorities seem to have a lively interest in this Asp. Have you considered giving them what you've learned, anonymously, of course, and letting them deal with him?"

Bruce was silent.

"Still fretting about Dr. Kinsolving, are we?"

"Alfred, I consider this discussion closed."

. . .

Asp fitted the cap to Shondra's head. "You may as well relax, Sandra. Or do you still prefer 'Shondra'?"

"Please, Benny, not again. Not after the slaughter in that village—"

"Ah. You know about that?" Asp adjusted a second cap on his own head.

"At the time, I just knew we'd done something horrible. Later, I heard you telling someone about it."

"A conversation I had with Fritz when I thought you were asleep." Asp was holding a hypodermic needle up in front of his eyes. He tapped it with a fingernail and squirted a tiny jet of liquid from the end. "And are you also aware of how we took a long-overdue revenge on Mother dearest?"

"Yes. I could . . . *feel* her die."

"Yes, pleasant, wasn't it?"

Asp jabbed the needle into Shondra's shoulder and thumbed the plunger.

"Benny . . . please."

"You *loved* what we did to the old witch," Asp said. "It's something you've wanted to do for years."

"No—"

"Yes. You hated her. You *had* to. As you hated the old man."

"I didn't want to . . . kill them . . ."

"But you *did*, little Sandra. And somewhere, deep inside, you're grateful to me for giving you the opportunity."

A roaring. She was in a black tunnel and wind was roaring around her, past her, through her. In the wind, she heard Benny's voice, his accusation—"You did, little Sandra"—and she screamed, "No, No," but she wasn't sure anyone could hear—

"But yes, Sandra. Yes, indeed. You have an anger inside you that's all the stronger for being so well hidden."

The tunnel changed from black to a fierce red, became a long tube of fire, and flames licked into Shondra's—Sandra's—heart, and she knew that what Benny was saying was true—

"Now," said Asp, "we turn our attention to Sir Hemingford Gray whom we met, briefly, outside the house at Monkleigh."

Shondra's lips formed the word: *Bruce.*

"He knew you. He obviously realized you were in danger."

Did he?

"He could have rescued you."

But didn't he try?

"Instead, he abandoned you. As your natural mother and father abandoned you."

And he lied to me. He lied about who he was. Lied from the very beginning. He expected me to believe his lies about being weak.

"They had no right to abandon you. *He* had no right to abandon you."

He had no right to lie to me.

"You hate him for that."

Do I?

"Let the energy pour out of you."

No, not hate. Not for Bruce.

"Let it come to me so I can amplify it and transform it and send it to—"

Sir Hemingford Gray. Bruce Wayne. She saw them, saw him, as clearly as if he were standing in front of her, and felt a surge of emotion. Love? Yes. Something she had always believed in but had never experienced. But—

"No no no," she cried because—

Bruce was disintegrating. His face was separating into sharp-edged pieces and the pieces were flying apart, as though he were a jigsaw puzzle suddenly caught in a high wind. And then there was nothing except a dreary room in a dreary cottage and Benny Asplin wearing a ridiculous beanie. . . .

"Master Bruce, are you all right?"

Bruce had suddenly stopped as Alfred was helping him from the car, leaned on his canes, and gazed with empty eyes at the sidewalk.

"Huh?" He met Alfred's stare and smiled. "Sorry. I must have zoned out." He began to limp toward the entrance to a hotel where Wayne Industries kept a suite. "I flashed on our fictitious friend, Sir Hemingford. I have this odd feeling that if he existed—"

They passed through the revolving doors into the lobby.

"—he would have died," Bruce concluded.

Shondra's head had fallen onto her chest.

"She okay?" Fritz asked.

"Yes. These little brain gymnastics apparently take a lot out of her," Asp said. "Personally, I find them invigorating."

"Yeah, well, how'd it go?"

"I don't really know. I have an odd feeling that something didn't work. When we directed our attentions to Mother dearest, I was *sure* the crone croaked. But Gray—I wish I could be sure. Ah well, we are in terra incognita. Who can *guess* what a particular feeling means? I have other matters to attend to, specifically the acquisition of fifty billion dollars. And possibly the murder of a world leader or two."

16

 The elevator doors had just slid open when Bruce felt the pain. His left knee buckled, and for a moment he teetered on his canes before he lost the center of gravity and toppled to the rug.

"Master Bruce," Alfred said, kneeling beside him. "What's wrong?"

"Don't know," Bruce said through clenched teeth. "Trouble standing."

"I'll get you to a hospital immediately."

Alfred scurried to the door of the suite, opened it with a key from his ring, and entered and used the telephone in the foyer. Within a minute, two uniformed hotelmen and a detective in a shiny blue suit were next to Alfred, hovering over Bruce. But there was nothing any of them could do. A quarter of an hour later, paramedics from Central Medical Center arrived. Smiling and murmuring encouraging words, they carefully put Bruce onto a stretcher and took him down to the lobby and out to a waiting ambulance.

One of them, a blond light heavyweight with freckles named Jimmy, remained with him as, outside, a siren howled and the ambulance crept through midtown traffic.

"Hey, Mr. Wayne, we got no problem here," Jimmy said cheerily. "Just routine. You're gonna be on your feet tomorrow, next day at the latest."

If Shondra were waiting for me at the hospital, I might believe that. Then, shocked, Bruce remembered. *Shondra isn't a healer anymore. She's a murderer. A mass murderer.* And then: *Can't think about that. Got to deal with the present. Get control of breathing. Focus on the pain. Stop fighting and let it happen.*

He was transferred onto a gurney and hustled through a corridor that smelled of antiseptic. A young man in thick glasses rolled up his sleeve and laid a needle against his upper arm.

"Is that necessary?" Bruce asked. "The pain's under control."

"Just relax," the young man said as the needle stung Bruce's flesh and the universe ebbed away.

And returned and went away several times in what some part of Bruce's mind knew were the next several days. He could have fought the drugs successfully—that was a trick he'd learned from *several* mentors— but he chose not to, and he didn't know why. The pain was present, but not bothersome and, anyway, not under his control. Finally, shapes hardened and colors muted; he stopped drifting through a nonplace and felt the crispness of the sheets over him and under him, the firmness of the mattress.

The young man in the thick glasses entered the room and smiled. "Dr. Hornaday. We've already met but you might not remember."

"You told me to relax," Bruce said.

"I did, yes, and you did. Good. Well."

"What's the prognosis?" Bruce asked and almost added, *Give it to me straight, Doc.*

"I wish I had better news, Mr. Wayne."

"I have a feeling that I'm going to wish that, too."

"But the truth is that your back was broken and you've done nothing to help the healing process."

"You're not the first doctor to tell me that." But at least Hornaday wasn't furious, as Holder had been. Rather, young Dr. Hornaday seemed bemused.

"Bottom line, it doesn't look good. I'm ordering you to stay in bed until we work out a treatment plan."

"Seems reasonable."

"If you want anything—books, television, tapes, whatever—just let the nurse know."

"I'll have my man Alfred bring some things."

"As long as he doesn't bring roller skates."

"I'll try to dissuade him."

At the door, Hornaday turned and said, "I'm glad you've kept your sense of humor, Mr. Wayne. It'll help. But please don't kid yourself. Your condition is serious."

"Noted, Doctor. And thanks."

So he'd have to let the trail get cold. Okay, he would. And when he was recovered, he'd find it again. More than once he'd located a fugitive by following a lead that was years old when he got it. Asp and Shondra would have to be somewhere on the planet, and as long as that was true, they wouldn't be able to hide from him.

Meanwhile . . . he hadn't read a book that had nothing to do with a pending investigation in years, nor had he seen a movie, or a television program purely for pleasure. He'd use his enforced leisure to discover what being ordinary could feel like. His only fear was that he might enjoy it.

"*Reported gunshots, possible domestic disturbance.*" Horror reduced to the formality of a police radio dispatch. A man, a woman, three children. The patrolmen who had answered that innocuous call had found all five slaughtered. Someone had changed their neat, well-kept suburban home into a butcher shop.

Batman had been busy with other matters—with a small-time hood named Roggy Benet—when the cops first got the report. He waited to see Roggy loaded into an ambulance and then returned to the Cave where, as he did every night, he listened to tapes of radio traffic. The usual stuff—robbery, assault, arson, burglary, and yes, murder; he was used to hearing it and resigned to being unable to do anything about most of it. But the slaughter of an entire family—even for Gotham that was horrifying. The kind of crime that Bruce Wayne would have certainly taken as a challenge. So Jean Paul Valley would, too. But he needed more information. Call Gordon? That would probably do, but Gordon's manner had been chilly lately. Better to get in touch with that fat detective, Bullock. Harvey Bullock. Harvey Bullock seemed to *like* this new Batman.

Batman's terse, infrequent conversations with Bullock were his only human contact since he'd exiled Robin. He never left the Cave during the day; he could sustain himself with emergency rations Wayne had stored: dried fruits, grains, vitamin pills. The Cave itself supplied water; a cool subterranean stream that widened occasionally into small pools trickled from one end to the other. He could bathe in the pools, and that was all the washing he needed to do; he saw no reason to launder his clothes, nor to shave, nor cut or comb his hair. His father had taught him, again and again, that mere amusements—theater, television, music—were not worthy; they had never been part of his existence and so he did not miss them. He didn't miss friends, either; he'd never had any. He understood *loneliness* only as an abstraction. He was pleased with himself, certain that as Batman he was serving everything that was righteous.

Without any awareness that he was speaking aloud, he began a familiar prayer: "I vow to walk the path of virtue each night of my life—"

"Then do you forsake *me?*"

Jean Paul whirled. Who had spoken? Who was in the Cave with him?

"Oh, faithless son!"

There, in the shadows, a figure in medieval armor glowed with an inner light. A *familiar* figure.

"Father?" Jean Paul breathed.

"He who begot you is dead. I am *his* father and your father and father to all who walk in righteousness."

"Saint . . . Dumas?"

The figure glowed brighter. "Why do you deny me by donning the mantle of another man?"

"I don't know what you mean."

St. Dumas swept his hand downward—a swift, slashing motion. *"The mantle of another man!"*

Jean Paul looked down at the costume he wore.

"First, you swear allegiance to this Bruce Wayne—"

"I never *swore*—"

"Silence! First Wayne, and now this Bullock!"

Jean Paul was on his knees, eyes downcast, hands clasped. "Only to get information. Bullock is nothing. I don't *like* him." Jean Paul struggled to find the words that would convince the saint of his innocence. "He's fat and . . . he smells bad. I deal with him only to better serve *you*."

Now St. Dumas's voice was softer, almost kindly. "Would that this were true."

"It *is!*"

"Perhaps."

"I will obey you—anything you say—"

"Yes." And now the saint's voice was deep, soothing. "Continue as you are. But hear me well, my son: what you do is in the final reckoning a test. Remember—Azrael does not protect. Azrael does not preserve. Azrael avenges!"

"A test? What do you mean?" But there was no reply, only a distant drip of water and a faint slapping that might have been the sound of bats' wings. Jean Paul raised his eyes. He was again alone in the Cave.

He remained kneeling for almost an hour, eyes closed, trying to fathom what had been said to him. It was confusing, contradictory. Only one thing seemed clear: *Continue as you are.* The saint had given him permission to visit Harvey Bullock.

Then something seemed to explode in the center of his brain: *What if the saint's visitation had been an hallucination? What if he had been giving himself permission to do what his own corrupt, selfish ego wanted to do? What if there was no St. Dum—*

Suddenly he was certain he could feel his body disintegrating, each atom separating and spinning away from its mates, leaving only a void. But the feeling passed. He opened his eyes and saw himself solid and intact, and he laughed at his moment of doubt.

Harvey Bullock's neighbors often complained of his cigars. Once a visitor was inside the front door of his apartment building, it was possible to smell them—no, impossible *not* to smell them. As the visitor climbed the steps toward Harvey's third-floor unit, the smell got stronger until, standing on his worn and filthy welcome mat, pressing his buzzer, the odor congealed in the visitor's sinuses and then expanded to fill first the visitor's head, then his body, and finally the universe. So the neighbors bitched. And Harvey flashed his badge and hinted that in about two seconds flat he could have anybody in Gotham City tossed out of their apartment and on their ass in the street. He'd hold up a pair of stubby, dirt-encrusted fingers. "Two seconds," he'd say, grinning.

Batman was having trouble breathing as he entered Bullock's place through a fire escape window. He remembered his father's descriptions of hell and wondered if the sulfurous pits stank like this. It was four in the morning; he expected Bullock to be asleep. But Harvey was wide awake, slouched in an easy chair in front of the television watching the holiday season's first showing of *It's a Wonderful Life*. Three empty doughnut cartons and two pizza boxes littered the bare floor around his feet. He had a beer can in one hand and a smoldering cigar stub in the other. A shoulder holster with a .38 Police Special was slung over the back of the chair, and when he heard Batman step into the room, he dropped the beer and reached for it.

"You won't need to shoot me," Batman said.

"Well, maybe not right away," Harvey said conversationally, as though masked vigilantes were to be expected at four in the morning. "You want a brew? I can't offer you nothing else—it's a little late for dinner."

"I want information."

"The killings out in the 'burbs, right? That'd be your kind of thing."

"What can you tell me?"

"Nothing you'll wanna hear," Bullock said. "Mom, Dad, two sons, eight and five, and a daughter, six, beaten, shot, cut up. Make you puke. We'll know more after the autopsies."

"Motive?"

"No vandalism, no sign of missing valuables. Nut case, probably."

Batman moved closer to Bullock. "What was the family name?"

"Old man was Kenyon Etchison. Worked for the electric company. Wife's name Sara—without the 'h.' Kids were William, Jane, Jonathan."

"Anything else?"

"You want to see what they looked like?" Harvey heaved himself to his feet and lumbered to where a trench coat was thrown on a scarred coffee table. He removed something from a pocket and handed it to Batman. "We took that from the bedroom. Boys down at the photo lab made copies."

Batman was looking at a color snapshot. In the flickering glow of the television, the five people in the picture seemed frail and ghostly. "Can I take this?" he asked.

"Sure, I can get another in the morning," Bullock said.

Batman turned toward the fire escape. "You'll hear from me."

"Hey," Harvey said suddenly as Batman was half out the window. "You the one took out Roggy Benet last night?"

Batman nodded.

"Pretty good, there. Ya know, for a long time you didn't show me much. But lately, I been liking your moves."

Later, in the Cave, Jean Paul stared at the photograph. Here, under powerful incandescent light, the Etchisons looked healthy, robust, cheerful—the ideal American family. Father, children, mother. The woman looked both sweet and strong, beautiful and kind of sexy.

"I wonder what *my* mother was like," Jean Paul said aloud.

Nobody, not even St. Dumas, answered him.

Bruce, who had been the best student in the history of Evelyn Wood's Gotham branch, read five books in the ninety minutes following the hospital breakfast, but one of them, *The Tao Te Ching*, was so short it hardly counted. At eleven, Alfred and four men in jumpsuits arrived. The men uncrated a forty-inch television and began installing it.

"Complete with cable," Alfred said, somewhat proudly.

"How'd you manage *that?*" Bruce asked. "Most hospitals don't have cable."

"This one didn't either, until an hour ago. I had a microwave dish installed on the roof—very quietly, I assure you. We shall, of course, be obligated to donate it to the institution once we leave."

"We will be glad to do so," Bruce said.

Using the remote, he switched on the set and channel surfed past talk shows, game shows, home shopping, a black and white movie, a rerun of "Magnum PI" and a cartoon called "Beavis and Butt-head," until he came to a newscast. He was about to skip that, too, when he heard a familiar name: *"—village of Monkleigh."*

He thumbed up the volume. *"Repeating our top story,"* the announcer said gravely into the camera, *"Undersecretary Folsome K. Feldon today told reporters that the president has received a death threat. According to Undersecretary Feldon, a note faxed to the White House said the president and four other heads of state would be killed unless they each deliver ten billion dollars to a Mr. Uraeus."*

"Uraeus . . . the sacred *asp* on the heads of Egyptian deities," Bruce muttered.

"What an astonishing thing to know," Alfred said.

"The note apparently cited the deaths of forty citizens of the English village of Monkleigh as proof of Uraeus's ability to make good on the threat," the announcer continued. *"The note also cited the death of Sir Hemingford Gray and said the leaders have until Thursday to answer the ultimatum. White House spokesmen indicated that the president has no intention of complying. Sources in the administration said that Undersecretary Feldon may be subject to disciplinary action for speaking to the press without the president's permission—"*

Bruce switched off the set and threw back the sheet that had covered him. He swung his legs over the side of the bed.

"What do you think you're doing?" Alfred demanded.

"This is Monday. I've got till Thursday."

Alfred put his hands on Bruce's shoulders, a liberty he had not taken in all his years of service to the Wayne family. "Absolutely not! You *heard* what the doctor said—"

Bruce shrugged free of Alfred's hands and reached for his canes. "Asp thinks Hemingford Gray is dead. Okay, we make a big noise about Hem being *alive*. Accuse the press of sensationalism. Threaten to sue. Press conferences, public outrages, whatever it takes. That gives me—"

"No!" Alfred's voice quivered. "Bruce, I have never questioned you before. Nor have I, for one moment, ever been disloyal. You have given

me an extraordinary life—a life I have cherished and hope to continue cherishing. But I will not be part of your self-destruction. Anything but that. If you do not obey the doctor's orders, I shall resign my post."

Bruce grasped a cane in each hand and planted them on the floor. He looked at Alfred. "Please try to understand. All I am is a man who serves an ideal. It's not something I can do halfway. If I've got to die in that service, the sacrifice would be regrettable, but if I shy back from the *possibility* of dying, my life has meant nothing."

Alfred stepped away, straightened, and announced, "In that case, Mr. Wayne, I hereby tender my resignation, effective immediately. Good day, sir."

He strode from the room.

Bruce stared after him. *I think he means it.*

Bruce put his weight on the canes and limped to the door, but the corridor was empty.

Alfred was gone.

17

Alfred stepped onto the sidewalk in front of the hospital and waved to a cabdriver who had just discharged a passenger. The driver motioned him into the cab. Alfred settled into the backseat and told the driver, "Wayne Manor, if you please. I shall direct you."

"You kiddin' me, pal?" The driver looked at Alfred over his shoulder and sneered. "That's more'n twenty miles outside the city limits."

"Ah. You are familiar with the area. An excellent quality for a taximan to possess. I commend you."

"Take a hike."

"If I do, it shall be directly to Commissioner Bartley, of the taxi and limousine department—a fine gentleman who has dined at the manor on numerous occasions. I shall tell him that"—Alfred leaned forward and squinted at the driver's framed license on the dashboard—"a Mr. Henry Goldwing refused a legitimate commission."

"Okay, okay," the driver grumbled. He put the car in gear and joined the traffic stream.

The city thinned until they were passing only occasional clusters of shops, and then only an occasional isolated house. It was a route Alfred had traveled often, thousands of times, and yet today, in the flat winter sunlight, it seemed alien. Alfred was startled when he realized that something inside him was aching.

The cab stopped in front of the manor's main entrance. Alfred handed the driver an amount of money he had carefully counted out.

"You call this a tip?" the driver shouted. "Lousy six-fifty? For alla way out *here?*"

"It is precisely fifteen percent of the fare. I believe that is the recommended rate."

"Stinkin' limies," the driver said, but Alfred had already shut the cab door and was moving toward the walk.

The driver spun his wheels, spraying gravel, as he sped down the drive.

Alfred looked at the lawn, the brown, dead winter grass littered with newspapers, and winced. He started to put his key into the lock and paused when he saw a cobweb hanging from the knob. "Disgraceful," he said.

He entered the house and stopped at the foyer table, ran a forefinger over the surface, and left a trail in dust. "Barbaric," he said.

"What do you want?" someone asked from behind him. Batman stood framed in an inner door. "I asked you a question."

"I came looking for you," Alfred said.

"You found me."

"May I ask you to remove the mask? And to speak in your normal voice?"

Batman was motionless for a moment. Then he slowly reached up and bared his face. He clutched the mask to his chest. Alfred thought, *How young he looks!*

"Okay," Jean Paul said.

"I have come to ask for your help," Alfred said.

"For yourself? Or for *him?*"

"For Mr. Wayne."

"Listen, he *quit!* I'm the Batman now."

"Yes, precisely. You are the Batman and he *needs* the Batman."

"Bruce Wayne needs *me?*"

"Someone very powerful will try to kill him soon. He refuses to take precautions. His only hope is for you to—"

"Not interested, Mr. Pennyworth."

"I could appeal to your vanity," Alfred said. "I could tell you that Mr. Wayne's enemy could be the most dangerous criminal on earth and that to capture him would be a splendid feather in your cap. But I shall not. Instead, I ask you a simple question: are you what you claim to be? *Are you the Batman?*"

"Yes, of course I am."

"And would the Batman refuse to help someone in mortal danger? Would the Batman condone murder?"

Jean Paul pressed the mask to his chest.

"Would he, Jean Paul?" Alfred said softly.

"Tell me about it," Jean Paul said.

"Mr. Wayne is a patient at Central Medical Center. If he's not there, you might look for Sir Hemingford Gray. *Batman* should require no more information than that."

"I'll find him. I'll save him." Jean Paul raised the mask and put it on.

"I'm certain you will," Alfred said.

"What are *you* going to do?"

Alfred gazed around the foyer, from the vaulted ceiling with its hanging chandelier, to the parquet floor, to the dusty table. "I shall clean this grand old house. For the last time."

Bruce maneuvered his wheelchair out of the elevator. He'd been in residence here, at the Ritz Gotham, for four days and he had yet to detect any sign of Asp.

Time to up the ante.

The man the staff of the Ritz knew as Sir Hemingford Gray took a deep breath and rolled his chair across the thick carpet of the city's most expensive hotel toward a six-by-six-foot painting depicting pink cherubs with white wings and gold halos playing silver harps amid fleecy clouds. It was an original by Oslo Frelgolard, a nineteenth-century romantic whose work is sometimes given credit for prompting the reaction that eventually gave birth to abstract expressionism.

"Going to do you blokes a favor," Sir Hemingford said to a bellhop. He stopped in front of the Frelgolard and peered at it. "Monstrosity," he announced loudly. "Insult to the eyes. Ugly as sin." Sir Hemingford fumbled in the pocket of his jacket and produced a platinum cigarette lighter. The hotel security chief, who had just arrived and was walking briskly toward the front desk, stopped to watch the eccentric Brit who had earned the enmity of the staff with his outrageous demands and their gratitude with the size of his tips when those demands were met. Sir Hemingford flicked the lighter, and when it was alight applied the flame to the lower frame of the painting. "Someone should have done this a hundred years ago," he said.

The security chief grabbed a fire extinguisher from behind the desk and charged past Sir Hemingford, who was leaning back in his wheelchair and rubbing his hands as fire began to nip at the ankle of a particularly chubby cherub. The security chief discharged a blast of mist from the nozzle of the extinguisher, saving the cherub and the rest of Frelgolard's masterpiece. He turned to Sir Hemingford. "What the *hell* do you think you're doing?"

"My bit to beautify the environment. Don't bother to thank me. It's very like me to be helpful." Sir Hemingford rolled forward, lighter blazing, reaching for the cherubs.

The security chief blasted mist at Sir Hemingford's lighter, grabbed the back of the wheelchair, and yanked. Sir Hemingford swiveled his neck and gazed up at the security chief curiously. "Copper, eh?"

"I'm the chief of hotel security, yes."

"Knew it. Knew you were either a copper or a garbage collector. Should have guessed copper. Garbage man would smell better."

"You're under arrest."

About time!

Sir Hemingford thrust out his wrists and waited for handcuffs.

18

"—and then he insulted the judge, the bailiff, the prosecutor, the mayor, the mayor's mother, and the American flag. And the Boy Scouts." Benedict Asp looked across the top of the tabloid at Fritz. "They finally fined him ten K and costs and turned him loose."

"Then he's in Gotham?"

"And we," Asp said, "are still across the ocean." He waved the newspaper. "According to this, he rented a yacht moored in Gotham Sound."

"That'd be well outside the city."

Asp shrugged. "Yes. That should make it easy for you."

"Meaning?"

"I want you to get him for me. Hire anybody you like, get any supplies you'll need, but don't fail me again."

"That mean I can pop him?"

"No. I've got to know who he really is and how he survived our attack. We'll put him through tests and *then* you can pop him."

●　　●　　●

A chill December fog was just beginning to billow in off the ocean, putting a halo around the lights on the pier and softening the edges of the sheds and pilings. The yacht, a forty-foot converted navy minesweeper, rocked gently beneath Bruce Wayne's wheelchair.

This would be a good night for them to come. Area's deserted. Poor visibility. If they escape over the water, they'll be almost impossible to catch.

Bruce wheeled himself across the captain's cabin to a dressing table. *Might as well get ready for company.* He inserted foam pads into his cheeks and dabbed a touch of gray onto his mustache. He inspected himself in the mirror. The disguise wasn't perfect, but it had fooled the hotel staff, a judge, and assorted journalists, bailiffs, and cops. It would probably also fool Asp's hired muscle for as long as it needed to—if they came tonight. If they *ever* came.

He waited while the fog thickened outside. Water lapped gently against the wooden hull; cables creaked; far away, a ship's horn moaned. He looked out the porthole. The end of the pier was completely shrouded, and the lights were now only dim circles in the mist.

Good. I was right to pick this place. No innocent bystanders to get hurt.

He thought about the past forty-eight hours and about what he was doing. Not being much like Batman, certainly. Batman would know exactly what he wanted to happen, and how he would act when it did, and how he would act if it didn't. Batman would have at least four alternative plans, tactics for each, contingencies for each. Batman would have an array of equipment either secreted on his person or within easy reach. Batman would try to leave nothing to chance but, like the good martial artist he was, would allow for the *possibility* of chance.

He looked in the mirror. Batman did not look back.

So what's old Hemingford Gray doing? Playing with a deck full of wild cards. Setting himself up as bait and hoping to improvise. Oh, he had a few little tricks. His canes were gimmicked to double as weapons, and there was a microwave transmitter hidden in the frame of his wheelchair. But he really had no idea how he might employ these things, or whether they would be of any use to him at all. Mostly, he was doing what Batman never did—trusting to the luck of the moment.

Again, he glanced into the mirror, and saw Sir Hemingford. *Maybe primitive peoples were wiser than we know. Maybe the mask* does *change the wearer.*

He thought he heard something hit the deck outside, but he couldn't be sure; the fog muffled and distorted sounds.

A man wearing a wet suit appeared in the doorway; he was aiming a silenced Uzi machine pistol.

" 'Bout bloody time," Sir Hemingford said, and sneezed. "Well? Where *is* it? I haven't got all night, y'know."

"What the hell you talking about, old man?" the gunman asked.

"The bloody *pizza*. I ordered it an hour ago."

An hour earlier, Jean Paul had finally learned where Sir Hemingford Gray was. He'd spent the day at the Cave's computers, scouring the world's data banks for information about Bruce Wayne's newest alter ego, and had found nothing. Frustration tightened his throat, making his fingers fumble on the keyboard. He was on the edge of rage: Alfred Pennyworth had smugly assumed that finding Gray—or Wayne—would be no problem. Well, it *was*. If locating Wayne was so important, why hadn't the butler *helped?* Because he couldn't? Because, for all his attitude of superiority, he was nothing more than a servant? That, Jean Paul decided, was the answer.

For a moment, the screen blurred and the Cave seemed to tilt. Jean Paul realized that something was wrong—with *him*—and was astonished when he identified what it was: he was hungry. He went to the rations bin. There was no food left in it, just a handful of empty wrappers.

For the first time in almost a month, he went up into the mansion to eat something, and while on his way to the kitchen, he heard the screech of brakes on the drive outside. He opened the front door and saw a newspaper delivery van, barely visible in the fog, moving slowly toward the gate. On the strip of lawn between the stoop and the driveway was a week's worth of the *Gotham Gazette*. He picked them up and as he went back inside glanced at the headlines on the top paper. The usual stuff: war in foreign places, government inefficiency and corruption—things Jean Paul had no interest in—and then:

BRIT TORCHES PAINTING
SIR HEMINGFORD GRAY ARRESTED

He ran down to the Cave and hacked into the Ritz Gotham's guest registration, and there it was: Sir Hemingford Gray—penthouse suite.

Jean Paul rubbed his eyes with his palms. Alfred had said that Bruce was under physicians' care, and so he had searched the data banks of hospitals and those area medical men whose records were computerized. But he hadn't thought of looking at hotels. Nor of reading the newspaper.

Well, okay, so I made a simple mistake. Overlooked something. I'm new at this detective business. I'll learn. And besides, I'm better than him at the things that really count. There's a lot less crime in Gotham City since I put on the mask.

Jean Paul glanced at the photo lying next to the keyboard, the one Bullock had given him. The family. Kenyon Etchison and the kids. That lovely mother.

This is what I should be working on. This horrible massacre. Not chasing an irresponsible fool who sets fire to pictures.

Sir Hemingford Gray, or Bruce Wayne, or whatever he was calling himself, could certainly wait another few hours. Jean Paul had more important work to do.

The kidnappers had come in from the water, boarded the port side of the moored yacht, and taken Sir Hemingford off the same way. As they were lowering his wheelchair onto the motor launch, he had been able to activate the microwave transmitter in the chair. It would bounce a distress signal off both onshore relay stations and a satellite partially leased by Waynetech. But would anyone detect, and home in on, the signal in time? He doubted it.

The launch bounded hard on the chop of the bay, sending spasms of agony from his back to the tips of his fingers. He almost welcomed the jab of the needle that dropped him through a hole in the bottom of his mind.

He awoke once, briefly, as he was being transferred to another boat, and again to a rain that stung his face as he was being carried ashore. Wind was howling, and he had an impression of sand and palm trees before he slid through the hole. . . .

He opened his eyes to a face that filled his vision. The face smiled and receded and spoke.

"Sir Hemingford Gray? Or *is* that your name?"

He was in his wheelchair, and Benedict Asp was standing over him. The room was spacious, furnished with rattan chairs and a low rattan table. A French window to his left was crisscrossed with duct tape. He could hear rain slapping it in waves.

"No matter," Asp said. "I'm less interested in finding out who you are than in learning how you survived my attack."

"Attack?" It wasn't easy to do Sir Hemingford's voice—his throat was dry, his mouth cottony—but he managed it.

"You weren't aware of it?" Asp pursed his lips. "Interesting, if true."

"You're the bloke from Monkleigh, eh? Dammit, man, you were damned rough back there. I've a mind to sue you for damages."

Asp chuckled. He got something off the table and showed it to Sir Hemingford. "I hope you weren't counting on *this*."

Sir Hemingford's brows arched as he looked at the transmitter.

"It was interfering with our navigation gear," Asp continued. "That's how we found it. Very nice. State of the art, I imagine."

"Dunno. Had it installed in Kenya. I've a habit of getting lost. Chap said that'd help."

"He was wrong." Asp turned and called, "Bring her in."

Two of the three kidnappers—Sir Hemingford recognized them from their body language—entered with Shondra shuffling, head bowed, between them. Her short hair was neatly coiffed, and she was wearing a crisp, clean, white linen dress and straw sandals.

"You two don't need to be introduced, do you?" Asp asked pleasantly. "No, of course not. Well, Sir Hemingford, you are no doubt wondering why I threw this little party."

"Can't say I give a damn."

"You will. Let me explain. My dear sister—the dark lady you know as Shondra—has perfected a technique for killing at a distance."

"Telepathy?" Sir Hemingford grumbled. "Some mumbo jumbo like that?"

"Something *very* like it. Shondra here generates energy which I focus and intensify."

"Changes it," Shondra mumbled.

Asp slapped her lightly on the cheek. "Please. Let's remember to speak when spoken to, shall we?"

Asp got another object from the table, a metal cap the size and shape of an old-fashioned beanie. "Recently, a Russian colleague developed this"—he lifted the cap to eye level—"a device that allows me to project Sandra's energy to anywhere on earth. I confess that I don't understand how it works. Pharmaceuticals are my area of expertise."

"Y'used that thing on me?"

"Ah, then you *are* aware of the attack. Yes, we used it on you and you survived nicely. That will *not* do. I've got to learn your secret so I can stop others from interfering with my plans."

"Such as the Yankee president?"

"Of course, you *would* know about that. It *was* on the news. Cost me quite a bit of trouble, that little bit of publicity did. I had to find a White House staffer—Folsome Feldon, I believe his name is—and addict his rather attractive young daughter to a certain stimulant. I promised to *un*addict her if he told the world what I wanted it to hear. Who knows? I may actually make good on my promise." Asp put the metal cap down. "By the way, do you have any idea where you are? Fritz said you slept during most of your journey."

"Judging from the smell of the air and those palm trees outside, I'd say the Caribbean."

"Close. Actually, we're on the coast of Florida."

Sir Hemingford cocked his head. "Sounds like a bad blow's brewing up."

"The season's first tropical storm. By morning, they say it may become a full hurricane. But you probably won't be around to see it." Asp turned to Shondra. "Sister dearest? Time to play our little game."

" 'S not a game." Shondra's words were almost lost in the loud hiss of wind and rain. " 'S bad. Please don't make me do it."

"But you know you *love* it."

"Shondra, listen to me," Bruce said in his own voice. "He's using a hypnotic drug on you—that's *got* to be the answer. But you can fight it."

"But she can't," Asp said smugly. "I notice your voice has changed— no more Monty Python pompous Brit. Is it a voice my sister recognizes, I wonder?" He leaned close to Shondra and spoke into her ear. "A voice belonging to one who has betrayed her as she has been betrayed by her mother and her father and everyone else . . . awakening all the rage and the hate she tries to suppress—"

"Don't listen to him," Bruce shouted.

One of the terrorists stepped behind the wheelchair and cuffed Bruce hard on the side of the head. "Not another peep," he whispered, and put his thick fingers around Bruce's throat.

Asp was behind Shondra, stroking her hair, his cheek against hers. "All that hate—let it go."

Shondra's eyes were wide and staring; tears coursed down her cheeks.

"See him," Asp murmured. "Let your energy go out to him . . . let it come to me and through me to him . . ."

Bruce stiffened. A vein throbbed in his forehead and a trickle of blood leaked from the corner of his lips. His fingers gripped the chair.

"Yes, yes," Asp hissed.

Bruce's mouth opened and he pushed on the chair arms, half lifting himself up. Then, as though the bones had vanished from his body, he collapsed onto the floor.

Shondra, too, relaxed. Her eyes closed, and she swayed slightly. Asp left her and knelt by Bruce.

"He's still breathing," Asp said. "Fritz, lock him in the next room for now. When the slut has recovered, we will try again."

"If it still doesn't work?"

"Then, friend Fritz, you will simply kill him."

19

 James Gordon glanced up from the report he was studying to the rain-streaked window of his office and the blurred lights of the city outside it. The weatherman on his car radio had said there was a tropical storm down south that might reach Gotham by morning. Maybe he should tell his officers to prepare for a blow. He'd monitor the situation, and if the worst seemed likely, he'd issue appropriate orders to the next watch.

"Commissioner Gordon," someone said from the shadows behind him.

Without looking back, Gordon said, "Son, someday you're going to get yourself killed, sneaking around like that."

Robin stepped around the desk into the light from the single lamp on it. "Not if I do it right. And I had a good teacher."

"I guess you did, at that. What's on your mind?"

"Someone said you'd have information about a kidnapping . . . or a threat against the president."

"That 'someone' is him. Your teacher. The real Batman. Not the sadistic clown who's taken his place."

"You know?"

"I'm not an idiot."

"Well, *do* you have the information, Commissioner?"

"He called me at home. Mentioned something that happened on a bridge once to prove his identity. Then he told me to monitor a certain radio frequency."

"A homing signal?"

"You got it." Gordon used a forefinger to push his glasses up his nose and leaned back in his chair. "He said I might find the bastards who wiped out that English village *and* the would-be presidential assassin at the end of it."

"Then *do* it."

"Can't, son. We lost the signal somewhere off the coast of North Carolina."

"Send somebody to wherever you last heard it—"

"We've been in touch with the Coast Guard. They've got a storm down that way, maybe a hurricane. They'll send out choppers when it passes. That could be a couple of days."

Robin moved closer. "In the meantime, there's nothing you can do."

"Afraid not. He's in trouble, isn't he?"

"I don't know. Yes."

"Spinal injury and he still goes after the bad guys."

"How'd you know about that?"

"Once upon a time, I was a pretty good cop. I haven't entirely lost the knack. We got reports of some big guy named Bane snapping Batman across his knee. Two of the witnesses were winos, and we pretty much discount anything they say, but another was a very sober elderly lady on her way to early Mass. Her account agreed with the winos' all the way. That's pretty good circumstantial evidence. But mainly, there's this clown I mentioned. Batman and me aren't exactly poker buddies. I never saw his face and I suspect I've never heard his real voice. But I know he's not a punk. And whoever's wearing his suit is."

"I won't deny anything you've said, Commissioner, except the punk part. He's not that. Maybe better, maybe worse, but not a punk."

"If you say so. I can still get in touch with you through the computer bulletin board?"

"Yes." Robin stepped back into the shadows.

"I'll do that if I hear anything."

"I'd appreciate it."

Gordon returned to his report. It occurred to him that Robin was just a kid, and no matter how smart he was, he wouldn't have all his mentor's moves. Gordon might be able to follow him, at least for a way, and get an idea of where he went. Did Gordon's contract with Batman extend to Robin? He decided it did.

Jean Paul stared at the photograph, as though the mute images might somehow be able to tell him who destroyed this family. But they did not. Should he pray to St. Dumas? Or was there something *else* he could do?

He tapped keys and brought the homicide squad's report up on the screen.

"All damage at the scene was related to the struggle. No vandalism and no evidence of theft. Might mean a crime of passion."

Jean Paul paused. Passion? That was something he knew about only from his reading. Like friendship, it was an abstraction to him. He shrugged and continued to scan the report. It was full of details that added nothing to his knowlege of what had happened to the Etchison family. He removed it from the screen and began to search for data on the family itself. There was a list of relatives, only one of whom interested Jean Paul. That was Kenyon Etchison's first cousin, Arnold, who seemed to have dropped off the earth ten years earlier. No record of illness, death, burial: just . . . nothing, suddenly. Without realizing it, Jean Paul began, silently, to ask for St. Dumas's help. And then he had an idea. He cross-referenced the prison population data base, and then the mental hospitals. The blur of words on the screen slowed and resolved into a file:

ETCHISON, ARNOLD
Age: 40
Height: 6'1"
Weight: 187
Hair: Brown
Eyes: Brown

Distinguishing features: Scar, left shoulder;
scar, right thigh.
AKA: Arnold Ektar; Abattoir

"Yes, thank you," Jean Paul said aloud. He opened the rest of the file and read eagerly. Arnold Etchison, alias Abattoir, was a serial killer specializing in family members, currently at large after the breakout at Arkham Asylum. He had twenty known victims, all but one of them related to him. According to the psychiatrists' reports, Abattoir claimed to "feed on the souls of his dead kinfolk."

Now it's twenty-five victims. He printed out the Abattoir information and went back to the Etchison family file, searching for the next nearest relative. The computer gave him the name of another of Abattoir's cousins: Graham Etchison. He found the name in the Gotham Telephone Directory and dialed Etchison's number. There was a click and:

"Hello. You've reached the residence of Graham Etchison. I can't come to the phone right now, but if you leave a message after the signal, I'll be sure to return your call just as soon as I can. Thank you for calling and have a nice day."

Jean Paul spoke as Batman: "Mr. Etchison, you may be in terrible danger. Please put yourself under police protection as quickly as possible. Call Commissioner James Gordon and mention 'Abattoir.' "

Jean Paul hung up and glanced at the printout he'd made, but he didn't need to; he'd already memorized its contents. Six months ago, Bruce Wayne had tracked Abattoir to the family crypt in St. Dymphna Cemetery. That was where Wayne, as Batman, had found and defeated him. So that was a place to start.

Forty minutes later, the costumed Jean Paul parked the Maserati next to an iron picket fence on a lonely road a few miles outside the Gotham City limits. He used the car's terminal to call up a map of the graves in St. Dymphna's, marked the position of the Etchison family plots, and after climbing over the fence, moved silently among the tombstones. The rain had stopped, but the wind that had driven it was still filling the air with cold. Fat droplets hung from bare branches, glistening in the light from the occasional lampposts; marble grave markers gleamed. The Etchison mausoleum was only about four hundred yards from the road, a large structure of white stone. The door was ajar. Batman shrugged his cape from around his arms to free them, slid his night-vision lenses into place, took a deep breath, and sprang through the doorway.

The low chamber was empty. On a bier in the center was an open coffin; its lid lay on the floor nearby. The coffin was empty except for a single bone from a human thigh. Batman lifted it and peered at the teeth marks at the splintered end—*human* teeth marks. He tossed the bone back into the coffin.

Assume the cemetery is well tended. A keeper would surely discover the damaged mausoleum soon after it was vandalized, within a day or two at most. So Abattoir was probably here after the quintuple murders.

Batman ran for the car. He had to find Graham Etchison.

For a long time, Bruce Wayne didn't know whether he was sleeping or awake. He could see nothing, and he heard only a roar of wind. When he tried to remember where he was, or what had happened to him, he felt a jumble of mixed sensations: a numbness in the center of his forehead, a burst of flame that seemed to start in his brain and spread throughout his body, a sudden assault that wrenched part of his being away to crumble and decay and dissipate. And something else, a *presence* that was kind and comforting. Gradually he became aware of the chair that supported him, and then, abruptly, he knew that he was captive in a house, in Florida, and a tropical storm was raging outside. The woman and the man, Shondra Kinsolving and Benedict Asp—they had tried to kill him. No, that wasn't precisely true: they had attacked something he had created, a second—no, a *third* identity. But *which* identity? He was Batman and he was Bruce Wayne and he was Bruce Wayne and he was Batman and . . . who else? He couldn't remember.

Bruce tried to move. He nodded his head. Okay, his head was intact. His legs: nothing. His right arm: yes, he was able to raise it, to flex the fingers, bend the wrist. His left arm: nothing.

The injury's worse. Left arm's useless.

He must have fallen unconscious. They'd taken him somewhere else in the house, almost certainly locked him in a room. Left him alone, but for how long?

Maybe long enough. He fumbled under the left armrest of the wheelchair, found the hidden compartment, slid it open, and located the small flashlight. He switched on the light and shined it around him. His guess had been right. He was in a small, barren room. No windows, one door. He put the flash in his mouth and wheeled himself to the door. Locked, as he'd suspected. He slipped lockpicks from the compartment.

Old lock. Piece of cake.

He twisted the knob, wheeled himself back, and pulled the door open. *Okay, good. Out into an empty hallway.* A second door four yards to his right, a flight of steps immediately to his left, a window at the far end. He wheeled himself to the steps, slowly and awkwardly because he could use only one hand; the steps were too narrow for his chair. He might be able to lower himself down them by leaving the chair and using his hands, but that was risky. Better to check out other options. He went to the window, to a pane streaked with rain, the glass slapped by palm fronds. For a moment he wished he had his night lenses, but he didn't really need them to know that he couldn't escape from here. The leaves meant he was parallel to the top of a tree, on the second floor of the house, or higher. Too high to risk climbing with no legs and only one useful arm. The door, then.

It wasn't locked. He inched it open, waited, listened, and went into a room almost identical to the one he'd just left, unfurnished except for a low wicker table and a small lamp. Shondra was sitting in the center of the floor, skirt high, legs splayed out in front of her, twisting her fingers and humming softly. Bruce remembered that he was supposed to be someone who wasn't either of his real identities and that he should disguise his speech. "Shondra, it's—" But he couldn't say the name, whatever it was, and the voice was his own.

Shondra looked up and smiled. It was a sweet smile he'd never seen before, and when she spoke, her words lilted. "Hi. I know who *you* are. You're not Sir Hemingford. That's not your *real* name. *Bruce* is your real name." The smile widened. "You can't fool me!"

For a moment, he doubted that this woman *was* Shondra Kinsolving. *Could Shondra have a younger sister?*

"You shouldn't *try* to fool me," Shondra said. *Definitely Shondra. A different Shondra, though. A Shondra full of sweet innocence. Perhaps she's running some kind of game.*

Bruce wheeled himself forward until he sat above her. He reminded himself that she had tried, twice, to do him harm and in fact *had* done something to his memory. He decided to bluff.

"Listen, I wasn't stupid enough to come here alone. There's a Coast Guard destroyer waiting for my signal. If they don't get it in about five minutes, they'll radio the Florida state cops and half the uniforms in the state will come charging in. They have orders to block every road within ten miles and send in SWAT teams. You can save yourself a lot of grief and maybe keep your brother alive if you help me get away."

"I want to get away, Bruce. This is a bad place. I don't"—her face wrinkled and her eyes filled—"I don't *like* this place."

In the next room, Benedict Asp leaned closer to a small receiver. He glanced over his shoulder at Fritz. "Ah, the slut and her friend. As I thought, she *does* know him."

Shondra's voice, thin and tinny, came from the receiver. "I *hate* this place."

"You want me to break it up?" Fritz asked.

"No, no. Let them talk. It might be very educational."

From the receiver, Bruce: "Shondra, look at me—"

Shondra wiped tears away with a fist and bit her lower lip. "Uh-huh?"

"Shondra, are you all right?"

"I'm fine, thank you," she said politely. Then she bowed her head and shook it violently, and when, after a minute, she raised it again, she reminded Bruce of a swimmer coming up for air. "No, I'm not all right." Her face had changed; pain and fatigue had replaced the innocence. "I keep slipping in and out of . . . childhood, I guess."

Bruce was sure she was telling the truth; no actress could be so convincing. "I don't understand," he said.

"I can't stand the things I've done. Monstrous, horrible violence." Slowly, she got to her feet and stood beside him. "Classic case of regression. The patient is unable to accept the present. She regresses back to an age when she was happy." She turned and stared at the wall.

"Go on," Bruce said gently.

"I have a power, something I can't name. It's an *energy* I generate. You may have heard of things like it. The Japanese have a technique called *Reiki*. The Chinese call it *Chi Kung*. Some American nursing schools teach 'therapeutic touch.' What I do is similiar, but far more potent. I first became aware of it when I was six or seven, after my stepfather took me from the orphanage. At first I thought it was good. It seemed to help people—to *heal*. But it could do other things too. It could kill. It killed him."

"Amos Asplin?"

"Yes. Benny and I together, we caused his death. The medical examiner said he died of heart failure, and he did, but we caused it. With our minds, we reached inside his body and . . . *disrupted* him."

"I know the story. It wasn't your fault."

"Yes it was. I hated him. I wanted him dead."

"Your brother, Benjamin—he did the killing."

"Yes, he did, at least he helped, but I was responsible for that, too. Benny was normal. A normal little boy until I changed him. When I came to live with the Asplins, he wouldn't talk to me, wouldn't play with me. I was lonely. So one day, I got inside his head and changed him into something like myself."

"You were a child. You can't blame yourself—"

Shondra ignored him. "I was scared. As soon as I could, I ran away and changed my name. I lived on the streets in New York, Minneapolis, Chicago. For a time, I lived in a commune near San Francisco. When I was nineteen, I bluffed my way into a small community college. I got good grades and in my senior year I was offered a scholarship to medical school. I accepted it because I thought I could make up for what I'd done if I were a doctor."

Bruce resisted an urge to reach out, touch her. "You didn't see your brother in all that time?"

"He didn't know where to find me. I'm still not sure how he did, finally. A couple of months ago, he just showed up at the clinic I run. He said something about a drug dealer describing me to him. Sometimes I think I *wanted* him to come."

"Why?"

"Because what we do together feels good. I hate it, but it gives me some kind of peace. I've been to four psychiatrists. Top men in the field. None of them even got close to the rage I carry inside me. Oh, I walk around smiling and doctoring, acting like Mother Teresa, but inside I'm seething, and it hurts. Benny can make the pain go away."

Bruce again felt the urge to touch her; this time he did not resist. He took her hand; it was cold and still. "I know a bit about rage and pain too—"

"Yes. You do. I knew that the moment I met you."

"It doesn't have to be bad. It can be useful. You've just got to channel it."

"I do. That's the problem. I channel it into murder."

"No, not always, Shondra. Certainly not necessarily. When you were a child, you used it to heal. You've probably used it to heal since then, without knowing it. You have a reputation as a medical miracle worker. Where does that come from?"

"I've been lucky."

"Shondra, my spine was snapped. Yet within a month, I was able to walk with canes, and you yourself said I would probably recover completely. How often does that happen? Was that luck? Jack Drake—every specialist in the country had given up on him. But not you. You were able to do what they couldn't. Did you have medicine they didn't have? Techniques? Skills? No. So what *did* you have?"

Shondra's fingers squeezed his quickly, and then she pulled them away.

"We've got to get out of here," Bruce said. "Can you drive? There has to be a vehicle—"

"*I* can't drive." The voice lilted. "I'm too *lit*-tle!"

She's regressing. How do I get the adult Shondra back?

"But *may*-be," Shondra the child continued, "*you* could take us for a ride, Mr. Bruce Wayne."

In the next room, Asp was grinning at the receiver.

Fritz said, "Bruce Wayne. Name's familiar."

"The Gotham City billionaire, you idiot!" Asp said. "Of course of course of *course*. Makes perfect sense. That's why he could withstand our attack. We were directing the energy at Gray—who didn't exist."

"So what if you shot it at Wayne?" Fritz said.

"Why, he'd die. He *will* die."

"Yeah, well, whatever you're gonna do, you better do it fast. That storm's a full-blown twister."

Bruce's words came from the receiver: "—big enough to wheel this chair, Shondra?"

"I told you, I'm not *Shondra*. I'm *Sandra*." She had resumed sitting on the floor, her legs open in front of her.

Asp entered the room, followed by Fritz.

"Yes," Asp said to Bruce, "her name *is* Sandra, and she is my precious darling. You are not. You have been a royal pain in my ass. Soon, you will be an *ex*-royal pain."

Asp nodded, and Fritz moved toward the wheelchair.

20

 Lanny Luchessi was late getting his sorry butt to the garage. The dispatcher, this creep, Something-*kowski* —they always had names a decent American couldn't pronounce, didn't they?—yelled at Lanny from his wire cage. "The charter's waiting already for you," the foreign creep yelled.

"So another five minutes won't kill 'em," Lanny muttered as he entered the locker room. He dropped his overcoat on a bench, opened his locker, and got out his uniform jacket. "To hell with the pants. I ain't putting on them pants. They don't like blue jeans, to hell with 'em." He pulled on the jacket and began to button it. The third button came off in his hand. "To hell with it." He finished buttoning and put on his cap.

Someone he didn't recognize came around the lockers, a white guy. "You new?" Lanny asked him. "Gonna snow today. Something *else* to give me grief."

"Not if you leave the driving to me," the newcomer said, and rammed a knife into Lanny's throat.

• • •

The weather was still bad in Gotham City—rain mixed with occasional sleet throughout most of the day—but Graham Etchison had decided not to call off the basketball team's trip to the mountains. He knew these kids had been counting the days until it happened for weeks, and he knew these kids had precious few opportunities to leave the grim, violence-ridden streets around Gotham's Oxylus Projects and smell fresh air, see things that were God-made instead of man-made, walk without fear of a bullet from a dark alley shattering their young bodies. That social worker, Leslie Thompkins, had done her part, raising the money for the trip. Now Graham Etchison would do his.

"Okay," he shouted. "All aboard."

A dozen boys, eighth graders wearing backpacks, began to climb into the battered yellow bus. After the last one was inside, Graham climbed the two steps and smiled at the driver. "Guess we can get going."

Gears clashed as the bus pulled slowly away from the Civic Center and headed for the bridge and the countryside beyond. Graham sat directly behind the driver and looked through the grimy window at fat snowflakes wafting down between the tenements.

"It's snowin'," one of the kids said.

"When we get to the mountains, you'll see some *real* snow," Graham promised.

The bus jolted as it hit a pothole and continued toward the bridge.

It was one of Bruce Wayne's cardinal rules: Batman never appeared during the day. Jean Paul admitted that the rule was a good one, but Bruce Wayne, while certainly smart, wasn't infallible. If Bruce were wearing the cape and cowl, he might very well sit in the Cave until nightfall, but if he did that, he'd be wrong because by nightfall Graham Etchison might be dead. *Would* be dead: Jean Paul was certain of it.

He checked the Maserati's screens and detectors; no vehicles on the estate or the access road. He accelerated and burst from the hidden exit into a blinding flurry of snowflakes. He braked and scanned the dashboard: where were the windshield wipers? The car was custom designed; things weren't labeled. Well, how smart was *that?* He pressed three buttons before, on the fourth, the wipers sprang from their hood recess and began arcing. He aimed the car toward the beltway.

He had spent the night doing the kind of work he hated, the work that Wayne told him was the most essential of Batman's activities: investigation. An area map told him that Etchison did not live in the city proper; he was one of those faceless hordes who, Monday through Friday, crossed the river to jobs in downtown Gotham—"Bridge people" the locals called them, usually contemptuously. A city directory informed him that the job Etchison commuted to was in a community center near the projects; he was a social worker in a program funded by Waynetech. Jean Paul next consulted a special directory Wayne kept in the Cave, one that printed telephone numbers next to street addresses, and called Etchison's closest neighbor. That person, a grumpy woman named Matilda Partridge, said Etchison was away for the weekend. Then, an hour ago, at six in the morning, Jean Paul telephoned Etchison's place of employment, the community center, and found out that Etchison was planning to take a grade-school basketball team on a trip west, to the mountains. This was bad. If Etchison went directly to the center from his weekend jaunt, he wouldn't hear the warning Jean Paul had left on his answering machine. And if Jean Paul could find him, Abattoir could too. Abattoir probably already knew where his cousin worked.

The beltway had traffic, but not much. Morning rush hour was past; most of the cars and trucks were going *away* from the downtown area. Jean Paul inched the gas pedal down and, traveling at almost a hundred, weaved effortlessly around the few vehicles he encountered. He was enjoying himself, amazed at his own skill. A month ago, he couldn't drive at all. Now, he knew proudly, he was as expert as anyone on earth, probably much better than Bruce Wayne.

He left the beltway at the downtown exit, ran three red lights, and sped onto the bridge. Somewhere ahead was a yellow school bus full of victims and, almost certainly, a maniac who wanted to kill again.

Fritz positioned Bruce directly in front of Shondra and stood behind the wheelchair as Asp prepared his hypodermic needle.

"Please please please," Shondra whimpered.

"She might not survive this," Bruce told Asp.

"Oh, I believe she will," Asp said. "She's a hardy one, is our little Sandra. *You,* however . . ."

"Let's get on with it," Fritz said.

"Why? You won't be going anywhere until the storm passes. We should *savor* what's about to happen here. How often do we get to watch a billionaire die?" Asp smiled at Bruce. "Surprised I know?"

"Not particularly. It figures you'd have the room bugged."

"But you weren't clever enough to keep Sandra from blabbing your secret, were you?"

Bruce shrugged. "I wasn't worried. I considered the quality of the opposition and decided you'd be too dumb to use the information."

"Dumb? *I'm* not about to die."

Bruce grasped the chair's right wheel and shoved it forward. The chair lurched backward, hitting Fritz's legs. Fritz grunted in surprise as Bruce reached over his shoulder, grabbed Fritz's collar, and pulled down. Fritz's chin hit the armrest. Bruce rammed his elbow into Fritz's jaw. Fritz toppled to the side, arms flailing. He caught a wheel of the chair and pulled it with him as he fell. Bruce grabbed the chair arms and shifted his weight to the left, but he was too late. Still sitting in the chair, he fell on top of Fritz.

Asp moved toward them, holding the hypodermic needle in front of him. Shondra wrapped her arms around his calves. "No," she gasped. "You can't hurt him."

Asp kicked her. She rolled a few inches, reached up, found his thumb, and twisted. Asp yelped and dropped the needle. He kicked again, effectively. His shoe struck her under the jaw, and she slumped onto her back.

Behind Asp, a window imploded. Tape tore and a piece of a park bench, driven by the storm winds, crashed into the room in a shower of glass and hit Asp across the shoulders, staggering and stunning him. He stood, arms hanging, staring at nothing.

Bruce grabbed Fritz's hair, pulled his head back, and then slammed Fritz's chin onto the floor. Fritz grunted and stopped moving. Bruce shoved his good arm between Fritz's body and the floor and turned Fritz over, then raised his right fist and brought it down on Fritz's unprotected face. Again. And again, savagely.

Fritz seemed to collapse inward and was still.

Bruce was panting. He felt Fritz's carotid artery and detected a faint pulse. *Never happened before. I lost control. Almost killed him.*

A gust of rain from the shattered window splashed him. He blinked away droplets of water and saw Shondra lying a few feet away. He called to her, but her name was lost in the roar of the storm. He began to crawl toward her, dragging his left arm, ignoring the shards of glass that ripped his right palm.

Suddenly the roaring of the storm quieted, becoming only a murmur. Bruce's voice was abruptly loud. "Shondra!"

Her eyes met his, and her lips moved silently.

"Something I have to tell you," he said. "Back when it all began, when you were kidnapped . . . I was on my way to tell you . . . to ask you . . ."

Panting, his brow glistening, he reached her. She looked at him curiously, as though he were some strange new pet. ". . . to ask if you'd marry me . . ."

"How very touching," Asp said. He was standing above Bruce and Shondra, aiming Fritz's gun at Bruce's head. "The tattered and wounded knight declares his intentions to the fair lady. Romance in the midst of chaos." He moved the gun barrel a fraction of an inch until it was pointing directly between Bruce's eyes. "But, alas, there will be no happy ending—not for you. For me, yes. I will escape with my dear sister and tomorrow we will kill a president."

Bruce's bloody fingers touched something hard and smooth: Asp's hypodermic needle.

"The next day," Asp continued, "I shall be rich. And you shall be among the missing. Even in your sorry state, you're too dangerous to live."

Asp closed one eye and squinted carefully at the gun's front sight. He lowered the barrel and pressed it into Bruce's forehead.

"The next sound you hear will be the last—"

Bruce jabbed the hypodermic needle into Asp's wrist.

Asp howled and dropped the gun.

He shook the needle free of his wrist and screamed, "You filthy bastard—"

Shondra reached out and touched Asp's ankle. "Brother," she said softly.

Bruce watched what happened to Asp then: watched the head bend backward as the bones and veins in the throat stretched the skin; watched the eyes roll back and their whites suddenly become red as all their capillaries burst at once; and watched the mouth gape open as the knees folded and the body dropped to the floor. Saw all that happening as Asp died, but heard only the sigh of the wind and the easy patter of the rain.

"I didn't think the drug would do that. I killed him," Bruce whispered.

"No," Shondra said. "I did. But I didn't mean to . . . any more than I meant to kill my father . . . I was trying to forgive them . . . help them . . . love them."

"It's okay," Bruce said gently.

"But somehow the love got twisted into pain and terror . . ."

Outside, the wind was louder, the slap of the rain more insistent. The storm was regaining its fury.

"Shondra, we've got to get away from that window," Bruce said. "I can't move, so you'll have to—"

"Don't worry," Shondra whispered. "You'll be fine."

Her hand slipped over his, and her fingers tightened slightly. He felt as though she were touching every cell of his body at once—soothing, quieting, healing. The world went away, then, ebbed away from him, and he was left alone with Shondra's touch in a place where there was no pain and no terror.

Later, Bruce would hear that Fritz's body washed onto a beach in Puerto Rico after being in the ocean several days. Sometime during that long night Fritz must have regained consciousness and tried to flee by boat.

Asp's remains were never found. When Bruce left the house that morning, Asp was lying where he had fallen. When the police inspected the premises the following afternoon, they reported finding no people alive or dead. The only explanation that made sense to Bruce was that looters had stolen the corpse for some dark reason of their own.

All this concerned him when he returned to Gotham. But this morning, the morning after the longest and most peaceful night of Bruce's life, none of it mattered. Shirtless, barefoot, moving as easily and gracefully as he ever had in his life, he lifted Shondra and carried her through the debris, down the steps, and out onto the beach. The sky was a gleaming blue, the sun warm on his shoulders, the air a tonic. He stood on the sand gazing out at a sea that seemed to be made of shattered diamonds, and he smiled until it was time to find a way home.

PART
3

 KnightsEnd

1

The snow was so thick, and so driven by the wind, that it was a white blur outside the 'mobile's windows. But Batman could still see clearly enough to make out the bus's tire tracks. He was on a road that branched off the main highway and led on an upward incline into the mountains. It wasn't used much this time of year— few families were interested in picnicking during a Gotham winter, and there wasn't much business in the area—and that made following the bus easy; there were no other tracks on the road.

The tracks were clear, despite the heavy snowfall. That had to mean that the bus was only a minute or two ahead. Batman briefly wondered if it would be foolish to accelerate further on a steep, slippery surface—he was already doing seventy—and then he did. Wheels spun, bit into asphalt, and the car lurched forward. It skidded around a curve, its rear end almost snapping into a tree, and straightened. Batman smiled; ahead, through the swirling white, he could see a smear of yellow. It had to be the bus.

•   •   •

Etchison tapped the driver on the shoulder. "Excuse me, but haven't you made a wrong turn? This isn't the way to the camp—"

The driver's free hand came up holding a large blue pistol that he jammed beneath Etchison's chin. "Then I guess we're all headed for a slight detour, cousin!"

"Dude's got a piece!" someone in the passenger section shouted.

Etchison jerked his head back. "Cousin? What do you mean? And put that thing away—"

The driver dug the gun barrel into Etchison's throat. "I'm *family,* cuz. And I want to thank you"—the driver nodded toward the back of the bus and the twelve basketball players—"for the *bonus.* A dozen *other* souls to consume. Not that they're as important as you. Only *you* will really nourish me."

"Who *are* you?"

"I told you. I'm your cousin Abattoir."

"You? You're *him?*"

"That's right. We haven't met, have we? Funny how I was never invited to the family get-togethers—the picnics, the graduations, the barbecues. I would have been a lot of fun at the barbecues."

Abattoir steered the bus off the road and braked only a couple of yards from a wooden railing. Beyond it was a short, steep slope ending in a drop of a thousand feet to a rocky valley.

"Whatever you want, leave the kids out of it," Etchison said. "There's no need to—"

"Shut up, Graham. I hate nobility. It doesn't mix with our family's blood." Abattoir yanked the lever that opened the bus door. "Outside. You first, cuz."

"Wait a minute. Let's talk about—"

Abattoir aimed the gun at a lanky young man with dreadlocks. "Him first. I kill him in three seconds if you don't do what I say."

The young man stared, fascinated, at the weapon.

Another of the basketball players, a teenager wearing baggy jeans and a team jacket, said to Abattoir, "Chill, man."

His teammates murmured in agreement.

"Chill *you!*" Abattoir shouted, waving the gun.

"Don't hurt them," Etchison said, moving toward the door.

"If you run, they all die," Abattoir said.

Etchison went down the two steps and stood blinking snowflakes from his eyelashes. Abattoir followed.

"I want to take my time with you," he said pleasantly. "Give the children something to watch."

Etchison heard something—an engine, loud and approaching fast. He turned his gaze away from Abattoir and that terrible gun. A black shape seemed to be growing behind the curtain of snow, enlarging and solidifying into a vehicle. There was a screech and the vehicle—some kind of sports car, Etchison saw—veered off the road and slammed into the back of the bus with a sudden, final crash. The bus lurched forward into the wooden railing, splintering it. The front wheels went over the precipice, and the bus hung, swaying; only its rear wheels were on solid ground.

Abattoir had apparently forgotten Etchison; he faced the car and stiffened as the door on the driver's side opened and a man in a mask and cape rose from it.

"You're Batman?" Abattoir said.

"Put down the gun."

Abattoir fired.

Batman twitched as a bullet struck his armor, then came around the car. He raised his right arm, and three small darts shot from his gauntlet. One passed over Abattoir's shoulder, but the other two buried themselves in his forearm. Abattoir dropped the gun, and Batman leapt. Etchison watched as the maniac and Batman closed in a violent clutch and fell.

He heard a crunching sound and moved his stare from Batman and Abattoir to the bus. It was swaying, tipping forward over the precipice. Through the windows he could see the youngsters' faces. Some of them started toward the door.

"*Don't!*" Etchison screamed. "*Stay where you are!*" He knew that if they went to the front, their weight would tip the bus over into a long, fatal fall.

He lurched forward, grabbed the back fender, and leaned backward. But he wasn't strong enough or heavy enough. The bus inched forward, sliding on the snowy dirt.

"Help!" He'd meant to shout, but the word was only a gasped whisper. He filled his lungs with cold air and tried again: "*Help!*"

Batman, straddling Abattoir, looked up, saw Etchison and the bus, and punched again. Abattoir stopped struggling. Batman rose from him and ran to Etchison.

"What's wrong?" he asked.

"Can't you *see?*"

And Batman did, then, see for the first time that the bus and its passengers were only seconds from death and for a second wondered how he could *not* have seen it earlier. He put his hands next to Etchison's and pulled. The bus slid another inch.

"Get them out through the back window?" he asked, but even as he spoke, he knew the idea was not good. The back window—*all* the windows—had metal mesh grates bolted across the glass. It would take more than a minute to loosen even *one* bolt—

What would Bruce Wayne do?

Find something to use. Batman glanced around. Nothing but the snow and the bus and the 'mobile—

And he saw a possible answer. The 'mobile's bumper was locked with the bus's. How *firmly* were they locked?

He ran to the open driver's door.

"Where are you going?" Etchison asked.

"Put the car in reverse," Batman said. "Maybe it'll hold the bus while you get the children out."

"It's worth a try," Etchison said.

Behind the wheel, Batman started the engine, reached for the gearshift, and—

He saw Abattoir, a dozen yards away, rising, trotting toward the road.

Over the front of the hood, the bus tipped. The 'mobile was pulled an inch.

He didn't need to ask himself what Bruce Wayne would do. But what should *he* do? Save the dozen lives on the bus and let Abattoir go free to kill maybe *hundreds?*

At the front of the car, he could see Etchison's lips moving: *What are you waiting for?*

Abattoir had reached the road.

Batman shifted into reverse and stepped on the gas. The powerful

Maserati engine whined. A moment later, the smell of scorching rubber filled the air as the 'mobile's spinning tires melted through the snow to the frozen soil.

Etchison scurried around the bus. Batman knew he would be helping the boys make the short jump from the bus door to the precipice, grabbing their hands, pulling them past the broken railing to safety.

Etchison appeared from behind the bus and held up his thumbs. Everyone was safe.

Batman stepped hard on the gas pedal. He'd either haul the bus up to solid ground or—

He heard a rending of metal and then the bus was tipping away from him, sliding over the edge, vanishing, breaking on the floor of the valley far below. The 'mobile, suddenly freed, bolted backward and crashed into a tree.

Batman was out and running before the fine white powder from the tree limbs had finished settling on the top of the car. He sprinted across the road into a stand of trees and stopped. Abattoir's footprints had been plain on the road, but here the ground was uneven. He knelt and peered at markings in the snow, unable to be sure which were footprints and which were merely natural depressions around roots, rocks, and twigs.

He had no idea of what to do next. He had never been in the woods before in his life.

What would Bruce Wayne do?

Easy. Wayne would do whatever was right because Wayne would have been in the woods, would have anticipated situations like this, would have trained for them years ago.

Batman returned to the car. Etchison and the basketball players were gathered around admiring it, examining the torn front bumper and crumpled rear end.

"Did you get him?" Etchison asked.

"No. But I will."

"Don't guess you could give us a lift back to town?"

Batman shook his head no, got into the car, and drove onto the road. Halfway back to Wayne Manor, he remembered to call a state patrol substation and report what had happened to the basketball team.

2

Bruce let himself into Wayne Manor through the front entrance and stood in the foyer. It was a place he had known since earliest childhood, and he'd been gone from it only a short time, but it seemed alien and artificial to him, not quite real: a stage set with very expensive props. He remembered Alfred comparing his life to grand opera and smiled, and then stopped smiling when he recalled that Alfred Pennyworth was no longer here. Bruce had called repeatedly, both the manor's general number and Alfred's private line, and had gotten no answer.

So Alfred meant what he said at the hospital. I wonder where he's gone. I wonder if I should go after him. And I wonder if anything else has changed.

He went to the grandfather clock and set the hands at 10:47. He stepped back, anticipating the opening of the secret doorway. But it didn't open. He curled his fingers around the back of the clock and tugged. No give. The hidden door was sealed shut.

Bruce was annoyed. Jean Paul had no right to make changes—

No, that's wrong. He does. He's been wearing the cape. And it won't be any big chore to change things back. But I wonder where he is. If he's in the Cave, he would respond to the alarm. Out? Out where?

Bruce searched the rest of the house. It had the air of some ancient ruin, long abandoned and forgotten. Alfred's room contained only the bed and nightstand; the closets were wide open and devoid of anything except coat hangers. Jean Paul's room was also empty except for a few articles of clothing tossed across the bed and a stack of textbooks on the desk. Bruce went to the master bedroom and his own closet and changed from his three-piece suit and calfskin boots into jeans, a sweater, Nikes, and a leather bomber jacket. He walked out the kitchen door and spent five minutes doing stretching exercises. His body wasn't what it had been. The joints were stiff, and the muscles soft. But his arms and legs moved freely, he could bend his back and move his neck in a full circle, all without pain. A miraculous cure, considering how badly he'd been injured, one he was certain conventional science couldn't explain.

Shondra, the miracle worker.

He did a final yoga asana, reaching past his knees and placing his palms on his shoulder blades, held it for a minute, straightened, and began to sprint across the snow-covered field that separated the Wayne property from the Drakes'.

He was slow. The mile run took a full five minutes. *I'll let Jean Paul mind the store a few more weeks while I get back in shape.*

Tim answered the door.

"Hello, Tim," Bruce said. "Long time no see."

Tim smiled, reached for Bruce's hand, hesitated.

"You're allowed to shake hands with a neighbor," Bruce said.

Tim grabbed Bruce's hand and moved it up and down as though it were a pump handle. "I don't know what to say."

"For openers, you could invite me in. It's cold out here."

Tim led Bruce to the kitchen and turned on an electric burner under a copper kettle. "I'll make us some tea."

"Sounds good." Bruce hung his jacket on the back of a chair. "How's your father?"

"At the moment, he's in Gotham at the doctor's. Some tests. But everyone seems pretty pleased with his progress."

"Good. Glad to hear it."

"What happened with you? Your back—"

"As far as I can tell, it's completely healed."

"Are you sure?" Tim asked. "I mean, is that *possible?*"

"Yes, I'm sure and yes, it has to be possible because it happened. But it *is* making me rethink a few ideas—or maybe they're a few prejudices. If I come to any interesting conclusions, I'll let you know."

"Where's Dr. Kinsolving?"

"She's on a long vacation. I'll give you chapter and verse later. For now, I want to hear what *you* have to say. How are things at the Cave?"

Tim folded his arms and stared at the floor. "I don't exactly know where to begin—"

"Which is my cue to say 'At the beginning.'" Bruce sat at the large oak table and looked at Tim expectantly.

Tim slumped into a chair across from him. "Bruce, I think Paul's gone off the deep end."

"Okay. And?"

For the next half hour, between sips of tea, Tim told Bruce everything: Jean Paul's changing the costume, his barring Robin from the Cave, his sudden bursts of temper, and most disturbingly, his increasing reliance on violence.

"You scare the bad guys without touching them, usually," Tim concluded.

"Part of my psychological arsenal. It makes them feel I don't think they're worth harming, gives them feelings of inferiority."

"Yeah, true, but it's more than that. You don't like to hurt people."

"No, I don't, Tim."

"I'm not sure that's true of Paul. He seems to get off on busting them up."

"I can't believe that's so."

"You haven't seen him in action. Bruce, don't take my word for it. Ask the cops—Gordon, Montoya, even Bullock."

"Okay, Tim, take it easy. I'm not doubting you." Bruce stood and stared out the window at the falling snow for a full minute. "I've got to talk to him."

"That might not be easy. He's holed up in the Cave and he's blocked all the entrances."

"Then we'll have to unblock one. Until I figure out the best way to do that, we'd better keep tabs on him. He's probably using wheels, so we should keep watch on the ramp exit and follow him. I know you're not supposed to drive—"

"No sweat. I have a special probationary license. The state issues them to kids whose parents are handicapped."

"Good. Always nice to be legal. Okay, you take the first watch."

"Won't he know I'm there? All that electronic gear in the car, all those hidden cameras—"

"I designed the system myself. I installed most of it. And I anticipated the possibility that I might want to knock it out some day. Don't worry. Within an hour, it'll be so much scrap wire."

"Bruce, this job you've given me. Is it a Tim Drake job? Or a Robin job?"

"Robin. A very *careful* Robin."

"Got it."

Bruce strode toward the front of the house. "Stay in touch by radio. You know the drill. I'll do my thing and relieve you in a couple of hours."

Bruce stepped outside, breathed deeply, and set off at a brisk trot toward the southern edge of his grounds. He stopped a hundred yards from the road, stooped, and pawed snow away from what looked like a clump of dead grass. He reached under it, found a small knob, and twisted.

That takes care of the electronics.

He trotted away, toward the mansion that was visible as a dim silhouette in the swirling snow.

I'll get into the Cave and have it out with Jean Paul. Maybe it'll be about nothing. Maybe Tim's misreading the situation. Maybe there are elements Tim can't know about. Maybe Jean Paul's protecting him from something.

Bruce's pace quickened.

And maybe Jean Paul has gone off some deep end. I'll have to take the cape and cowl away from him and then I'll have to figure out my responsibility for whatever harm he's done and ask myself how I could have made such a terrible mistake.

3

Jean Paul paced frantically around the Cave's computer complex. "But it wasn't my fault," he said aloud for the twentieth time. "The road was icy. *Anyone* would have hit that bus."

But he knew he was lying to himself. Bruce Wayne would not have hit the bus because Bruce Wayne would have taken the weather into account and Bruce Wayne was a more skillful driver—

"No, *I'm* better than he is."

That was also an obvious lie. Wayne was the superior driver, and Wayne would not have let Abattoir escape—Wayne would have chosen among a dozen possibilities, any one of which would have stopped Abattoir cold.

Jean Paul felt as though his mind were splintering. He didn't know what he thought, nor what he felt. He wanted to take some action, but he didn't know what to do, how to begin. Where might he find one man in a city of seven million? He paced, trying to focus, to reason, and could not. Finally he knelt and closed his eyes.

"Most Holy St. Dumas, I beseech thee—"

"Yes?" The familiar voice of the saint, deep, comforting, just a bit impatient. "You want to find this Abattoir?"

"If it is thy will, Most Venerable—"

"What would Bruce Wayne do?" the saint demanded.

Jean Paul moaned.

"I'm waiting," St. Dumas said, impatience now dominating his words.

"Detective work," Jean Paul mumbled.

"You wear his mantle. Do as he would."

"As thy will would have it."

"But," the saint said, suddenly thundering, *"once you have* found *your quarry, do as I would have you do."*

Jean Paul raised his eyes. He was alone.

He rose, went to the computer, and began tapping keys. He wasn't aware that he had a plan, but he moved his fingers deftly, calmly. A list scrolled onto one of the monitors. Jean Paul looked at it and smiled. It was all quite simple, really. Abattoir was obsessed with his family, would be likely to know everything about it, and the Etchisons were real estate people—next to the Waynes, *the* real estate people in this part of the state —with property on both sides of the river. Bruce Wayne's excellent database had a list of their holdings—Bruce Wayne's, not Batman's; Jean Paul had found what he wanted in the Waynecorps files, not the Batman files, and somehow that pleased him. Most of the Etchison property he could eliminate at a glance—the apartment buildings in upscale neighborhoods, the big mall east of the city, the few downtown offices that Wayne *didn't* own. But there were other places, most of them in a decaying industrial area across the bridge largely abandoned when factory owners left the area in search of cheaper labor and larger tax abatements—*those* were possibilities. One in particular, a bowling alley empty for the last four years . . . it was worth checking out. He could be there in less than an hour.

"Hello, Jean Paul."

Jean Paul whirled, dropping into a defensive crouch, at the unexpected sound of Bruce Wayne's voice. Wayne was standing at the bottom of the steps that led up to the mansion. Something was . . . *wrong* about him.

"How did you get down here?" Jean Paul demanded. Wayne's presence was an outrage, a blasphemy. The Cave was desecrated by his presence.

"You changed the combination on the clock," Bruce Wayne said, "but you didn't change the lock itself. Any medium-competent safecracker could have beaten it."

"What do you want?"

"I'll decide that after we talk."

Jean Paul knew what was amiss about Wayne. He was dressed casually, grinning a lopsided grin that had charmed scores of husband-seeking debutantes, and he spoke in the high baritone that had uttered vapid pleasantries at a thousand tony parties. But he was Batman. There was nothing soft or stupid in either his steady gaze or his relaxed, alert posture.

"I have nothing to say to you," Jean Paul told him.

"You've just convinced me otherwise. You *should* have things to say— plenty of them. If you don't, something's wrong."

"Get out of here."

"Maybe soon. But not now."

"I'm warning you—"

"Of *what,* Jean Paul?"

"*I'm* Batman now."

"That might be true. Let's discuss it."

"I have work to do."

"Maybe I can help." Still smiling, Bruce strolled toward Jean Paul. "You've got a case?"

"None of your business. I told you—*leave me alone!*"

Bruce looked past Jean Paul to the monitor screen. "Something cooking on the computer?"

As Jean Paul began to swing, he saw Bruce's left arm rising, Bruce's weight shifting. But too slowly. Jean Paul's fist caught him on the cheekbone. Bruce fell to the floor of the Cave and in the same motion rolled and scrambled to his feet.

Jean Paul stared at him, struggling to contain his fury. "I'm leaving now. I've got work to do—*important* work. You'd better not be here when I get back."

"Or you'll do what, Jean Paul?"

"Whatever I have to. Don't try me, Wayne. Don't *test* me."

Jean Paul ran to the 'mobile, opened the door, looked back at Bruce. "I never want to see you here again. Don't you understand? *I'm* Batman now!"

Robin saw the 'mobile burst from the hidden exit. Obviously, Bruce's disabling of the security system had been unnecessary; Jean Paul wasn't worried about being seen. Robin, driving his father's Lincoln station wagon, followed the 'mobile out onto the access road; Jean Paul was heading for the beltway and, presumably, Gotham City. It was a few minutes after five; the winter sky was steel gray, and night was coming fast. That meant that the strange, sleek vehicle might not be noticed— *might* not.

The dashboard telephone buzzed. Robin picked it up as he was guiding the Lincoln onto the beltway ramp. Although Bruce was only two miles away, his voice sounded as though it were coming from an unimaginable distance. "You on him?"

"Yeah. We're heading for Gotham. What's going on?"

"I'm not sure. Just don't lose him. And *don't* confront him."

"Something bad's happened, hasn't it?"

Bruce ignored the question. "Give me a call when he stops. You'll probably be hearing from me in a few minutes."

"Okay." Robin replaced the receiver and concentrated on keeping Jean Paul in sight. The black 'mobile was moving at the speed limit, but not above it, and staying in the middle lane. Jean Paul was driving carefully. Robin noticed the damaged rear end and wondered if that had something to do with Jean Paul's uncharacteristic caution.

Robin followed Jean Paul off the beltway and onto the bridge. Across the river, the traffic thinned, and thinned further still when Jean Paul entered what had once been an industrial area. Robin had never been here and didn't like what he was seeing—block after block of empty corrugated steel buildings with shattered windows and bars with cement blocks sealing doorways. Once these desolate, vacant streets had been the state's industrial hub; now they were a preview of the night after the final war.

Only one factory was still operating, a smelting plant that Jean Paul passed twice. Obviously, he was searching. But for what?

The street was easy to miss. It was a single long block that began at one huge, dark factory and ended at another. There were four low buildings on one side that had once housed bars and diners and, on the other, a single large structure with a low domed roof. Robin saw the shape of a huge bowling pin silhouetted against the last dim glow of the western sky. Jean Paul guided his car to the curb and stopped. A hundred yards away, Robin wondered if he should try to get closer or keep what he considered to be a safe distance. Bruce would know. Robin was reaching for the telephone when he saw Jean Paul—it was impossible to think of him as Batman—leave the car and begin running.

Robin hesitated, his hand hovering near the phone. No time to consult his mentor—the decision had to be his. He switched off the Lincoln's engine and began to chase Jean Paul.

It had taken Jean Paul longer than he anticipated to find the bowling alley, but he convinced himself that it wasn't his fault. This was a ghost town—no lights, no street signs, nobody to ask for directions. When he did find it, he realized that he had no plan.

What would Bruce Wayne do—?

No. To hell with Bruce Wayne. Bruce Wayne was a pathetic has-been who could be dropped with a single punch. *Jean Paul* was Batman. He would devise his own tactics—

Then he saw a side door open and someone leave the bowling alley. Even in this dim light, he instantly recognized the man he'd seen running into the woods the previous afternoon. He yelled, *"Abattoir!"*

Abattoir turned and began running. He rounded a corner of the building and vanished into the shadows. But he wouldn't escape again. Jean Paul couldn't see him, but here, on the kind of ground that Jean Paul was used to—city ground—Jean Paul could hear him, could distinguish the sound of footfalls from other noises.

Abattoir burst from the shadows and trotted up the middle of the next street.

Jean Paul lengthened his stride. "You can't get away!" he shouted and thought, briefly, that he sounded silly.

Abattoir came to a chain link fence, reached over his head, clutched the wire, and climbed. He rolled over the top and dropped to snow-covered asphalt on the other side.

Jean Paul hit the fence at full run, jumped, grabbed the pipe that ran along the top, and vaulted. He came down running.

Ahead, Abattoir was limping—he'd hurt himself getting over the fence. He hobbled past a row of cars parked along a wall. Jean Paul realized that they were in a parking lot behind the factory he'd passed while he was searching for the bowling alley. A rectangle of orange light appeared in the wall—a door had opened—and a man dressed in cover-alls emerged holding a cigarette. Abattoir elbowed the man aside and entered the building. Jean Paul caught a glimpse of the man's outraged face as he followed, heard the man screech, "Son of a bitch—"

The heat, after the cold outside, was like a slap, and the noise, a hideous combination of roar and shriek, was almost painful. Jean Paul slowed and scanned the area. He was in a foundry: concrete floor thick with grease; high, peaked ceiling crisscrossed with catwalks; directly ahead, a gigantic vat with gouts of steam and flurries of red sparks rising from the top. He saw three men wearing leather aprons over jumpsuits at the base of the vat: one was looking at him and yelling, the others were gazing upward. Abattoir was climbing a ladder toward a catwalk. At the top he paused and looked back at Jean Paul, then rolled off the ladder and under a guardrail. Jean Paul went after him.

Here, on the catwalk, the heat was intense and the light, a blue-orange glare, filled his vision with sprays of brightness and looming shadows. But he could see Abattoir, fingers wrapped around the handrail, taking slow, fearful steps outward. But Abattoir couldn't go far. The catwalk ended directly above the vat. There was no ladder, no other exit.

Jean Paul advanced and Abattoir stepped backward, into a cloud of steam that rose from the vat, until his back hit the guardrail. For a moment the two men stared at each other through the white mist. Then Abattoir unbuttoned the top of his overcoat and tugged a gun from inside it. Batman raised his right gauntlet. Three darts shot from it; one buried itself in Abattoir's wrist; the other two caught in the thick cloth of his coat. The gun dropped. Abattoir opened his mouth to howl, but his voice was lost in the roar. Batman stepped within arm's length of the killer and suddenly struck him on the chin with the heel of his right hand. Abattoir's head snapped back, and he toppled stiffly over the guardrail; his body somersaulted backward as he began to fall toward the vat. His left fingers caught the edge of the catwalk and he hung, feet dangling. He mouthed the words, "Help me," but again, Batman could not hear him. Batman reached down toward Abattoir's hand.

"Once you have found your quarry, do as I would have you do."

Although the din of the foundry was as deafening as ever, the command was clear. Batman looked around for St. Dumas. Was that him over there, in the shadows? Or was Batman seeing a mirage, an illusion compounded of steam and flickering light?

Do as I would have you do.

Regardless of whether the Venerated One was present, his wishes were unmistakable. Batman stood, turned, strode to the ladder, and climbed down.

He met Robin at the bottom.

"You've got to help him," Robin shouted.

Jean Paul glanced over his shoulder. Abattoir was still dangling from the catwalk.

He shook his head.

"Then *I* will," Robin said, and reached for the ladder. Jean Paul grabbed him, pinned his arms, flung him to the floor, and again glanced over his shoulder. Abattoir was gone. The steam rising from the vat was no longer white—it was crimson and gray now, and tiny flames rocketed high in the air and arced downward. The roar seemed louder than ever.

4

"I saw him die," Tim said. "I was lying on the floor and I looked up and watched him drop into the vat of molten metal. What a horrible end—"

"Take it easy," Bruce said. He reached for Tim's shoulder, and then withdrew his hand. He didn't know how to be physically comforting, and he realized for the thousandth time that he would have made a terrible father.

"Maybe you're used to things like that, but not me. I'll never forget the sight of that man falling as long as I live."

"I hope not. If you do forget it, you'll have lost something of immense value."

"Have *you* lost it?"

"I don't think so. No, I haven't."

"I'm sorry, Bruce. I'm pretty freaked out."

"It's okay."

They were in the library of the manor. Jean Paul was somewhere below, in the Cave. Bruce leaned back in the huge old easy chair and stared into the cold fireplace. *What's he doing? What's he feeling? Regret? Remorse? Triumph? If I knew, maybe I'd know what to do next.*

Tim was pacing back and forth in front of the windows. Beyond him lay acres of snow-covered lawn, glowing in the wan light of the winter moon. "I just thought of something," he said. "Couldn't you—Batman—be charged with a crime? With manslaughter or something?"

"I guess it's possible. According to the newscasts, the men at the foundry are telling a pretty garbled tale. There was only a skeleton crew working last night and only three of them actually saw you and Jean Paul. By the way, they're not calling him Batman. He's changed the costume enough for there to be doubt."

"But what if they *do* charge you?"

"I guess the police will have two reasons to be after me. Technically, I'm still wanted for questioning in connection with the murder of those women."

"But they've got Bane."

"And maybe he's confessed. Or maybe not. That's another problem." Bruce looked up from the fireplace. *Now's the time. I've got to tell him now.* "Tim, I've got more bad news."

Tim stopped pacing. "I'm afraid to ask."

"And I'm afraid to tell you. But it wouldn't be fair not to."

"Okay."

"I've been in touch with Gordon. They found Graham Etchison."

"Who?"

"The man Abattoir was looking for."

"How is he?"

"Dead, Tim. Abattoir killed him."

Tim bowed his head. "Oh, geez."

Bruce hesitated. He had to finish it. "He was in the bowling alley. Abattoir buried him under a pile of bricks in the basement."

"When?"

"He died this morning in the hospital."

Bruce watched Tim understand.

"He was alive last night?" Tim said slowly. "When Paul was chasing Abattoir?"

"I'm afraid so."

"He was alive when *I* was there?"

"Yes."

"If I'd stopped . . . if I'd searched the bowling alley . . ."

"Tim, you had no reason to believe there was any point in bothering."

"Would *you* have done it?"

Bruce was silent.

"Answer me!" Tim's voice was shrill, and there were tears in his eyes.

"After Abattoir died, I would have gone back to see if anything had been overlooked."

"And you'd have saved Etchison's life."

"Maybe. But I've had years of experience. Tim, you can't blame yourself—"

"Why the *hell* do you think I blame myself? *I* didn't do it." Tim pointed to the floor. *"He* did. That bastard who's sitting in your lousy cave down there—*he* killed Etchison."

"I'm not arguing."

"There's only one question you've got to ask yourself, Bruce . . . what are you going to do about it?"

"You sound like you blame me, Tim."

"You picked him." Without looking at Bruce, Tim crossed the room and went into the foyer.

"Can you get home all right?" Bruce called after him. A moment later, he heard the front door slam.

Bruce sank further into the chair. He had a lot of techniques to calm his mind, disciplines he'd learned from every kind of guru there was: yoga, meditation, deep relaxation, self-hypnosis, active imagination . . . The list was long. And at this moment, useless. He could focus on nothing. He was wearier than he'd ever been in his life.

I created him, he's Batman, and Batman is a monster. Maybe Batman's always been a monster, a childish, demented phantom that allowed me to escape from grief and loneliness, and my vanity wouldn't let me admit it. My pathetic vanity.

Bruce got up and turned out the lights, then lay down on the rug and stared into the darkness. He would lie there, sleepless, all night long, and in the morning he would rise and begin doing whatever had to be done.

•   •   •

Maybe it was time to retire Batman. But before Bruce could do that, he had to *become* Batman again.

He set himself a training regimen as rigorous as any he had ever undertaken: a twenty-mile run before breakfast, through snow, in work boots, carrying a backpack filled with sand; a thousand sit-ups and push-ups mornings and another set evenings; weight training for the major muscle groups on alternate days; chin-ups; squats; two hours of yoga midmorning and another two hours late afternoon—he'd converted the South Drawing Room to a fully equipped gym and to hell with the antique furnishings.

The months of partial inactivity had been costly: although he had no hint of pain in his back and neck, he was stiff and his muscles were lax. At first he was shocked at how weak he'd become. A thousand push-ups? His arms refused to flex after three hundred. Run twenty miles? After six, he stopped and stooped, hands on thighs, breath erupting in white clouds from his mouth. But years of disciplined conditioning hadn't been totally lost, and at the end of the second week, his body was responding to his demands. He wasn't yet his old self—far from it—but he was confident he soon would be.

Bruce called Tim at least once every day. Occasionally Tim would actually pick up the telephone, but he was always in a hurry, always vague about his plans.

Bruce read the *Gazette* and watched the local newscasts. No mention of Batman, nor of any unexplained violence. That was good. It could mean Jean Paul was inactive, or it could mean he was operating very secretly. Bruce wished he could believe that it meant his protégé had retired, but he remembered the mask of fanaticism that had been Jean Paul's face at their last meeting and the hate in his voice—"*I'm* Batman now"—and knew it couldn't be so.

Bruce considered entering the Cave again—there were several ways that could be managed—and trying to speak with Jean Paul. But he decided it wasn't a good idea. If Bruce were to succeed in avoiding a final, physical confrontation, Jean Paul would have to see he was dealing with an equal, not a supplicant.

He wanted to avoid that confrontation. But it was a possibility, even a probability, and he had to be ready for it, assume it would happen. He was rediscovering his strength and agility. Next he would have to regain his combat skills.

He would begin with some basics. A *kata*—a prearranged series of combat moves that superficially resembled a dance, but only superficially; it was actually a rehearsal for repelling several attackers at once. He chose a sequence from the Shaolin *gung fu* school, which he had first mastered at age eighteen. After his run on the Tuesday of the third week, he dropped his backpack into the snow and trotted to a wide stretch of lawn behind the north portico. He assumed the horse stance—legs wide, knees bent, hands at hips—and snapped out his right fist.

Lame. That punch wouldn't have bothered a hummingbird.

He punched with his left fist—

Lame-o—

—straightened and kicked to an imaginary opponent's solar plexus. He was a half second late straightening his knee, the kind of mistiming that a seasoned attacker would turn to devastating advantage. Worse, he almost lost his balance.

Am I stiff from the run? Is something wrong with me?

He did three backflips.

All systems go.

He tried another kick: another failure.

Okay, maybe gung fu *isn't a good style to start with. Let's try something gentler.*

He assumed the opening stance of Yang-style tai chi chuan and began the slow, rhythmic moves of the most peaceful, and potentially most useful, of the martial arts. He put his feet in position and waved his arms according to the form, but he knew he wasn't doing real tai chi; he could feel no movement of internal energy, no sense of flow, no harmony. He felt like a clumsy adolescent shoving his first date around a dance floor.

I've lost something. And I'm not sure what.

He picked up his backpack and went into the house, through the kitchen to the library. He sat in the lotus position on the rug. He asked himself: *What have I lost?*, stilled his mind, and waited for an answer. It came in the form of wordless images:

Amos Asplin slapping a small child.

His mother's pearls spilling into the gutter.

Bodies strewn around the narrow streets of an English village.
Benedict Asp twitching on the floor of a house in Florida.

When Bruce stood, he was trembling. *I've lost my capacity for violence.*

He now despised what had been an essential tool—what he had chosen to *make* an essential tool. He'd have to regain it. And he knew only one person could help him do that.

5

It took Bruce two days to locate Lady Shiva, and when he did, he learned that she was only about two hundred miles away. The procedure, which he'd learned years earlier, was to place an ad in the personals section of a New Delhi newspaper and wait for a reply. That was a problem: he couldn't sign the ad "Batman" and add a telephone number. So he placed the ad and, with some reluctance, went to visit Tim.

"I could use some computer help," he said. Tim led him to the wide room in the rear of the Drake mansion that was filled with Tim's property, including a computer array that looked like the slightly younger brother of the one in the Cave.

"Is this a Robin job or a Tim job?"

"I have a feeling that Robin is in temporary retirement. So call it a Tim job."

Tim nodded. "Okay."

"I need you to hack into a newspaper data base and get me the address that goes with a name."

"Local paper?"

"Not exactly. It's in India. The *New Delhi Gazette*. It's an English-language daily."

"I wonder if theft of data is illegal in India."

"Probably. That's why I'm not asking you to do it. I'm only saying I could use some help."

"What's the name you want an address for?"

"She signs herself 'Kali's Sister.' "

"Okay, give me a few hours. I'll call you."

At the door, Bruce said, "If Robin ever wants to get back into action, he could probably be accommodated."

"Robin thinks he'll stay in limbo until some questions are answered. Maybe finding out who Kali's Sister is could help answer them."

Bruce finished the day's workout, ate a spartan dinner, and was preparing for an early rest when the phone rang.

"It was a lot harder than I thought it would be," Tim said. "But I finally managed it. Kali's Sister gets her mail as Ossie Isis, General Delivery, East Cottage, Pennsylvania. I looked it up. It's a hamlet in the Alleghenies a bit east of Bedford."

"I'll find it. Thanks, Tim. And the Robin job offer's still open."

"Let's see how well Robin's boss does *his* job."

"Robin's boss will do his best. He only hopes Robin believes that. Thanks again, Tim."

The following morning, Bruce took a commercial flight to Pittsburgh, rented a car, and before noon was driving west on the Pennsylvania Turnpike. Traffic was sparse. Seeing snow falling in large slow flakes reminded Bruce that it was Christmas Eve. The holiday had never meant anything much to him, not since early childhood, and so he was aware of it only if it bore on work he was doing. Today it didn't.

At three in the afternoon, he passed an accident site. A black Pontiac Grand Prix was overturned in the middle of the highway. He slowed, planning to offer help, but he saw that an ambulance was already there and paramedics were loading a man and a woman onto stretchers; he wasn't needed.

He arrived at East Cottage an hour later. It was almost too small to be called a town—a single street with only a few small stores on either side. It was as picturesque as a calendar painting and as vacant; at four in the afternoon, the sidewalks were empty, the layer of new snow covering them untrodden, the buildings dark. Christmas Eve. Folks at home with folks. But not a childish, demented phantom created to let an orphan escape from grief and loneliness; no, that morose warrior was prowling the twilight searching for a woman who would school him in mayhem. Ho ho ho.

Bruce found an open gas station and questioned the attendant, an old man wearing a sheepskin jacket and a Steelers cap eager for conversation. He talked as he pumped gas.

"No, there ain't nobody like you describe living in town. I lived here all my life and I'd be safe in saying I know everyone. 'Course, some people come in only to shop and get their mail. Them I don't necessarily know. Some of them live way up the mountain. 'Course there ain't much point in going up there tonight. Roads'll be bad and if you don't know where you're going you could get in trouble. Gets real cold. You could freeze to death and I mean that. It's happened. I was you, I'd head on back to the highway and find a motel. You could get an early start in the morning. Won't be as bad then. County'll have the roads cleared, at least some of them. Unless it snows again."

Bruce took a hundred-dollar bill from his wallet and handed it to the old man.

"You got anything smaller, mister? I ain't got change for this."

"But I'll bet you know somebody who could use a few extra dollars," Bruce said. "You'll be doing me a favor if you give it to that person and tell them to have a merry Christmas."

"Well, thanks. And you have a merry Christmas too."

Bruce drove back through East Cottage to a crossroads. He stopped and got out of the car. To the right, a mile down a winding strip of icy asphalt, he could see the turnpike, a blue ribbon hazy in the snow; to the left, more icy asphalt that blurred into darkness.

No contest. I'll always choose the night.

He got climbing boots from the trunk, put them on, and locked the

car. He would play a hunch, he would search for Shiva. It wasn't rational
—the old man's advice was what was rational here—but it felt somehow
appropriate, and he'd learned to heed feelings when there was no obvious
reason to ignore them. Sometimes his subconscious was smarter than his
conscious—not often, but sometimes.

He began to hike.

At midnight, Bruce reached the end of the road. But he could see a
path leading sharply upward through a stand of pines. He took a small
flashlight from an inner pocket of his parka and played the beam on the
path: tiny depressions in the snow—footprints, almost covered.

He climbed.

At three, by his watch, the snow stopped and silver-rimmed clouds
slid away from a full white moon.

Ahead, at the top of a ridge, there was a squat, square structure, a
cabin—the only man-made thing in sight, harsh and unnatural—and in
front of it something else, something smaller; although Bruce was too far
away to see it clearly, it seemed as natural to the vista of mountain peaks
and trees as the cabin was foreign.

He pulled a ski mask from his pocket and pulled it over his head.

He walked on.

Lady Shiva was sitting cross-legged in the snow, back straight, short
hair stirring in the breeze, eyes staring straight ahead, open palms up-
turned on her knees. She was naked and beautiful.

Without looking at him she said, "If you come any closer, I'll kill
you."

"You haven't changed," Bruce said. "Good."

"Do I know you?" Shiva asked, not moving.

"We met about four years ago through Vic Sage. We had a little
workout on a pier."

Shiva smiled. "Yes. You wore a different mask then, and a cape. You
had promise." She rose—or rather, it seemed to Bruce that her body
transformed from sitting to standing so quickly and smoothly he wasn't
sure he saw it happen.

"You'd probably consider me a chauvinist if I offered you my coat,"
he said.

"Not necessarily. But I think I would break two bones in your forearms and drive the sharp edges into nerve clusters. That would cause you great pain."

"Then I won't."

"Why are you not wearing the other guise? The cape? The mask of the Bat?"

"That's all been usurped . . . altered . . ."

"Perverted?" Shiva's smile widened and she ran her tongue over her lower lip.

Can she know about Jean Paul? No. She's deeply intuitive and she's the world's greatest reader of body language. That was just a lucky shot.

"Yes," Bruce said. "Perverted."

"And now you want it back?"

"I want to redeem it."

"Why bother me with this?"

"I want you to train me."

Suddenly Bruce was sitting in the snow. He'd been watching her hands and so she must have kicked him. But he hadn't seen her do it. His chest began to hurt.

"You are not ready," Shiva said.

"I know. *Make* me ready."

"Why should I?"

"For the only reason you do anything. It might prove interesting."

"You are not worthy of me."

"Not now, not yet. But once I was. Remember the pier? Bring me back."

Shiva turned away from him. "You were *never* worthy of me. You refuse to kill."

I almost did kill. Back in Florida. Because I was desperate and my body would not obey me. But that's something she can never know.

"That will never change," Bruce said.

"Then coming to me was an insult."

"No, it was a tribute. I need nothing less than the best and that's you. But if you refuse, there's nothing I can do about it." Bruce began walking down the slope.

"As you said, it might prove interesting." Shiva was moving up the hill toward the cabin, stepping so lightly that her feet barely indented the snow. Bruce followed, trudging, feeling clumsy as an elephant. Saying nothing, she led him into the cabin. It was what Bruce expected: stark, functional—a futon, a glowing charcoal brazier, a few candles. The only ornamentation was a large yin-yang symbol hung on one wall. Shiva motioned him to sit by the brazier. She put on a flowing white silk robe that somehow emphasized rather than concealed her incredible sensuality.

"Will you drink tea with me?" she asked. Her voice now held none of the contemptuous authority Bruce had heard in it earlier.

"It would be my pleasure." Bruce rolled the bottom of the ski mask to his upper lip, above his mouth.

"Wouldn't you like to take that off?" Shiva stared at the mask for a moment and then slowly, deliberately, slid her gaze down his body.

"I'm shy," Bruce said.

Holding a china teapot, Shiva knelt in front of him and placed it on the brazier. The candlelight glowed on her pale skin and caught reddish highlights in her jet-black hair. "And I wonder," she said, "what it would take to *cure* that shyness."

The acrid odor of burning charcoal mingled with another scent that seemed to waft from beneath the woman's robe, and Bruce felt himself wanting to reach for her.

Fifteen years' worth of world-class sublimation is now cleaning out its desk. Whoa.

Bruce coughed and said, "I have to admit, it's a much better opening line than asking my sign—that bit about curing my shyness, I mean."

Shiva raised an eyebrow. "You do not find me alluring?"

"Lady Shiva, you are very probably the sexiest woman alive, which is probably not exactly a late-breaking bulletin to you. But I really don't want my forearms broken. It would bitch my tennis game all to hell."

Shiva laughed. "You have passed your first test. Now take off your clothes."

"The direct approach?"

"Take them off and go outside. Sit in the snow until I summon you."

"Is this part of my training?"

"Yes. It is the part that freezes your ass off."

"Can I keep my mask on?"

"Only if it does not cover your ass."

Later, after he'd been sitting for two hours, naked and shivering, watching the sun rise over a distant peak, Shiva came out of the cabin. She was again nude.

"Stand up." No breath in her voice, and not much of anything else, either.

She walked around him, inspecting. "Much muscle."

"Is that good or bad?"

"It is neither. It is a fact. You are strong so we will use your strength. If you were not strong, we would use something else."

"What if I had nothing?"

"Then you would be dead and beyond my help."

In the past, he'd had many kinds of masters, ranging from thugs whose fighting skills made them nothing more than what they wanted to be, highly accomplished bullies, to gentle, wise Kirigi, the ancient Korean who refused further instruction when Bruce would not swear to forsake violence forever. But none were remotely like Shiva. Once she must have been a daughter, a student, perhaps even a lover; now, she was only her art. There was no technique, from any discipline Bruce had ever heard of, that she had not perfected, and many he found completely baffling.

She injured him, often, and when she did, she repaired the damage. An abrupt twist and a dislocated shoulder was restored with no hint of stiffness; a poultice held in place for fifteen minutes and a cut closed; a cup of foul-tasting brew and a raging nausea caused by a kick to the belly vanished. There was no concern in her ministrations, just an incredibly efficient restoration of functioning. She was a healer, as was Shondra, but there the similarity ended. He had sensed that Shondra desperately *wanted* her patients to be healthy. Shiva, he was certain, cared nothing for his well-being, only for the potential she saw in him.

In less than a week, he stopped being aware of the passage of time. No hours, minutes, seconds, no day or night: everything was reduced to conditions—of heat, cold, light, dark, pain, fatigue, exhaustion. And each condition had a remedy and, ultimately, a use.

Occasionally, in the rare moments when Shiva was not absolutely controlling his existence, Bruce wondered about Jean Paul. What was

Batman up to? Brooding in the Cave? Or dunking the odd serial killer in molten metal? But Shiva never allowed him more than a few moments' reverie before demonstrating a new technique or proving, usually humiliatingly, that he was inept in the execution of an old one.

He almost forgot about Gotham City.

6

Batman had fifteen minutes before his appointment with Sergeant Harvey Bullock. Time enough to cruise the streets near the river and search for crime: muggers, carjackers, burglars, crack dealers—he might find any or all of them in this neighborhood. It was nearly midnight on New Year's Eve. A mile away, revelers were gathered in the theater district drinking alcohol and cavorting like animals. They were not his worry.

He passed a tenement. Even in the wan glow of a streetlamp half a block away, he could see that its facade was grimy, its fire escape rusted and sagging. It was a dwelling for the poor, the hopeless, the lost, yet three of its windows were rimmed with colored lights and he could see a Christmas tree in a fourth. He remembered his holidays with his father. There hadn't been many of them; usually his father was away, traveling, he now knew, on errands of violence. But some Decembers his father joined him and they shared a meal—pizza, pastrami sandwiches from a delicatessen, bags of potato chips. They never exchanged gifts.

"The magi brought presents," his father had explained. "The angels had no need to. Their mission was to serve. We are as angels."

He had no idea what that meant, not then. Now he did. His father had been Azrael and Azrael bore, not gold, frankincense, and myrrh, but a fiery sword.

At midnight by the dashboard clock, he turned into a narrow alley between two loft buildings. Bullock was already there, leaning against his battered Dodge, holding a cardboard carton and stuffing a doughnut into his face.

"Yo," Bullock said as Batman approached. "Happy New Year."

"What do you want?" Batman asked.

"And they say *I* ain't got no gift of gab. Okay, let's get to it. You maybe noticed there ain't been much activity on the police band lately."

Batman nodded. It had been a week since he'd last learned of a felony by listening to the radio.

"You wonder why? Reason is, Gordon put out the word. We ain't supposed to use the squawk box except in case of emergency. We're supposed to carry quarters and call on pay phones. Or use one a' them portable phones, which Gordon says we gotta pop for ourselves. Eighty, a hundred bucks for one a them things and that ain't counting what they charge to put 'em in service. Anyway, I figure the commissioner's freezin' you out. He don't like your style these days. Me, I don't agree. I think you're doing fine. I make it was you who put Abattoir down coupla weeks ago, which was long overdue, and I'm damn sure you been kicking ass and taking names all over town. That's my kinda police work. I gotta tell you, I used ta think you was a pussy Boy Scout. Not anymore, though. Whatever you're having for breakfast these days, I'd like to feed it to the whole damn department, starting with Gordon."

"Thanks for the information." Batman turned and started for his car.

"Hold on a minute," Bullock said, taking a rolled sheaf of papers from the pocket of his overcoat. "I got something that might interest you. I got into the commissioner's private files and did some copying. It's a list of lowlifes we know are dirty but we ain't been able to nail—not in a way that'd stand up in court. I figure you might be able to do something about them. Keep you busy."

Batman accepted the papers.

"You get done with that bunch, gimme a call and I'll give you some more," Bullock said.

Batman got into the car and put the list on the seat next to him. He would return to the Cave and study the information Bullock had provided. Then he would go to work.

Shiva fell backward into a deep drift of snow, tried to roll, and couldn't; for a moment, she floundered. He watched her struggling to regain her footing and felt a sudden, savage joy. He had taken her arrogant confidence and, if he chose, he could dominate her, humble her—now, while she was helpless.

A bruise was already forming on her chest where his heel had struck her. There were four similar bruises on her body. Yesterday morning, there had been none.

"Excellent," she said.

"It's time for me to go," he said.

"Oh? I do not recall saying that."

"You didn't."

"Is it because you enjoy beating me?"

"That might be a good guess. But only a guess. I don't really know. I'm not prepared to find out."

Shiva shook her head ruefully. "Why do you struggle with yourself? Accept what you are."

"You're asking me to accept your *definition* of what I am. No deal."

Bruce went to the cabin, dressed, put on his backpack, and started down the path. The sun was almost directly overhead; the snow all around him was glaring.

Shiva stepped in front of him. "If you stay, I will make of you the finest martial artist who ever lived."

"Some other life."

"I could stop you from going. I could force you into a fight to the death."

"You could try."

"You doubt my ability?" Shiva laughed.

"No. But if you insist on mortal combat, I will disable you without killing you."

"You will fail. I will kill you."

"I accept the possibility. It doesn't change my mind."

Shiva bowed and moved aside.

"I'm grateful," Bruce said. "You have given me what I came for. If you need anything, get word to me. Now I have a final request. Don't ever come to Gotham City. Please."

"I promise nothing."

"I didn't expect you to. Good-bye."

When Bruce was at the bottom of the path, he heard Shiva call, "You will return to me."

He continued walking. *You have given me what I came for,* he'd told her, and it was true. Yesterday morning, as the sun had just begun to glint off the distant peaks, he'd blocked a punch to his face and retaliated instantly with a palm strike—the first of Shiva's bruises—and in that instant, he'd regained his capacity for violence, and something more, something he had never known was his: the pleasure of physically dominating another human being. An hour ago, as he watched Shiva fall, it had erupted into the purest joy he could imagine.

So I've been kidding myself all these years. I didn't despise the violence—I reveled in it.

Deep within himself, Bruce felt the stirring of a long-dormant fear, and he knew that if he lived through the coming week, if he survived the confrontation with Jean Paul, he would have to undertake the terrifying task of stripping away all the masks he wore to learn what kind of man lay beneath them.

Bruce's car was where he had left it, but completely buried under snow. In the month he had been with Shiva on the mountaintop, he had been only peripherally aware of the snowfall; it was just another part of the erratic cycle of pain, exhaustion, and rest that was life with Shiva. He hiked to the gas station and arranged for a tow, and while he was waiting for the tow truck driver to return, he idly listened to the cashier's radio and learned that the Northeast had been assaulted with some of the worst storms in history while he had been away.

He paid cash for the tow and a few minor repairs, tipped generously, and got in the car. It seemed strange to him, as though he were occupying some alien artifact—a vehicle from the fourth planet of Cygnus, say, assuming Cygnus had planets and those planets were host to beings who wanted to go somewhere. Cautiously at first, he guided the car down the steep road to the turnpike; once on the pike, he regained confidence and accelerated to the speed limit. The pavement had been plowed and the night was clear; he was back in Gotham by midnight.

He didn't want to risk a confrontation with Jean Paul—not yet, not until he knew what the situation was. So he checked into a downtown hotel, remembering to assume playboy Bruce Wayne's shambling walk, slightly unfocused gaze, and the tenor voice that just missed being shrill.

"I met a wonderful man in Charlotte Amalie," he explained to the desk clerk. "An absolute *guru*, in my opinion. He said it is absolutely *essential* for a person such as myself to get away from ancestral influences once in a while. Too much of their ectoplasmic vibration can be *stifling*. Well, my house is *crawling* with ancestral influences at any time at all, and *tonight* I felt the ghosts were breathing into my face. Invisibly, of course. Not that I believe any of it, but what's the harm in being careful, as my great-great-grandfather Solomon Wayne used to say. So I decided to spend the night here. Say, do you people serve kippers for breakfast?"

In the room, he considered calling Tim and didn't; at two in the morning, Tim should be sleeping, and Bruce didn't want to risk waking Jack Drake. He shed his clothes and lay down on the king-size bed. He couldn't get comfortable; he felt as though he were sinking a mile into a vast, feathery mire. After an hour he got up, placed a blanket on the rug, did a quick relaxation technique that he had learned when he was seventeen, and slept.

At seven o'clock he was awake and refreshed. He ordered room service breakfast—as a matter of fact, they *did* have kippers, but he opted for pancakes instead—and while he was waiting for it to arrive, telephoned the Drake house.

Tim sounded relieved. "Bruce, I was beginning to worry."

In the playboy's tenor, Bruce said, "Well, it *was* a longer trip than I anticipated, but the scenery was *delicious*. And how's by you?"

"No problemo."

"Our friend?"

"A few developments, but no real change other than with the costume. *That* he's changed a lot."

"Well, we should bang this around a bit. Any chance you can get into the city, Tim?"

"Sure. Where are you staying?"

"At the Gotham Towers, but I'd rather meet somewhere else. How about the park?"

"Southern entrance? By the bus stop?"

"Fine. Or the big birdcage. How'd that suit you?"

"Big birdcage it is. I should get there by eleven."

Bruce ate breakfast, which seemed heavy and cloying, and read the *Gotham Gazette*. Then he scanned the television for news programs and talk shows. Then it was *still* only nine o'clock. He yearned to run, or to punch the hell out of a bag, and either of those activities was possible; the hotel had a gym and the park was near enough for a run. But both were distinctly un–Bruce Waynelike.

He found he was actually *missing* Shiva's foot in his face.

You have given me what I came for, he had told her, and now he wished he could give a little of it back.

He sat and for the next ninety minutes slowly relaxed and contracted every external muscle in his body, one at a time, focusing, concentrating totally. This was Shiva's modification of a popular exercise technique, one that added elements of tai chi and hsing yi; it was as effective, if not as satisfying, as a morning at the gymnasium.

Tim was waiting for him at the birdcage.

"Let's walk," Bruce said, and they began to circle the zoo. It was Saturday morning: there were hundreds of mothers and nannies, and thousands of children—making angels in the snow, building snowmen, throwing snowballs. The park was a field of innocence. But Bruce scanned it anyway, and even after he was satisfied that there were no listening devices nearby, spoke in a near whisper.

"Fill me in," he said. "What've you been up to?"

"Algebra, Spanish, Civics, American History, English Composition, and Lunch," Tim said solemnly, and grinned. "Oh, you mean on the redbreast front. Well, Algebra and the rest of that stuff have been taking most of my time, but I have managed to plant a tracer on the 'mobile—"

"How?"

"By getting into the Cave. You shut off the alarms, remember?"

"I didn't want you taking any chances—"

"And I didn't. I played it supercareful. Not that I think Paul would hurt me. I really don't. Anyway, with the tracer I've been able to monitor him sometimes and I've even got a few photos—"

"Tim, that *had* to be dangerous."

"Safer than crossing the street. I used a telephoto lens. I wasn't within a hundred yards of the action."

"What kind of action?"

"Name it. If it's illegal, he's hurting it."

"How *much* hurt?"

"He's broken a lot of bones, but nobody's dead."

"Is he developing the leads himself?"

"Hard to say, Bruce. Not likely. He's not exactly a poster child for detective work."

"Then somebody's feeding him."

Tim packed a snowball and pegged it at a No Parking sign. "The last couple of nights he's been cruising up and down Burnett Avenue a lot. Seems interested in an apartment building in the four hundred block—"

"Four-fifteen?"

"How'd you know *that*, Bruce?"

"That's where his father was shot. An arms dealer named LeHah owned a penthouse there."

"Arms dealer? Hey, this plot is beginning to thicken. He busted an arms shipment a few nights ago. That's one of the things I photographed."

"When can I see the photo?"

"How about right now?" Tim reached into an inner pocket of his parka and produced a business envelope. "I've got the negs and small contact prints."

"This'll do."

Bruce took the envelope and removed a slim sheaf of photographs:

Batman punching; Batman slashing with his bladed gauntlet; Batman shooting his darts; a crate full of what looked like assault rifles; four men in windbreakers running; Batman kicking; Batman holding a small round object up to a lightbulb.

"I'll take these," Bruce told Tim.

"Consider them a homecoming gift. I didn't have time to shop for flowers."

"You want some lunch?"

"Not unless you need me. I told Ariana I might give her a call this afternoon."

"She'll be better company than me."

"I have learned never to argue with my elders, sir."

"You give me hope for the younger generation. Off you go."

Bruce turned and started to cross the path toward the park's softball diamonds.

"Bruce," Tim called. "You'll stay in touch?"

"Sure." Bruce waved and watched Tim trot toward the street.

I should have thanked him, Bruce thought. *One of these days I'll have to learn to be human.*

Waynetech's Gotham City headquarters were on the far side of the park. At noon on Saturday, the tall, grim building was deserted except for a skeleton crew of security guards. Old Tom Joseph, who had been a Wayne employee for thirty years, was manning the desk in the lobby.

"How be you, Mr. W?" old Tom said as Bruce strode to his desk. "Ain't seen you since before Christmas."

"Life grows ever more demanding," Bruce said. "Sometimes I do not know how I keep up."

"What can I do for you?"

"Not a single, solitary thing. Actually, I think I left a bottle of wine here someplace—a Château Lafite something-or-other. I happened to meet a rather intriguing young woman who confessed to a passion for the Château Lafite product. Thought I'd surprise her with an early Valentine's Day present."

"Help you look?"

"No, no, Mr. Joseph. I'll just stumble around myself. You go on about your business."

"You need anything, holler."

"That I will."

Bruce took the elevator to the computer laboratory on the sixteenth floor. He dropped his coat and hat onto a chair and noticed that the large, shadowy chamber was chilly; there was no heat in the building on weekends. Bruce went directly to an IBM mainframe with an array of peripheral equipment attached, snapped switches, and started working. He scanned one of Tim's photographs into the machine.

A hunch. Nothing more than that. But it won't hurt to know what Jean Paul was looking at.

On the monitor, Batman peered at the round object. Bruce tapped keys. The image sharpened. More tapping: a box appeared around the object. Tapping. The object seemed to grow and move forward until it filled the screen. A medal, probably of gold, bearing the likeness of a stern man with a halo around his head.

Yes. The sigil of the Order of St. Dumas.

Bruce looked away from the screen to the small photograph on the table in front of him.

What was Jean Paul thinking when this was taken? What did it do to whatever's left of his sanity?

7

 He had beaten the gunrunners into submission, and as he was making his way to the car, he had glimpsed the golden disc on the floor of the warehouse, gleaming in a stray beam of light shining through the grimy window. He picked it up, peered at it, and gasped. He had seen its twin only once, lying in his father's palm, but he would never forget it because his father had said, simply, "St. Dumas," and suddenly often-heard syllables had meaning to his seven-year-old mind.

This *is St. Dumas. This* man. *St. Dumas is a* man. *It's a* man *that father is always talking about.*

At first, standing in that riverfront garage, surrounded by crates of automatic weapons, he thought the medal was a sign from heaven, or somewhere in that celestial region, a sign that he was doing good and righteous work. He felt a rush of approving virtue. Then he realized that *of course* he was doing good work—had not the Venerable Saint himself approved of it?—and that the medal must have been dropped by one of the criminals. He was confused. What would a criminal be doing with the sigil of the holiest and most secret order on earth?

He heard sirens. Sergeant Bullock had said he'd give Batman a first crack at the mooks but then he'd send in the cavalry. The cavalry was coming, was almost here.

Batman left by a side door. He was speeding up a rear alley as four GCPD squad cars were arriving at the front of the warehouse.

Batman went immediately to the Cave, removed the medal, placed it on a table, and waited. St. Dumas did not appear. Neither did his father. Neither did anyone or anything else that might have answered his questions. So he had to think. He had to be a detective, which he hated. But it didn't really require much thought—hardly any at all—once he remembered that his father's killer, Carleton LeHah, a renegade member of the Order, had been in the arms trade—indeed, was almost certainly the only arms dealer in Gotham City. As a member, he could have possessed a duplicate of the medal the elder Valley carried.

Okay, this detective stuff isn't too hard once you get into it.

LeHah was dead. Jean Paul himself had administered the killing stroke. But he could have dropped the medal sometime before he died, or left it somewhere, and an associate could have gotten it. The associate could have been one of the men Batman had just vanquished.

Batman lifted the telephone and called Harvey Bullock's home number. He asked about the gunrunners. Bullock responded with a brief précis of their arrest records, prison sentences backgrounds, aliases, and known employers, none of which interested Batman.

"I make the Patrick mook the honcho," Bullock said, his words muffled by something—almost certainly a doughnut—in his mouth. "Mostly 'cause the rest don't seem bright enough to light a Christmas tree bulb."

"Tell me about him," Batman said. "About Patrick."

"I just did. You oughtta learn to listen. Okay, I'll run it by you again. Age, thirty-four. Arrests for extortion—"

"Not his history," Batman said impatiently. "Anything odd he said or did. At the police station."

"Yeah, the most amazing thing. He swore he was *innocent.* I told him we was real sorry we inconvenienced him, but he'd have to stay anyhow and could I maybe get him a glass of lemonade."

"Anything else?"

"Yeah. He accused the arresting officer of stealing his lucky piece when he was getting out of the lockup. Some kinda gold medal, he said. I asked him how lucky could it be with him getting busted like he did."

"Getting out?" Batman asked angrily. "You let him go?"

"Hell, his lawyer was here waiting for him with a writ from a judge that's dirty as a whore's panties. He wasn't behind bars an hour. Funny how fast the system works for the bad guys."

Batman broke the connection without replying. The gold medal, the sigil, belonged to this Patrick and—

And?

Now what? What was he supposed to *do* with this information?

Then he remembered. LeHah had help when he killed Jean Paul's father. He didn't know how he knew—maybe something his father had said in those final, terrible moments, or something Bruce Wayne had figured out, or something St. Dumas himself had spoken. But Batman was absolutely certain LeHah wasn't alone in sending bullets into his father's body—in fact, LeHah may not have actually pulled the trigger at all. This Patrick—if he was close enough to LeHah to have LeHah's medal, LeHah would have entrusted Patrick with an important murder. Perfectly logical.

This detective stuff isn't too hard . . .

"Kill him."

Batman looked around. The Cave was empty. So who had spoken? No matter. Kill him. A good idea. An imperative.

He called Bullock and got Patrick's address: 415 Burnett, penthouse. LeHah's address. This confirmed it for Batman: if Patrick lived in LeHah's apartment, he *had* to have been his father's executioner.

Perfectly logical.

The next night, he drove past 415 Burnett. There were no lights on in the penthouse. He came back an hour later, and an hour after that, and twice more. No lights.

Same the following night. Two nights with nothing to show.

A third futile night.

Then he got an idea: detective work. He phoned the building and talked to the doorman. He said he had a package for Mr. Patrick, and Mr. Patrick wasn't answering his calls and could the doorman help?

"Mr. Patrick's outta town," the doorman said. "Be back Friday, Saturday. But if you leave the package with me, I'll be sure he gets it—"

No. I'll be sure he gets it.

Friday night: no lights.

Batman returned to the Cave early Saturday morning and sat down to wait. In twelve hours, it would be dark again.

Bruce went from the computer lab to his office on the top floor of the Wayne Building. He stood at the window watching Gotham City brighten itself: first the tiny dots of headlights as drivers realized night was upon them; next the hazy blue of the streetlamps; finally the gaudy glare of the theater district, which contained far more bars and topless joints and hotels that rented rooms by the hour than theaters.

That's where Bane broke me the last minute I was Batman.

He turned from the window to a large, framed daguerreotype of downtown Gotham as it was in 1883, taken by his great-great-grandfather with an experimental camera—a rough approximation of Gotham to come; the streets were cobblestoned and crisscrossed with power lines, but the buildings were almost all of the grim, windowless style that professors of architecture the world over presented to their classes as examples of how not to build a metropolis, the style that still made the city an easy laugh-getter for lounge comedians everywhere. The picture frame was hinged, and when he swung it open, he was looking at a safe, which he ignored. He slid the plywood backing from the frame and removed folded cloth from under it. He shook out the cloth and held up a gray-black costume. It was of silk: a *summer* costume, but after the month with Shiva, he knew he wouldn't be bothered by the cold outside.

He removed Bruce Wayne's finery and started to put on Batman's combat garb.

He hesitated, not knowing why. A part of him was resisting this return to what he had been for so long. He shrugged and dressed in the tights, the tunic, the gloves, the cape. Finally he started to pull down the mask and again hesitated: with the mask in place, the transformation would be complete; he would no longer be Bruce Wayne.

But he was. Even with the mask on his face, he did not experience the internal shift that had always characterized his assumption of the Batman identity. He was merely Bruce Wayne in different clothing. That was bad; that could be dangerous. Bruce Wayne was never a match for Batman's enemies.

He considered putting his ordinary clothing on over the costume; that would certainly simplify getting out of this building and traveling the half mile to 415 Burnett Avenue. But if he couldn't pass old Tom in the lobby and a few strollers he might meet on the way without being seen, he had no business wearing a cape and cowl, much less matching himself against gunrunners and maniacs.

Old Tom was no problem; he would go to his grave never knowing that a shadowy figure passed within two feet of where he sat reading the sports page of the *Gotham Gazette*. The strollers weren't difficult either; Gotham City's architectural and design eccentricities—the high, windowless walls, narrow streets, few light sources—made sneaking through it an easy pleasure. Rudimentary technique was all he needed: move quickly but smoothly, stay close to walls, use alleys where feasible, use fire escapes and rooftops when possible.

I may feel more like Bruce Wayne than Batman, but at least Bruce isn't a complete klutz.

Burnett Avenue was the widest core city thoroughfare in Gotham— three short, tree-lined blocks lined with luxury apartment buildings and condominiums all constructed since the Second World War. It ran between the rim of the theater district and the river, and it was mostly inhabited by old-monied men and women who wanted "a place in the city" in addition to their inevitable suburban mansions, and new-monied men and women who could not yet afford suburban mansions but would be able to soon.

Bruce found a comfortable spot behind a chimney on the roof of a condo across from Carleton LeHah's penthouse and waited for Jean Paul Valley to arrive. He might not, of course; he may have lost interest in the four hundred block of Burnett Avenue or be busy elsewhere tonight. But if Jean Paul *did* appear, it might be an opportunity to observe, judge, and if necessary, stop him.

Bruce had no idea what Jean Paul had seen in the medal, or deduced from it. But his finding the gold sigil and his sudden interest in LeHah's property couldn't be a coincidence. Bruce mentally reviewed what he had learned about 415 Burnett when he was pursuing LeHah last year. It had a mere fifteen units, all three bedrooms and larger; rents started at around forty-eight thousand a year and climbed to whatever the market would bear. There was a laundry room in the basement—nice for the hired help —and an attached parking garage. There was also a novelty, a helicopter landing pad on the roof that the tenants were now forbidden to use because of a zoning ordinance. LeHah owned the building. His own unit was the largest, fourteen rooms with terraces on all four sides. There was a doorman, for show, and a private security force—at least four men armed with shotguns and automatics on duty at all times. The building was probably Gotham's most luxurious fortress.

He had been waiting for ninety minutes when he saw lights go on behind LeHah's penthouse windows. LeHah was dead, of course; Bruce had seen him die in a blazing New Mexican oil refinery. But a man like LeHah would have an organization, and maybe a few leftover odds and ends stashed around the old domicile—Swiss bank account codes, for instance. His associates—accountants, attorneys, assassins—would look for whatever LeHah had left that could be turned into power or profit and were almost certainly looking for it at this moment. But they weren't Bruce's concern, not tonight, and maybe never.

He leaned over the parapet and scanned the street. A black custom-built Maserati sped from the darkness at the corner, glided to a stop in front of LeHah's building, and a caped figure sprinted from it to the glass entrance.

Bruce moved. He had looped his line around the chimney and was sliding down it when he heard the first shots. He hit the ground running.

Okay, here we go. Let's see how good Shiva's training was.

A uniformed doorman was sprawled just inside the entrance to 415 and a guard lay a few feet away, his body almost completely covering a .12-gauge shotgun. There was a bank of elevators immediately ahead and, to the left of them, fire stairs. Bruce knew Jean Paul would be on the stairs; even amateurs were aware that elevators were traps.

Bruce ran.

The two men in the lobby had been easy. Batman had dropped them without missing a breath.

Did Wayne ever handle himself better? No, not a chance.

The one at the top of the stairs was no harder. His weapon was only half out of its holster when Batman punched him into the door to the penthouse. As he was falling, Batman kicked, and the door slammed open.

There were two of them in the spacious living room. Batman shot darts into the one nearest the door. The second, who was in the process of replacing a section of the fireplace, had his hands full of a heavy stone. He was lifting it to a throwing position when Batman's gauntlet split his scalp.

Batman glanced around the room. There was the gleam of metal behind the gap in the fireplace: a safe. Across the thick, creamy rug were French doors opening onto a concrete terrace and near them two bulging suitcases. Obviously these criminals had come here to obtain illegal funds hidden earlier. Batman had no idea why they couldn't simply put the money in a bank, nor did he care; that was a matter for Sergeant Bullock. Batman was here to kill Patrick and—

But which one of the men he had dropped *was* Patrick? He did not know what Patrick looked like. He had never seen a picture, nor even gotten a description. Bruce Wayne would have certainly not have made that mistake—

Well, Wayne had his methods and Batman had his. The answer to the problem was obvious: kill them all.

"What the hell?"

The man who had spoken was standing in a door Batman had not noticed earlier, a dozen feet to the left of the entrance; it led to an inner room, a bedchamber probably. He was holding a small radio—a walkie-talkie. His eyes moved, and he said, "Shit." He backed through the door and slammed it. Did he really think it would stop Batman?

The door split down the middle when Batman struck it. The man was next to French doors, duplicates of those in the living room, muttering into his transmitter, "—no, dammit, not the heliport—*here!*"

"Patrick," Batman said.

"Hey, I don't know what your beef with me is—"

"Then you *are* Patrick."

The man looked flustered for a moment. "No, no, Patrick's not gonna show—"

"You lie." Batman advanced.

"Don't." This time the speaker was behind Batman. He recognized the voice. He whirled. A second caped, masked figure stood just inside the shattered door. For a moment Batman didn't recognize the newcomer.

Another criminal? St. Dumas in another guise? No—

"Geez, *two* of 'em," Patrick said.

—Bruce Wayne, come to meddle.

"Stay out of this," Batman told him.

"We'll bind them and leave them for the cops," Bruce said.

"Not him." Batman jerked a thumb in Patrick's direction. "He dies."

"No."

Batman raised his gauntlet to shoot darts, but Bruce was already coming, low and fast. The darts passed over his head. He hit Batman at the knees, and both men tumbled to the carpet.

From high overhead, somewhere in the night sky, came the whine of an engine and the sound of rotors whipping the air.

Patrick slid open a glass door and slipped onto the terrace.

Batman slashed at Bruce. His bladed gauntlet ripped open a sleeve and tore into flesh. Bruce rolled away and vaulted to his feet. He glanced down at his bleeding arm. "I'll let you have that one," he said. "But not another."

The engine noise was close, just above the building. Through the glass, Batman saw Patrick standing on the terrace, gazing upward.

A *helicopter.*

Batman stood.

"Let him go," Bruce Wayne said.

Batman ignored him. Bruce grabbed Batman's shoulder, spun him around, jammed his hip against Batman's, dropped, and lifted—a perfectly timed, perfectly executed judo throw. Batman somersaulted and landed flat on the floor.

There was a thump over their heads. The engine noise was deafening.

Batman kicked Bruce Wayne in the stomach and scrabbled across the carpet. At the French doors, he got to his feet and bolted onto the terrace. A helicopter trembled on a flat platform atop the penthouse; its rotors blasted Batman with wind. Patrick was stepping off a short ladder that ran from the terrace to the platform. Batman ran to it and climbed as Patrick was hopping into the helicopter.

Bruce Wayne burst from the doors, vaulted to the wall of the terrace, and from there leapt to the platform.

The helicopter rose.

Batman jumped and caught one of the helicopter's landing skids.

Bruce Wayne caught the other.

The helicopter seemed to slew to the side and then rose further, passing over the rooftops, over the riverfront, and out over the river itself. It spun on its axis and flew downriver, toward the red lights of the Gotham Bay Bridge. Batman grabbed a strut and pulled himself up onto the skid.

Patrick and a leather-jacketed pilot were in the cockpit behind a plexiglass dome. Batman punched through the plexiglass and struck the pilot in the face. The helicopter tilted and began to drop toward the water a thousand feet below.

On the other side of the dome, Bruce Wayne yanked open a door and reached across Patrick to the control yoke. But Patrick, panicked, tried to shove him back.

The helicopter spiraled downward.

The red lights on top of the bridge towers seemed to slide up from under the aircraft, followed by the steel suspension cables of the bridge itself.

The aircraft's tail assembly struck a cable, and a moment later the cockpit smashed into a tower.

Batman leaned away from the skid, closed both hands around a cable, and began to slide. His armor would protect him.

The helicopter dropped a yard and stopped, snared in bands of steel. It hung like a grotesque insect caught in a spiderweb. A rotor snapped off and wafted slowly into the river.

Bruce slapped Patrick lightly on the cheek. "Don't move," he said. "Help will be here shortly."

"What the hell's going on?" Patrick whimpered.

The helicopter swayed and creaked as a gust of wind hit the bridge. Patrick clung to his seat.

Bruce clung to a cable and looked down to the roadbed. It was too dark to see anything clearly other than the headlights of a dozen vehicles stopped or slowing.

I have to assume that Jean Paul's there someplace. There, or in the water. Could he have survived a fall all the way to the river, even in his armor?

Bruce simply couldn't know. But he had to assume that Jean Paul was alive.

He had more immediate problems. He could hear sirens. Police and firemen would be here in a minute, followed by reporters who would ask questions he didn't want to answer. The cops would have questions too, and demands that he accompany them. That was not on his agenda.

He was wearing silk clothing. If he tried to slide down a cable, the friction would shred the cloth and then rip the flesh from his bones. He looked at the nearest tower, a yard away. In the red glow of its lights he could see ladder rungs sunk into the masonry. He opened his right hand, swung, caught a rung, opened his left hand, and was flat against rough stone.

Shouts from below.

He found a rhythm. Grip, drop, grip, drop, grip, drop . . .

The stone in front of his eyes became a reddish blue, darkened, brightened . . . A police cruiser, its dome light flashing, was on the roadbed immediately below him.

More shouts.

Grip, drop, grip and—

He pushed away from the tower and dropped a final time, beyond the bridge railing to a narrow catwalk that hung between the railing and empty air, and landed on his toes.

"Freeze," someone yelled—a cop.

Bruce ran, certain that the cop would not shoot.

If Jean Paul were alive, he would go back to Burnett Avenue, to his car. Approximately two miles. He wouldn't be able to move as quickly as Bruce, not in that bulky armor. But he had a big head start. Bruce couldn't catch him. Once behind the wheel, Jean Paul would head for the Cave; he had nowhere else to go.

Bruce himself had no vehicle—he didn't even have cab money. He might be able to steal a car or a motorcycle, but that was risky. The Wayne Building wasn't much further than Burnett Avenue; that would be his first destination.

He went to a service door, picked a lock with the tab of a soda can he found on the pavement, and entered. An alarm would sound, a guard would check, find nothing, and if he were doing his job properly, note a possible electrical malfunction in his watch log.

Bruce went up the back stairs to his office and put his suit on over the silken costume.

Forty minutes later, Tom Joseph saw his boss emerge from the elevator.

"Find your wine, Mr. W?" he asked.

"No such luck. What time is it?"

"Midnight, close to."

"Darn. The shops will be closed. Listen, Mr. Joseph, are there still company cars in the garage?"

"Couple of Chevies."

"Could you bring one around for me? Better yet, just give me the keys."

"Sure thing." Tom detached a pair of keys from the ring he wore on his belt and handed them to Bruce. "Silver one'll get you in the garage. Other one's for the Chevy. Green Nova, parked near the stairs. I'll open the exit for you."

"Thanks a whole bunch."

"Shame about the wine."

"Yes, it is. I wonder if my lady friend would settle for a weekend in Aruba."

Tom chuckled and shook his head.

As he was guiding the car down the ramp into the Cave, Batman had a vision . . . no, not exactly a vision—more like an inspired idea. He got out of the car, checked the alarms, and discovered that they had been disconnected. For how long? How long had he been vulnerable, unprotected, a potential victim? He didn't know, but he did know who was responsible. Bruce Wayne. A devil incarnate. He couldn't blame himself for not having seen Wayne's true self earlier: it was part of being a devil to be clever and deceptive. Cleverness and deception were almost inevitably hallmarks of evil beings—his father had certainly been right about *that*—and there was little even a vigilant man could do to guard against them. Still, he wondered how Wayne could have fooled him for so long. It wasn't until earlier that night, when he saw Wayne in a costume—a mocking travesty of the *true* Batman garb—that he realized the fullness of his enemy's depravity. He could almost feel the recognition blast from the center of his being and hit Wayne, and watch all Wayne's cleverness and deception shatter and fall away.

Batman spent the next hour reconnecting the alarms and adding to them, wiring them to various weapons. If anyone entered the Cave, they

would not only advertise their presence, they would almost surely die. Which was as it should be.

When the task was finished, he went to his favorite place, a spot on the stone floor near the computer bank but out of the overhead lights, and sat to think. He reached up to remove his mask, hesitated, and decided to leave it on. The mask and costume were part of who he was; without them, he didn't feel like himself.

He needed to plan, but before he did that, he needed to establish priorities.

All right. Patrick had to be executed—that fact had not changed; in fact, the urgency was greater than ever. But there was one obstacle between him and his father's slayer: Bruce Wayne. A false idol. A false Batman. And—the idea stunned him—perhaps his father's *real* assassin. Why had he thought it was LeHah, or Patrick, when Bruce Wayne was the better suspect? Wayne had entered Batman's life barely a month after his father's death—could that possibly be a *coincidence?* No, no. Batman felt awed at the ability of the foe to prevent him from seeing the obvious. But ultimately, the truth would out.

Before he could destroy Patrick, he would have to destroy Wayne. No, that wasn't quite right: Patrick could live, Patrick wasn't important. Wayne was his only concern. He would have to find the enemy, but that shouldn't be difficult. He knew Wayne's secrets—that had been the *enemy's* big mistake, to let Batman know so much. In fact, it suddenly occurred to him, he might not have to do any more than wait. Wayne had visited both the Cave and the house above it before, and he might again. Batman would lurk until the enemy appeared and strike as he was taught to strike, swiftly, declaring vengeance in the name of St. Dumas—

"Have you forgotten you are excommunicated?"

The Most Venerable One was floating above him, surrounded by a blinding aura as dazzling as the sun but casting no light into the surrounding shadows.

Batman could find no answer; a terrible dread began growing within him.

"Have you?" The saint's voice seemed stern, but Batman was certain he could hear compassion in it. "Yes, you have."

"You have often graced me with your presence—"

"—Since you disobeyed the commands of my Order," St. Dumas said, finishing the thought Batman would not have been able to utter.

"Yes." Batman bowed his head.

"Though you have disobeyed, I have neither forgotten nor forsaken you," the saint said. "You are mine. You can never be anything *other* than mine. Don't you know that, foolish child?"

"How can I serve you?" Batman said, feeling tears fill his eyes.

"You *are* serving me. You *have been* serving me. As Batman, you are far more useful than as Azrael. Others can don the garments of Azrael, but there is only one Batman."

The dread within Batman's soul was transformed, instantly and completely, into joy.

"Only one Batman," St. Dumas repeated. "You are he."

Batman looked up. St. Dumas was gone, but his presence filled the Cave.

An alarm sounded. Someone was entering Wayne Manor. Batman smiled beneath the mask.

During the drive from Gotham to the manor, Bruce considered and rejected several tactics. He had to assume that Jean Paul had reactivated the security system and was prepared for an assault. That didn't eliminate a sneak attack, but it did compromise its chance for success, unless he used the one entrance that neither Jean Paul nor Tim knew about—and that he would employ only as a last resort. He would much prefer to avoid violence, although the encounter at the penthouse proved that Shiva's instruction had been effective.

I don't want to hurt him. But why not? Jean Paul is dangerous, and I've never hesitated to solve his kind of problem with force before. Why not now?

He didn't know. Later, maybe, he could find an answer. Now, he decided, he would again try to talk with Jean Paul. Meet him in the manor. Keep the costume hidden under his Bruce Wayne finery. Avoid threatening him in any way. That might work.

He glanced at his Rolex: 2:45. The darkest part of the night. The time

when Batman was usually busiest. He wondered if there would *be* a
Batman after tonight.

*If there is, he won't be the same, regardless of who's under the mask.
For better or worse, this is the night Batman changes.*

He turned off the access road onto the drive to the manor. Twice his
car stalled in snowdrifts and he had to use considerable skill to free it; the
drive hadn't been plowed. Normally Alfred would have seen to that, but
Alfred was gone, probably forever.

He parked in front of the main entrance, tramped through the snow,
and opened the front door, mildly surprised that Jean Paul had not
changed the lock. He stepped into the foyer, switched on the chandelier,
and stood waiting. The alarm should have sounded; Jean Paul would be
aware of his presence.

Bruce heard a grating sound. The grandfather clock swung open and a
grim figure stepped into the foyer and shouted: *"No!"*

"Hello, Jean Paul," Bruce said.

"You are not the Batman!"

"I guess that's what we have to discuss."

"*I* am the Batman. Now—*get out!*" The voice was full of rage—rage,
and something darker and uglier.

"I'm not here to fight with you, Jean Paul."

"I am not Jean Paul. He is gone—forever. I am the Batman."

"Okay, Batman, let's talk."

"We have nothing to talk about. Do I have to tell you again? *Get
out!*"

"Look, I'm trying to understand you. Can we agree that I *do* own this
house? It's mine—"

"Because someone *gave* it to you." Jean Paul flung a hand backward,
gesturing at the framed portrait of Thomas Wayne on the wall behind
him. "*He* gave it to you. Your *father.* You don't deserve to own Wayne
Manor any more than you deserve to be the Batman."

"You can't believe that. Batman is my creation—"

"*Is* he? Somehow I doubt it. I don't think a privileged, pampered
weakling like Bruce Wayne could create something like me—"

"Like *you?*"

"—but let's say you aren't lying. Let's say you *did* create Batman. You were too weak to continue being him—too weak and too cowardly. You couldn't defeat Bane. He broke you like a twig and what did you do? You *ran*. Ran off and left me to do the dirty work."

"Jack Drake and Shondra—Dr. Kinsolving—were kidnapped. I had to find them—"

"So you say. So you'd have us believe. I will tell you one final time— *get out!* Do what you do best—slink away to your women and your cars and your parties and take"—Jean Paul whirled, reached up, and tore the portrait from the wall—"your precious *daddy* with you." He lifted the portrait over his head and snapped it across his knee. The ancient wooden frame broke.

Bruce could not believe what he was seeing.

Jean Paul tore the painting in half and flung both parts at Bruce's feet.

Bruce looked down at them numbly. He had never anticipated something like this, had never experienced this overwhelming, paralyzing fury. His fists clenched, and he began to move forward. He wanted to hurt this insane interloper more than he had wanted to hurt anyone since that night, so long ago, when he saw a revolver buck in a stranger's fist and watched his mother and father fall. He stopped and through his anger remembered that he was determined to avoid violence. He controlled his breathing for a few moments and said, "Until this moment, I wasn't sure. I'd heard that you'd lost control, that you'd become a savage, devoid of kindness, compassion, simple decency. I even heard that you'd done what none of us can ever allow ourselves to do. I heard you killed a man. But I wasn't sure. I didn't want to believe any of it. I denied what I knew to be true. I can't do that now. You're guilty. But the responsibility is at least partially mine. I helped make you what you are."

"You did *nothing!*"

"I wish that were true, Paul. But it isn't. We've got a lot to do together, you and I. We begin here and now. Take off the costume."

"Never."

There was rage in Jean Paul's voice, and something else that Bruce now recognized: fear. Jean Paul was afraid. Of what?

Jean Paul raised his gauntlet, but Bruce was already down and rolling, knowing what was about to happen. The darts passed through the space his head had been occupying and thudded into the wall. Jean Paul lowered his arm and shot another volley. Bruce grabbed the halves of Thomas Wayne's portrait and raised them in front of his face. The darts penetrated the canvas and the wooden backing, caught, stopped an inch from their target.

How many does he have? Can I get to him before he shoots again?

Bruce reached over his head and flicked the light switch. He was at a momentary disadvantage as his eyes adjusted to the sudden darkness, but Jean Paul would be having the same problem, and Bruce had been familiar with this foyer all his life. That would give him an edge.

He heard a creaking and the click of a lock. Jean Paul had gone through the hidden door behind the clock, had fled back to the Cave.

Bruce got a flashlight from the kitchen; he didn't want to chance turning on the chandelier. He examined the clock. The combination had, as he expected, been changed, but that was no problem. Bruce had designed and helped build the mechanism. It took him only moments to decipher the new combination and open the door—

He hesitated and decided on caution. He dropped to his knees and finished opening the hidden entrance. There was a hiss, and a hail of Jean Paul's darts sped across the foyer to join their mates in the wall.

Okay, I didn't expect it to be easy. There are probably other booby traps on the stairs behind the clock and at the car exit. Probably by Tim's trapdoor, too. He'll have all the ways in and out covered—all that he knows about.

Bruce left the manor by the carport and began trotting across the snow-covered lawn and onto the open field behind the garden. Thick gray clouds hid the moon, but Bruce knew exactly where he was going. He leapt a fence, ran another dozen yards, and stopped. There was no marker here, no shrubbery, nothing to distinguish this patch of snowy ground from the acres of snowy ground that surrounded it. But he knew it, went to it unerringly, knelt and ran his fingers into the dead brown grass, seeking and finding the seam hidden beneath. He allowed himself a few seconds to remember. . . .

The day had been as bright and sunny as any the six-year-old Brucie ever saw. Mommy and Daddy had put up a badminton net next to the garden, were idly batting a birdie back and forth, talking and laughing.

Brucie wandered away on an exploration. He chased a butterfly. He blew the fuzz from dandelion stems. He rolled in the tall, prickly grass and suddenly the ground didn't feel *right,* and suddenly there *was* no ground and he was seeing the day shrink to a narrow blue slit and something struck his back and his legs curled to his chest and he couldn't scream and he was sliding away from the blue slit into cold and dark and terror. After a while he could whimper, and a while after that he could shriek. He heard Mommy:

". . . down *there,* Tom . . ."

And Daddy:

". . . get him out . . . hole's too damn small . . ."

Mommy again, sounding like glass breaking: "Daddy's coming for you, sweetie. Can you hear me, Brucie? Daddy will rescue you."

Time passed and Brucie thought maybe he was dead. This was how he thought of death: cold and dark and hard and, more than anything, lonely. He must have slept. He blinked and Daddy's face, all blurry and smudged with dirt, was inches from his. Brucie was lifted up, through the blue slit and out into a day that was no longer sunny, lifted into Mommy's arms. She hugged him until he hurt. Her cheeks were wet. She carried him back to the house, put him to bed, gave him a glass of chocolate milk, and pretty soon a doctor came. . . .

Bruce had fallen through a narrow fissure that may have existed, unnoticed, for tens of thousands of years. When Thomas Wayne found it that day and realized how his son had vanished, he got a sledgehammer from the tool shed and smashed away the rock until he could squeeze through it. Later, he had wedged a wooden baffle into the ground over the hole and dumped a bucketful of concrete around the baffle's edges.

"Will that be enough, Tom?" Bruce recalled his mother asking.

"It will be if we keep our eyes on the boy next time."

"Shouldn't you get a workman—"

"No, I shouldn't. If word of the cave gets out, we'll have everybody from geologists to historians poking around. You want that, Mart?"

"I really wouldn't mind . . ."

Thomas Wayne put his hands on his wife's shoulders. "Marty, Marty, Marty. Are you *ever* going to stop being my little worrywart?"

Thomas Wayne had been an excellent physician and a mediocre hole plugger. Bruce easily dug away the crumbling concrete, slipped his fingers over the baffle, and lifted. He slipped through the hole and slid down a steep incline to the floor of the cavern. He took the kitchen flashlight from his pocket and swept it around him. He was in a tiny, dome-shaped chamber no bigger than a large pantry. He'd assumed that it would be huge; to a terrified six-year-old it *had* been huge. He stood still and listened, hearing nothing more than the distant drip of water and the flapping of bats' wings.

There was a narrow round opening in the cave wall to his right; it would lead to the main chamber below the house. He wondered if it was wide enough to accommodate him. Ever since he had returned to Gotham a decade ago, he had been intending to explore and map the cave, but something urgent was always delaying the project.

My consolation is that Jean Paul probably hasn't done any exploration either. So there won't be any nasty surprises waiting for me in here.

He started toward the tunnel, stopped, found the baffle, and wedged it back into place.

Why am I worrying about the thing now, when I've ignored it for so long?

The only answer he could think of was that it seemed worth doing and he had learned not to ignore the promptings of his subconscious. Ignoring those promptings, insisting on pure logic, had almost killed him several times the first year he wore the mask.

He squeezed into the tunnel, duckwalked, and then began crawling. The stone was rough; it scraped his palms and tore the knees from his trousers. The tunnel narrowed. His overcoat bunched at the shoulders and caught on something, stopping him. He wriggled out of the coat and continued. His shirt ripped, and then the silk tunic underneath it ripped. He crawled.

It took him almost two hours to travel a thousand yards.

When he was beginning to wonder if he had miscalculated, if the tunnel led anywhere he wanted to be, he saw a glow. He closed his eyes for a full minute, then opened them. The glow was illuminating the gray stone ahead. He crawled forward. The tunnel widened, turned. He stood and crept to where he could see the Cave—the vast chamber filled with computers, books, labs, gymnastic equipment, all the tools of his vocation.

Flattening himself against the wall, he scanned the area. Jean Paul was sitting on the floor, his back against the mainframe computer, silent and motionless. He seemed alien to the electronics that surrounded him, as ancient and elemental as the cavern itself.

What's my move? Nothing between us except the trapeze bar, and that's well off the floor. No cover, but I could probably reach him before he could stand, run zigzag to avoid his darts. Then a flying kick to his head. A good, solid kick would bounce his skull off the inside of his helmet, disorient him, cause a concussion if I'm lucky. Then he's mine.

Bruce remembered his father's portrait, torn, lying on the foyer rug, and again felt the fury. He breathed deeply and let the emotion ebb from him.

He's mine. And then? Take him downtown? Gordon would have to ask the hard questions—he wouldn't want to, but his dedication to his job, his sense of honor, would force him to. That would be the end of Batman. Maybe that would be best, maybe that's inevitable, but I'm not prepared to do it. Not yet. Talking to him didn't work before. But it might now, if I don't give him a target. It's worth a try.

He cupped his hands around his mouth and shouted, certain that his voice would reverberate throughout the stone chambers, that it would seem to come from everywhere at once: *"Jean Paul Valley—"*

Jean Paul twitched as though stung.

". . . listen to me . . ." The words echoed, as though the stone itself were speaking.

Jean Paul rose to his knees and raised his arms. "Is that you, oh most venerable St. Dumas?"

He thinks I'm that phony saint!

"Have you come to me again?"

Maybe I can use this, pretend to be Dumas. No, I won't lie to him.

"St. Dumas is dead," Bruce shouted.

Jean Paul sank back to sit on his heels; his arms dropped.

"Your father is dead. It is time to free yourself of them . . . and of Batman. There is no Batman. Batman is a fiction—"

Bruce listened to the echoes as though listening to a stranger saying something utterly astonishing. Had he actually said that? All these years he had believed that *Batman* was the truth, *Bruce Wayne* the fiction.

"No Dumas," he continued. "No Batman . . . only you, Jean Paul Valley . . . the others aren't real . . . you are. . . ."

10

Batman was transfixed. He was almost accustomed to visits from St. Dumas, but who was *this* speaking to him? Someone with more authority than the Venerable One, of that he was sure. Someone higher in the heavenly brotherhood. An angel? An *arch*angel? Someone even higher? But what was he saying, this heavenly messenger? Things that did not make sense—

". . . *stop hiding behind something that does not exist. Let yourself be yourself. Take off the costume.*"

Yes. Oh, yes. It was plain to Batman now. The slyness, the cunning—the deceiver almost fooled him. *Almost.*

"Take off the costume." The exact words the defiler had used earlier. It was no angel speaking, it was a coward afraid to show his face. Batman smiled. Cunning and deception? Batman would *show* him cunning and deception.

Careful, now. Sound humble. "It's you, isn't it? Bruce Wayne?"

Batman waited for a reply. None came. He added a note of weariness to the humility: "All right. I'm tired of fighting, tired of running from you." Batman astonished himself; he sounded so *sincere.* "Come on out. Let's discuss a truce."

Bruce Wayne emerged from darkness—how appropriate!—and stood beneath the trapeze bar. "We have no need for a truce, Paul. We're not enemies. But as I said, we have a lot to do together."

Batman stood, careful to put his hands at his sides, palms forward and open. "Not a lot, really. Just one task—and its *mine,* not *ours.*" He moved toward the enemy, slowly, casually. "Upstairs, in the house, I tried to kill you—I *could* have killed you, you know." *Careful: don't boast, don't threaten.* "Then I changed my mind. Instead of finishing what I'd started, I came down here to think." *The astonishing part of this is, I'm telling the truth. But isn't that how deceivers work? By using truth to cloak lies? Father once told me that the devil quotes scripture for his own purposes.* "That was a mistake—" And now he was raising his hand in what he was sure looked to the enemy like a simple gesture. "Thinking is foolish and weak. *Action* is what counts—" He was close enough. *"This* action."

He slashed at Bruce Wayne. The blades on his gauntlet ripped through the enemy's white shirt, through something gray underneath it and into flesh. But Wayne had moved back an inch; the cut was superficial, just deep enough to draw blood, which began to stain the shirt.

"Jean Paul," Wayne said, "this is *wrong.*"

Batman slashed again and missed completely. Wayne leapt straight up and caught the trapeze bar. He swung, somersaulted, and landed behind Batman.

"You're a victim, Jean Paul," he said. "Your father and that hellish Order he served twisted your mind from infancy on and you didn't even know it. But you do now. You can stop being his puppet and—"

"I am Batman!" Batman roared, springing to face Bruce Wayne. "Because if I am not—" He stopped and gulped air. His throat burned, and he knew that the next words he said would be true and unbearably painful. But they *had* to be uttered. "If I am not, I am *nothing.*"

It was monstrous, it was unbearable, that the enemy had heard his deepest secret. He had succumbed to the enemy's wiles, allowed the enemy to draw from him that devastating confession. The enemy must not be allowed to seduce him further. The enemy must be sent to hell.

He ran, slashing, but Wayne seemed to vanish from his path. Batman's momentum carried him into the computers. His gauntlets shattered glass, and blue flame danced around him. His armor was insulated; he was unharmed.

"I will not be nothing!" he screamed.

Bruce Wayne seemed to materialize next to him. "Jean Paul, please. You've got to understand that what you're doing, what you're thinking . . . it's sick. Let me help you."

Batman swung. The edge of Wayne's flat hand struck his forearm, halting the blow. Batman punched with his left fist, but again Wayne seemed to melt into emptiness and reappear a yard away. He began inching backward, out of the light.

"It won't do you any good to run. You can't hide. I'll find you."

"Not on the best day you ever had," Wayne said. *Now he reveals his true essence—smug, arrogant, corrupt.*

"I will find you," Batman repeated.

"Not until I want to be found." Wayne turned and ran into darkness.

Bruce easily outdistanced Jean Paul.

His costume's bulky. It makes him powerful, but it also makes him slow and clumsy. That's my edge.

Bruce dropped to his hands and knees and crawled into the narrow tunnel.

How long has it been since Paul's taken his costume off? Probably not for weeks. It's become who he is. The exoskeleton's replaced the man. I should have understood that much earlier. It's something we have in common.

Bruce paused until he heard Jean Paul behind him, then crawled on. Finally he had a plan—not one he could explain, but one that was filling him with certainty and purpose.

By now he'll have put his night lenses into place. They won't do him much good, but he'll be wearing them anyway.

"You can't escape," Jean Paul called from behind him.

I don't intend to.

He arrived at the narrowest section of the tunnel, the tiny neck barely able to accommodate him if he thrust his hands and arms out over his head. The flashlight dug into his belly. Something soft was in his way: his overcoat. He squeezed past it. His shirt caught on a tiny stalagmite and he felt it rip. He inched through to the other side and on, until he could crouch. A minute later, he heard Jean Paul stop, mumble.

The next few seconds will make all the difference. If he stops now, or removes the mask—

"Giving up so soon?" Bruce shouted.

He risked the light—a quick flash to the top of the tunnel, nowhere near Jean Paul. It was less than a second, but it was long enough to glimpse Jean Paul wriggling out of the armor. If he also removed the mask, their conflict would surely have to end, finally and drearily, in physical combat. But Bruce heard the sound of metal against stone as Jean Paul continued his approach; that meant he'd left the mask on.

Bruce duckwalked to the end of the tunnel, the dome-shaped chamber where he had entered the Cave—how long ago? He glanced at the luminous face of his watch. It was nearly seven; the sun had been up for an hour.

He waited, listening to the distant drip of water, the flap of bats' wings, and the grunts of the approaching man who was both his pursuer and his quarry. Jean Paul was out of the tunnel, was entering the chamber—

Bruce raised his hands, found the wooden baffle.

"End of the line," he said.

Jean Paul's voice was loud and near. "Yes. You've got no more room to run."

"Neither have you. It's over, Jean Paul. Please believe that. There's nothing to be gained by fighting."

He heard the faint rustle of cloth and sensed Jean Paul moving, preparing to strike.

Bruce's fingers curled around the edge of the baffle. He pulled. The cave was abruptly filled with sunlight.

Jean Paul's hands jerked up to cover his eyes, the eyes of his mask, too late. The glare stabbed into lenses meant only for starlight. He stumbled as though struck. "I can't *see*—"

Bruce looked at him, a heavily muscled man clad in a torn T-shirt and sweatpants, and a grotesque headpiece, arms over his face.

I could hit him now—

Jean Paul wrenched off the mask. His face was young, younger than his years, his yellow hair drooping to his shoulders, his cheeks and chin covered with light blond down. His mouth was open and he was blinking.

Bruce tensed. *I could vanquish him. Put him on the ground.* He felt as though he were caught in some strange interstice between moments of time. *If he reaches for me, I'll finish him—break and humiliate him so utterly that he'll never recover. If I must.*

Jean Paul dropped to his knees and stared up at Bruce. "You are the Batman," he said. "You've *always* been the Batman. And I am nothing."

No rage in the voice now, no fear—just a loneliness Bruce realized had been there from the beginning.

"You'll take me to the police?" Jean Paul asked.

It was the question that Bruce had not answered for himself. "I should," he said slowly. "If I don't, I'll be denying a lot of what my life has meant." *I'll be changing myself forever.* "But no, I won't take you to the police."

"Why? Isn't that what you *should* do?"

"Jean Paul, we're more alike than you know. You see things in black and white. Right or wrong. Good or bad. Saved or damned. I do too, or at least I did until now. But I can't deny my part in your actions. I panicked and forced you into something you weren't ready for. What happened was my responsibility and yet I thought I was only doing what was right, what *had* to be done. That's how you feel too, isn't it?"

Jean Paul nodded.

"So maybe the road to hell is paved with good intentions. Maybe if I'd been there, if I'd seen you kill Abattoir, I'd have to take you in and ask them to put the cuffs on me, too. But I *wasn't* there. I *didn't* see it. That allows me to give you the benefit of the doubt."

Jean Paul rose and hugged himself. He was shivering.

"I guess I'm letting you go," Bruce said slowly, "because I don't know what else to do. But if you ever kill again, I'll come for you. I'll find you and I'll bring you down regardless of cost or consequence. Do you understand?"

Jean Paul nodded.

Bruce gestured to the bright rectangle behind him. "Many years ago, I fell through that opening. I haven't really ever *stopped* falling. Maybe it's time to go the other way. Time for both of us to leave the dark."

Bruce climbed up, out onto the wet brown grass, and reached down to help Jean Paul. The sun was a hard, hot ball in a blue, cloud-flecked sky. It was a beautiful morning.

"You were wrong when you said you're nothing," Bruce said. "You just don't know *who* you are, what you might become. But you might be able to learn. It won't be easy and you might fail, but you've got to try."

"Then you forgive me?"

"Yes, I suppose I do."

Someday, I may even forgive myself.

"You need clothes, money—"

"I'll be fine," Jean Paul said.

Bruce pointed to the horizon. "Go now, and don't ever come back."

Jean Paul nodded and smiled—a shy smile, the smile of a child. He began to walk away.

"Remember," Bruce said, "you're not me, and you're not your father."

Jean Paul continued walking. Bruce called, "I wish you well." But he didn't know if Jean Paul heard him.

Then Bruce turned toward the house. Below was a region of cold and eternal night, and it might be that this was his true home, a destiny he had created and could not escape. Soon, perhaps, he might return to it.

But not today.

Epilogue

It was eight o'clock on the last Sunday in March when Bruce Wayne picked up Tim Drake at the front door of the Drakes' mansion. As they left the property, they saw Jack Drake, out for his morning constitutional with his private trainer; he waved his cane to them and both Bruce and Tim waved back.

For the first hour they were silent. Bruce seemed intent on operating the car and Tim gazed out the window, apparently enjoying the country-side. It was, emphatically, spring; the most savage winter in Gotham City's history had vanished as abruptly as a coin disappearing from a magician's fist.

Finally Tim shifted in his seat, adjusted his safety belt, and said, "We really haven't talked, have we?"

"Not since Jean Paul left."

"Maybe we should, Bruce."

"If you have any questions, shoot."

"Okay, for openers, what's with Bane?"

"I'm told he's still in the prison ward of the state mental hospital. He has no coherent memory and very little physical strength. The doctors say that drug he was addicted to completely tangled his central nervous system. He's not expected to recover."

"What about his pals? What were their names—"

"Bird, Trogg, and Zombie."

"Bird, Trogg, and Zombie," Tim repeated. "Yeah. What happened to them?"

"Bullock and Montoya rounded them up. They're in Blackgate Prison. There's talk of extraditing them back to Santa Prisca. By the way, Bird's trying to cop every plea in sight. He's already told the cops that Bane's responsible for killing the street girls, which gets Batman off *that* particular hook."

"Okay, now the tough question. Jean Paul. What's with him? You have any idea?"

"I got a postcard from Amsterdam. Two words: 'I'm fine.' "

"He knows everything—"

"All my secrets, yes. I've got to trust him not to reveal them. Not much else I *can* do."

A pretty teenager was riding a bicycle along the side of the road. Tim craned his head around to keep her in view as they sped past.

"How's Ariana?" Bruce asked, smiling.

"You saw me look at the cyclist, huh?"

"I *am* a trained observer."

"Ariana's fine," Tim said, turning again to gaze at the countryside. "I think I may love her, but what do I know about love? A lot of *other* girls are very interesting to me, too. How about you, Bruce? You ever have a, uh . . ."

"Lover? Not exactly. I sowed a few wild oats when I was knocking around the world—back when it wasn't suicidal to do that—but I've never made a commitment to anyone."

"Did you ever want to?"

"Hey, if this is going to be about my personal life, let's discuss baseball—"

For several minutes, Tim watched Bruce drive. Finally he said, "Tell me about the Arkham inmates."

"Most of them are in Blackgate until the asylum gets rebuilt. The

Joker's still free and that's the worst possible news. It's like waiting for the other shoe to drop—"

"And the shoe's loaded with high explosive," Tim said. "One more question. I don't know if I have any right to ask this, but . . . have you heard from Alfred?"

"You *do* have a right to ask—he's your friend, too. Unfortunately the answer's no. No calls, no letters, no contact of any kind."

"Can't you find him?"

"If I want to, probably. If I ever think he *wants* to be found, I'll try. But I don't. I have to respect his decision. I owe him that."

They were approaching an estate surrounded by a stone fence. Bruce parked the car outside the gate, and he and Tim walked across a wide lawn toward a large house with a garden on three of its sides.

"This is where she lives?" Tim asked.

"Yes. I bought this place for her and staffed it with trained nurses. A physician looks in twice a week. He's always on call—he lives five minutes away."

"What's her condition?"

"Pretty much like Bane's. Barring some unforeseen medical breakthrough, there's no hope for her recovery. But she's safe and she has everything she'll ever need."

A matronly woman in a white dress came around the house and beamed at Bruce. "Mr. Wayne! How good to see you!"

"Nice to see you, Mrs. McFarland. This is my neighbor, Timothy Drake."

Tim and Mrs. McFarland shook hands, and the three of them continued walking past the house.

"How's our girl today?" Bruce asked.

"Mr. Wayne, she is just the sweetest thing," Mrs. McFarland said.

They entered a playground area, with swings, a jungle bar set, a seesaw, and a sandbox as large as a tennis court. Someone was sitting on the grass, playing with a stuffed unicorn.

"Remember," Bruce said to Tim, "her name is Sandra now."

Bruce and Tim squatted next to the woman they had once known as Dr. Shondra Kinsolving. Her curly hair hung loosely around her shoulders; she was wearing a long, flowing gown of bright yellow silk.

"Hello, Sandra," Bruce said.

Sandra raised her eyes and frowned, as though struggling to remember something important.

"I'm Bruce and this is Tim," Bruce said.

The frown vanished and Sandra smiled. "Hello." Her voice, though still a rich contralto, was that of a child, as soft and bright as her gown.

"You feeling all right today?"

Sandra's smile widened. "I feel *won*-der-ful."

"I'm glad," Bruce said. He stood and then leaned down and kissed Sandra's forehead. "I'll come and see you again soon."

Sandra nodded and returned her attention to the unicorn.

Bruce and Tim said good-bye to Mrs. McFarland and walked silently back to the car.

Bruce sat motionless, not turning on the engine, just resting his hands on the wheel and staring out the windshield.

"Bruce, is there still a Batman?" Tim asked finally.

"Damned if I know," Bruce said.

End

Afterword

There are nine and sixty ways of constructing tribal lays,
And every single one of them is right.
                                                —Rudyard Kipling

He's had a number of personalities in his fifty-five years of existence. He's been a grim avenger; a swashbuckling fantasy adventurer; a cheery solid citizen; a Sherlockian ratiocinator; and on television, a self-mocking comedian. Because he's inhabited that vast, unbounded mirror world known as Popular Culture, where realities shift from day to day and change is the only constant, the Batman has had to remake himself every decade or so or risk almost certain extinction. He has survived, and in the mirror world, that is an achievement.

I'd like to think that, despite the many guises he has assumed in the past five decades plus, there *has* been one other constant: his soul. Now when we're discussing a fictional character, "soul" doesn't mean quite what it means when we're discussing your next-door neighbor. (You and your neighbor, and Father O'Malley, and Rabbi Goldberg, and Lao Tzu, and Zoroaster, and Martin Luther, and Mohammed would probably also disagree about the exact definition of the word, whether applied to real or unreal people, but that's irrelevant.) Let's agree that in this context, "soul" means whatever prompted the creation of the character. A Jungian, or a student of mythology, might argue that our hero is an *archetype* —an idea or image that's part of everyone's psyche—and I'm not sure I'd disagree. If that's the case, he wasn't created so much as discovered, and then adapted to fit the needs of the moment. Mythologists tell us that's how it usually works.

But if he is an archetype, he should have had earlier incarnations. Other denizens of the mirror world certainly do. Superman is a modern version of Gilgamesh, Hawkman is Daedalus, the Flash is Apollo, the Hulk is Hercules—it could be a pleasant rainy-day diversion for a trivia freak with a scholarly bent to complete the list. But if we look for earlier versions of our man, we find little or nothing that can be labeled "hero." We're successful if we search for him among the villains: the demons, the bloodsuckers, the were-creatures, all the dwellers of dark places, all those who shun the light. Look at Dracula, squint a bit, and you see the Batman.

This is a good guy?

Well, yes. He has that half-century's continuous publication to prove it. But I wonder about how the metamorphosis worked, exactly. What changed the dark-dweller from monstrosity to savior, and why has he remained popular for so long?

Start with this: the Batman is nothing if not urban. So maybe the answer is in how people have come to regard cities. Once, cities were havens: bulwarks against wild beasts, savages, all the manifestations of a cruel and capricious Nature. But by Dickens's time, cities were recognized as themselves cradles of evil. The devil doesn't live in a bog miles from civilization; the devil lives upstairs. The devil is Rosemary's Baby. That being so, where is a citizen safe? Certainly not in New York City, nor in New York's mirror-world counterpart, Gotham. I've long believed that Batman's Gotham City is Manhattan below Fourteenth Street at eleven minutes past midnight on the coldest night in November. Take a walk. What is that in the doorway? The man in the black jacket, the one crossing the street there—is he wearing something over his face? Why is he running? And—oh my God—he's coming this way. Now imagine this: the runner speeds past you and strikes down the person in the doorway, who is your worst enemy, who is insane, who has an ax. The runner is

Batman. What I'm suggesting is that we have co-opted the grimmer arche-
types, embraced them, declared them, with all their ferocity and relent-
lessness and inhuman competence, our allies. One of the names we call
them is Batman.

Why? Well, it's been a pretty rough century, and it's probably getting
rougher. It might be easier to co-opt a devil than to believe in an angel.

Of course, we're not glum all the time. We don't always want to be
shaking hands with Beelzebub. Optimism and pessimism seem to be cy-
clic. The reason Batman survived and other saturnine worthies—particularly his immediate forerunner, the Shadow—did not may be the
adaptability I mentioned earlier. If the decade favors the Protestant virtues—citizenship, family, patriotism, good old churchgoing American Decency—our man becomes the Batman of the fifties. If the decade is
questioning such virtues, our man caricatures them as did the sixties
Batman. The secret of this adaptability is simple: many different artists
and writers and editors have worked on the Batman. Although he was
created by Bob Kane and Bill Finger, dozens of later craftsmen, including
me, produced his stories. We were all reacting to the moment, to whatever
was shaping our lives at the time, and the lives of our editors and publishers and readers, and our reactions in turn shaped him.

Which is not to say the stories bear no individual stamp; they do.
Writers like Steve Englehart and Len Wein have given us a normal,
healthy Batman with a romantic streak. Others, such as Frank Miller and
Jim Starlin, have presented Batman as a tormented obsessive. There
hasn't been as much latitude in the graphic representations—he's always
had the bat silhouette, the flowing cape, and the dark colors—although
the Batman has certainly looked different from decade to decade. Neal
Adams's approach is generally considered the best—some say definitive.
Neal's rendering is basically realistic. He once told me, "If Batman existed, he'd have to look the way I draw him." But it is a heightened
realism or, to borrow a term from German painters and Latin American
novelists, "magic realism." In Neal's work, people and things are recognizable, but idealized and subtly exaggerated, given a unique drama and
purity. It is a style particularly appropriate to a character who, while a
super-hero, is not superhuman: who manifests both an ideal of human
perfectibility and a reflection of human terror.

Having said all that, I must reiterate that the character as a whole is a consensus. No one individual guided the Batman, and so he could not be the victim of one individual's getting old, cranky, isolated, out of touch. That may be antithetical to great art, but it is almost a condition of folklore—a myth is a story that generations have agreed on—and any character who's been visible for more than fifty years has to be a folk hero. He's been molded by too many disparate influences *not* to be.

Appropriately enough, this many-authored folk hero is as versatile as he is adaptable. He has visited virtually every area of pop culture. He's been the star of movies, radio, games, television, cereal boxes, short stories, public service announcements, even an amusement park attraction. (I'm told that the Six Flags "Batman: The Ride" is a heart stopper.) And books. Most recently, *this* book. *Knightfall* is not the first Batman novel, but it is the only one that began in Batman's original and truest domain, the comics.

To understand how such a sprawling plot could evolve, could even exist, in lowly comic books, which usually have fewer than twenty-five story pages, you have to understand what comics have become. When comic books were first published in the thirties, they were basically anthologies. There would usually be a lead feature, often but not inevitably touted on the cover, followed by a miscellany of whatever do-gooders the public seemed to find amusing—cowboys, spies, spacemen, private eyes, magicians. The early Batman adventures were no exception. He was introduced, with no fanfare, in *Detective Comics* #27, dated May 1939. Although he was, like Superman a year earlier, an instant success, all his early exploits were typically brief; he shared the pages of *Detective* with such swashbucklers as Slam Bradley, Speed Saunders, and Buck Marshall Trail Detective, as well as several gag strips and a page of text. In 1940 he was given his own quarterly title, *Batman,* but his stories remained brief; there were several of them in a single issue, none more than thirteen pages long. It wasn't until February 1963 that his first full-length adventure, "Prisoners of Three Worlds," was featured in *Batman* #153, and it was concluded in all of twenty-five pages. No continued stories in those days. Comics were available only on newsstands, and newsstand distribution was notoriously spotty. Conventional editorial wisdom decreed that, since a reader couldn't be sure of getting the *next* issue, everything had better be wrapped up in *this* issue.

That's changed, enormously. The comic's main venue is now the specialty shop—there are, at this writing, about five thousand of them in the United States—which virtually guarantees that any interested reader can get the next issue, and the one after that, and last month's, and last *year's,* if he's missed something or wants to complete his collection. Editors are, of course, aware of this and know also that the modern comics audience demands continuity; readers insist that the characters' biographies, and the fictional universes they inhabit, be consistent, logical, and self-referential. We don't produce mere stories anymore; we produce something that hasn't really been named yet. "Metafiction"? "Macrofiction"? Let's settle for *saga,* and define it, tentatively, as a series of heroic tales that, although complete in themselves, are serially related and are part of a much larger fictional construct. Batman, the character, appears every month in *Detective Comics, Batman, Shadow of the Bat,* and *Legends of the Dark Knight.* He often appears in *Robin* and *Catwoman.* And he *might* appear in any of the other forty-plus titles that comprise the DC Universe group of publications. Nothing he does, or is, in any of these venues should be inconsistent with anything he does or is in any of the others.

A typical comic book in the nineties is a strange amalgam of fiction, instant mythology, and imaginary history. We're in a perpetual terra incognita. No storytellers have ever worked with these elements in this combination before. We're continually making it up as we go along, and I'm afraid we don't always fully understand what we're doing. We just know that our odd backwater of publishing has become fiercely competitive—we're vying for the same dollars that are spent on videocassettes, cable television, movies, and other comics—and *whatever* the hell it is we're doing had better be done innovatively and entertainingly.

Which brings us, finally and circuitously, to *Knightfall.* It began when I guessed that our readers—the comics fans who support all the comics specialty shops—might lose interest in Batman after the release of a big-budget movie, the Fox television series, and the toys, T-shirts, graphic novels, and video games that would inevitably accompany them. I knew that in the summer of 1992 there would be a lot of Batman out there, perhaps too much. I could imagine a reader becoming just a bit weary of our Dark Knight, his friends and foes and the faux New York they inhabit, and beginning to favor a less-ubiquitous super-hero. My task, as editor of the comics, was to give these readers a reason to continue their loyalty to our magazines. My coeditors, Scott Peterson and Archie Goodwin, and I decided to use the opportunities afforded by the saga form we worked in and create the longest, most complex story arc ever attempted, one that would span the six comics we edited and, perhaps, cross into other DC titles. We met with our artists and writers and began to discuss ideas.

Our theme was suggested by questions that had nagged at us for several years. Was our man too tame for the nineties? Sure, he'd changed over the decades, but had he changed enough? Despite his grim mien, his kinship with vein-biters and hellspawns, Batman always maintained one pious virtue, his unspoken insistence on the value—the sacredness—of human life. The movie heroes embodied by Eastwood, Schwarzenegger, Norris, Gibson, Seagal and their legions of wanna-bes casually totted up body counts that threatened to rival the casualties of medium-size wars. Was that what "hero" had come to mean—a macho slaughterer? Batman, though he thrashed and bashed, never killed. Did that make him a sissy? A wuss? A doddering old anachronism? We didn't think so. We certainly hoped not. Instead of continuing to ignore the possibility, we decided to confront it. It would be what *Knightfall* was about.

But not *all* that *Knightfall* was about. We weren't, and aren't, in the homily business. When someone buys an entertainment about a guy in a mask and cape, they expect fantasy, melodrama, grotesquerie, a world a hundred times larger than life. We wouldn't disappoint them. Nor were we compromising our collective integrity: we absolutely love writing and drawing that stuff. There would be plenty of it in *Knightfall,* but, we realized, it would be put at the service of our question: *Was* our relentless, night-shrouded avenger passé?

We launched *Knightfall* and we got our answer. The reception of the series, and the vehemence of reader mail, assured us that the audience liked a Batman who was at once avenging and compassionate. That ambivalence may indeed be intrinsic to his appeal; remember, he is fashioned from contradictions.

Knightfall's comic book success generated enough interest to spin off a British radio series that will be released in the United States by Time Warner AudioBooks. It also made executives at DC and Bantam Books wonder if the story couldn't be reshaped into a novel—actually, two novels, one for young readers and one for adults. I agreed to try writing the adult version, not knowing, then, how *much* reshaping would be needed. Ask me now and I'll tell you: comic book series and novels are very different things. *Knightfall*-the-book is a second cousin to *Knightfall*-the-comics, and they're both clearly, but sometimes distantly, related to the radio program of the same name. Take a note: form *does* partially determine content.

Where, in all this media welter, is our pietistic archetype, our Batman? Being altered just a little, probably. His argot, his style, even his wardrobe may change post-*Knightfall*. But his soul, I'm pretty sure, will remain intact.

But wait. Can a soul, even the soul of a composite, survive so many mutations? Certainly. The Batman archetype is the creature of darkness who serves the common good, the devil on an angel's mission; that's the image always at the center of the stories. It is what individual artists and writers react to—either embrace or deny, or even lampoon, but can never totally ignore. Unless humanity has a sudden, unprecedented attack of sanity, and we need no longer fear the darkness, it will probably keep him popular for at least another fifty-odd years.

"Yes, Sir. May I Please Have Another?"
A POSTSCRIPT

Be careful what you wish for, they say. It just might come true.

In the fall of 1993, Bantam Books had published *The Death and Life of Superman* by Roger Stern. For the next five weeks the hardcover novelization remained on the *New York Times* Bestseller List. Combined with the publication of a bestselling children's novel and an award-winning radio drama—all timed to be released on the same day in which the comic containing the return of the Man of Steel from the dead went on sale—the publishing of these projects was an unqualified success.

Returning to the other books I'd been editing, I enjoyed my new-found sense of time. Whereas *The Death and Life* had taken seven months from conception to publication, most of the other manuscripts on my plate had the usual one-year lead time. I could stop to take a deep breath, the pace much more manageable. When I looked out the window at the end of the day, it was still light out. I actually had the time to go home and have a life. I even found myself reading for fun once again.

Picking up a Batman comic from the pile that had been accumulating on my floor for the better part of a year, I got sucked into the storyline I'd been hearing so much about. Something called *Knightfall*. Batman is crippled by a supervillain named Bane, and a new vigilante called Azrael rises to take the place of the Dark Knight.

As I read, the obvious struck me. If we pulled off a publishing trifecta with Superman, perhaps we could have the same success with Batman. Besides, the writers, artists, and editors had made it so easy. The storyline they were working on had all of the elements that made *The Death and Life of Superman* work so well: A hero who had been around, by then, for more than fifty years, in a story that challenged our understanding of who he was exactly.

I remember turning to my girlfriend at the time, carefully broaching the subject. "What if...?" I began hesitantly, then pitched her what I was kicking myself for even thinking.

"You have to do it," she agreed. "When else would you ever have the chance?"

Knowing I would never forgive myself if I didn't, I walked into my boss's office the next morning and pitched her the idea. She in turn pitched it to her boss, then Bantam Books, Bantam Young Readers, the BBC, and Time Warner AudioBooks. Before long, the team was back in place, and the wheels of instant publishing geared up once again, ready to crush everyone who stood in its path.

Although it seems like an obvious choice now, at the time, assigning the adult novelization to Dennis O'Neil took some convincing (even though as far as I was concerned, there was no one else who could have written it but him). Besides being the editor of the comics I had been reading, he was also an amazingly accomplished writer. For the better part of forty-something years, he has written some of the industry's best, and most important, comics.

Not surprisingly, I grew up reading Denny's work. In fact, I have in my office a framed copy of *Shazam!* #1, his 1973 comic that heralded the return of the original Captain Marvel. It was one of my favorites as a kid.

But how does one go from being a fan, a reader/admirer of someone's work, to being that writer's editor? In what universe does that make sense? Truthfully, it doesn't. But somehow that part of one's brain shuts down. Even though I never lost the awe I felt, I had a job to do—so I threw myself into it, and was fortunate enough to become friends with Denny in the process.

Fast forward nine months. As detailed in Denny's introduction, the novel was written and published in a series of events that would make even Rube Goldberg shake his head.

I don't think I'm giving away any secrets by saying Denny made it through the process thanks in large part to the support of his amazing wife Marifran. And thanks to her lemonade and chocolate chip cookies, *I* survived as well.

On June 17, 1994, we arranged a press conference announcing the return of Bruce Wayne as the one, true Batman. The event at a school here in New York was well attended. The students we had gathered for the press asked some amazing questions, and the writers on the panel—Chuck Dixon, Alan Grant, Doug Moench, and Dennis O'Neil—fielded them like pros. Later than night, we went home to watch the coverage on television. Imagine my surprise when I tuned in to see a white Ford Bronco racing throughout the Southland of Los Angeles.

An hour later I picked up the phone. "I don't think they're going to run our little Batman story anytime soon," I remember saying to Denny. They didn't, either.

Knightfall, however, did go on to become a national bestseller. In fact its first week on sale, it simultaneously hit #11 on the *Wall Street Journal* Bestseller List, #10 on the *Walden* Bestseller List, and #13 on the *Barnes & Noble* Bestseller List. At the time, and especially in retrospect, it was worth all of the effort.

Since its publication, the novel you have just finished has been read and enjoyed by many, confronting our conceptions about what it means to be a hero. It's a story all the more apropos in this new post-9/11 millennium, a time when we need heroes perhaps more than ever.

And here's our hero, flaws and all. Like us, Batman is only human. And thanks to *Knightfall,* he's back. Better and stronger than he ever was.

CHARLES KOCHMAN
NEW YORK, NEW YORK
JANUARY 2004

ABOUT THE AUTHOR

DENNIS O'NEIL is a group editor at DC Comics and the guiding force
behind the Batman mythos. As editor and writer, he has helped return the
character of Batman to his roots as a dark, mysterious, gothic avenger.
O'Neil began his career in the mid-sixties as Stan Lee's editorial assistant
at Marvel Comics and went on to become one of the industry's most
successful and respected comic book writers and creators. As a freelance
writer and journalist, he has produced several novels and works of nonfic-
tion, as well as hundreds of comics, reviews, teleplays, and short stories.
A frequent guest at conventions and on television, O'Neil teaches writing
at the School of Visual Arts in Manhattan. He currently lives and works
in New York with his wife, Marifran.